CONTRACTS & CATS

CONTRACTS & CATS

MEOW: MAGICAL EMPORIUM OF WARES
BOOK ONE

TONI BINNS

BARDHWOOD PRESS, LLC

Paperback ISBN: 979-8-9853073-4-4

KDP ISBN: 979-8-2657643-2-4

Library of Congress Control Number: 2025918714

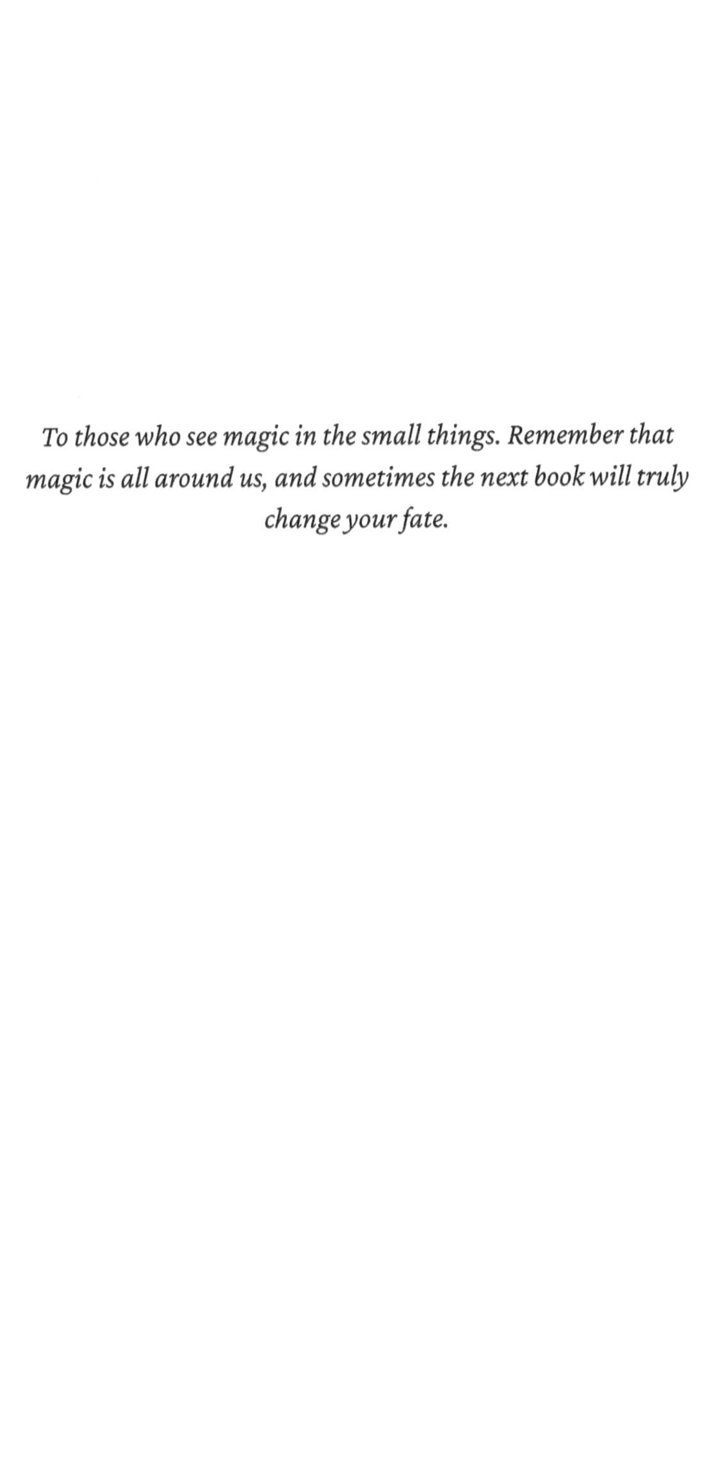

To those who see magic in the small things. Remember that magic is all around us, and sometimes the next book will truly change your fate.

ONE

The job ad seemed normal enough. It had been in an email along with a long list of other ads from one of those job sites. I'd signed up on such a website hoping to find something, anything, after graduating last week. Those student loans were a heavy weight waiting to drop.

Barista and caretaker for a bookstore. Experience wanted. Room and board included plus student loan repayment. You must like cats. The shopkeeper is going to retire and needs someone to help the Cat, run the small shop, and keep the coffee flowing.

I mean, any job with student loan repayment was amazing on its own, but this one involved cats too. That was why I stood outside the storefront in the sunshine. A wooden sign depicting a cat and a book hung out above the door, and the writing in the window seemed to sparkle in the sunlight: *Meow: Magical Emporium of*

Wares. The window showed stacks of dusty books, along with an old wingback chair that held a knitted throw.

All I wanted to do was curl up in the chair and never leave. Still, I needed to pass this interview.

I'd received a reply almost immediately after I'd sent my resume in, which was a positive sign. It said they were looking forward to chatting with me and to show up at a certain time. I couldn't find an online presence for the store, but directions came up when I searched for them. The interview time was in five minutes, and I hoped to explore the shop first.

The latch on the bright-blue wooden door opened silently. The door itself rattled, and a ringing bell filled the space.

I jumped ever so slightly at the jarring sound. Eagerly, I glanced around the bright room. In front of me and to the left, bookshelves lined the wall, filled with books of different sizes. Wooden signs hung above the very top of the shelves, noting the various genres. Nonfiction books were first before changing into my favorite section, fantasy and science fiction.

On my right were big bright windows with the chair I'd seen from outside, but the center of the room was a wide-open space.

Along the wall stood a long wooden counter. It had to be someone's pride and joy since the wood almost sparkled in the sunlight streaming in from above. An old-fashioned cash register sat on one end. The register had buttons like on a typewriter, along with a more modern screen that faced the shopkeeper. On the other end of the counter stood a high-end espresso machine.

I did a double take. *Look at that baby.*

The Yas400 in bright red. Getting to use that was worth almost anything. The cost alone to buy one could keep me alive on a decent budget for almost a year. I'd never be able to afford one.

I moved closer before catching something out of the corner of my eye. An old-fashioned poster hung on the wall over the register:

> Do not upset the Cat.
> The Cat is always right.
> Do not go behind the counter.
> Do not upset the Cat.

That was strange. They spoiled the Cat for sure.

Note to self: do not upset the Cat.

That would be the key to acing this interview. Inside my head, all I could picture was a cat in a tie asking me questions. Too much caffeine and not enough sleep.

An old bell sat on the counter next to the register, and I figured I would need to tap it to get some help. After tapping the bell, quiet returned to the space slowly.

"Meow!"

A cat suddenly jumped up onto the wooden counter. Bright-green eyes stared right at me. I totally felt judged.

"You must be the Cat the sign is talking about. Do you like pets?"

He was such a pretty black cat, and his eyes were a vivid color. All I wanted to do was see if he was a cuddler. Some cats loved pets, and others hated them.

I held out my hand for him to sniff. Hopefully, he

liked me and wouldn't get upset. It was in the rules, after all.

The cat meowed again loudly. Talkative cat. That was new. All the cats I had been around didn't really make much noise, unless it was time to eat. Or *I* was eating.

"Coming!"

The voice came from above, and I jerked back my hand and looked up. Woah, the ceiling towered over me. The bookstore hid a second floor up there, with a railing above the counter. This place was bigger than it looked from the outside.

An older gentleman came out of what looked to be a doorway and peered over the railing. "Ah, you must be Sable. I will be right there. Too many emails today."

He then vanished. The sound of someone going down wooden steps followed, and I walked closer to the counter before the white-haired man came out from a different doorway behind the counter.

I hadn't noticed that doorway until just now. So many secret nooks and crannies.

He could be someone's grandpa with his short white hair, thin glasses, and kind look. A knitted vest covered a white button-up, and his pants looked pressed.

"I totally get having a ton of email, especially with that job ad. This is like a dream job." I couldn't help but blush as the words tumbled out.

This was not the impression I wanted to make, but either I would get the job, or I wouldn't. I would rather they saw me for who I was.

His bright-blue eyes studied me and flicked up to my hair. At the moment, my hair was short and a neon purple, but his eye color made me want to change it to blue. It had been a while since I'd last changed colors.

The cat meowed again and broke the tension, drawing my focus back to the black furball.

"Well, we are looking for a great fit. That matters more than anything else. This place is special, and the person who gets hired needs to be special as well." He motioned to the edge of the counter. "How about you come around this way and make us some coffee? That will get a big requirement out of the way."

I motioned to the sign. "Are you sure? I know what the rules say."

"Come, come. You have permission," the old man said with a smile.

I scooted behind the rounded edge of the counter, and my jaw dropped at how much room stretched behind it. The red machine seemed to glow in the light.

I smiled at the man. "What would you like to drink?"

I resisted the urge to rock back and forth in place. I would actually get to use this baby even without getting the job. No matter what, I would make her sing.

"I am simple. What is your favorite?" he asked.

I thought for a moment, then replied, "I will drink just about anything. How about a few shots? Then I can make a mocha for you to try, and I'll have a latte."

Everything I needed sat nearby. There was a grinder, plus a mini fridge under the counter, syrups in a line near the wall, along with a canister for the used grounds. It was a nice little setup, but it was clear that while this bookstore made drinks, they must not have a morning rush.

The last coffee shop I worked at had a morning rush, and this setup was just a little inefficient. It was off in one corner without a staging area to line up multiple drinks and get them done quickly.

Still, maybe the personal touch was what they were going for. Especially considering the clear space on the counter, which gave a direct line to chat with the customer.

I started my dance with the orders. If barista work paid just a little bit more, or if I hadn't gone to college, I would have stuck with it, but everyone had pushed me to go, so I went.

Under the counter, a row of different coffee mugs sat, along with mismatched teacups. Way too cute. I couldn't help but reach for the teacup.

"I would like a latte. I love the foam," came a voice from over my shoulder.

The grinder was going, but I still heard the soft request. It sounded simple enough. I nodded in response.

The shots were easy to pull, and I tasted the first to make sure it was okay. Then I poured the second shot into one teacup for a straight espresso. Next up was a mocha and then finally the latte. For that one, I went with a cute flowery mug and topped it with a ton of foam.

Finally, after a small breath, I turned back to my audience. Both the shopkeeper and the Cat were watching me.

"Have at it..." I motioned with my hand.

The cat padded over directly for the latte, and I glanced at the man in confusion. Caffeine and cats... I wasn't sure if that was a very good idea. Not to mention he was taking a drink requested by the shopkeeper. Plus, who let their cat drink coffee? It couldn't be normal.

The cat's black head darted into the mug, lapping eagerly. I didn't know if I should stop him. The cat was always right, after all. His whiskers came out covered in foam. It was so cute, but I resisted taking a picture with my phone. I needed to be professional.

"He can decide on what he wants," answered the gentleman.

He didn't seem worried at all.

The old shopkeeper took a sip of the espresso, and then the mocha. "Both are delightful. How about you make yourself a drink, and then we can walk through the shop? I want to make sure you know what you're getting into."

I must not do a happy dance. Play it cool, Sable. You got this.

I grabbed a bigger mug that was a bright-blue color with glittery gold stars on it. A vanilla latte took little time, and it would be tasty. All the ingredients were high-end, from organic milk to imported coffee beans, with only the vanilla syrup looking homemade.

"Who does the ordering?" I asked to keep the conversation going.

More information was good. Plus, I had trouble with silence.

"You will, eventually. You can do it on the register."

That made things easy. Usually, someone else was in charge of that, and it sucked not having any input.

"What about the syrups?"

He chuckled. "I made them. The recipes are in the kitchen. I can show you if you want to follow me."

He headed through the doorway that he'd come through earlier.

"This door on the right is the storeroom for dry goods." His fingers tapped on the door, but he kept moving. To the left-hand side, a staircase led upstairs. "We will go upstairs after the kitchen."

The short hallway opened up to a gigantic industrial kitchen. It wouldn't be out of place on a cooking show. It had a large, gorgeous island with a wooden countertop made of the same wood as the counter out front.

My eyes grew wide while I looked around. "Isn't this a little overkill?"

I didn't know how to put this big, nice of a space to good use. Why was it here?

"It depends. I like to cook, and this is the kitchen in the building. While the shopkeeper's room is upstairs, it only has a mini fridge and an electric kettle. So any of your personal cooking will be down here."

I spun around in the giant kitchen. A list of different things I could learn how to cook or bake came to mind. I had put off learning how to cook since I'd eaten cheap fast food and ramen during school.

But with this as an option, I would learn. Somehow. I would find some good cookbooks in the store. Plus, with board included in the compensation package, I had a decent budget for food.

"The store only serves coffee, right? No food service?" I asked.

"Only beverages, unless you want to change that.

Sometimes, I had to order cookies or something for events, like book readings or such in the store. This is a creative job with lots of flexibility as long as you follow the rules."

"That the Cat is always right?" I asked with a grin, though he didn't grin back.

"Yep, that's the big one." He shook his head lightly. "Let's head upstairs. You can get a good view of the shop."

He turned, slowly walked up the wooden steps, and vanished around the corner. He moved quickly on his feet once out of sight, and I had to rush to keep up.

Bookcases stood along the walls, but I didn't see another staircase. This must be all private space.

"This is your area. Customers aren't allowed up here." He motioned to an opened door. "That is the studio with a private bathroom. Feel free to look around."

I'd take any excuse to snoop around, so I headed into the bedroom. The hardwood floors continued in this room from the rest of the shop. Bright skylights covered the ceiling. A big queen bed sat against one wall with a desk on the other. A small counter with cupboards and a mini fridge stood in one corner, along with a kettle. Multiple suitcases sat on the otherwise bare floor.

Another doorway piqued my interest. White tile and a massive clawfoot soaking tub came into view.

You will not squeal, I thought to myself.

This shop was perfect. This studio was absolutely perfect. Now I just needed to get the job.

When I turned around, he looked at me with an eyebrow raised.

"Does it meet your expectations?" He smirked at the joy I radiated.

It took everything inside me to not start gushing about the room.

"So, I man the coffee machine and the register. I order supplies on the register. What about the bookshelves and merchandise?"

"You won't be ordering that. The owner will be."

"That sounds fantastic."

I would do this job well. Very well. Plus, maybe I could put my business degree to use, after all.

I headed back out of the room and leaned on the railing, looking at the bookshelves below. The balcony wrapped around three walls. On the far side, a wall of glass stretched to the ceiling, with what looked like plants growing along it in pots. There was so much I kept missing.

"Ah, that's a small rooftop garden. I do not have a green thumb, but there is some space if you want to plant things."

Warning bells went off in my head then.

This place was too perfect.

CHAPTER

TWO

"Tell me about the benefits," I said.

I had to say something. Otherwise, this might seem weird to him, especially depending on how many people he must have interviewed already.

I tasted my vanilla latte and wished I could crawl inside it and take a bath. This was a dream come true. I couldn't believe that I'd have lattes on tap for the next year. This whole thing was a little unbelievable.

But at some point, you just had to win the lottery, right? *Right?*

"We listed the compensation in the ad. I'm not in charge of that. I can forward any of those questions to the owner. Just send them to me tonight."

Hold up.

"Wait, I thought *you* were the owner." I'd assumed he owned the place and was retiring to a warmer location.

He chuckled and shook his head. "I'm just the shop-keeper, though I'm retiring. My contract is up, and I'm excited to step away from the place. I don't own the store, but I get to pick the replacement."

The cat hissed.

I jumped, glancing around for the little guy, but I didn't see him.

"And the Cat. He gets a majority vote, if I'm being honest here."

That cat must be someone special.

"Good to know. The compensation is fine. I was just wondering about things like health insurance. I know the student loan stuff was mentioned."

The cat appeared at the top of the stairs and padded toward us. He rubbed against my ankle.

Health insurance be damned. The cat was worth it. He was so fluffy.

I bent down to scratch him on the head, careful to not spill my drink. Not to mention I didn't want to share it with him.

"The compensation is higher than normal since it is a twenty-four-hour job, because of looking after the cat. The work schedule is six days a week, and the store is open six to eight hours a day. You are the only one on staff. We are only closed one day, and it's your only day off."

I hadn't ever lived on the property for a job before.

"And the Cat can be a tough master."

I reached down and scratched his head. "Awww, can this awesome little bud be a tough one?"

Maybe he drank out of any cup left out. He had gone after that foam like no tomorrow. Or he might knock over glasses like on the internet.

"If I'm the only one working, what happens if I get sick?" I asked.

He frowned. "Well, if you get sick, you can close the shop early. Your health is a priority here."

"So if I have to close the shop for a week because of the flu, the owner doesn't get upset?"

Most jobs freaked out if someone had to miss a shift. Being the only one on staff had some down sides.

"If needed, the shop can be closed, or the owner will find someone to help temporarily. That's not your responsibility."

All right, so I didn't need to find a temp employee if I was down with the flu. That was a good thing. I did not want to upset the owner or risk my job because of illness. Not that I got sick all that often, but while in college, I had once gotten strep from my roommate. That had sucked.

I had nothing else to ask, so I dug deep to keep the conversation going.

"So, are you happy to be retiring? This position seems like the kind of thing you wouldn't ever want to give up."

He shrugged. "I have done this job long enough. I'm ready to not have to deal with customers anymore, and while I like cats…"

The cat glared at him. The man might be sick of the cat as well.

I understood getting tired of customers. Customers could make or break a job, and after a certain point, you were just done with them.

"Are you interested in the position?" asked the shopkeeper.

"I am." Yep, I was in with both feet. "I think I would be a great fit, and I can handle everything we have gone over."

Or at least I would fake it until I learned everything.

"Great. I will get the contract for you to sign and go over." The guy headed down the stairs, whistling a merry tune.

The cat stared at me from the top of the stairs.

"Sounds like we're going to get to know one another," I said to the black, whiskered face.

After climbing toward him, I leaned down and scratched behind his ears. He purred, and I melted. This cat was so adorable and fluffy.

The realization that I got the job, and this would be my life over the next year, stretched my whole face with a grin.

"Are you coming?" the man's voice echoed from below.

The cat darted down the stairs before I had time to respond.

"Be right there." I glanced once more over the railing at the sun-filled room below.

The bookshelves gleamed in the light, and little bits of cat hair floated in the air. I would need to put a cleaning schedule in place to deal with the cat hair, but it was still so worth it.

I would get to work here, every day, and run this little bookshop. This would be my home.

The paperwork was just a couple of pages that I barely glanced over. It was a yearlong contract to stay on the property, run the shop, and take care of the cat. The details were light, and I didn't have questions.

It caught my eye that I was required to find a replacement before leaving the position. It made sense. The owner probably didn't want to close the shop.

By the time I finished my latte, I had signed and dated the last page. The shopkeeper flashed me a bright-white smile, and his shoulders relaxed.

"So, what time do you want me here tomorrow morning?" I asked.

"Around 8:00 a.m. would be perfect. It will give you time to settle in upstairs. I don't think we will be open tomorrow to give you time to unpack and get some training in. I will have a copy of this for you tomorrow, once the owner signs it."

He held out his hand, and I shook it.

"Sounds good. I will see you tomorrow."

The cat wound around my ankle one last time before I headed out the door.

It was time to pack! I couldn't wait.

The bell rang behind me as I headed out the door and into the sunlight, grinning from ear to ear. Still, concern over how perfect this job was lingered. Determined to hold onto my good mood, I shoved the concern aside. Whatever hidden down side there was, it would be worth it.

CHAPTER
THREE

I owned little, so packing was easy. A suitcase of clothes and then two more—one full of books and the other my bedding. I was broke while in school, so I'd kept things simple.

I'd paid my rent through the end of the month, but my roommates wouldn't have a problem finding a replacement, since our apartment was cheap. I needed to remember to let my family know that I'd found a job, but I wanted to wait until after I got settled first.

The taxi dropped me off in front of the bookstore and disappeared in a flash. It took a hot minute to get everything inside. The door made a racket with the back and forth of getting my bags through. Several other suitcases sat by the door, the ones that had been upstairs yesterday.

"Meow," said the cat.

He appeared as soon as I set my first bag down and went back out to grab the rest. He sniffed everything before padding back to the counter and jumping up near the register.

Realization dawned then. I didn't know the shopkeeper's name. The owner was Mr. Cearnachain, but the shopkeeper wasn't the owner.

"Ah, Sable, you're here. Good, good. I have a flight to catch. I don't want to be late." He appeared out of nowhere from behind a bookshelf.

"Wait, what?"

Today was supposed to be for unpacking and training, not being thrown into the deep end.

A horn honked from the street. He grabbed a bag and set it outside the door.

"The extra copy of the paperwork is on the counter near the register. Feel free to bring your stuff upstairs. The room has been cleaned and straightened."

"But…"

He really was leaving me here. In the really cool bookshop with the awesome coffee machine.

I grabbed one of my bags and moved it closer to the counter. The espresso machine seemed to glow. I needed a coffee to handle this.

"Do you want any coffee for the road?"

Hopefully, he would slow down and talk.

"Nope." He moved another few bags outside. "I'm good to go."

"Are you sure? Caffeine is important."

A stack of papers lay on the counter, and I pulled it closer.

"I'm sure. Good luck, and I hope your years fly by."

"Wait, *years*?"

But he was gone, with suitcases in each hand. The door closed softly behind him.

The contract was only for one year. I breathed deeply. This was actually happening.

The cat jumped onto the counter next to the pile of paperwork.

"Looks like it's just you and me, bud. Time for some coffee."

The beautiful red machine called my name, and I patted its top. The contract could wait. Caffeine was first on the list; second was checking the paperwork.

"We're going to get to know one another so well. Hmmm, let's start with a cappuccino."

"I would like a cappuccino as well, extra foam. This time in a teacup, please."

The metal cup to froth the milk tumbled out of my hand, and I spun around. What the heck?

The cat stared at me.

"Use the teacup so I don't get my whiskers covered in foam," a voice echoed in my mind. "I don't want to clean my whiskers again."

This wasn't possible.

"You can talk?"

"I am the Cat. You agreed to be the Shopkeeper. So yes, we can talk." He ran a paw over his face, then stared. "Are you going to make that cappuccino?"

Nope, nope, nope.

I grabbed my backpack and the suitcase handle for my books and headed to the door. Then I froze. My two other bags were gone. They had been right next to the door.

"I'm not doing this." My hand hit the doorknob, and I pulled it open, the bells ringing loudly.

But the door was blocked. A smooth invisible surface in the doorway stopped me. I couldn't get out. I dropped the handle of my suitcase, and it banged to the floor. I ran both my hands along the invisible boundary.

I spun around in place, glaring at the Cat. "Let me out. Now."

"You signed the paperwork. You are now the Shop-keeper for the next year. I thought you said the compensation was fair."

"Not for being trapped! How are you freaking talking to me? What the actual fuck?" My words came out in a rush.

My hands shook, and I didn't know what to do. The Cat was somehow talking to me.

I held my backpack tight in my arms. This couldn't be real. I had to be dreaming. It was time to wake up. This dream needed to end.

The Cat jumped down from the counter and ambled forward.

"You heard me bright and clear yesterday, then you made a great drink. The hearing-me part was the most important requirement." He stopped about a foot away from me. "Come on. You have some coffee to make, and you need to unpack. Tomorrow is going to be your first actual day on the job. I'll keep it simple."

Deep breaths.

I wasn't waking up. No one would believe me. What was I going to tell my family? I got a job at a bookshop, and the Cat talks. I knew the money had to be too good to be true.

"Where did my stuff go?"

The Cat's tail flicked in the air. "To your room, of course. Unless you *want* to lug it up the stairs. Chop chop. I would like some coffee."

The suitcase stayed where I'd dropped it. My backpack hung from one shoulder as I skirted past the Cat back to the coffee machine.

I did not want to upset him. If he could move my bags, what else could he do? Where was I actually working?

"What *is* this place?"

"The Magical Emporium of Wares, of course."

"A magical bookstore?" I shook my head and set my backpack on the counter.

When I looked again, my suitcase had vanished. It must have happened once I took my eyes off it.

A calm feeling washed over me, making me wonder about this place.

"Something like that," the Cat answered. "Any of the teacups will do. Several years ago, a friend got them for me as a present."

My hands continued to shake as I worked my magic on the lovely machine. What was I going to do now? I couldn't leave. The money was great, and this place was awesome. This was only a dream, right? The contract was for a year. It had to be better than school. Somehow, I would deal with the Cat.

I poured a shot into the small teacup then followed

with the milk. As soon as I placed it on the counter, he tiptoed over to it and lapped it up.

"So you are a cat that likes coffee?"

"Who doesn't like coffee? Cat or otherwise."

"Good point." I quickly made my drink and poured it into the bright-blue mug with stars.

The mug had sat in the same spot since yesterday.

At least I had superb caffeine. That helped. I sipped at the coffee and took another deep breath. The job paid well, but I was stuck in the building. At least for now. The contract had to have more answers, but I'd save that for later.

I ignored the Cat as I touched the strange cash register's screen. It flickered on. The front page had various tabs for inventory, ordering supplies, and checking out customers. At least that seemed normal enough. The ordering supplies section had a grocery spot as well.

They better deliver.

"So, you are the one who does inventory ordering, right?"

No answer.

I peered over in the teacup's direction. Empty, and the Cat was nowhere to be seen.

Just great. Magical cat, locked in the bookstore, and no more answers. For now, at least.

I cleaned up the espresso machine and gave it a pat on the top, then I turned toward the kitchen. I'd had a quick breakfast on the way here, but lunchtime would be here quickly. Time to see what the pantry had in the way of foodstuffs. Otherwise, groceries needed to be ordered as soon as possible.

Dream or not, I just had to do the best I could. I hoped it would all seem normal soon enough.

FOUR

Half the time I wrote something down on my pad of paper, it would magically show up in the next cupboard. Or in the fridge. Weird, but kind of cool.

But not everything showed up. Avocados never arrived, nor did a fancy cheese I once saw on a menu. So there had to be limitations. It would take time to find out what they were. First was snacks, like crackers and cereal. Then I tried things like milk and steak. Like, a really expensive steak.

It showed up in the fridge wrapped in butcher paper. It was crazy. Or I was, but it was worth it.

I currently had a plate of chocolate chip cookies, cheese crackers, and some iced tea on the counter. Best nibbles ever. It was all pre-made snack food. Nothing that was healthy for me in any way. The amount of sugar on my plate concerned me, but for a reward, it was fine.

I'd survived coming to terms with the fact that magic was real, cats could talk, and this was my next year. Given some of the questionable things I'd done in college, this wasn't the worst thing that could happen to me.

I tapped my fingers on the pad of paper, which felt artisan. Not even the pen was basic. Instead, it was metal with a fine tip—not something I'd get at an office supply shop.

I glanced at the simple grocery list on the pad of paper. Avocados, cheese, bread, and lunchmeat. Sandwiches would be an easy lunch. Dinner was a little more complicated since I didn't really cook. I'd have to figure out what to do about that. Maybe read some of those books. Or maybe the shop could cook?

"Hey, Cat?" I called out.

No response.

That was not helpful. I didn't know what he ate or didn't eat. Since he drank espresso, I wasn't sure if cat food or people food should be on the list for him. Should I cook for him? It depended on what the contract said. I'd signed it, so I guess I was stuck with it.

Having to look back at the paperwork made me feel like I did when I'd gotten the first notice for my student loans. Like I had screwed up and now needed to figure out how bad of a hole I'd dug for myself.

I grabbed the plate and the list and headed to the counter in the shop. I opened the grocery section and added what was on my list. It was like any other grocery app.

A stool sat off to one side, and I pulled it closer to the counter.

"All right, let's get this done." I grabbed the stack of papers and started reading.

It was exactly what I had signed yesterday, as far as I could tell. The owner's signature line was signed. It did not mention the talking cat, magic, or being stuck here, though it said to remain on the premises for the year. Yesterday, I thought that just meant living here. Now, I knew better. "Remain on the premises" really meant "never leave."

I shook my head and headed back to the kitchen to refill my plate. I set it on the counter and took a step backward.

"Can the plate be moved up to my room? Like the suitcases?" I whispered into the kitchen, hoping that talking to the shop was okay.

When I glanced away and back, my eyes went wide at the empty counter. *It worked.*

Rule One—magic didn't happen when I watched.

Rule Two—talking to the shop was okay.

Rule Three—just go with the flow.

I added the third, since as long as the check cleared my bank account and my student loan payment went in on time, I couldn't complain. Especially given how my roommate had wanted her boyfriend to move in and for me to get out. I knew I should have gone to the same school as Jackie, my best friend from back home. Instead, I'd decided to be daring and try a school even farther away.

That didn't matter now. I had a job, a place to live, and fantastic food to eat. I had a year to go to figure out how this magic stuff worked, but for now, it didn't seem so bad. Room, board, a fair salary, and benefits. Plus magic. I couldn't forget the magic.

Time to go unpack and see what other magical secrets I could uncover.

This human was strange.

I tried not to creep around and stare at her, but the smallest of magics seemed to bring her such joy. Her emotions radiated outward and rippled through the shop.

Arnold had been different. His fear and need to leave had made the shop almost unbearable. I'd endured. I'd had no other choice.

But this one was different.

Food motivated her. It was easy enough to provide. The shop needed someone to take care of it, and having this human here brought the shop a quiet contentment.

Not "this" human. Sable. I needed to get her name in my head.

The shopkeeper had to be on the "must not let them die list," since the shop must have a keeper. If something happened to her, it would not go well. I needed to make sure nothing happened to...Sable.

The shop already felt different. Arnold had ignored the magic as much as possible. I'd known it was time for a change when the coffee machine appeared. Arnold hadn't made coffee like that, and I knew he didn't want to renew his contract. He didn't even need to say anything.

I thought he had been a perfect fit at the beginning.

Someone older, retired, who didn't have enough money and was looking for somewhere to stay. I was wrong.

So on to yet another human. Someone else who would need to learn and bumble around. They always took so long to figure things out, and to understand their part in the order of this place.

Sunlight drenched the chair in the front window. It was the shop's way of trying to put me in a better mood. I padded in that direction. A spot of warm sunlight after a wonderful coffee was perfection.

Tomorrow, we had much to do, appointments to keep, and things to check off in the book. But for now, a warm nap sounded perfect.

I didn't need to worry about anything else today.

FIVE

The blank screen stared up at me, and I did not know what to say.

Mom, Dad, I got a job at a magical bookstore, and I don't need to sleep in the basement after all.

Somehow, I didn't think it would go over well. How could it?

Dad would think I was joking, and Mom would roll her eyes at the two of us. One of my brothers would show up within twenty-four hours to find out what was really going on. I didn't need any of that.

I leaned back in the wooden chair and closed my eyes. Keeping it simple would be key. I nodded and reached for the keyboard.

Mom, Dad,

I got the job I was hoping for. It's this cute little bookstore in midtown. The espresso maker is to die for. It includes taking care of the Cat, who is adorable. My first day went well, and I think I'm going to love it here.

Love,
Sable

"That should be perfect," I muttered.

"It sounds good."

I spun my head around so fast I almost tweaked my neck. The Cat sat near my feet.

His green eyes stared up at me. "I wanted to see how you were settling in...and see if you had any questions."

I'd already put away my clothes, and my books lined some bookcases in the room. Artwork had appeared on the walls that I'd already fallen in love with—giant splashes of bold colors of a sunset over some mountains and trees.

"How much can I tell my family?" I ask. "We're close."

The Cat's tail flicked. "What you have is good."

"But what about the magic?" I pressed.

"Who would believe you?" The Cat stood and padded toward the door. "From your world, at least?" He glanced back at me. "Just keep the magic out of it would be my advice."

I shook my head. "So just a boring bookshop with coffee."

He disappeared through the doorway. But he did not know. It would not hold up with my family. Not at all.

I hit send on the email, then I set the laptop off to the side and grabbed some hair dye. The goal was to get it into my hair before they called.

But my cell phone rang as I pulled on the gloves to

keep my hands from turning purple. Thankfully, I hadn't opened the hair color yet.

"Hi, Mom. Warning: I'm going to be working on my hair as we chat."

"You got the job!"

A smile broke out on my face at the happiness that came over the phone. "I did. It's this cute little bookstore. I love it."

"You're staying there, too?"

"Yeah, there's a shopkeeper's room on the second floor. I get a day off per week, but the pay makes up for it."

"What about your roommate?" asked my mom.

"She didn't care. She wants her boyfriend to move in with her, and the others have jobs in other places. Everyone is really going their own way or trying to get into grad school. Which I was not going to do."

"Schooling was good for you."

I let the groan of frustration slip through my lips as I separated my hair out into sections. Going to college hadn't been on my list, but everyone in my family encouraged me to go.

"I know you didn't think so... but your brothers can be overbearing, and getting away from the family was a learning experience."

Something sounded off in her voice, and I paused with my hair.

"I feel like there's a 'yet' coming."

"Well, we all thought you would come home after you got your degree."

I couldn't help the giggles that rolled out of me. I had

to be careful not to set my purple fingers down on the bathroom vanity.

"So let me get this straight. Everyone wanted me to go to school and experience the world. Now I'm finding my own way, and you want me back home?"

"That's not it at all. We miss you." My dad's voice came over the line. He was ever the joker, but he cared about each of us so much. "You are so far away. When was the last time you visited?"

"I came home for the holidays."

"For two days, and you didn't want us to visit at school."

I got what he was saying. I even knew where it was coming from. My frustration at feeling like they'd pushed me to go to college had rolled into an attitude that I didn't want to see any of them. I'd also picked the school the farthest away I could get.

"We knew the fab four were going to be breathing down your neck and figured some time away from them would be important, but the assumption was there that you would move back home closer to us afterward."

"You know what they say about assumptions."

My dad chuckled.

I could feel Mom rolling her eyes at him.

"It's a year-long contract. Afterward, I will see where it takes me. But I have to warn you, the espresso machine is amazing."

Mom's laughter burst out from the phone, and I kept working on my hair.

They both knew the way to my heart involved food,

caffeine, and a good book. Still, our conversation left a sour taste in my mouth. Couldn't they be happy for me?

EVERY TIME I tried to move a paw, the carpet fought against me. The shop wanted me here. Right outside her open door, for some reason.

So I sat. And listened. My heart ached. She was loved. Her family loved her and wanted her to come home.

I understood the feeling when I let myself dwell on the past. I cherished my children, until I didn't. Obsession, and my ego, had been my downfall.

I flicked my tail and brushed the past away, then I padded toward the observatory on the other side of the second floor.

Sable would serve her year. She'd signed the contract, after all. But she would need to go after she'd fulfilled its terms.

Family was important. I'd learned that lesson too late.

SIX

It wasn't a dream.

Sunlight barely peeked into my room from the giant skylights, but my internal alarm clock had gone off. It was time to get up, no matter what the clock said.

Unpacking last night hadn't taken long, but soaking in the tub had ended up being a two-hour affair, because I found name-brand bath bombs in the bathroom cupboard. It was a good way to unwind after the call with my parents.

This place was the best. I was smitten. I just needed to deal with the Cat.

Opening the door to the balcony that overlooked the store was a glorious experience. Except things looked different. Like, the shop itself looked different.

The bookshelves down below had multiplied, and off to one side was a children's section with beanbag chairs and books on lower shelves. A few more skylights crowded the roof as well, but I wasn't going to complain about it. Sunlight was my jam. Especially when it looked like it was going to be a beautiful day.

I made my way downstairs to the espresso machine. First stop, caffeine. Then breakfast.

"Good morning, Betty. How are you doing?" Yes, I had decided to name the espresso machine. She needed a name, and I thought Betty fit the job well. "Let's get going and make an Americano. Something to wake me up."

Not that I needed to wake up. I was already awake and wondering what the day would bring. It was my first real day on the job, and I couldn't wait.

"Who are you talking to?" asked the Cat.

I jumped. *Shit.* It didn't matter that I'd expected it.

I glanced over my shoulder and spotted the Cat on the floor, staring at me.

"I'm talking to this lovely machine. She is glorious and needed a name."

He didn't blink.

I shrugged and went back to the shot I was pulling.

"Don't name things. It can be dangerous."

I rolled my eyes at the Cat. The Cat who was talking to me in a magical bookstore. He did not get to comment on my naming of the coffee machine.

"Did you want a coffee?"

"Not yet. It's early for caffeine. Breakfast first."

He could have his opinions on caffeine, but for me, it always came before breakfast.

I sipped the espresso in the teacup and headed to the kitchen, careful to not step on him. "So, what does taking care of you include? Like, you can talk. Am I really needed?"

"You have thumbs... and I can't just talk to everyone. Only certain people. Speaking of thumbs, how about some breakfast?"

Breakfast did sound good. I opened the fridge and found everything I could possibly need for a hearty meal. Bacon, eggs, and cheese, plus a variety of veggies. I turned the oven on to preheat, and before I could grab a pan, it dinged.

"Uh, the oven is a little fast." Strange, since preheating usually took forever.

"Did you really want to wait for it?" sassed the Cat.

That was a very good point.

I put the bacon on a pan and into the hot oven. Then I grabbed some veggies for the eggs. While I didn't really cook much, I could make a good breakfast. Umber, one of my brothers, didn't have time to cook breakfasts when I was growing up, so it was the one meal I could handle.

The Cat jumped up on the counter next to the cutting board.

He glared at the red peppers. "Are you putting vegetables in that?"

I stared at him. "Yes, veggies are good for you. Well, us. Actually, are you eating the same stuff as me, or is there cat food around here somewhere?"

Maybe I could get some answers about what I should do. I knew normal cats shouldn't eat vegetables, especially not onions or garlic, but he was a magical talking cat, right?

"I am not eating cat food." The Cat's full body

twitched. "I will have eggs. Without peppers in them. And bacon."

"Dude, these are sweet peppers, and they will fry up with the scallions."

You could not live off of eggs and bacon, or at least *I* couldn't. He could eat what I was eating.

"It will be tasty. I swear."

Part of me couldn't believe I'd just argued about vegetables with a cat.

He just stared, and I kept chopping the peppers. Every time I went to reach for something, it was right there. It sped everything up considerably.

The bacon timer went off, and I laid it out on some paper towels to crisp. Then I tossed the peppers in a skillet with some bacon grease. The eggs were super quick to scramble.

"How many slices of bacon do you want?" I loaded my own plate up with four, along with a big helping of eggs.

On his slightly smaller plate, I put the eggs with the peppers and scallions. Then I added bacon slices one by one.

"That should be good," rumbled the Cat.

I set both our plates on the island and grabbed a fork. By the time I turned around, half his bacon was gone.

"Woah, don't choke."

He was even eating the scrambled eggs and the veggies. Though I didn't see him actually bite the food. It just vanished.

Still, I couldn't help but smirk. Overall, it was a really

good breakfast. Probably one of the best things I'd cooked in a good while.

"So, what does the rest of today look like?" I asked.

"You man the register."

Was that really all he was going to give me? I motioned with my hand for him to continue. But then he didn't.

"That's it?"

"Yep."

This had to be about the peppers in the eggs.

I rolled my eyes and grabbed a water bottle out of the fridge. I set the dishes down in the sink and cleaned the rest of the kitchen. It didn't surprise me that the dishes were gone by the time I turned to get them washed. The dishwasher in the corner turned on by itself. I guess if you could move things around without touching them, getting the dishes done wasn't hard.

"Thank you," I whispered to the kitchen.

I disliked doing dishes. It was a major reason why I didn't cook much. Cleaning up afterward was not my favorite thing to do.

All right, time for more coffee before the day really started. I was ready. For the day. At least, I hoped so.

CHAPTER

SEVEN

I was bored as heck.

The Cat had me unlock the front door over two hours ago, and still nothing. A stool had appeared behind the counter, and the Cat dozed off to sleep in the chair by the front window. I didn't know what to do with myself.

Finally, I decided to wander through the shelves to see what I could read. I'd unpacked my books upstairs, but I'd read each of them multiple times. As much as I liked the idea of digital books, they weren't my jam. I needed to touch the paper to sink into the story.

The bookshelves were just like any other bookstore's. Each had a sign displaying the genre. Everything from self-help to business, to fantasy and young adult. The children's section was much bigger than it had been yesterday, and the number of adorable kids' books impressed me.

I swung by the cooking section and grabbed a book on cooking from the farm. It seemed interesting, and at least it would keep me busy.

The bells over the door rang, and a little girl darted into the store. She went right to the children's section, her jacket discarded in the middle of the floor. Not a glance around her, or at me. Just to a particular spot on the floor, and then she pulled out various kids' books.

I quickly made my way back to the counter with the cookbook under my arm.

The Cat still slept on the chair.

Okay, guess I would man the register on my own.

About three minutes later, a tall guy came in.

"Molly, you can't be darting off like that. You know better..." He gave me a smile and headed over to the kid, grabbing the fallen coat on the way.

"But dinosaurs, Dad! I have to read about dinosaurs!" announced the little girl, Molly.

He crouched down next to her with a big smile on his face. "One book only, and then we need to go. This is supposed to be your daily walk, not your daily reading time. We do that at home."

The dad patted her on the head and stood. He walked in my direction, and I couldn't help but smile. My dad was that type of dad, too. Patient.

"Can I get you something to drink?" I asked as he approached.

The girl's father had brown hair and deep-brown eyes. He had at least ten years on me, but he was still cute.

He studied me from behind his glasses. "Sure, can I get an Americano to go and a small hot chocolate for Molly?"

"Coming right up." I turned to my coffee machine, got the grinder going, then the shots.

"You must be new here. I don't think I've seen you around. I know Arnold talked about retiring. You look like you know what you're doing with the new machine. He had drip coffee on tap."

I couldn't help but shiver. "I can do better than drip. Yeah, I just started here. My name's Sable."

When the Americano was done, I glanced around. Under the counter sat a stack of to-go cups. They were not there yesterday.

I pulled one out and handed over the coffee. "Next up, a small hot chocolate."

"Did you hear that, Molly? If you clean your books up, you can get a hot chocolate."

The little girl started moving much more quickly.

I couldn't help but grin at the antics. I poured the hot chocolate into its own small cup and took it with me over to the register. I quickly rang them up, and he used a tap card.

"Can I have my hot chocolate?" asked Molly.

"Of course, little one. Here you go!" I smiled at the look on her face.

"Thank you!"

"You're welcome. Have a good day!" I waved at the pair.

This was going to be the easiest job ever.

As they headed to the door, it opened yet again, and the dad moved quickly to hold it. Someone was carrying a box inside.

"Thank you!" said the delivery guy.

He headed to the counter and set the box down. I could now see his jacket and the company he worked at.

Something black darted nearby, and I jumped as the Cat made his way to the counter.

"Hey, little guy." The delivery guy gave him scratches. "I got two more in my truck. I'll be right back."

Of course the Cat had awakened when packages arrived.

The guy came back and nudged the door open before adding another box to the counter. His name tag said John.

"Hey, I'm John. You must be new," he said to me.

"I am. I'm Sable. Are you the usual driver?"

He flashed a very white smile at me. He had to bleach those teeth.

"This is on my weekly route, though I can't believe Arnold finally retired." He shook his head. "I swore that he hated his job."

I wasn't sure how anyone would hate great coffee, magic, and unlimited food, but then again, you needed to deal with the Cat.

"Anyway, more stops to make. I hope to see you around!" John literally winked at me.

I gave him a small wave and tried not to roll my eyes. Staying on good terms with the delivery guys would be important.

I grabbed a box cutter and opened the lid. Then the Cat blocked my way, peering inside.

"Good, good. I hope everything is here," mumbled the Cat from partially inside the box.

He climbed back out. Inside the first box was a weird

collection of items. Bright-blue paint, a three-pack of tennis balls, some more children's books, and some plain cotton rolls of fabric.

"Grab the paint out. You can take this box into the supply cabinet. Open the next one first." He pawed at the next box and quickly sliced the top open with his claws.

I grabbed the first box and carried it over to the door I hadn't explored yet. It opened without a sound, and I peered inside. A row of metal shelves lined one wall, but not much else was in there. I set the box on one of the shelves and headed back to the counter.

"What about this one?" I asked, trying to see what was inside, but it was filled with crinkled paper.

The Cat had pushed some of it out of the box. I took over the job of removing the packing material. It had rows of glass vials that looked to be from an old-fashioned apothecary.

"Look for the peppermint oil and the rosemary. The supply closet should also have a pouch of black powder. The rest of this can go into storage," the Cat said.

I took out each bottle and squinted at them to decipher the horrible handwriting. Some sort of really small cursive. It took me longer than I would have thought to find the peppermint oil and the rosemary oil.

I set those on the counter and headed back to the supply room. But something was different. A small leather pouch rested next to the first box. I set the box of vials down and picked up the bag. The handwritten paper tag read *Black Powder*. The only black powder I knew of was gunpowder.

I headed back to the counter and carefully set the leather bag down.

"All right, what's in the last box?" I asked.

This was definitely a more interesting inventory than any other job I'd had.

He sniffed the box. "Well, open it and we can see... Though I think it's the diamond powder."

"Diamond powder? That's a thing?"

The Cat nodded. "Lab-grown, much cheaper than anything else, and it is the same thing. Works just as well as mined diamonds, but with less bloodshed."

The much smaller box had a tub labeled *Diamond Powder*.

This collection of items was strange. Blue paint, herb oils, black powder, and diamond powder.

"So, why do we need all of this?" I motioned at the items.

The Cat didn't answer, flicking his tail instead.

"Okay, does the diamond powder go in the supply closet?"

"Yep."

I added that to the shelves and then closed the door. After a moment, I opened the door and peeked back inside.

Empty metal wire shelves.

"Huh," I said, not really surprised anymore, but still unsettled.

Where did everything go?

"While you are playing around over there, can you grab a clay crock from inside and then a wooden spoon from the kitchen? It should have a green handle."

Now I felt like a go-fer. He really meant it when he'd said I was hired because I had thumbs.

The clay crock sat on one side of the storage room that I hadn't seen, and the spoon lay on the island in the kitchen.

"All right, now what?" I asked.

The Cat sniffed everything and nodded. It looked so strange from a cat.

"Now it is time for magic."

I blinked. Then blinked again. "Magic?"

EIGHT

The Cat turned and looked at me. "Yes, magic. This is a magical shop, is it not?"

His green eyes glowed and stood out against his black fur.

"It is a bookshop," I answered slowly.

The shelves had changed a little, and things moved on their own, but it was still a bookshop.

"Right now, it is a bookshop." The Cat sat down. "But it won't be one tomorrow. This needs to set overnight, so pay attention. Fill the crock to the line inside with the blue paint, and try not to get it everywhere."

"Shouldn't we do this in the kitchen?" I asked before I could stop myself.

The Cat glared at me, so I closed my mouth and opened the paint. It was mineral paint, and it didn't look mixed.

"Should I mix this?" I showed him inside the container.

"Yes."

I closed it back up and started shaking it. Then I rolled it around on the counter. At least it was only one container.

The Cat's tail twitched each time it rolled in front of him. His paw moved only once when it came too close to him.

"So what type of magic is this?"

"Important magic."

Okay... He was not in a talkative mood.

I opened the lid to check to see if it was good. It was all one color now. I carefully poured it inside the clay pot, making sure not to spill it. Getting paint off of the wooden counter would be a pain, and I knew the Cat wasn't going to clean it up.

"All right, what's next, Jedi Master?"

"I am not a Jedi. And next are the oils. Three drops of rosemary. Then all of the peppermint."

How did he know what a Jedi was?

I did as he requested. These instructions were easy enough.

"Now stir it with the spoon." He moved much closer, his face right next to the edge of the rim as I stirred.

I tried to be careful not to spill any of it. The whole area stank of peppermint. Thankfully, I liked the smell. It completely covered any smell from the paint.

His whiskers twitched, and he nodded. "All right, now on to the black powder."

"Is this gunpowder?" I asked.

"No. Dump the whole bag into it carefully. It stings if it gets in your eyes." The Cat moved backward from the crock, putting a good distance between him and the black powder.

"While stirring?"

"You can stop stirring."

That was a relief. I didn't know how I wasn't going to get it all over the place if I had to stir it. The black powder was a little more difficult than the oil had been, since it was in a leather pouch with only so much structure. But I got it all on top of the blue paint mixture and tried to make sure I didn't breathe any of it in. Who knew what was in it?

I moved to grab the spoon.

"Don't!"

I flinched at his tone and froze. I held the spoon up, but I didn't move. I wasn't sure if I could.

The Cat darted forward and leaned over the opening. His nose touched the powder piled up. Bright light pulsed from his nose and slowly covered the black powder. When he pulled away, it had turned a deep silver color.

"Now you can stir it."

My muscles relaxed at once, and I almost stumbled. The Cat had turned the black powder into something that looked like glittery nail polish. I moved the wooden spoon slowly, and the silver sank into the blue. It really did almost look like nail polish. The silver did not dissolve. Instead, it floated, little silver flecks in the blue paint.

I tried to keep the smirk off my face. "You know, glitter might be cheaper."

"It's magic," grumbled the Cat.

His eyes stayed on the mixture as I kept stirring.

"Whatever you say," I said.

After all, he was a talking cat, so maybe it was magic? I kept my unease to myself.

The hair on the back of my neck prickled. He had frozen me in place. I wasn't sure how to feel about this. Not to mention whatever he had done did seem like magic. But the magical bookstore seemed safe somehow. Whatever he had done, didn't, though.

For now, I ignored the goose bumps.

"You can put it in the fridge now. We will need it tomorrow. The magic needs to rest to combine with it."

"Will it do anything to the food inside the fridge?"

The Cat shook his head. "Put the lid on it."

Cats shouldn't shake their heads. It looked so wrong.

"Okay, just checking. 'Cause I don't know much about this magic stuff."

I STUDIED her as she carried the crock into the kitchen. She was being super careful with it, taking slow steps to make sure she didn't spill or drop it.

This one was weird. The magic didn't seem to scare her much, and me, not at all, even when I froze her. I didn't mean to. It happened automatically. I spoke, and it happened.

Starting over would have taken too much time. Not to mention we didn't have any more paint or peppermint oil. The supply closet was running low on several items, some normal and others magical.

Whenever the shopkeeper changed, things slowed down. The place needed to get used to the new energy, and so did I. There was just a never-ending list of things to do, places to go, and things to keep in order.

I couldn't help but glance at the book she hadn't noticed yet. It lay on the chair I'd slept on earlier. Soon she would need to see it, and maybe understand what we were responsible for.

But not yet. It was good that she liked the shop. And she did make good bacon.

"I am going to be placing a Walmart order. Make sure you add anything you want to the list. You have twenty minutes."

That should do it. Right on time, she popped out of the kitchen.

"For real? Anything I want?" she asked.

"Even more of that purple hair dye. Just make sure it's in stock."

The smile on her face lit up the whole shop. More sunlight streamed in from the new skylights. She was already making so many changes, and she didn't even know it. The longer it stayed that way, the better.

I had to admit, the new light in the room was nice. I liked it. Which was strange. I didn't like anything, not anymore.

More and more, the years weighed down on me. Everything was about the book.

I snuggled into the chair a little bit more and closed my eyes. The next delivery would get here soon enough. Sable's fear had vanished with the bribe. I didn't want her to fear me.

And that was new, too.

NINE

Sometimes you fail, and that's okay. At least the kitchen didn't smell of burnt rice anymore.

It wasn't like it hadn't been edible, there was just a smaller amount than expected after getting rid of the burnt bits. Still, at least I could prove my worth with breakfast. That I could nail without a problem.

Hopefully, this evening I could Skype with my mom and catch her up on the job. Edited, of course. Mom would probably flip if I told her about the magic stuff. Flip, or decide I was lying about the whole thing and really was in some sort of danger. She could be a bit dramatic that way.

The Cat appeared on the counter.

"Good morning. Do you want veggies in your eggs or not?" I wanted a little more instruction for my day.

"Make me the same as yesterday."

Ha, I knew it. He had liked the eggs, and he'd cleared his little plate.

Yet, I said nothing. I just smiled and went on with making breakfast.

"So, today will be a busier day. We will have customers for most of the morning."

I paused scrambling the eggs. "How do you know what the day is going to bring? Like, I get there is magic and all, but..."

"We will need the paint today. The customers are coming to pick it up."

I nodded slowly. Okay, that made more sense. Whoever had ordered the blue magic paint was coming in, so that's how he knew what was going to happen.

My shoulders relaxed a bit, and I loaded both plates up with eggs, plus some reheated bacon. Bacon every day would go to my thighs, but I would not resist. I mean, it was bacon. Resistance was futile anyway.

"Anything else I should know?" I asked hesitantly.

He was being a little more talkative, and I wanted to keep it that way.

"Just a normal day at the shop."

"Okay, sounds good." I sipped the coffee I had made before breakfast. A refill would be nice. "When are we going to open?"

"When we are ready." The Cat inhaled the plate of food, and for the second time, I wondered where it went.

He wasn't a fat cat, but I had given him a ton, forgetting that he was only a cat and not the size of a human.

I nodded and finished my breakfast. I wrapped the last of the bacon and put it in the fridge. The Cat was already heading to the front counter.

"Do you want me to grab the paint?"

"Yes."

Okay, here we go.

I grabbed the paint and left my coffee on the table.

"Thanks for cleaning up the kitchen. I'm coming back for the coffee," I whispered.

I knew it had to be the Cat cleaning up after me, but still. It felt weird thinking about saying it to him directly. After all, if he could clean up, why did he even need me?

The main shop looked different. I knew it as soon as I stepped out of the doorway. The counter was the same, but beyond that, the bookshelves lined the walls, but no books were on them. Instead, unique pieces of wood stood all around the room. They looked like branches that had been cut off of trees. Each leaned up against one of the shelves.

I carefully set the clay pot on the counter and noticed the register was gone. The Cat sat in his place. When I glanced the other way, my eyes widened.

"No... Nonono... Where is Betty?"

A stack of old rags and jars with paint brushes in them filled the space.

"Betty?" the Cat asked.

"My espresso machine?!"

"You don't need a cup of coffee that bad."

I turned to the Cat, my fingers clenching into fists for the first time since joining the shop. He dared tell me how much caffeine I needed? He loved a good cup of coffee as well, and I knew he hadn't had one yet.

His head jerked backward, and he blinked at me.

"Give me back my machine!" I yelled.

How could he not warn me it was going to be unavailable today?

"We don't have time for this," muttered the Cat.

He seemed tense as he glanced toward the door, which, of course, let out a tinkle of bells as someone opened it.

I spun to give them a fake smile but then froze. I dropped below the counter, my breathing frantic. They were green, had horns, and were giant! Like, their heads touched the doorway, which had probably gotten bigger just for them. What were they?

"Sable?"

I glanced up, and the Cat peered over the edge of the counter at me.

"Are you okay?"

I shook my head. Clouds must have crossed over the windows, and the skylights darkened momentarily.

"They're trolls, perfectly safe. The paint is for them. Well, the spears are for them, but the paint is as well."

I shook my head again. Trolls were real? More information would have been nice.

He jumped off the counter and nudged my hand, which was plastered to the floor.

"You need to get up and greet them." He nudged me again. "You can do this."

I tried to relax my shoulders and my fingers, but it was slow going. Footsteps moved around the shop but didn't approach the counter.

The Cat nudged my fingers again.

"I should have warned you. Please, get up." He stared at me with his bright-green eyes. "You're worrying me."

They are just like anyone else.

I could do this. They were people. Big, green, horned, not-at-all-normal people.

Deep breaths.

First, I calmed my breathing, and then I carefully stood. I did not squeak, even as I realized more of them crowded the shop besides the one at the door. Five or six of them looked at the branches. As soon as I came into view, one of them approached where the register had been.

He was the tallest one of the bunch. His bright-blue horns curved back from his forehead, the same color as the paint in the pot.

I glanced down to confirm it. My coffee mug sat next to the pot. Steam rose from it. I flicked my gaze to the Cat, but he stared at the troll.

The troll bowed his head to the Cat. A necklace rattled against his chest. It was made of different teeth, strung on a cord.

My stomach shook, but I ignored it. I rushed to my coffee mug, letting the warmth seep into me.

"Our new warriors have come for the spears! They have passed the rites," the troll said.

How the heck did I understand the troll? There was no way he spoke English. The sounds were wrong. Or, well, not normal, but I understood him anyway.

The Cat nodded. "Vulug, let them find the wood that calls to them. Then once they carve the point, we will use the magic."

The troll turned to me, waiting.

But I didn't know what to do.

CHAPTER
TEN

"Repeat it, Sable. He doesn't know what I said."

I opened my mouth, quickly repeating what the Cat had said.

The troll nodded and turned back to the others.

I tightened my grip on my coffee mug and took a sip. At least I had a little bit of coffee left, and it was still warm.

Hopefully the Cat realized he had royally screwed up by not warning me.

The more I watched the trolls admiring the various pieces of wood, the more I relaxed. They were here to buy things, just like anyone else. They were just green and tall. Why was everyone so tall?

"So, is this their first spear or something?" I quietly asked the Cat.

"It is the one they will take into their great hunt. Vulug visits each year with the ones who are now old enough and have passed whatever rites or rituals there are among his people. It is an honor to be involved. He is a great Elder for the trolls."

I assumed the large one was Vulug.

That made sense, in a way.

"They can't do the magic themselves?"

The Cat lay down on the counter, his head resting on his paws, almost like a dog. "Their shaman used to, but he died without a successor."

Inside, I winced.

"They pray another will be born who has the power. Maybe one of these warriors will be that one. Until then, we provide the magic so that their people's rites can continue."

This had to mean something big to these people, but they couldn't do it themselves anymore. That had to be rough on them.

But since we were here, we could help them. Warmth filled me.

My shoulders relaxed a bit more, and I studied everyone in the shop. Every time one of them picked up a length of wood, they looked at it every which way. They would run their green hands along the length and hold it up to their shoulders as if they might throw it.

It mesmerized me.

Vulug approached the counter with a smaller troll by his side. It was then I realized that the ones looking at the wood stood a little shorter and had fewer muscles. They had to be the new hunters or warriors.

"Does this shaft match this warrior?" asked Vulug.

The Cat sat up as they approached. He motioned for the younger one to hold his spear out. The Cat leaned forward and touched his nose to the wood. Then he sniffed the troll before nodding.

"Good, good." Vulug motioned to the troll. "Go carve your point."

The potential warrior then headed out of the shop. The door stood propped open, but the Cat said nothing about it.

"You asked questions about us," said Vulug. "You are new. This is the first time I see you."

"Yes," I said hesitantly. "I was wondering about how we help your people."

He nodded, and his eyebrows pulled together.

"A new shaman will be born when the time is right. Our old shaman's son, Dorz, and daughter, Horza, are both the correct age. We will see if either has the power during the hunt." Vulug smiled at both of us. "Then you and the Cat can be guests at the ceremony."

The Cat froze at the words, then he shook his head.

"It will be so, old friend. You have helped for many years." The troll's hand hovered above the counter before he set it down with force. "Someday you will visit and meet the rest of our people."

His dark eyes stared at the Cat for a moment, before he turned back to the others in his party.

The Cat's head lowered, and he turned around on the counter before curling into a ball.

I didn't know what to do to break the mood he seemed to be in. He was strange, even for a cat, but not normally, well, sad.

The smell of wood smoke drifted into the shop, but the

pleasant scent cheered me up. I loved a good campfire, and marshmallows to roast over it. Outside, a small fire burned with trolls surrounding it. Usually, I couldn't see far through the hazy windows, but today the glass was clear.

The Cat was still curled up, and I carefully reached out and petted him. He slowly relaxed and unfurled out of the ball.

As time went on, one by one, the rest of the trolls approached the counter. Each time, the Cat would touch the wood with his nose then nod or shake his head. If it was a no, the troll would go back to find a different piece of wood that spoke to them. With the first rejected troll, I worried about what the youngling would do, but he nodded at the Cat with a smile.

"They would rather it be right for the hunt," the Elder commented to me. "It is important."

"That makes sense. So they take these spears, and you go on a big hunt?" I could ask the Cat, but he seemed to still be in a bad mood. And Vulug seemed willing enough to indulge my curiosity.

"Yes, we will all go into the plains and hunt great enormous beasts," said Vulug. "It takes several spears to take them down. They have thick fur and large tusks. This is their chance to prove they are warriors to the clan."

Finally, it was down to one troll who wasn't outside already carving a tip and hardening the point in the fire. Or, at least, it looked like that was what they were doing. I wasn't sure. Spear-making was not on my resume. Though, if I could, I totally would make one. Heck, if the

Elder offered to help make me one, I would take him up on it in an instant.

The only troll left was the woman, Horza. She went from shelf to shelf looking for something that called to her and that the Cat might approve. She came up to the counter by herself, as the leader stood outside, helping with the next step.

"Hello. Hold it out for the Cat."

Horza looked to me then to the Cat, who was napping. "Yo, Cat. It's time to do your thing."

He glared at me and climbed to his feet. She held out the wood, and he sniffed it before nodding.

"Great, you are good to go!" I announced.

The female troll was dressed like the others in some sort of cloth. Bracelets of wooden beads covered each of her wrists, with each painted different colors.

"I like your bracelets. They're pretty."

"They are potent magic. My father made them before he passed. I have added to them." She paused. "But I don't have magic. At least not yet."

"You might though. Your leader said something about it."

Horza frowned then nodded. "Yes, they hope my brother's magic comes out after the hunt."

"Yours too, right?" I asked, but she shrugged.

A mask came over her features, covering any emotion.

Vulug came in and smiled when he saw her at the counter. "Ah, good. One spoke to you. Time for carving, and then magic."

She gave me a tight smile and then headed to the

door after Vulug. She hadn't answered my question about her magic.

"Doesn't she want magic?" I asked softly.

To my surprise, the Cat answered. "She might not. Women warriors are highly respected by the trolls. They usually become great leaders for their people. If she has proven herself enough for the hunt, becoming a shaman might not be what she wants."

I hadn't even thought about the downsides of having magic. I thought magic was awesome most of the time, but it wouldn't change what I had to do for the next year. No matter what, I would be here in this shop. Yet for her, if she had it, everything would change.

"So, does the magic happen after the hunt?"

The Cat nodded. "It usually shows itself during the hunt. The trolls' magic is potent during the first hunt, and that can ignite other magics as well."

"Are shamans the only ones who use magic? Can she become a magic warrior or whatnot?"

Learning about the trolls' culture interested me, much more than any of the classes I'd taken in college.

The Cat tilted his head. "It hasn't been done. I don't think."

"Ah, so you don't know everything."

The Cat didn't respond to that. Instead, he jumped down from the counter and padded over to the chair in the window. He jumped up and peered outside.

I finished my coffee and then headed to the open door. I did not try to cross the threshold, but leaned against the doorframe. The trolls who had picked out new spears stood scattered about, plus several who had not come into the store. Some still carved points and waved them over the wood smoke. They spoke, but they were far enough away that I couldn't hear them.

The woman caught me watching her, and she gave me a genuine smile. She held up her spear with glee, and I smiled in return.

They weren't as frightening as I thought at first. Just people.

For my first official morning, I'd call that a win. Who knew what the rest of the day would bring?

ELEVEN

The seven trolls outside slowly finished their spears and then stood in a line. Vulug walked up and down the line, inspecting each of the spears. Some had carvings in them; others kept theirs plain.

Two stood out to me. Horza's and the guy's who stood next to her. I assumed that was her brother, Dorz.

I kept glancing back at their weapons, even though I tried to look away. It was weird.

Vulug eventually nodded and turned back toward the shop.

My eyes widened, and I quickly made my way back to the counter. The Cat had beaten me and sat on top of it.

"Is it time for the magic now?"

The Cat nodded. "Get your brush ready. You will need to coat the tip of each spear. I will do the actual magic."

The crock of paint still sat on the counter, and I moved over to the brushes that lay in the place Betty usually sat. Footsteps sounded near the door, and I quickly grabbed a towel and a brush.

The trolls stood all lined up, one behind the other, holding their spears with the butt to the ground. The first one stepped up and held out his weapon.

I looked to the Cat, who nodded. I dipped the paintbrush into the bright-blue paint and slowly coated the pointed tip. The silver flecks had seemed to vanish. The blue seemed to soak quickly into the blackened wood. Once I'd covered it, Vulug and the one holding the weapon both whispered something as the Cat touched it with his nose.

A bright-white light flashed. The tip of the spear now had two gold lines running down the point on opposite sides of each other.

The troll grinned. "It is done."

The Cat nodded, and the now-blessed warrior walked out of the shop. The next troll in line waited until they'd left before stepping forward. We repeated the ceremony four more times.

Then it was the two siblings.

This time, when the brother held out his weapon, the Cat moved before I could. He sniffed at the point, and all the trolls froze. He didn't touch it, but the swirls young Dorz had carved in a ring around the tip glowed as the Cat hovered.

"Paint it," whispered the Cat in my mind.

I carefully painted the tip of the spear as the trolls whispered to themselves. The Cat then touched it. Once the bright light fled, I gasped.

The gold wasn't just in two lines. Instead, it had spread to the swirls the young troll had carved.

Dorz smiled widely at the Cat, and his gaze moved to Vulug, who nodded at him. He turned to leave the room but paused at his sister. He said nothing, but a look passed between them. Both their eyes sparkled.

Once he left, Horza stepped forward. She had carved two distinct rings around the top part of her spear. One was like her brother's, but the other was more geometric, like a band. Below that was a cord of what looked like leather wrapped three times around the wood and a string of three wooden beads dangling from the end.

"What do the carvings mean?" The words slipped out of my mouth before I could stop myself.

Horza leaned back for a moment. "The first ring is for the magic of my bloodline, of my father. The second is the one I earned from winning the games at the clan gathering."

She paused. "The beads are for my mother."

I nodded like all of that made sense, and held out the brush.

While we had spoken, the Cat had sniffed at the spear. He nodded to me. Again, I painted the tip with the blue concoction. The Cat touched it with his nose. This time, the gold filling the designs didn't shock me. What did was that the wooden beads turned the same deep blue as the paint.

Yet Horza frowned, and Vulug seemed confused as well.

"But my brother has the shaman magic?" asked Horza.

"You both have the potential," answered Vulug. "You both are still in the running."

Horza slowly left the shop after shooting a glance at the Cat, but he didn't respond.

Vulug hung back.

"Could both of them be shamans?" asked the Elder.

The Cat took his time responding, his eyes turned skyward. "As you said, they both have the potential for strong magic from their father."

I repeated the statement from the Cat.

"The clan won't like this. We can only have one shaman."

"So, only one can be the shaman? Why does it matter if they both have magic?" I asked.

Vulug shook his head but didn't respond as he left the shop. The door stayed open behind him.

"Is that all?" I asked.

"No, they will go on the hunt and return. Hopefully, one will be a shaman, and our duty will be done."

"And if not?"

"Then this will repeat each year until they do." The Cat jumped off the counter. "How about lunch while we wait?"

"Wait, lunch? How can you be thinking about food? Who is going to be the shaman?" My voice carried after the Cat into the kitchen, but he remained silent.

I rolled my eyes and walked after him. Having the door open made me nervous, and suddenly it closed with the jingle of the bells.

"Thank you!"

Sometimes the Cat was a nice guy.

I DECIDED against anything fancy and made hot dogs for lunch. If I knew how to roast meat, I would have done that, just to keep with the feel of the day, but hot dogs were the closest that I could do.

I set one hot dog in its bun on a plate for the Cat.

"What do you want on it?" I asked.

The Cat stared at it. "What is it?"

"A hot dog... Tubed meat with a bread bun," I said. "I usually put ketchup, mustard, and relish on mine. If I were being fancy, I would have made chili and melted cheese."

The Cat stopped staring and sniffing at the hot dog to turn and look at me. His chin tucked closer to his neck and his eyes went wide. I was pretty sure that was his confused face.

"Do whatever you do."

"Okay." I grabbed the condiments and copied what was on my two hot dogs.

I couldn't bring myself to put two of them on his plate, he might explode from that much food.

"Eat up." My stomach growled, and I started eating my first hot dog while monitoring the Cat.

He took a bite out of the end of the hot dog. He didn't get any of the bun, but he got mustard on his nose. I kept eating my lunch to remain quiet.

He didn't eat like a normal cat. He'd take a bite, and it would be gone, with no chomping. Nothing like that. It wasn't even like a human chewing. Just a bite, and it vanished immediately. My brain hurt watching him, so I glanced away to finish my food.

"Hot dogs are okay," stated the Cat loudly.

I took a sip of my water.

His plate sat empty, and he must have cleaned up his face already since the mustard was gone.

"Better than your breakfast."

"I'll keep that in mind." I motioned to the front of the store. "How long is this going to take?"

The Cat tilted his head to the side. "It depends on how long they take to find one of the big animals they hunt."

I glared at him. "Fine, so it should be soon. We shouldn't be here more than a few hours more."

I leaned back on the stool, careful not to fall over.

"How do you know where we need to go?" I asked.

"It is part of my job." The Cat moved on the counter so his back faced me and he could look at the entrance to the hallway and then the store. "We should go back to the counter."

If he thought that would stop my questions, he had another thing coming.

I put both of our plates in the sink and then finished my water. A pitcher of iced tea sat in the fridge, and I filled my glass with that. It was my only caffeine source, since my poor espresso machine had vanished.

I made my way to the front of the store, and the door opened. The Cat sat in the chair by the window, and I moved to the door.

"So, how did you get the job?" I asked the Cat.

The Cat shuddered.

"I will not speak about this. Do not ask me again." His voice sounded icy, and I couldn't help but shiver.

The store darkened, and a shout came from outside the door.

Peeking out, I saw a line of trolls marching toward the store. They were a distance away, but many of them dragged a large sled behind them.

"Ah, the hunt was successful." Every trace of coldness had gone, and the normal Cat was back in its place.

"Can you see that far?" I couldn't make out faces, only that it was a large group.

"They killed the animal, and they partially butchered it. They will need to finish that tonight."

"What about the siblings? Are they different?" My curiosity bubbled inside me. I needed to know more.

Then again, what happened to the curious cat?

I peeked back at the Cat. Did his curiosity get him in trouble?

The Cat took his time responding, instead staring outside. "They are both near Vulug and have been painted. You will need to ask."

"Painted?" I leaned forward and ran smack into the barrier that prevented me from leaving.

I jerked back, stumbling. My nose hurt, but at least it didn't break. I had misjudged by a few inches.

"Are you okay?"

"Fine," I grumbled, rubbing my nose.

By the time I moved back to the doorway, the trolls had come much closer.

Vulug marched toward the door, and I jumped back to give him space. The Cat sat next to me near my feet.

Vulug entered with a giant smile. "The hunt was a success! We have a shaman and six new warriors."

"That is success indeed, Vulug."

"Who is the shaman?" I asked.

"Dorz is a shaman. His sister has talent, but decided that she will focus on being a great leader for our people. We will paint stripes on her horns. They all fought bravely."

"This is it, then," said the Cat. That drew my attention. "This is farewell."

Vulug's eyes narrowed. "I invite you, Cat, and the Shopkeeper, to the great gathering next year when we present our shaman to the clans. I name you guests of honor, and honor must be fulfilled."

The Cat said nothing, only bowed his head.

Vulug gave me a nod and then strode out of the shop.

I caught a glance at Horza, her arm wrapped around her brother's shoulders, both laughing at something. Then the door closed. I blinked, and everything vanished.

"Cat?" I hadn't seen a shift before, when the store moved.

Outside the door was a street now, nothing like the campfire and gathering of trolls.

The Cat still had his head bowed, and I crouched down on the floor to peer at him.

"Hey, Cat..." I ran a finger along one of his ears, and he trembled.

Without thinking about it, I scooped him up in my arms. "We will figure it out... Don't worry."

It only took a few moments before he jumped back

down out of my arms. "That is done. Tomorrow will be another day."

As he walked off, I knew that there was a lot more to this than just a magical bookshop. Even if that was saying a lot.

And despite the fact that the Cat was sometimes annoying, I wanted to help him be at least a little happier when I could.

Somehow.

CHAPTER

TWELVE

I woke up ready to go.

I made my shower quick, and I put on my favorite shirt that had a picture of a cat curled up with a book. I almost didn't, but if the Cat had a problem with it, he could deal. Nothing would destroy my good mood.

I swung open the door with force and a bright smile and stepped out onto the balcony into a sun-filled room. The shop down below looked different, but not as drastically different as I'd hoped for.

The bookshelves lined the three walls, and several others created stacks like in any bookstore. A table sat in front of the rightmost wall with a chair behind it. The store had piled a stack of ten books on one end of the table. From here, I couldn't read the cover of the top book. The glare from the sunlight was too much.

"So a normal bookshop day... Maybe..." I said to myself.

I headed down the steps, taking two at a time, praying that he hadn't touched Betty. As I came around the corner, there she sat, right where she belonged. A sigh escaped my lips before I could help it.

"The coffee machine was only gone for one day," said the Cat.

He jumped up to the counter from the other side.

"One day was too much," I said with a smile.

My normal mug of dark blue and stars sat cleaned and ready to go. I still couldn't get over the fact that things cleaned themselves here. Or at least were loaded into the dishwasher and then put away. I needed to figure out how the Cat did it, and I made a mental note to follow up on that.

"What do you want to drink today?" I asked.

His green eyes studied me. "Your choice. Something fancy in a teacup."

I pulled out a teacup from below the counter with a saucer. It was a light-blue color with light-pink roses dotted over it. Gold rimmed the edges. The cup was in pristine condition.

I set it carefully on the counter. "Hmmm, how about a flat white with a dash of chocolate on top? Or maybe a little hazelnut with the espresso..."

My mind started racing with a couple different combinations, but hazelnut sounded so good this morning, I kept coming back to it.

First, I dribbled a little hazelnut syrup into his teacup then into my mug. I followed it with two shots of espresso for his cup then another two for mine. Last came the steamed milk, and I topped both cups. To give his a little more flair, I sprinkled a little cocoa powder on top.

"Here you go, fancy."

He sniffed the cup and licked a small bit of the foam off. "Should it be stirred?"

I nodded. "Most people stir it after the barista gives it to them all pretty…"

I found several teaspoons in a cup under the counter, and I grabbed one.

"Do you want me to stir it for you?"

He nodded. "Thank you for the fancy drink."

"You're welcome," I said with a bright smile. "Now it's time for bacon."

"And cookies," said the Cat.

I paused as I picked up my drink. "Cookies?"

The Cat nodded and pawed at his drink. "Yes, we have a book signing today. We said we would provide cookies."

My good mood wobbled. "Ugh, I can't bake cookies from scratch… I mean, I can learn, but I don't know how to do that off the top of my head."

I swear he smiled at me.

Then someone knocked on the door.

"That's what the cookie dough order is for," he replied smugly.

The Cat jumped off the counter and headed for the kitchen, leaving his teacup behind.

The person knocked again.

After setting my mug back on the counter, I made my way to the door. An older woman gave me a hesitant smile as I unlocked the store and motioned her inside. She carried a large plastic container.

"I hope this is the right place for the cookie dough," she said as she stepped inside.

"Yep, you found us."

"Perfect! This order was a lifesaver. Sales have been really rough this month, but this gets me in a much better place." She walked in and set the container on the counter.

I noticed the teacup was gone.

"I have instructions on these index cards," the woman said, "and if you need anything, just call me. My number is on the back."

She'd pulled her dark hair into a ponytail, but it was messy and all over the place. Her shirt had flour on one side, and she had a handprint on the right leg of her jeans.

She held out the index cards. "I mean it. If you need any last-minute orders, or anything. My name's Sandra."

I took the cards. "Thank you! This event is a little last minute, so I really appreciate this. I am not a baker."

The name on the card said *Sandra, Cookie Master*, and in the corner was a cookie with a chef's hat on it.

"I need to get back to the shop, but thanks again!" Sandra headed out the still-open door, leaving the plastic containers behind.

The cards pulled at my attention, so I flipped through them. Instructions for the temperature to bake the cookies, along with storage instructions, were written in neat handwriting.

Step one: Preheat your oven to 375.

My eyes widened, and I darted into the kitchen to

turn on the oven. One oven was already at 400 and the other at 375.

"Is it time for breakfast?" asked the Cat.

"I need to figure out what to do with the cookies, and then I will make bacon. How much time do I have until this book signing?"

The Cat lapped at his teacup before pulling away. "It starts at ten, and we will open the doors at 9:00 a.m."

Never had I been so happy to have gotten up at 6:30. At this point, it was only 7:30, and I had plenty of time.

My shoulders relaxed, and I went back to the storefront to grab the containers of cookie dough. By the time I set them on the countertop, my coffee sat next to the Cat.

"Thank you for grabbing my coffee."

The Cat didn't respond and looked curiously at me.

"I didn't have enough hands. All right, let's get the bacon in along with the first batch of cookies. What flavors did you get, anyway?"

Hopefully with the help of the shop I wouldn't burn too many cookies.

CHAPTER
THIRTEEN

The Cat must love cookies.

Three batches of cookies later, I was missing over seven cookies across the board. I hadn't touched one yet.

He had gotten several varieties, each with two batches of twelve. So far, I'd baked batches of snicker-doodles, double chocolate chunk, and old-fashioned peanut butter cookies. The peanut-butter ones I put on a cake stack with a glass covering over them.

"Should I make more?" I asked the Cat.

"Yes, make a batch of the chocolate brownie ones. And shortbread."

I blinked at his tone and paused what I was doing.

"Please."

I gave him a nod then grabbed another baking sheet out of the drawer. Each time I went to grab one, another one sat there, and I tried hard not to think about it. The same went for the silicon sheets that went on top of the metal pans.

The cookie woman had been right—all I needed to do was space the balls of cookie dough out on the pan and pop them in the oven. It was magic.

Well, not magic like the Cat's magic, but magic anyhow. Though maybe baking was magic like the Cat's magic.

I sipped my coffee and pulled the tub of cookie dough closer. It had round balls stacked next to each other, covered by a layer of parchment paper, then another layer stacked on top of the first. One side I hadn't touched, and it looked like little cylinders of dough. Per the tag, it was a coffee shortbread cookie. The other was a buttery shortbread recipe. I went with the coffee one.

I placed each cylinder two inches apart, then I placed the metal tray into the oven. This cookie took a little longer than the others at twenty minutes.

Next, I grabbed the container for the brownie cookies. I did not know what a brownie cookie was. These weren't balls or cylinders. Instead, thick batter covered the bottom of the container. The directions said to scoop out one-fourth of a cup three inches apart.

I shrugged and followed the directions, but it made a mess. Chocolate batter got all over the place.

The Cat chuckled at my antics to get the batter on the pan.

"Like you could do better," I grumbled.

If these turned out round, I would be shocked.

I flung a finger at the Cat, sending a glob of the batter his way. He jumped back, and it missed him by a mile.

He moved forward and sniffed it before licking it. "It's tasty."

The smell of the coffee shortbread cookies filled the air. Slowly, I brought all the cooled cookies out to the front of the shop. A glass case had appeared next to the register, and I slid the metal trays inside. The peanut butter ones in the cake stand I set next to the register.

I checked the time, and we were doing okay. We still had thirty minutes before we would open the shop.

"So, Cat, what is this book signing about?"

The Cat said nothing, and I peeked around to find him. I narrowed my eyes at the crumbs on the counter. Another cookie was missing from one of the trays.

"Cat, you can't eat all the cookies!"

He didn't respond, but black fur flashed up on the balcony near all the plants.

I rolled my eyes and made another flat white for myself. It had turned out superb earlier, and it went with the cookies pretty well.

I must ignore the peanut butter cookies.

The timer went off in the kitchen, and I headed back in to get the next batch out of the oven. They needed to cool a bit before they went into the case.

Time was ticking.

Okay, I failed.

Three peanut butter cookies were gone from the stack, and this time I couldn't blame it on the Cat. These cookies were just too good. The Cookie Master should rake in millions for her cookies. I made a note to leave a review about how good they were.

We had five minutes until the doors opened, though they were already unlocked. The Cat was still nowhere to be seen, but I swear he was running around upstairs like he had the zoomies.

The bells on the door jingled, and a woman entered the store. She had on a bright-red hat, a trench coat, and a big red bag. She smiled as soon as her gaze landed on me.

"This is such a cute little bookstore! I can't believe this is the place." Before I could reply, she twirled around the shop. "Look at the shelves!"

The shelves were rather nice in the deep wood, with a great finish. The stacks were dust free and filled with many books. I hadn't had a chance to walk through them yet, though the setup was like when I'd first taken the job.

"I'll ditch my stuff over by the table then come get a cup of coffee before the masses descend."

Again, I didn't need to say a word as she approached the table and set the bag on the chair along with her coat and hat.

"Just so adorable," she muttered as she approached the counter. "What do you recommend?"

"Today's special is a hazelnut flat white. It goes great with any of the cookies we have for the signing," I said.

"Oh, that sounds perfect."

The Cat took that moment to jump up onto the counter.

The woman jerked back. "You have a cat?!"

"Well, the shop is called Meow..."

She reached out and scratched him behind the ears.

"He has had a case of the zoomies this morning." I quickly made the drink for her and motioned to the cookies. "Do you want a cookie?"

"Just the drink for now." She studied the offering. "Can you set aside one of those brownie cookies for me?"

"Sure, I'll set one under the counter."

The Cat's voice whispered in my mind. "You don't need to charge her for any food or cookies. The first cookie will be free to everyone. After that, the prices are in the register."

I set her drink on the counter in one of the nice mugs. It was black with deep-red roses on it. The leaves had flecks of gold in them.

"Here you go..."

Once she turned away, the Cat glared at me. "What are 'the zoomies'?"

I giggled to myself but didn't answer.

The bells rang out as more people entered the store. This time it was three women, all clutching books to their chests. The author quickly made her way over to the table. Two of the women headed in that direction while the other headed to me.

"Welcome to Meow. Our special today is a hazelnut flat white. Plus, we have a free cookie for attending the signing."

"I'd love one of those peanut butter cookies, but can I get an Americano?"

"Sure," I said as I grabbed a to-go cup to begin her coffee. "So, what's the book about?"

I motioned to the book she'd set on the counter. The

title was *The Singing Waves,* and it had gold filigree on the edges with a splash of water and a fish's tail.

She blushed and giggled. "No judgment, please, but it's a very spicy book about Sirens."

I couldn't help but lean in. "How spicy?"

"It starts in chapter four and just takes off from there. The main plot is about what happened to this chick at a beach, but she goes through a roll of guys. It is so good!"

I nodded and set her Americano on the counter. "I'll have to check it out."

"It's hot," she said as she took her coffee.

It looked like she might be sweating ever so slightly.

The bells on the door rang again, and another two people entered.

I rang up the Americano, and before she could scan her card, the door opened yet again.

From there, the pandemonium started.

FOURTEEN

My feet hurt, but it had been a fantastic day. The ebb and flow of people throughout the hours had been pretty intense.

I regretted making a special of the day, since I had made so many hazelnut flat whites.

The store was closing in ten minutes, and I was so ready to be done. The author had just signed yet another book, but no one else waited in line. Either line.

Not only had I been busy with coffee, but it seemed the fans had hit the romance section hard. Then again, maybe the bookstore had refilled the shelves when no one had been looking. I didn't have time to put out books. We must have sold at least twenty; I'd scanned at least that many.

Right after lunchtime, there had been a lull, and I'd tossed some more cookies in the oven. Plus, I'd grabbed a sandwich. The coffee shortbread cookies had been a big hit, and the same with the double chocolate chunk.

I spotted the Cat here and there during the day, but he didn't seem to do anything. Right now he sat in the chair in the front window.

The author grabbed her bag and slid on her coat.

"I think that's a wrap," she called from across the store with a grin.

"I hope so," I replied.

I wiped down the counter and pulled out a small paper bag that I'd slid the last two brownie cookies into. While they were good cookies, they were not my favorite. Thankfully the peanut butter cookies were gone. The rest of the cookie dough stayed in the freezer, which would help my willpower.

I held out the bag.

"You didn't need to do that..." She grabbed the paper bag.

"Well," I said, pulling a book out from under the counter. It was a copy of *The Singing Waves*. "One last signature?"

She laughed. "Sure, are you a fan?"

"I haven't read it, but that many people can't be wrong."

"I'm warning you. It's spicy, and I normally don't write books like this. I stick with fantasy with some romance, usually." She shook her head and pulled her pen out to sign the book.

"Good to know," I said. "I hope it was a good signing for you."

"Are you kidding? It was great! I hope I have time to come back and wander the shelves." Her expression fell, and she suddenly looked tired. "Though, I am excited to go hide from the world for the rest of the night, and probably the week."

"Have a good evening!" I said to her.

She waved and headed out of the store, nibbling on a cookie.

"Cat, can you lock the door?" I looked away, and the lock on the door clicked. "Tonight might be a night for takeout. What do you want?"

The idea of trying to cook something sounded like pure torture. Hopefully, the Cat knew what takeout was, given that he'd ordered the cookie dough.

"How about Chinese? I like the spicy beef," came his reply.

I started laughing, and I couldn't stop. Spicy beef—it was just too much.

"I can do that. What was up with the signing, anyway? Like, why did we host it?"

The Cat jumped down from the chair and padded across the store. He slowly jumped up to the counter, like he was thinking about how to respond.

"You didn't do any magic today, did you?" I asked.

"No, today had nothing to do with the book."

"What?" I leaned down toward him. "Why, then?"

He glanced at the cookies.

"You've got to be kidding me." I straightened back up and spun toward the kitchen. "We did this because you wanted cookies?! I could have just ordered you some cookies! We didn't need to host a book signing."

My feet ached with every step as I headed to the stairs.

"What about food?" asked the Cat.

"Ugh." I spun back to the register.

The ordering app was on the tablet connected to the register. Unless I wanted to pay for it myself, I had to order it from there. Until I got paid, my bank account was a little low.

"All right, two orders of spicy beef coming up."

While in the app, I noticed the Cookie Chef Bakery in the recent history. I chuckled and wrote a five-star review. Then I took out my phone and checked a few other websites to see if they had any ratings.

I added my review to a couple of different places. I said how she was a lifesaver and that the cookies were a hit. Not to mention the instructions were easy to follow for someone who couldn't bake to save their life. I took a picture of the few cookies I had left that I had moved to the cake stand.

My feet still ached, but food was on the way, and the freezer had some cookie dough in it. Now that my frustration had faded, I smiled.

"Those were some good cookies." My stomach grumbled. "I hope the food is quick. I have a book to read."

I RESISTED the urge to correct her. Yes, we'd held the event for the cookies, but not because I wanted cookies. The sweet treats were delicious, but I didn't like what the sugar had done to me. I think those were the zoomies she had mentioned earlier. Either way, it was something for me to study.

As soon as she submitted the first review, I relaxed. Our mission for the day was done. Now we both could enjoy some food and some solitude.

The call of cookies from the kitchen did, however, increase the odds of additional zoomies.

CHAPTER

FIFTEEN

It was a boring day. Well, not completely. I hadn't screwed up breakfast, and I'd made a fantastic egg scramble with bacon and cheese.

Now I was reading a book on how to bake muffins. After all the cookies this week, plus the amount of cookie dough that I'd frozen, I was looking for something a little less sweet but still a treat. Somehow, that led me to muffins.

The store was in its bookstore formation, with bookshelves lined up across the store. The cute signs for each genre were back, along with the oak bookshelves. They were always dust free, which I appreciated. The children's area was the smaller version of just a few shelves without a reading nook for kids. I assumed that meant Molly would not be visiting today.

Bright sunlight streamed in from all the skylights, and the front windows looked out to some nondescript street. The smell of the Cat's latte hung in the air, but as soon as he had finished that, he'd vanished to the chair in the front window. As far as I knew, he was napping.

I sat on a stool with the book open on the counter. I had iced coffee for once, a cold brew I'd started last night. I needed to experiment with it a bit more so it'd be smoother. Still, it was definitely drinkable.

Taking a sip, I turned my focus back to the baking book. The next section was about how to mix a muffin blend you could leave in your pantry. Then, whenever you wanted muffins, you just mixed in the wet stuff, plus the sweet stuff like fruit or nuts, and boom. Pop them in the oven. It sounded easy, but who actually knew? I'd never baked anything that complicated.

My thoughts stopped as the door opened and the bell rang. The ringing washed over the space, and I snapped the book shut. I slid it under the counter next to the teacups.

A tall man with long, deep-brown hair and striking brown eyes entered the store. He shut the door softly behind him and turned to study the room. His eyes skidded right over me and kept going until he spotted the chair. The Cat stared at him from his curled-up position.

"There you are," said the man.

The Cat flicked his tail and reluctantly stood. He jumped down and padded silently across the floor toward me. He vanished behind the counter before jumping up next to the book. Once the Cat stood on the counter, the man approached.

"So, do you have any work for me?"

The Cat turned and looked at me, then back at the man.

"Fine." He looked at me for the first time. "Hello, my name is Alas. I'm a leather worker, and I do work for the Cat when he has a request."

He ran his fingers through his long hair, revealing pointed ears.

I blinked, then smiled. "Nice to meet you. I'm Sable, the current Shopkeeper. Can I get you a coffee?"

This was a real-life elf. Or was he a fey? I needed a primer on the various races so I didn't lose my cool when someone entered the shop. Coffee would distract me from asking all the questions about elves.

"Uh, sure. Something warm would be nice," he mumbled. His gaze went back to the Cat. "At least I now know why you have answered none of my messages..."

"You can let him know that yes, it's because you just started. I didn't want to overwhelm you," said the Cat.

Yeah, like he'd overwhelmed me with the magic spears and trolls. Messages were nothing compared to that.

I gave the Cat a nod as I started to make some espresso for Alas.

"Yeah, the Cat said he didn't want to overwhelm me." I shrugged. "But after this, he is going to show me how to check his messages."

"That was not what I said," muttered the Cat, his tail flicking through the air.

I gave him a bright smile as the espresso dribbled out of Betty. Next, I grabbed a teacup from under the counter and poured the hot brown liquid inside.

"Here you go. It should perk you right up."

"Thank you, lass." He carefully picked up the teacup and took a sip. After the first one, he downed it in one go. "Normally, it isn't this long between messages, and I just wanted to make sure the old coot was okay. Can't have him dying on us."

The elf stared at the Cat, who looked away first.

"Tell him I have an order for a pair of boots. Or I will soon," said the Cat.

"Wait, we get orders?" I asked. "How do I check for orders?"

I headed to the cash register and flipped through the menus. There was a button for orders, but I'd assumed if it was important, the Cat would have said something.

Alas glanced between the Cat and me. "Yes, you get orders. I don't know how the Cat deals with them. I just send messages. I'm not sure where they go."

"I can explain them later," said the Cat.

I clicked on the button and pulled up a list of orders. All of them had *Filled* next to them. The descriptions were all different, and some didn't even make sense, like *floating apples* and *book of greats*. Book of great what?

"Focus! Boots!" the Cat demanded.

I rolled my eyes at the Cat and turned away from the register to Alas. "He says there is a pair of boots."

Alas leaned against the counter, his eyes narrowed. "What kind of boots?"

"Boots with a secret compartment. One on each boot. For a knife," said the Cat.

I relayed the information to Alas.

He stood up straight and lightly nodded his head

before touching his chin. It was like he wasn't in the room with us anymore.

"Any magic?" he finally asked.

"Only for comfortable walking and longevity," said the Cat.

I hated being his mouth, but I did it anyway. This was my job, after all. Still, magical boots were a thing. That was cool.

"How can *I* get a pair of magic boots?" I asked the Cat.

I wanted in on this action.

Alas chuckled, his face shifting into a grin. "Well, I can handle the boot part, if you want a pair, but the magic part is up to the Cat."

This time, the Cat glared at him.

"The hidden compartment part is also up to the Cat. All boots I make have charms for wear and comfort."

"So, how do I order a pair with the charms for wear and comfort? What types of boots are possible?"

Alas shook his head. "The walking kind. I'm not talking about fashion boots. I'm talking about boots for adventurers or riding horses through the fields. Boots for being silent while hunting monsters who are eating your animals."

His voice took on a musical lilt, and I leaned in.

An image of dark trees and glowing red eyes closing in on me filled my head. My heart pounded as the creature took form with black scales, six legs, and a tail with a stinger.

The bells on the door rang, snapping me back to the bookstore. I blinked, but no one was at the door.

"What was that?" I muttered, shaking my head.

"Sorry, lass. I didn't mean to ensnare you."

The Cat glared at him.

"Well, I'll be getting on my way." He pointed at the Cat. "As soon as that order comes in, have her message me. There is talk of war with the demons..."

Alas gave me a nod then walked out of the shop. The door slammed shut behind him.

Wait, demons?

"Demons are real? War?" The questions tumbled out of my mouth.

"You don't need to worry about that. It's not on your world." He stared at the door and shook his little head. "Now you know how to check orders. Though the machine gives a notification if one comes in." The Cat moved next to the register. "My messages are in a different folder."

I moved in front of it and waited for direction.

"Check under orders, then messages."

There was a button in the corner for recent messages, and when I clicked it, only Alas showed up. The most recent was *Cat, are you there?*

"Do you get lots of messages?"

The Cat shook his head. "The order will be in-person and after lunch."

"Do you have preferences for lunch?" I asked the Cat.

We still had time before lunch. At least an hour before I normally would make something quick.

The Cat didn't reply; he just jumped off the counter and padded across the store back to his chair.

Well, he wouldn't answer my questions about elves

or demons, or even lunch. At least right now. Hopefully he would eventually.

I went back to my book on muffins and pondered.

My fingers itched to go back and look through the messages on the register, but I resisted. *All in good time, Sable,* I told myself.

CHAPTER

SIXTEEN

The register taunted me and broke my ability to get lost in the cookbook, so I gave up after only a few minutes. Instead, I found myself wandering the shelves, hoping to find a guide or something on the various races that I might come across in the shop.

As far as I knew, the Cat still lay asleep on his chair. Lunch was hot dogs again, and this time, the Cat didn't complain. He just ate them in that weird way of his. I still wanted to know where all the food went, but at this point, I assumed it was a mystery of the universe.

The shelves weren't dusty, but sometimes I thought they extended out longer than they should. Like, from upstairs, the shelves were only five deep, but down here while wandering, it felt like I was seven or eight rows in. That shouldn't be possible.

The wooden sign marked *Magic* caught my eye, and I quickly jumped ahead of the animal section I had been in. Some titles were in languages I couldn't read.

Hopefully, this was the good stuff.

Bells rang from the front of the store, and I almost stomped my foot.

"Coming!" I gave the shelf one last glance then headed to the front.

I'd have to circle back to this area later.

I came out from behind the frontmost bookshelf and found someone standing in front of the register. He was looking at the sign on the wall. I knew what it said by heart.

> Do not upset the Cat.
> The Cat is always right.
> Do not go behind the counter.
> Do not upset the Cat.

All I could see of the guy was that his shoulders were broad, and he had shorter blond hair. It looked like a buzz cut that needed to be trimmed. It was just long enough that it was starting to lie down, and to be honest, it looked really good. He held his hands together behind his back.

Military. He had to be military.

He wore a dark-gray shirt and black cloth pants with combat boots. He turned at the sound of me approaching. Bright-blue eyes met my gaze.

"Hello. I was shelving books. How can we help you?" I quickly made my way around him and to my correct position behind the counter.

His blue eyes landed on the Cat, then came back to me. "I'm looking to purchase a gift of a more magical nature?"

My eyes widened.

"Is this about the boots?" I asked.

The Cat's head snapped to me, but I ignored him.

The guy's lips parted, and he nodded.

"Yes, I want to order a pair of boots for a young woman I know." His eyes narrowed and he tilted his head, but the expression quickly cleared from his face.

Whomever this young woman was, she had to be important to him. After all, magical footwear that was comfortable and lasted a super long time was no first-date kind of gift. Maybe I could order two pairs and get one for myself.

I grabbed a pad of paper from beneath the counter, along with a black pen. "What size boots does she wear?"

The Cat shook his head with his eyes aimed at the ceiling.

"Ask him who they are for and why he wants them. Sizes, shapes... We can figure that out later," said the Cat. "The magic can make them fit, anyway."

The guy's gaze went back to the Cat. "She's a size eight, and calf length. Something good for being on her feet."

"Well, he wants to know who they are for and why you want them." I took down what he'd said then pointed at the Cat.

The guy nodded. "I want them for a traveler. She will do plenty of walking, and it should have space for a knife or two. Hidden, if possible."

The Cat nodded.

That didn't sound special at all. Boots for someone

who traveled and did plenty of walking. Didn't Alas say they would be boots for hunting monsters and riding through fields?

"So why do they need to be magical?"

This time the Cat made a grumbling noise at me, almost like a purr, but deeper.

"Sorry, never mind my questions."

The guy chuckled. "It's okay. Like I said, these are for a Traveler."

I still didn't get what he meant, though I thought I heard a capital *T* that time.

The Cat made that noise again before adding, "A Traveler is a special type of person. They can go between worlds. I thought we talked about this. Let him know it will be a couple of weeks, but he can leave a number. We'll let him know once they're in."

"The Cat wants your name and a number to reach you. It should only take a few weeks to get them made," I replied.

"It's Carter, and here's my card." He pulled out a business card of all things.

Carter, Guardsman, it read, and had his number listed. Nothing else was on the white card.

"Thanks. I'm Sable, by the way," I said.

I didn't know what to do with the card, or the guy still standing here.

"Do you know how much it will cost?" Carter asked.

"Set the card down and tell him we will discuss it once he's seen the boots. I know he's good for it. It won't bankrupt him, and she will need them," said the Cat. "The boots are important."

I glared at the Cat. This sounded like a creepy back-alley deal, and I didn't want to be that type of person.

I set the card down next to the Cat. "Once you see the boots in person, we can discuss the price, though the Cat said she needs the boots, and he won't bankrupt you. I'm sorry. I haven't had to do an order like this before for magical boots. I swear I won't be this awkward next time."

His laughter spilled out of him and filled the room like a blast of warmth. It took a few seconds to fade away.

"That's okay. I haven't purchased magical boots either, but I've heard of Meow. Plus, my grandfather recommended I come here if I ever wanted anything magical. Until now, it hasn't come up. So we're in the same boat. It's a first for both of us."

My shoulders, which I hadn't even realized were tense, relaxed. The feeling like I was failing at a test vanished, and I gave him a smile.

"Would you like a coffee for the road? I can make just about anything."

"Sure," he said with a smile. "How about a mocha?"

"Coming right up."

The Cat looked between us and picked the card up in his teeth before setting it closer to the register.

I quickly pulled a to-go cup out from under the counter and then ground the espresso beans. "So this Traveler... She must be special to you. I mean, magical boots! I'd kill for a pair."

"You work in a magic shop. You must have access to all sorts of things," said Carter.

The Cat sneezed, and we both looked over.

"Okay, maybe not, then."

"Nope." I steamed the milk with some thick chocolate syrup in it. The scent of bittersweet cocoa wafted from the cup. "This is a new job for me. I'm still learning about all the magic stuff. The coffee part... Now that I have down. The rest of this stuff? It will take all year for me to understand what's going on."

I added the espresso to the cup and then carefully poured the milk in to create a flower pattern before I set the to-go cup on the counter.

"Thank you. How much for the coffee?"

"You can pay for it with the boots." I set a lid on the counter next to the coffee, and he grabbed it.

"I'll wait for that call." He gave the Cat a nod, headed to the door, and opened it with one hand.

"Wait," I called out.

He turned to look at me.

"What world are you from?"

"Terra. Of course..."

"Right."

He tilted his head at me and stepped out.

"Terra," I muttered to the Cat. "That's definitely not Earth."

SEVENTEEN

My first day off. To say it excited me was an understatement.

I'd just settled into a chair on the outside deck to soak in some sun in a bathing suit, when I heard a knock on the door.

I pulled my sunglasses down and concentrated to make sure I'd really heard what I'd heard. When it didn't repeat, I pushed the sunglasses back up my nose.

I was ready for my day of rest in the sun, reading a spicy romance novel to pass the time. Life was good.

The patio was off of the conservatory on the second floor. A stone wall surrounded the space so I couldn't see outside, but sunlight streamed down from above, and the roof opened to the elements. Raised garden beds surrounded the space, and in the center was a fire pit, along with lounge chairs. I couldn't name anything in any of the beds, and two were just dirt.

Finally, it was time to relax.

The bells jingled.

"Are you going to answer that?" asked the Cat.

I hadn't even noticed he'd joined me on the patio.

"It's my day off," I answered. "We aren't open."

My phone vibrated next to me.

"I think it's for you," said the Cat.

I grabbed my phone and noticed it was a text from Cyan, one of my brothers.

I read the text aloud.

"*I think I am at your place...* You've got to be kidding me!"

I knew it disappointed my parents that I wasn't moving home, but I thought we'd all agreed to let that settle. It was just a year. Now Cyan was here.

I set down my sunglasses and climbed to my feet. I grabbed the cover-up draped along the back of the lounge chair and headed back inside. Cool air hit me as I entered the shop.

"I'm coming!" My voice sounded loud in the space as I padded across the balcony and toward the stairs.

It didn't take long for me to make it to the front door. The shop was in its bookstore configuration, the same one that had greeted me on my first day visiting. Just a normal shop.

Through the glass door, I spotted Cyan staring at me. I unlocked the door and swung it open. Before I could say anything, he wrapped me in a hug.

"I found you, Nugget!"

I pulled away from him, rolling my eyes at the nickname.

"What are you doing here?" I asked.

"Why are you in a bathing suit?" he asked at the same time.

"Come in, you dork." I stepped back to let him inside the shop, and I locked the door once he stepped inside. "Sunbathing. It's a thing. I wasn't expecting company."

He stood in the middle of the shop, turning around slowly. "You're lucky it's just me. You could have had Onyx and Umber as well."

"Was Cerulean too good to be invited?" I asked with snark.

Cyan shook his head. "Nope, he's off on another adventure."

Cerulean was the second oldest and an adventurer at heart. He did mountain climbing for a living, and we never knew when he would take off on another climb or quest to visit some remote place. He would be gone for a few months then be home for a few months before leaving again.

Yet no one gave him grief for not being near home. I wasn't bitter or anything. I swear.

"Well, do you want anything to drink?" I pointed to the coffee machine. "I can make you just about anything."

"Something chilly would be nice." He moved closer to the bookshelves.

Cyan was a bookworm, just like me, and if I didn't want to lose him into a book, I needed to get him upstairs.

I quickly darted over to the machine and started on an iced latte.

"We can head upstairs and back into the sunlight to

talk." It didn't take long for me to set a glass with a straw on the counter. "Come on. I'll show you the patio."

He followed me quietly up the stairs then paused, looking over the bookstore from the railing. "This is a delightful view."

Out of all of my brothers, the bookstore would draw him in.

"Yeah, I love it up here. The second floor is mine, and customers stay down below. I have a studio. It's that door." I smiled.

The door stood wide open since I didn't see a reason to close it. No one was supposed to be here but me and the Cat.

Speaking of, I didn't see the Cat anywhere.

"That's a lot of plants, sis. How do you keep them alive?"

"I just gotta water them."

I'd killed plants left and right at home. Gardening was another skill I simply was not good at. Umber was the plant guy. He grew a massive garden each year. He was also the one who'd learned how to cook from mom.

To be honest, I hadn't been watering the plants, and I didn't know if I needed to. I didn't actually know how they were still alive. That was going to need to go on the question list to ask the Cat. Along with my questions about elves, demons, and Travelers, oh my.

Sunlight streamed in through the glass ceiling and wall. I opened the sliding door that led to the rooftop patio. Cyan stepped through, and I glanced around.

"Take a seat." I grabbed the spot where I'd been

sitting before and picked up my sunglasses and my own iced latte. "So what brings you all the way out here?"

"Can't I want to visit my little sister?" he teased.

"I thought Mom and Dad were good after my call."

"They'd planned a coming home party, with a barbecue and everything."

It felt like he'd punched me. Thankfully, the sunglasses hid my eyes.

"You've got to be kidding me." I grabbed my drink, needing something to steady my hands.

"Nope, they really thought you would be back. There was even talk of if you were going to take over Tess's cafe."

I leaned back in the chair and took a deep drink of the caffeine.

"So everyone else was busy planning my life like normal?" The acid in my voice was perhaps a bit thicker than Cyan deserved, but this was a sore subject.

They didn't have any problem with the boys going out and having their independence, but me?

"Nug—"

"You know it as well as I do. It's one reason I went to college all the way out here. I need to live *my* life and not the life that you all want for me."

"We just want you safe and sound."

"What about my happiness?" I asked.

"Of course we want you to be happy! Just closer, where we can visit easily." He took a deep breath. "You know Onyx doesn't fly, and it's one heck of a drive here. It feels like you're hiding from us!"

I tilted my head to one side. "I'm not hiding. I found a job I enjoy, and I'm living my life."

He didn't reply.

The Cat jumped up on the end of my chair.

"Cyan, meet the Cat. Cat, meet Cyan, one of my big brothers."

"You got a cat?!"

Cyan wasn't a fan of animals. He didn't hate them, but he was neutral about having them. He was not the brother on my side when I wanted to get a family pet.

"He came with the job."

"You couldn't come up with a better name besides Cat?" asked Cyan under his breath.

"I heard that." He rolled his eyes at me.

"So what now?" Cyan asked.

I took another sip of my coffee. "I'm here for a year. After that, who knows? I might sign on for another year."

"Woah." He raised his hands. "Don't be hasty. Don't sign any more contracts until you talk to us, okay? Please?"

He never said please. Like, ever. It was strange.

Cyan stared down at the Cat, his eyes wide. I realized that they both had green eyes. He caught me staring and turned to look at me.

He gave me his begging look, and I sighed.

"Okay, I won't sign another contract until I talk to everyone." A thought hit me like a brick then. "They aren't in your car or anything, right?"

I wouldn't put it past my family to come on a road trip to visit without telling me. I'd send Cyan in as well, if

I were to pull a stunt like that. Which I wouldn't, of course.

"No, it's just me."

That was a positive, and my posture relaxed just a little. Now I just needed to figure out what to do with my brother without leaving the shop.

Or him discovering magic.

EIGHTEEN

"So, this is your brother," said the Cat.

His voice sounded soft in my mind.

I took another sip of my drink. I didn't have a way to respond without talking in front of Cyan. The Cat moved closer to sniff him.

Cyan jerked back.

"Hey, Cat, Cyan doesn't really like cats..." I said, leaning forward to pick him up.

To my surprise, the Cat let me move him to my lap.

"It's not that I don't like cats. It's just that I don't know what to do with them," muttered Cyan.

"Animals are easy. You be nice to them, speak kindly, and give them pets if they want." I scratched behind the Cat's ears, and he purred at me. "Now, cats, you just need to treat with a little more respect."

Cyan rolled his eyes. "So, how is the new job treating you?"

I smiled at the Cat then stopped scratching him to take another sip of my drink.

"Great! I'm slowly learning the ropes. We had a book signing here this week. I learned how to bake cookies from cookie dough and handle a bigger crowd than normal." I motioned to the spicy romance novel on my chair. "See? I even got a signed copy. I was planning on reading it today."

"You made cookies? Miss 'I can't cook to save my life; please save me, Umber…'?"

So, he had a point. Throughout high school, I'd do anything to get out of cooking any meal other than breakfast. Umber was such a better cook than I that it was hard to eat anything else.

"It's cookies from custom cookie dough. There's a great shop we order from." I shook my head. "I'm not making them from scratch. Though, I can toss a few in the oven, if you're brave enough, that is, to eat one."

Cyan stood. "What cookies do you have?"

"Old-fashioned peanut butter or double chocolate chunk." I grabbed my drink, rose, and took a few steps toward the sliding door. "Both are amazing."

I glanced back at the Cat, who still sat next to my book. His dark fur glistened in the sunlight. I didn't know how to ask if he wanted any of the cookies.

I slid open the slider and motioned for Cyan to head inside. "The kitchen is behind the register. Give me a moment to grab my stuff in case it rains."

"You're gonna lose me in the stacks," warned Cyan.

"Have fun! Maybe you'll find something to read."

He strolled away from me and toward the stairs.

I darted my eyes back to the Cat as I approached my chair to grab my book.

"Do you want any cookies? You can join us if you want company," I said quietly.

"Enjoy your time with your brother," said the Cat.

I gave him a nod then headed inside. Maybe he *would* get lost among the stacks. I could make cookies then get him on his way.

The sunlight called my name, and I wanted to read that book. I loved my family. I really did, but they were a lot to handle.

By the time I made it to the kitchen, Cyan was nowhere to be found.

The ovens were already at temperature, and I grabbed a few cookie sheets. The frozen cookie dough had slightly longer cooking times, but I didn't care. Following directions was a strong suit of mine. Most of the time.

I set the timer on my phone and got the cookies in the oven.

"Woah, this is a kitchen Umber would die for," said Cyan.

I spun around to find Cyan staring at the giant space. "Yeah, I'm glad I don't need to use it, besides the basics."

"You have two ovens?!"

I nodded. "It comes in handy when cookies have two different temperatures. My assumption is at one point, the shop offered more baked goods. Right now, we only offer them for events, and then we get pre-made dough."

Cyan sat at the counter on a stool. "So you actually like this job?"

"I do. For once, I feel like I'm good at something." I snorted. "Plus, each day, things are different. You never know who's going to come into the store or what they're going to be looking for."

"My sister, a bookseller."

"Shopkeeper. I'm the Shopkeeper," I immediately corrected him, surprising myself.

"Sorry, shopkeeper. Sable the Shopkeeper. It's like a video game or something. That one that Onyx plays."

"How is the rest of the family doing?"

Going to school had cut off daily conversations with my brothers. Every week I'd call home, but my mom was a phone hog and wanted to know about everything.

"Cerulean is off somewhere, though he said he's going to take a vacation after this trip. Maybe he'll stick around for more than a few months."

We both knew that Cerulean didn't take vacations for long. He got paid well taking rich guys on mountain trips, but he also loved exploring on his own.

"Yeah right! Isn't the longest he's lasted, like, six weeks?"

Cyan shrugged. "Umber finally paid off the land next to the house, and he's going to build his own house on it. His farm's doing great. Every week he sells out at the farmers' market."

I nodded. "Is he seeing anyone?"

Cyan blushed in response.

"Who?"

"I don't know. He won't tell any of us. We were hoping you could figure it out when you came home."

Umber was a homebody. Talented chef and farmer, but he didn't really want to travel the world. He wanted to keep his people close and make sure everyone was taken care of.

"I'll call him."

"Yeah, maybe poke at Onyx as well." Cyan studied his fingers. "You can get everyone to talk. They open up to you. Right now, the family feels off."

I leaned forward across the counter. "Mom sounded fine on the phone..."

"Mom doesn't want you to worry. Something's just off with the family. She's planning a big party for my twenty-fifth, and we still have six months to go. For the rest of them, it wasn't a big deal, but for me, she's acting like it's huge. I think she's hoping you'll come home for it and not leave."

That was a trap. Mom sometimes did that. It was with love, but still a trap. Just like all of them planning my life out.

"I'll call and talk to both of them. Don't worry about Mom. I can handle her."

The timer on my phone went off, and I grabbed an oven mitt before taking out the baking sheet. As soon as I cracked the oven, the smell of chocolate filled the kitchen. The dark cookies had melted bits of chocolate in them.

I set the pan on the counter. "They need to cool for five minutes, or they're lava in your mouth."

Cyan jerked back his fingers, which had drifted toward the edges of the pan.

I grabbed the peanut butter cookies out as well. I'd only made nine of the chocolate and six of the peanut butter. Otherwise, we'd eat way too many cookies.

"Okay, these look amazing." Cyan gave me a smile. "I need to bring some of these home to Umber. Maybe he'll spill his secrets to me."

"You can take half home."

The first bite of the chocolate chunk cookie seemed to unlock something, and then Cyan chatted about *his* life for once.

"The art show went well. I sold three paintings. People are really loving my forest scenes. Cerulean promised to take some shots of some mountains, and I'm going to try them next. I can only paint so many trees until I need something else."

"Are you still dating Amy?"

He shook his head immediately. "She discovered the small town wasn't for her. It sucks, but it is what it is. Our town is close-knit, and I'm not moving away. I love it there. More than I loved her."

My hometown was freaking tiny and hard to get to, but the natural beauty always amazed me. Still, I thought he'd fallen head over heels for her.

"I'm sorry. Are you okay?" I asked.

"That's the thing. It really didn't bother me. It was more of a relief. She didn't get along with Mom, and she hated hanging out with the family. Like, I thought she and Onyx were going to get into blows once."

"Onyx, gentle giant Onyx, who wouldn't hurt a fly?"

"Yeah, he wouldn't speak of it, and she didn't say what happened."

"Huge red flag there."

Cyan nodded. "Yeah, hence why I'm not bothered. I

think I'm gonna put off dating for a while. Maybe the right person will just show up? You never know."

Stranger things had happened to me this week, so I wouldn't argue with him.

"Anyway, I need to get on the road. There are a few places I want to snap photos of on the way back. It'll give me something to paint while I wait for Cerulean to get back."

It didn't take long to pack up a bag with most of the leftover cookies. I'd already eaten one of each, and I kept one of each in case the Cat wanted one later.

"I love you, and safe driving!" I said as he headed out the door with the bag.

"Love you, Nugget!"

THERE WAS magic in her family. More than it took to be a Shopkeeper. I knew Sable had some, since she had found the ad, along with the store. Plus, the shop responded to her like no other in many years.

Yet, the spark of magic in her brother was stronger. It was caged inside him, trying to find a way out.

Strange.

Something to think about in the coming weeks.

Sable eventually came back to the deck and sat down in her chair. She set a plate with two cookies next to me.

"I saved you some," she said.

The sunlight warmed my fur as I studied her. Her own spark of magic had shifted. Not by much, but there was a change. It had grown.

I took a deep breath, and Sable scratched my ears.

The contract was signed. It could not be broken. Who knew what could happen if Sable accessed the spark of magic she had?

Yet, she'd saved me cookies and gave me scratches, like she hadn't a care in the world. She must not know what she could be...

Should I tell her?

Another thing to ponder, after a nap in the sun.

NINETEEN

"Sable..."

Something hit my foot, but I ignored it. The blankets were warm, and my bed was comfortable.

"Sable! You need to get up!"

Something pounced on my back, and the covers slipped down over my head. Bright sunlight streamed down from the skylight in my room, and I...

Wait. Bright sunlight?!

I sat up quickly, flinging the blanket off of me, and the Cat as well in the process. My eyes shot open, then closed, then open again.

My phone sat on my bedside table, but it wasn't plugged in. It had died at some point during the night. How had I not plugged in my phone?

"Oh god, I'm late!"

The Cat slowly crawled out from under the blanket that now lay wrinkled at the end of my bed.

His head popped up from the edge of the blanket,

and he stared at me. "Yes, you are. The Bookseller will be here shortly."

I jumped up and pulled on jeans before his sentence sank in. "Bookseller?"

"Yes, we can't be late." The Cat pulled himself the rest of the way out from under my covers and padded across my room toward the barely open door. "We might need to skip breakfast."

His voice sounded so depressed at that.

I paused, then I moved faster, grabbing a bra and a shirt to go over it. At the very least, we needed coffee, and I still had to brush my teeth. It didn't take too much longer before I walked down the stairs in my socks, skipping shoes entirely. If the day was like most, I'd have some downtime to finish getting ready after the customer left.

The Cat sat at the counter next to the cash register as I made my way out to the front of the store. The shop was set up in what I called the normal arrangement. Bookshelves with no tables or special areas. The wooden shelves lined the walls, and there were rows with signs that showed each genre.

After a quick glance around, I smiled, but then I snapped my head back. Not the normal arrangement at all. There stood an extra door! Not the front door that was always there, but between two bookshelves stood a curved archway that showed another room beyond it. The room didn't seem to have any lights, and I couldn't make out what was inside.

"Coffee would be good," said the Cat.

I pulled my eyes away and started quickly grinding

some espresso beans before getting the machine going. I needed something to get my head on straight. I pulled a teacup out first for him and added the espresso. I topped it with some heavy cream, just enough to lighten the shots.

"Here you go." I moved the teacup closer to him. Then I made myself an Americano and also added a drop of heavy cream to mine. "I'm sorry I overslept."

The Cat lapped at his coffee. "It's fine. I was just concerned something was wrong with you."

"Nope, just my phone didn't get plugged in." I shook my head. "I swore I plugged it in like normal. It's strange. I have no idea what happened."

I always double checked to make sure I'd set my alarms. I hated to be late for anything. It always made me anxious.

Before I could say anything else, the bells rang as the front door jerked open.

A man entered, covered in flowing robes of dark-green cloth. Short silver hair covered his head and high-lighted the sharp-pointed ears on the sides of his head. The numerous earrings in each of his ears sparkled in the sunlight. His large, woeful brown eyes reminded me of a puppy's, and they turned to gaze at me. The man, or elf, or whatever, carried a basket in one hand, which looked like it was made out of reeds.

"Ah, I've found you after all..."

The Cat nodded from his perch.

"I wasn't sure after our last encounter that you'd still want to do business with me. Oh, but you have a new keeper." He snorted. "That'd do it. I didn't like that old man."

No one seemed to like the guy from before me, though he'd seemed perfectly lovely to me. Then again, he hadn't warned me about the contract.

The customer moved confidently into the room, moving across the space quickly as he chatted. The door shut quietly behind him.

"You can call me the Bookseller," he said to me while bowing his head.

The closer he got, the taller he appeared to be.

"Tell him you're the Shopkeeper," said the Cat, his voice coming out frosty.

"I'm the Shopkeeper," I said, following instructions.

This was the first time the Cat didn't want me to say my name. That had to mean something. Who was this person? *What* was this person?

The Bookseller set the basket on the counter.

The Cat moved forward to sniff at it before he nodded his head again. "Let him know we are looking for five books..."

Before I could say anything, the Bookseller reached into his basket and pulled out one book, then another, and then a third. He stacked them on top of one another next to the Cat. His fingers were long, and his nails were sharp talons. While the rest of him was human-shaped, ignoring the ears, his hands betrayed him as something else. Probably not an elf, or at least not like I'd seen before.

"He said he is looking for five books." My voice came

out strong, but I couldn't help but wonder where the books were coming from.

The basket had a lid on it, preventing me from seeing inside, but the three books he'd pulled out were much too big to have been inside. Each was cloth-bound, and two of the three were a dark blue, while the third was a deep green. Deeper than his robes, almost black.

"Of course he is," muttered the Bookseller. He then added another five books to the top of the stack. "Are any of these the ones you are looking for?"

The Cat peered at each of the spines and touched two of them. The bookseller moved those two in front of the register.

"Only those two?" asked the Bookseller, tapping on the counter. "Are you sure?"

"Tell him to try again," said the Cat.

I took a sip of my coffee first. "He said to try again."

This was interesting. The Bookseller had obviously worked with the Cat before.

He grabbed each of the books left in the stack and shoved them one by one into the basket. Then he pulled a black leather-covered one out. The Cat nodded before he touched the counter, and the Bookseller put it on the stack by the register.

"I haven't lost my touch yet," whispered the Bookseller.

The next book was a deep-blue color, and for some reason, my fingers itched to grab it. Inlaid in gold was an oak leaf on the front cover.

I gripped my coffee mug tighter to keep my hands to

myself. Yet I couldn't help but lean closer to it. I didn't see any writing on the cover, just that oak leaf.

The Cat nodded again, and the Bookseller set it on top of the stack. As soon as it touched the other books, the urge to snatch it vanished. The tension disappeared, and I let out a breath.

The Bookseller's eyes snapped to me, and they didn't look brown anymore. Instead, they were a deep black, as though something else stared out of him.

Everything in me wanted to freeze, but warmth flowed from my coffee cup.

"There should be one more book." My voice came out softer than I wanted, but it caused him to flinch.

The Cat moved closer to me and glared at the Bookseller.

"You are a strange one," he said before looking away. "You found yourself someone special this time, Cat. Lucky, lucky Cat. Though you're stuck here, so how lucky can you be?" A dark chuckle came out, and he reached again into the basket.

This book was smaller than the others, and dusty.

"Is this the last one?" he asked with a sneer.

The Cat nodded.

The Bookseller placed it on the stack. "Now, as for payment..."

The Cat's eyes narrowed, and he moved closer to the Bookseller.

"Now, now, I know you won't give me her..."

My eyes went wide and shot to the Cat, but his focus remained on the Bookseller.

He reached into the basket one more time and pulled

out something that shimmered. Its form stretched before settling into the shape of a book with a clasp holding it shut. Cold air rose from it, visible wisps that dissipated slowly.

I took a step back, and focused on the warmth steaming from my cup. The sunlight grew brighter from the skylights, falling directly on the Bookseller and what he held. The cold wisps shrank and pulled back into the book. The clasp moved and seemed to tighten.

"You can guard it. Keep it." The Bookseller's voice was almost pleading. "Free me of this burden."

I couldn't move from my spot.

His fingertips dug into the book. Slowly, dark lines grew from his contact with the book up his fingers.

"It has to be time," the Bookseller said. "Surely I have paid my debt to you."

The Cat stared at him, then looked at me, his green eyes glowing. "I need you to take the book from him and carry it into that room. The one with the arched doorway."

The dark lines stretching from the book clutched in the Bookseller's hand darkened, and I shivered.

I needed to touch that book? Could I?

TWENTY

"Will it hurt?" I softly asked inside my head.

"I hope not," said the Cat, his green eyes staying on me. "I cannot touch it, or I would do this thing."

"And if I say no?"

The Cat sat down and his ears drooped. "Then the Bookseller will need to keep it until your contract is up. He cannot go into that room, but the Shopkeeper can."

The Bookseller glanced between the two of us like he knew we were talking, but didn't know what was being said. "Please, it has to be time."

I took a long swig of my coffee and set it down on the counter. I had signed a contract to do my job. Of course, that was before I knew it involved magic and books that did strange things.

"Does it hurt you?" I asked the Bookseller.

"It is like a weight on my shoulders, increasing with every breath. At first, it was a leaf, and I could barely tell it was there. After the first year, a scarf. By the hundredth year, a rock the size of my head." His hand trembled. "Now, a crushing weight that makes me tremble getting up in the morning."

My eyes narrowed. He had to be carrying this for a reason. "Why are you bound to carry this burden?"

The Bookseller's eyes flickered to the Cat, then back to me.

"I once sought to trick a Fey Lord and steal from him. Yet, he was trickier still, as all Fey Lords are, and I stole something which should have remained where it was. It was this"—he paused—"book. Now I must carry it until another can guard it."

"Guard it from what?"

"Escape." His voice came out in a rush, and the dark lines on his skin pulsed.

I glanced back at the Cat, who still stared at me.

"Can the bookstore really guard it? Is what he said true?" I asked the Cat.

The Cat nodded twice.

Whatever that book was, it was bad news. I had no desire to touch it. Especially now that I knew more about it. Who would want to willingly take it? I still didn't know what it was, only that it needed to be put in that room. And then the bookstore would deal with it?

If I didn't do it, then the next person who signed on for this job would have to. That felt like a dick move, not to mention it would force the Bookseller to keep it.

It had to be important. I held out my hand for the book.

The Bookseller's eyes grew wide, and his body flickered. For a moment, instead of the tall Elvish-like person, something else stood there. He stood much taller, with bright-silver hair, sharp pointed ears, and deep dark skin with dark eyes and a bare chest with puffy pants. Then I blinked, and the image was gone, replaced by how he looked before.

I touched the book, and ice swept through my veins, running up my hand and wrist. It wasn't painful, just cold. Like someone running an ice cube along my skin. The light in the store flared brightly, and the chilly sensation stopped traveling up my arm. Or rather, it slowed down.

I took a deep breath and my first step. I could do this.

Yet that step broke the contact with the Bookseller, and the cold came back.

Stronger.

I couldn't feel my fingertips anymore, and the icy trail up my arm ached.

I had to move. Somehow, I had to put this book in that room across the store. Quickly. Yet, I felt like I couldn't step forward anymore. I stood frozen in this spot, holding the book that spread ice through me.

"Sable, you can do this. I believe in you."

Something nudged my foot, and I could move again.

My next step away from the counter shook my muscles but I gritted my teeth. As soon as I stepped out from behind the counter and into the sunshine, it got easier.

The Bookseller stood still by the counter, but as soon as I'd taken the book from him, he stood frozen. I didn't see the Cat.

"Keep moving," the Cat whispered in my mind.

With the first step out of the sunlight, pain shot up my wrist, and my hand shook. Yet I didn't let go. The next was the same, but the door wasn't that far. I was close enough that I could see inside the archway. The room was empty except for a table, right in the middle.

Each step hurt, but the one where I crossed the threshold my whole body trembled. The book did not want to move forward into the room.

"You can do it!"

Yet another voice responded, "I can free you...from the contract...from the Cat..."

It was a seductive voice, a pleading voice, but one that I knew I couldn't trust.

I gritted my teeth and yanked on the book, using my chest to force it forward through the doorway. The resistance suddenly left as soon as I crossed the threshold. After a quick three steps, I set it in the middle of the plain table. I backed away slowly from it, not turning my back on the book.

When I made it just outside the doorway, the room heated up. I turned back to look at the counter, and in that split second, the door behind me closed with a bang.

"Dumb book. That contract is gonna pay off my student loans..." I muttered under my breath as I shook my head.

Whatever was inside that book didn't understand the amount of debt I had.

The Bookseller still stood frozen next to the counter, and the Cat was still missing. Slowly, I made my way back to my coffee cup. The Cat jumped up on the counter, and he gave me a nod.

As soon as I touched the coffee cup, the Bookseller moved, glancing around in confusion. His hand still hovered in the air, and he yanked it down.

"You took it?" whispered the Bookseller. His gaze switched between me and the Cat. "You really took it, my Lord."

His fingers stretched toward the Cat, but then he must've thought better of picking him up.

"I'm free... Truly free..." He grabbed the basket and took off for the door, running at full speed.

"No one is free," muttered the Cat, but the Bookseller didn't hear it.

The door snapped open right before the Bookseller got to it, then closed softly behind him.

"What was that?" I asked.

"The Bookseller? A fey. He stole from a Lord, thinking the book would teach him power." The Cat shook his head. "Now we will guard it."

I snapped my gaze to the doorway, but it was gone. Solid bookshelves lined the walls.

"What was that book?"

"Some things should never have been created. That is one such thing. You don't need to worry about that. Over time, it will die and vanish," said the Cat. "I could use another coffee. Maybe something sweet."

Something sweet could be good.

He glanced up at me then nudged his teacup. "You could use another as well. I liked those hazelnut things you made for the book signing."

I rolled my eyes as I rubbed my hands. Echoes of the cold still remained. Then the Cat sat there while I scratched his ears. The warmth of his fur banished the last of the cold.

"I can do that." I turned back to Betty and started the process of making more espresso. "Cat, how long will it take for the book to die?"

Not to mention, how the heck did a book even die?

SABLE SEEMED nervous as she went about making the coffees I'd requested. I hoped it would help steady her after that event. Her hand had been icy cold where she'd touched the book.

Its power had tried to escape, even bound as it was. Being with the Bookseller had weakened the binding, but it was better now that the shop would take care of it.

Somehow, her magic had reacted to the cold. She had brightened the shop, bringing warmth.

"It won't take long for the book to die," I said in response to her question.

She didn't need to know that the shop would eat the creature. The one of dark and ice.

All energy came from somewhere, and thanks to the Fates, the shop could run on all different types of energy and magic.

How strangely things worked out. Little did I know that the day that the Bookseller stole the book, it'd lead to the death of the creature of dark and ice, a far better outcome than the risk of failing to imprison it.

TWENTY-ONE

The shop smelled like fall, and I didn't understand why. Per my calendar, it was still the middle of summer, but as I got dressed, it was somehow fall, with crispy leaves on the skylight and that crispness in the air. By the time I got downstairs and made my first cup of coffee, I was certain.

"Cat, why is it suddenly fall?" I asked.

The Cat didn't appear, so I walked into the kitchen. The oven was already preheating for the bacon, and a sheet pan lay on the counter.

"You are so amazing," I whispered.

At the sight of the pan, my brain went to the last of the cookies we had in the freezer. The cookie dough supply had been dwindling slowly, but I had enough to make a few batches. It all depended on the schedule for today.

"Cat, what…"

"Yes?" asked the Cat.

I turned, and he sat on the island, staring at me.

"There you are! What's the schedule today?"

"It's All Hallows Eve."

I blinked. "You mean Halloween, right?"

"That's what your people call it now, yes. Halloween." The Cat rolled his eyes and sighed. "We will have children visit us for candy."

I burst into action. Energy roared through my veins as I got the bacon into the oven.

"I need to get some cookies out and see what else we can get from the cookie place. Do you think I can order Halloween cookies from there? Like, is it that time of year on Earth?"

The Cat's eyes grew wide at my frantic questions. "I bet you could order whatever you wanted from her store, and it will be here pronto. Why are you all excited?"

"Halloween is the best! I love all of the holidays. Doesn't matter which one, but I do really like Halloween. How much time do I have to prep?"

By the time I turned back to the counters, more pans had appeared, along with the tubs of cookie dough. I quickly grabbed the silicone sheets, lined the pans, and tossed little balls on each of them. I set the timer and then quickly headed to the register.

The listing for the cookie dough place already lit up the screen, so I grabbed my phone to call Sandra.

She answered. "This is Sandra, the Cookie Master."

"Hey, Sandra, this is Sable from Meow. You—"

"Oh my god! I can't tell you how much your review meant to me. My sales spiked after you posted everywhere. I even hired a person to help. How can I help you?"

"This is a weird one. Do you make Halloween cook-ies? Something orange and black. Cute, but not scary?"

"Of course... It's a little early, but I bet I can whip something up. Do you want them already baked?"

"If possible? I'm throwing a little themed party for some friends, and their kids are dressing up. So, make it a pretty large batch of cookies. Maybe four dozen? I'm gonna use up the dough I have in the freezer as well."

"I got you." She called for someone named Jenny. "I'll deliver them as soon as possible."

"Thank you so much! Just charge the card on file."

"Thank you!"

I hung up and found the Cat staring at me.

"We could just give out some candy."

"Cat, I know you can't understand this, but we are a magical bookshop. On Halloween. That is actual magic. Like, we are going to go all freaking out."

Warmth and the smell of cinnamon filled the air. A timer went off in the kitchen, and I dashed in to get the bacon. We couldn't live off of only cookies.

This was going to be fun.

"Cat, I need to know exactly what we need to accom-plish today."

The Cat followed me into the kitchen and accepted a hot piece of bacon as a tribute.

"There will be several groups of children who stop here."

I glared at the short answer, and his eyes widened before he continued.

"One or two need the magic of this night to fuel their

dreams. Think of a butterfly's wings changing the world. That sort of thing."

"This is going to be the best day ever. Time to find out what we have in storage."

I didn't know if the Cat paused time in the shop or how it worked. All I knew was that what should have taken all day, didn't.

I asked the Cat for cauldrons, a fake fire, and spooky decor. He rewarded me with anything I would need to decorate the front room like a witch's cottage as he slept on the counter. Bottles of all shapes and sizes with candles inside lined the front window. I set out an old chair next to the cauldron. The deep-red glowing stones I set on top flickered like flames.

I asked him to move the bookshelves around to make it seem like a smaller space, then I headed into the kitchen. When I came back, the room itself appeared smaller. The counter still sat there, but Betty hid behind some fake stone paneling. The bright wooden floors were a darker color, and dusty stacks of books lay all over the place. Candles topped a few of them.

The small table near the door was where I'd place the cookies. It gave kids enough space to come in but not wander around too much.

"Do we have any lanterns?"

By the time I turned back to the counter, a few lanterns had appeared around the space. After standing in front of the door and looking around the area, I moved a few things here or there. Then I cackled in delight.

"Be careful. Some of these items are magical," said

the Cat, opening his eyes. "Like that cauldron. It amplifies magic."

A knock on the door interrupted my thoughts, and I quickly opened it.

Sandra held out several large containers. "Woah, you went all out. I bet once the lights are off and the candles are lit, this is going to look amazing."

I grabbed the trays and carefully set them on the counter, which would be shrouded in darkness when the time came. There were over four dozen cookies in the shapes of ghosts, witch hats, and pumpkins. Sandra, or her assistant, had drawn a few quick details on each, like eyes for the ghosts and buckles for the witch's hats. The pumpkins had little jack-o-lantern faces on them.

"You outdid yourself," I said.

"Well, Jenny is now prepared to make many cute Halloween cookies for this fall. I also brought some more cookie dough for your freezer." She pulled off a backpack and took different tubs out of it. "You shouldn't run out soon. I have a new recipe for you to try as well. It's on the house. Let me know what you think."

"Awesome! Thank you so much again for this order."

Sandra smiled. "Of course. You have no idea how you changed everything. Any time you need an order, just let me know."

She headed out as I set cookies on the stand.

A thought crossed my mind, and I paused, cookie in hand. "Cat?"

"Yes?" He sat next to the register, which hadn't moved.

His nose hovered directly over one of the sugar cookies, like I had caught him sneaking a snack.

"That book signing... Was that for the cookie place?"

The Cat didn't answer, but a cookie vanished in that strange way he ate things.

"It was, wasn't it?"

His tail flicked in the air, and I shook my head.

The shop and I had changed her life, and how her business was doing. She'd hired someone to help, and things were looking up for her. That happened because of *this* place.

Warmth filled me as I began to hum and flutter around the room.

Halloween would blow that out of the water. I just knew it!

CHAPTER

TWENTY-TWO

I slid the black dress on and headed into the bathroom to do some makeup. I wasn't that great at it, but a little sparkly eyeshadow and some eyeliner looked good enough. Plus, a deep-red lipstick. All I needed was a hat, and I'd ordered one online for rush delivery.

"No costume for me?" asked the Cat from his perch on the toilet lid.

I was pretty sure he was joking, but one never knew. "I thought about it. Instead, you can be my familiar."

The Cat jerked backward, almost falling off the toilet. "I am not a familiar! I am The Cat!"

"Don't worry. No costume required. You're already a black cat with glowing green eyes." I reached out and scratched his ears.

He purred before he realized it and then stopped. "Still, I am not *your* familiar. You can be *my* witch."

"Whatever you say."

Someone knocked on the door, and I quickly fled the room, heading for the stairs.

"Coming!"

My normal delivery driver, the one who brought my groceries, stood outside with a black cloth hat. I unlocked the door, and he held it out to me.

"Here you go. Looks like quite a party you have set up."

"Hopefully. Gotta surprise a few kids who love Halloween."

"That's a really great idea." He nodded and then walked off toward his car, which he'd parked at the curb.

I closed the door and looked over the hat. It was dark black and made of heavy wool. It had a soft point at the top that bent ever so slightly backward. Absolutely adorable. I almost wished I had a small one for the Cat.

"You would look good with a small one of these," I said.

"No."

I shrugged and took the tag off the hat, and then I carefully placed it on my head. "Okay, I think we're almost open for business. Cat, can you lower the lights... Yep, just like that..."

The store dimmed, and all the candles suddenly snapped on. Little flames danced, filling the space with pleasant warmth. The red crystals under the cauldron glowed, making the whole thing look amazing.

I moved to the front door and swung it open. Darkness greeted me, and I used the doorstop to prop the door open. The smell of dried leaves filled the room, and I smiled brightly.

"This is amazing," I mumbled, looking over the scene in the shop.

The sound of children's voices came from behind me, and their excitement was palpable in the crisp air. I only had a quick glance before I moved back into the shop, but leading the pack was a girl dressed as a fairy.

They must have seen me open the door, and the girl popped her head into the shop. Her fearless eyes grew wide. She had delicate wings shimmering with glitter. She stepped inside, looking every which way before noticing me standing behind the cauldron.

"Come in, come in," I said.

"Happy Halloween!" Her voice kicked off a chorus of voices as the others followed her in.

They had a daring pirate with an eye patch and a toy sword, a ghost with a sheet, and a few superheroes I didn't recognize.

"Trick or treat!"

"Cookies are on the table." I pointed to the table near the front window.

Each child grabbed two, and some started nibbling. "Thank you!"

Then they were off, back into the night.

The Cat came out from under the chair.

"You could sit on the chair and look menacing," I said.

"This whole thing is ridiculous..."

Still, the next time a group came in, the Cat sat on the chair, staring at the children with his deep-green eyes. The kids fawned over the decor and then were on their way.

The night continued like this for hours, and the darkness grew deeper.

The Cat suddenly sat up from the ball he had curled up in and focused on the door. My feet hurt from all the standing, but I kept the cookie plate filled.

Three kids popped into the shop, slightly older than the crowds before, solidly in their teens. They had more complex costumes. All three were werewolves of some sort. The makeup was incredible on one of them. The other two hadn't put in as much effort.

"Trick or treat!"

"Welcome. I have cookies for each of you," I said.

I gave the first two teens two cookies each. The third one reached out, but his fingers were wrong, pointed with claws. He noticed my pause, and his hand trembled, pulling back slightly.

I quickly grabbed a third cookie for him and held it out.

"Our little secret," I whispered.

His yellow eyes glowed as a big grin broke out over his face. The two others quickly hauled him out of there, their voices low and muttering about not getting caught. He glanced back once more, and I gave him a wink. Then they were gone, off into the night.

"Well, you handled that well," said the Cat.

The deep howl of a wolf rattled the shop.

"I think he liked the cookies." I ignored the fact that I'd just given a real werewolf cookies and just went with the flow.

It was Halloween. Who knew what magic was in the air?

After that, I peered carefully at the "costumes," seeing traces of real fur or fangs. Once, I was positive the wings were real. For each of these, I gave an extra cookie. All seemed thankful yet shocked at my appreciation for their costumes.

Eventually, the cookies started to run out.

"We can close up anytime now," said the Cat. "We've done what we needed to. More than that, in fact."

I nodded and moved to the door. Two figures formed in the darkness, a mom in a witch's hat like mine and a little girl, also dressed as a witch. She had on a black dress and held a plastic cauldron. Her eyes locked with mine, and she darted forward, dragging her mother toward the shop.

"See, Mommy! Another witch! Witches go trick or treating!"

I stepped backward into the shop before they arrived at the doorway. The mom stuck her head in, and her eyebrows drew together. Yet the girl made her way around her mother's legs and began to explore the space.

"Oh, so much magic."

"Of course. It's Halloween. Magic is all over, if you know where to look," I said.

The mom glanced all over, but the girl drew my attention. Her fake Halloween basket was empty.

I squatted down next to the cookie table and held one out. "What do you say?"

"Trick or treat!"

"That's right. I have some cookies here for you."

The little witch held out her bucket, and I placed three cookies, each covered with a little deep-purple paper bag, inside.

"Angela," whispered the mother.

Her voice sounded slightly panicked.

I found her staring at the Cat, her eyes wide.

"He means you no harm, not on this night." The words rolled off my tongue without even thinking about them.

"Momma, I got three cookies!" The little witch smiled brightly at me. "Can you do magic for me? Momma says witches don't do magic on Halloween, but I think witches should."

I climbed to my feet, my thoughts racing with what I could do.

"What do you think, Cat? Can we do some magic for the little witch?" I asked out loud.

The Cat just stared at the mother.

I moved close to the cauldron and prayed the Cat wouldn't let me down. Extra cookies sat on the counter behind us in the dark. I could do this.

> "Cookie, cookie, come to me.
> Abundance this night,
> of three times three.
> May it harm none,
> and bring joy to see.
> Cookie, cookie, come to me."

I reached into the cauldron. Three more cookies appeared in my hand.

The little witch clapped and held out her bucket.

I placed the cookies inside with a soft smile. "Here you go!"

The mother grabbed the little witch's hand and pulled her to the door.

"Thank you for the cookies," she whispered.

"You're welcome. Happy Halloween."

Then they were gone, and the door snapped shut behind them.

SHE HAD DEFENDED me and then called the cookies to herself. They moved from the counter to the cauldron. Her little spell was unneeded. As soon as her thoughts had pictured the cookies in it, they'd appeared, out of sight.

The cauldron had been excited to taste some magic, as it'd been without for many years. Yet it hadn't done any of the lifting. That was all the shop. It wanted her to use the magic that was given to the Shopkeeper. Its excitement filled the air, and it hoped she would use it more often now.

Sable sat down in the chair and took off her shoes.

The shop grew brighter, and all the candles went out. The shop did not like flames, but had wanted her to enjoy the evening.

"That was so much fun, Cat. Did you have fun as well?"

"I did," I replied.

There wasn't another truthful answer. Watching her figure out that not all who came to the shop were human fascinated me. She treated each one a little extra well, though I knew not why.

Still, that was who she was.

Sable, the Shopkeeper.

This little detour was worth it, since her fear of the book had gone.

LATER THAT EVENING the shop seemed restless. It jostled me from my sleep in my small bed.

I padded along the hallway, trying to find what was causing the problem. The endless shelves parted before me, but it wasn't anything that we kept. Looking up, the second floor called me.

Sable's door opened as I approached, and I only stuck my nose in. She deserved privacy and rest after what she had done for the shop and the Fates.

She mumbled in her sleep, the sound making me sneak closer to get a look at her.

The downside of being a cat was that I had to jump onto the bed to see her face. Even under the thick comforter, she shivered. The room was warm, but an echo of the creature's power flickered even here.

I placed each footstep carefully as I crossed the bed, making sure not to wake her. Finally, I sat right next to her face.

Again, she mumbled, something about fingers.

I touched my nose to her forehead and pushed the nightmare away by sheer will. My powers weren't used to such actions, but I could use them to defend the Keeper in any way she needed, and I deemed this defense necessary. Her mumbling stopped, but despite that, she shivered again. I walked around her, heading to the foot of the bed.

Here, I paused.

I glanced back at her, studying this human who could do magic. She shivered yet again.

Shaking my head, I curled up on the blanket near her hands, which were ice cold. Heat radiated off of me, and she snuggled closer.

I might not be able to banish all the dreams, but I could at least keep her warm.

TWENTY-THREE

The smell of bacon filled the air, and I was thankful for the grocery delivery person. The fact that I could place an order and then food would magically show up without actual magic was unbelievable.

Then again, it would be magic to someone not from Earth.

I hadn't slept well, with nightmares of a book trying to eat each of my fingers. A shiver crossed my body just thinking about it. I took a long chug of hot coffee to chase it away. The Cat had taken one look at me this morning, asked for an espresso, then gave me my space.

Next thing I knew, my head rested on the counter, and the timer dinged, letting me know the bacon was done. Yet, I felt a little more awake. The caffeine had to be hitting me.

I took the bacon out, plated it, and quickly made some scrambled eggs. All simple things for me to make that I rarely screwed up.

"Cat, breakfast!"

The Cat suddenly jumped up on the island in the kitchen, making me wonder if he was just staying out of sight.

"Are you doing better this morning?" asked the Cat.

"I... Yeah. Didn't sleep well, but the espresso is helping. I'll make some lattes before we open the store."

The Cat nodded and then dove into his eggs and bacon. I couldn't watch him eat. My brain screamed it was wrong how the food just vanished. No chewing or anything. What *was* the Cat? Was he like the creature in that book?

I shook my head. This morning wasn't for dark thoughts.

The bacon was the perfect amount of crispy, and the eggs were good enough.

"Today should be a calm day compared to the kids from yesterday," said the Cat. "Just a normal buying and selling day. Someone wants a book we picked up, and we want the trade goods she has for it."

That did sound like a simple day. "Nothing strange about this one?"

The Cat shook his head, and his tail flicked. "No, but I'd love a latte in my cup."

"You got it."

I forgot to put my plate in the sink, but by the time I turned back, it was already gone.

"Sorry, I'm running a little slow today," I whispered to the shop.

I didn't care if the Cat controlled it. I still felt bad that I wasn't keeping up with the normal flow.

Yet, a warm feeling washed over me. Like someone

patting me on the shoulder and telling me it was okay. I opened my mouth, but I didn't know what to say.

"You coming?" asked the Cat from the hallway.

He'd already vanished to the front of the shop.

I quickly left the kitchen and made my way over to Betty. The glorious red espresso machine was my pride and joy. It made making espresso an art form, and espresso was just a type of magic only some people understood. The machine was already warm, so I ground the beans and tamped them down before pulling the shot. The fresh smell of warm coffee filled the air, and I smiled.

"There is nothing like that smell," I mumbled. "Baked goods also rank up there."

"Like the cookies," added the Cat.

"Yes, like the cookies."

He normally didn't engage in small talk with me, but this morning, things felt a little quiet. Still, I went with the flow, just like with the shop patting me on the shoulder.

Next, I steamed the milk until it was nice and frothy. His teacup needed little milk after the espresso, and the rest went into my dark-blue mug. I added an extra shot to mine, along with a little vanilla and hazelnut. Now the shop smelled like coffee and baked goods.

With the first sip, the warm, frothy milk made me relax even more.

The teacup was already empty, and I raised an eyebrow at the Cat.

"It was tasty."

I moved his teacup under the counter as the Cat moved into his starting-the-day spot next to the register.

"I'm ready," I said before he could ask.

I cupped the warm mug in my hands and took another sip. This I could do.

The sound of the door unlocking echoed through the store. Everything was set up in the same basic layout that I loved. Bookshelves on the back wall, with a second row in front of them. The large table in the center with various items on it. Today it held more books. As I looked around, it was just books today, no other goods. Just stacks and stacks of books, including next to the chair in the window.

Well, the Cat said our next customer was looking for a book.

My mug ran low when the jangle of the bells on the door snapped my head around.

"Good morning. Welcome to Meow," I said. "Can I get you a coffee while you browse?"

The Cat looked at me but said nothing.

"A coffee would be lovely. Something sweet," called the woman.

She looked middle-aged and had an air of curiosity surrounding her when her gaze went to the books all around. Her hair was a deep brown but had streaks of gray running through it. It was tied back into a bun. She reminded me of a librarian, not one I knew, but what you thought about when someone described one in a book.

She even had a pair of glasses dangling from her neck on a chain. Yet, as she stepped into the stacks, I noticed a slight limp. It wasn't the only distracting thing about her. The green flowing dress she wore had some sort of runes stitched into the hem, and they glittered gold in the light streaming down from above.

I turned away to leave her to her search, and sought a specific mug. It had a plain white body, and the only color was a deep-green leaf embossed on one side. It was round with a thick handle, and you could hold it nicely. Once I set it on the counter, I began grinding the beans.

Something sweet, she'd said.

I pulled out a jug of maple syrup and poured a few tablespoons into the bottom of the mug. Once I frothed the milk, I stirred an inch into the sweet syrup before filling the rest of the mug. Last came the shots of espresso. I tried to do a little design, but it wasn't my strongest skill.

I nodded to myself while looking at the cup. It felt right, like it fit her, or at least the impression I got from her.

"Your coffee's ready," I called out.

The woman came out from the end of the stacks and made a beeline to us at the counter.

"Oh, that looks perfect." Her long fingers reached for the mug, and she picked it up and carefully took a sip. "Sweet, but not too sweet."

"So what are you looking for today?" I asked.

The Cat stared up at the woman, who then nodded at the sign.

"A special tome, one that helps restore artifacts..." said the woman. "And I think I've finally found the correct place to get it."

The Cat nodded at her.

"Ask her again what tome she is looking for," said the Cat.

"He wants to know what specific tome you want," I relayed.

She glanced between the two of us, then she nodded softly. "I'm looking for a tome to help restore the golden acorn. Once it's restored, I can fix the fighting between the dryads and the huntsmen."

TWENTY-FOUR

The Cat gave me a look. "That's a powerful book. Dangerous in the wrong hands."

I gave her his speech.

"I know," said the woman. "To prove I want it for that reason, I've brought the guardian crystals from my home." She let out a sigh. "I don't want to part with them, but I need that book, and the fighting needs to stop. Both of my people are dying, all because someone messed with the natural balance of things."

Her voice rose at the end.

The Cat nodded.

She reached into her dress and pulled out a smooth bright-blue crystal. It was the size of my fist, and I couldn't help widening my eyes. Something moved within it, and uncertainty crept up my spine, making me look away. I quickly shifted my gaze into my mug.

"The water guardian, a mermaid with the power of the deep." Next, she set down a chunky deep-amber stone.

The presence on the counter felt heavy.

"The earth golem with the power of stone and sand." She brought out a spiky fiery-red stone.

Jagged edges covered all sides, such that it seemed impossible she wouldn't cut herself. It flickered with an inner light.

"The fiery phoenix with the heat of the sun, and last..." she said.

A small clear stone with streaks of purple running through it.

"An airy sylph with the power of the winds." She took a deep breath. "They have guarded my home for centuries, but ending the war is more important. If I can stop the fighting, then I don't need the guardians."

Her gaze hadn't left the stones as she spoke.

She glanced at the Cat. "So do you have something that can fix the golden acorn?"

It felt like such a serious moment, but I really wanted to ask about the golden acorn. Like, was it a normal-sized acorn that just happened to be gold? What did it actually do?

I couldn't help myself. "What does this acorn do?"

I swear the Cat sighed.

"Sable..." said the Cat.

Yet it was too late.

The woman's gaze snapped to me.

"Every one thousand years, the great oak tree drops a golden acorn, then the tree withers and dies. The golden acorn is then planted, and another great oak grows in its place." She shook her head, wisps of gray hair escaping her bun. "Without the power from the great oak, the dryads and huntsmen are dying out."

That wasn't good.

Her gaze flicked back to the stones. "My family has guarded the great oak after planting it to help it grow, but something went wrong. The golden acorn didn't grow. Somehow, it lost power, and I need to fix it."

Now this was an epic story, though I was glad I didn't live on a planet that had magical trees that people died without.

"Satisfied now?" asked the Cat.

I gave the Cat a nod.

"There should be three books stacked in the center of the table. Bring them over here. Any of them should do," said the Cat.

"One moment," I said, setting my mug down and coming around the counter.

The large center table had stacks of books all over it. Yet in the center stack of five books, three looked different. All were a deep green, and one even had green pages. I shuffled the books around until I had the ones I was sure the Cat spoke about.

I headed back to the counter but realized the woman still stared at the crystals she had placed on the counter. Her fingers wrapped tightly around her mug, but she wasn't drinking from it. Instead, she gripped it like it was a security blanket.

"Any of these three should work," I said.

I set each one down on the counter next to the four unique stones. One had the same oak leaf on it that matched her mug, another had something in writing I couldn't read, and the last was blank on the cover.

"Any of them will work?" asked the woman.

The Cat nodded, drawing her attention.

"And you will trade one book for the stones?"

Again, the Cat nodded.

Carefully, she touched each of the books but didn't flip through the pages. As soon as she touched the first book, her fingertips turned a deep green. The second caused her hair to shimmer, and I swore small horns appeared. Nothing changed when she touched the last book.

"Each has power, but how do I choose? What if I choose wrong?"

The Cat said nothing, only stared at the woman.

The silence became too much for me to handle.

"Is there really a wrong answer?" I asked. "If any of them will fix the problem, which one calls to you?"

This time, she set her whole hand on the cover of the first book.

"This one calls to the dryads," she stated with reverence. She pulled away reluctantly, then she set her palm on the center one. "This one calls to the huntsmen."

That might explain the green fingers and horns.

Her fingers darted back from that book much quicker. Yet she didn't place her hand on the last one; she just pointed.

"That one doesn't call to either, which is probably the point. One shouldn't have power over the other. We need both for the forests to thrive."

She nodded to herself, and her gaze landed on the crystals.

"They have been in my family for the last two hundred years, but the forest is more important. I'll take the last book." After her statement, she drained her mug dry.

I picked up the first two books and set them under the counter.

The third I picked up and held out to her. "This is yours, then, and we will take the crystal guardians."

"Thank you." She grabbed the book, and it vanished somewhere.

Once more, she glanced at the crystals and then set the mug down. Her hands trembled, and she stepped back.

"Good luck with the golden acorn," I said.

The Cat moved forward to the edge of the counter and sat in front of the stones. That seemed to shake her from her hesitation. The woman turned and fled the shop. The bell rang behind her as the door closed.

"Well, that was different," I said. "What was the book?"

The Cat snorted and turned to look at me. "Nothing special. Some story about planting seeds in new spots with flowing poetry and care."

"Wait," I said. "You traded her magic stones for a normal book? How is that going to solve the golden acorn problem? You can't be tricking customers..."

The Cat chuckled.

"I solved the problem." He nudged one of the stones.

I flicked my gaze to them, and energy danced inside each of them.

"You're saying the stones were the problem, not the acorn?"

"You're on the correct path. Keep going," said the Cat.

I sipped the last of my latte and automatically went to make another. Thoughts flowed easier if my hands were doing something.

"She mentioned her family had gotten them a couple hundred years ago, and I assume the gold acorn failed to thrive." I turned after grinding the beans and poked at one of them. "They look magical enough, but do they use the same type of magic that the acorn used to grow?"

"Correct," said the Cat. "The stones drew on the magical energy in the land, which stopped the acorn from sprouting."

"So, the book talking about planting in new soil will hopefully direct her to plant it in a different area where there is still more magic?"

"Close enough."

I chuckled. This magic stuff was strange, but it seemed to be all about transferring energy. Like the Cat's magical paint for the trolls' spears.

I shook my head and finished making the latte. "Do you want this? I probably should lay off the caffeine a bit."

"Sure, fill my cup."

After grabbing his teacup out from under the counter, I filled it.

The four stones glowed on the counter.

"So, what about these now? These guardians?"

The Cat's tail flicked. "I needed to get them away from her. Right now, they'll go into storage until they're needed."

"Are we just a magical thrift shop that solves problems?"

"We are not a thrift shop," growled the Cat.

We were totally a magic thrift shop. We had to be with his tone like that.

I chuckled and filled my cup with the rest of the latte.

Who needed sleep anyway?

SHE HEADED UPSTAIRS, and I turned back to the stones, sniffing each one. My magic poked out and touched them, but they were what she'd said they were. Guardian stones, with the spirits of each of the elements.

Normally, I knew what each item was going to be used for. Most of the time, it was needed soon, but occasionally, it would be years.

But these... I had no idea, and that worried me.

TWENTY-FIVE

I was tired. It felt like I'd gone out drinking, but I hadn't.

Still, I felt sluggish and had a sickly sweet taste in my mouth.

I slowly rolled out of bed, and the skylights showed it was still early. In this case, that was a good thing. A hot shower, some caffeine, and I'd be back on track for having a good day.

I hoped.

By the time I started grinding my beans for espresso, I felt more awake. Awake wasn't the right term, but maybe more solid. The thick scent of coffee filled the air, and I couldn't help but lean forward.

This was heaven. No rush to make coffee or breakfast.

I blinked, then I snapped out of my caffeine haze.

"Cat, what's your preference today?" I called out.

I took a sip of the latte, and I added a touch of vanilla

for a hint of sweetness to the drink. Maybe the Cat would like one of these.

I peeked into the kitchen, but it was empty. The bookshop itself was still in the normal arrangement, with nothing strange that I could see. The wooden bookshelves lined the back wall, and the small kids' section stood right where I expected it.

As I glanced around, there was nothing special. It was still early, though. Normally, I'd be getting out of bed right now.

I paused.

Why did I wake up early?

The warmth from the deep-blue mug in my hands centered me. Something had woken me up. I never woke up early. I loved to snuggle in my thick comforter until my alarm said it was time. At that point, sunlight usually filled my room and made it feel magical. But today, I'd crawled out of bed before my alarm, showered, and made coffee.

"Where's the Cat?" I muttered, tapping my fingers on the countertop.

The more I stood there, the more I felt like something was wrong. Today wasn't a day off. I had one more workday this week, with whatever strange thing we had to do would need to be done.

I set my mug down on the counter.

"Where is the Cat?" I asked, louder. "I need to find the Cat."

Something sparkled at the edge of my sight, and I spun around. Paw prints led up the stairs, glowing faintly, almost like glitter. My lips parted, but then the first prints vanished. I dashed up the stairs, following the paw prints down the hall past my room. They led around the balcony toward all the plants.

Then I spotted a dark patch—the Cat curled around a tree in a wooden container. It was a sapling with a few leaves. A dead leaf lay next to the Cat.

"Cat?" I whispered.

That feeling of something wrong increased when he didn't respond. I knelt and touched his fur, which didn't look like it was moving. As soon as my fingers made contact, he gasped, jerking.

"Sable?" His normally bright-green eyes looked dull. "What are you doing?"

He glanced around, taking in the situation before carefully climbing to his paws.

"I couldn't find you, and I was worried," I said. "Are you okay?"

He glanced at the dead leaf next to him.

"I'm fine. It was just a rough night." He marched off the way I'd come. "I need some caffeine."

I looked back at the dead leaf. None of the plants had needed any tending, and none had dead leaves. Everything was always bright and green in this area of the shop. With the giant windows, sunlight normally poured in.

I picked up the dead leaf and realized the little sapling was an oak tree. It had several other leaves on it, all still bright green.

"Poor little guy. We just need to give you a bit more attention." I set the dull brown leaf at the base of the tree and patted the pot. "I'll figure out how to take care of you. This is a bookstore, after all."

I climbed to my feet and glanced around at the plants, but from what I could see, nothing else was different. Only the sapling. A puzzle to solve, and I loved puzzles.

The Cat waited for me on the counter next to my mug. "You didn't make me a coffee..."

I chuckled. "I didn't want it to get cold. I couldn't find you, and like I said, I was worried."

I reached out and scratched his ears, and he leaned into my touch. Something seemed off with the Cat, so I scooped him up into my arms and gave him more attention. He purred quietly as I sat on the stool I kept behind the counter.

"I'm glad you're okay."

We stayed like that for several minutes—me holding the Cat in one arm to my chest and the other petting him. That raised red flags all over the place. He liked some scratches on occasion, but he usually resisted being picked up unless it was his idea.

"You can talk to me about anything," I whispered. "I'm here for you."

"I'd like a latte. Yours smells good," answered the Cat, pawing at my hand.

I set him back on the counter and turned to make a latte for him. "What's on the schedule today?"

"I haven't checked yet," answered the Cat.

I spilled the steamed milk when I poured it into his teacup. It splashed onto the counter, and I jerked back so I wouldn't burn myself. I grabbed a rag, but the mess was gone by the time I turned back. I shook my head, grabbed the espresso shot, and added it to the milk.

"Here you go. A latte like mine. It should warm you up." I grabbed my mug and took a sip of the still-warm beverage.

Maybe I'd get to see that book he kept hidden, the one with the appointments.

The Cat glanced at me and at his beverage.

"Please go into the kitchen and start breakfast," demanded the Cat. "I know you want to see the book, but you're not ready for it."

I glared at him. "Really?"

"Really." He nodded. "The magic can be dangerous, and I don't want you to get hurt."

He stared at me, and he looked sincere with his head lower than normal.

I stood from the stool and turned to go into the kitchen. He waited until I'd made it down the hall, and then a bright light flared behind me. I rolled my eyes and didn't look back.

Yet, what if the Cat was right? The magical book from the Bookseller had been cold. So freaking cold it hurt. This book had a bright light, so what if it burned me?

That kept me going into the kitchen and focused on breakfast. I could get the bacon cooked, along with some eggs. Boring breakfast food was still tasty.

Sable, thankfully, went into the kitchen as I'd asked. I'd worried she was going to resist and push the issue.

I wasn't ready for that, and I didn't think she was either. The pressure of who we answered to weighed heavily, and I didn't want it to break her. I had to protect the Shopkeeper, even if it hurt our relationship. She deserved to be free at the end of her contract.

Still, I worried.

She had found me near the...

I pushed the thought of the dead leaf away. I had a job to do, and my focus needed to be on that. We had to check items off the list, keep the balance that I had so ignorantly shattered, and someday heal it whole.

"Cat, we have bacon!"

I closed the book, shaking my head. Today was a simple day, unless I wanted to add a harder task to it. I jumped off the counter as the book vanished.

Maybe next time. Not today.

TWENTY-SIX

Breakfast was tasty, but quiet. I ate more bacon than the Cat, which wasn't normal. As I headed into the main shop to make another latte, the Cat followed me.

"Do you want another?" I asked.

"No, thank you." The Cat jumped up onto the counter. "Today will be a simple day, and then you can start your day off early."

"Early?" I asked, hesitating.

He nodded.

I wasn't sure if the Cat would just vanish like he normally did on my days off. Normally, the shop would appear somewhere warm, and I'd crash on the rooftop deck for a tropical vacation with unlimited books, coffee, and sunlight. Would that be good for him, too? He seemed like he still needed some attention.

The shop hadn't changed, which normally meant deliveries and bookstore people, not people from other worlds.

"So, what's on the schedule today?" I finished making my second latte and sat down on the stool.

"Deliveries and dealing with dogs, of all things," said the Cat.

"Dogs? Like, the pets, dogs? Or dogs, like you're a cat, dogs?"

The Cat turned to stare at me, his eyes wide.

"Somehow, I understood your broken thought process." His tail flicked, and I swore he snorted. "Actual dog-like creatures."

"What are they going to buy?" I asked, leaning against the counter.

"They aren't." He turned toward the supply closet. "I need you to go get the tube of tennis balls."

Again, no answers today, but that was pretty normal. The more he spoke, the more normal he became.

I opened the supply closet door, and the shelf to the inside of the door had a tube of three tennis balls in it. The easiest supply run ever.

"When I tell you to, I need you to throw one of the balls as hard as you can out the door," said the Cat.

I stared at him. "Excuse me?"

"You will need to open the door and toss the ball," answered the Cat. "I can't throw it. I don't have thumbs, remember?"

My hands shook. "How far?"

The Cat shook his head. "Just as hard as you can. It doesn't matter how far. It'll go where it needs to."

"But what if it doesn't? I don't have a throwing arm," I said, squeezing the tube. "I make coffee for a living."

"You are the Shopkeeper, and you will do this." His voice rattled around the shop, and I took a step back.

He stared at me, his eyes glowing.

"Okay... don't get your panties in a twist," I mumbled.

"Panties?"

I shook my head and grabbed a tennis ball. It was like any other tennis ball I'd seen before. Nothing special.

The door stood closed as I approached, and I couldn't see out.

"Get ready," whispered the Cat, his voice more normal than before.

My fingers tightened around the ball, and I let out a breath.

"Now!"

I swung the door open and flung that ball as hard as I could.

Then I froze.

Right outside the door, a massive battle raged. Creatures the size of Great Danes tore into each other with giant sharp claws. Others chomped down with jaws on necks or legs. The smell of mud, and the copper tang of blood, hit me.

The bright-yellow ball flew, distracting several animals, including two giant ones on top of a hill. They were bigger than all the other dog creatures. Howls rose at the sight of the ball.

Something yanked me back, and the door slammed shut.

I stumbled backward but landed in the nice chair that normally sat in the window display.

"What was that?" I whispered, my eyes wide. "Cat?!"

He jumped up into my lap. "That was us changing the course of a battle and saving lives."

He purred as he kneaded my legs before curling up. My hands automatically petted him while he kept purring.

There had been so much blood.

"Those were dog creatures, fighting each other." The warmth of the Cat in my lap stopped me from trembling. "Why?"

"To decide who was going to be top dog."

The pun hit me, and I snorted unintentionally. "Top dog? Really?"

"Really. That was two princes trying to figure out who would be king. It shouldn't have become a massive battle. It spiraled out of hand."

"What did I do?" I asked.

Did someone die because I tossed that ball? Did I now have blood on my hands?

"The fighting stopped. To you, it looked like a tennis ball. To them, it was an orb of divine right. Whoever got to it first became King," explained the Cat. "You saved lives."

"So, I didn't just end up killing someone, right?" The question came out as a whisper.

"No, you didn't." He nudged me with his nose. "I wouldn't ask you to kill someone, Sable."

I nodded and focused on petting the Cat. Something solid. That scene, with all of those creatures fighting... I shook my head slightly. Those poor creatures were all fighting about who would rule. How many had already died?

"Drink some more of your coffee. It will help," said the Cat.

Next to me stood a short table with my mug now sitting on it. Somehow, he had moved it, without me even noticing. I smiled softly and picked up the mug.

"Thank you. I wasn't expecting to see that when I opened the door." I took a sip of the warm beverage. "Did they see me?"

"No," said the Cat. "The shop's magic hid you. Only people who are supposed to come to us, do."

"Including me?" I asked.

"Including you," replied the Cat. "Plus, now…"

The bells above the door jingled.

His head tilted to the side, and the Cat sighed. "Well, we have one more item on our checklist for today. You should get back behind the counter."

I quickly made my way there, and by the time I glanced back at the door, the chair sat in the window once again.

The Cat gave me a quick look, then the door opened.

In walked a man, who might've been human, wearing a deep-red cloak.

"Ah, you're finally open." He glanced at me behind the counter and then at the door he'd opened before shaking his head and stepping inside.

He flashed a friendly smile, but as I returned it, something felt off.

The cloak was a deep shade of crimson, but it was

like it absorbed the light. It covered most of his body as he stepped closer to the counter.

"Welcome. How can we help you today?" I asked.

"Ah, help, yes. I'm looking for a particular book," he said, moving closer. He glanced at the bookshelves but continued until he stood in front of the counter. "I think someone sold it here a few weeks ago."

"Given that this is a bookshop, I need a little more to go on," I said, glancing at the Cat.

The Cat stared at the man without blinking.

"It's a cold book. I know the book—"

"No," said the Cat.

The word came out as a meow, making the man pause.

I swallowed thickly. I knew what book he was searching for, and there wasn't a chance it was leaving this shop.

"That book is not for him," the Cat continued. "Tell him he is not welcome here."

"The Cat said no, and you are not welcome here," I told the man, my voice coming out flat.

The guy's black eyes narrowed. The warm smile vanished. "Now, you listen here—"

"I said, you are not welcome here!" This time, my voice boomed out, and the bookshop shook.

The door flew open, and he stumbled back against a table.

CHAPTER

TWENTY-SEVEN

"Leave!" Again, my voice rang out, and something shoved him out the door.

He crashed into the stoop and fell before climbing to his feet. He patted his pockets, and the door slammed in his face.

My legs went out from under me, and I crashed to the floor.

The Cat peered over the counter. "Are you okay?"

"Yeah, just strangely exhausted." I climbed back to my feet, still feeling unsteady.

"Well, now we are done for the day," said the Cat. "So take as much rest as you need."

I nodded and downed the rest of my coffee. Today had been just too much. We'd only been open for an hour; I could just pretend I'd slept in.

Then, maybe, start the day again later with, hopefully, better results. If needed I could always try to bake something. That always helped.

Into the kitchen I went to make some cookies.

I tossed a batch of double chocolate cookies into the oven and pulled out a book from my stack.

The perfect amount of sunlight streamed in from the skylights, and as soon as I finished making some boba tea, I planned to read and get some sun. I'd gotten some kits and tried a regular milk tea with boba. Prep was super easy, and it turned out perfect and not too sweet.

The smell of melted chocolate was so freaking enticing. I pulled down a plate and waited until the timer went off. I used an oven mitt to pull the tray out, then I danced around the island, waiting the five minutes they needed to cool on the pan. Once that timer went off, I added six cookies to my plate.

It was time to get some sun.

Yet, as I moved to go up the stairs, I heard something from the shop area. The Cat had vanished shortly after I'd decided to just relax. He hid wherever he did when I couldn't find him, but I didn't know who else could have made a noise.

"Hello?" I called.

The front door was still closed and locked, and the shop lights were off. From the skylight, the sun brightened the room, but it wasn't a perfect light casting shadows from above. I set my plate on the counter, along with my glass of iced tea. A chirp came from the table in the center of the room. I moved closer, when something moved on the table.

"Holy smokes," I mumbled.

Right next to one of the books sat a tiny purple dragon. It stared at me with bright-green eyes that reminded me of the Cat. Yet, it was tiny. The size of my palm, tiny.

"Hey, little guy... It's okay. I won't hurt you."

The dragon backed up right into the spine of a book sitting on the tabletop.

"Are you hungry?"

The dragon blinked at that and nodded.

It freaking nodded.

Where was the Cat when I needed him? I didn't know what tiny dragons ate, or how to take care of them. Where did this little guy come from, anyway?

"I don't know what you eat..."

I held out my hand for him to crawl into. He hesitantly moved forward and scrambled into my palm. His claws wrapped around my thumb as I moved him closer to me.

"Let's head into the kitchen and figure out what you eat, and what you're doing here."

The kitchen lights were still on, and on the center of the island sat a chunk of meat. Like someone had set out a few pieces of cut beef for stew. As soon as the dragon caught sight of it, he jumped off my palm and flew toward the plate. He tore the meat into little pieces, eating all of it.

"Well, now I know you eat meat..." I grabbed a cookie from the pan and munched on it.

The chocolate was gooey and still warmer than I'd have liked, but at that moment, I was a little preoccupied.

"Now, what are we going to do with you?" I mumbled.

Yet, as soon as the meat vanished, the little dragon curled up tightly and went to sleep.

"Hm... No reason my plans need to change. I'll just bring you along. Maybe when the Cat shows up, he can let me know what you're doing here."

I woke up from my nap. I'd ignored the cookies earlier to give Sable a chance to regain her footing. The battle between the dogs had shaken her, along with the magic she had used to get rid of that creature in the cloak. I huffed, wondering why we'd even had to deal with him. The book hadn't said, which wasn't unheard of, but it was unusual.

Something important had happened. I just didn't know what.

Still, there were cookies to eat, and I should check on Sable. I wanted to make sure that she was okay.

It was the only honorable thing to do.

By the time I polished off two cookies and made my way to the roof, something tickled at the back of my head.

Sable wasn't alone.

I raced toward the roof. No one should be in the shop without my knowledge. The door hadn't opened, and the portals were closed.

This wasn't possible.

"You're a book dragon. Did you know that, little one?" I asked the tiny dragon dozing in the sunlight.

The tiny purple dragon had been napping on and off since eating.

On my way up to the roof, I'd discovered a book on different dragons. I still had no idea where the little guy had come from, but I knew he shouldn't eat cookies. Or boba tea.

That meant more for me and the Cat.

I wondered where the Cat had gotten off to. It surprised me he hadn't made an appearance, given something was happening, even if that something was mostly napping. Still, I had a handy book all about dragons to read, and the little guy seemed happy enough. I'd fed him, gotten him some water, and he lay curled up in a hand towel next to a book.

From what I'd read, book dragons guarded books, but they could also eat books and get stronger. Or maybe it read books and got stronger? I wasn't sure. The dragon book I was reading was in English, but a weird form of it. It wasn't from my world, and so trying to understand what the words meant was harder than I thought it would be.

The dragon only knew a few words when I spoke: hunger, water, sleep, and other very simple concepts. The book made it seem like book dragons were scholars. My only assumption was the little guy was very, very young.

Finally, the sound of the Cat padding down the carpet reached me.

"Hey, Cat, we have a guest."

He darted through the door I'd left open, his fur all poofed out. "Where is it?!"

"Shhh, you'll wake the little guy..." I pointed to the towel.

The Cat jumped up on my lounge chair to see what I pointed at.

"This has to be a joke," said the Cat, sitting.

"It's a book dragon," I said. "Though, I don't know where he came from. I fed him meat and got him some water. Now he's napping."

"She, and you can't keep it," said the Cat, leaning forward to sniff at the dragon.

"She?"

"Purple ones are usually female." The Cat shook his head. "You need to pick her up and set her outside the door."

"Woah, woah, woah..." I whispered, holding up a hand. "I am not leaving a baby dragon on our stoop. That's just wrong. Bad cat."

The Cat jerked back. "What?"

"You can't do things like that. What if this little guy, uh, girl, is supposed to be here? Isn't that what we do? Help things we're supposed to?"

The Cat's lower jaw moved, and his eyes narrowed. "Don't you move. I'm sorting this out."

The Cat jumped off the chair and vanished into the bookshop. The dragon still napped, and I grabbed my last cookie.

I rolled my eyes and nibbled on the chocolaty goodness. The sunlight felt divine as I waited for the Cat to reappear.

It took longer than I thought it would.

He slowly slinked his way back to the chair. "She can stay until I figure out where she needs to go. You must not let her out of your sight. There are things, even books, in the shop that could kill her."

"I won't. I swear." I held out half of the cookie to him.

"No, thank you."

"Where did she come from?" I asked, finishing the cookie.

"I have no idea, but I'll find out." The Cat had a grim look on his face as he left.

I leaned closer to the napping dragon.

"You get to stay," I whispered.

The dragon curled tighter and sighed a sigh of sleepy contentment.

I wouldn't let anything happen to this baby dragon. No matter what.

TWENTY-EIGHT

Who knew that keeping a tiny purple dragon in your sight at all times would be so freaking hard? While we had lounged outside in the sun, I'd been on easy mode, and I hadn't even known it.

Now that I was trying to cook dinner, things had gotten more difficult. The Cat was nowhere in sight as the dragon hopped around on the counter, constantly in my way as I tried to get the veggies cut and in the pan.

Fajitas should be an easy meal. The meat was already pre-cut and seasoned. All I had to do was slice peppers and onions then cook everything. Put it in a tortilla, and boom, a great dinner.

Add in a tiny purple dragon that had to smell everything, and in some cases lick it, and, well, things got messy.

I finally contained the dragon in a bowl with a piece of meat. She didn't really seem hungry, but the spices distracted her as I tossed the veggies in the hot pan.

As soon as they were done, I put them onto a clean

plate and then placed the meat into the hot pan. Steam rose, and the spicy scent filled the air. I kept one eye on the dragon as I flipped strips of meat.

"It looks like you're doing as I asked," said the Cat.

I spun, almost hitting him with the tongs in my hand, but I realized who it was quick enough to stop myself. "Sorry, I'm a little on edge."

Quickly, I spun back to the stove and resumed work. "I'm keeping her close."

"Not close enough," mumbled the Cat.

The bowl sat empty. I glanced over my shoulder to find the purple dragon staring at the Cat, her green eyes wide, like she hadn't ever seen something so perfect as the black cat.

He glared back at her then looked away. As soon as he did, she took another step forward.

It took everything in me to not laugh as I turned back to the stove and adjusted the heat. By the time I set the plate of cooked meat on the island that the Cat sat on, the purple dragon lay only a few inches away. The Cat's tail flicked back and forth, but he didn't move.

I grabbed the rest of the stuff for the fajitas and made three. Two for me, and one for the Cat. The dragon hadn't been interested in anything but the meat so far, and she had stuffed herself twice today already. I set the Cat's food down in front of him and grabbed a stool for myself, joining him.

The spicy fajitas made my eyes water a little, but they tasted good. Something was missing, but I didn't have a clue at what else I should add.

The Cat ate like normal, the bites magically

vanishing as soon as he bit down. I couldn't watch him; it made my head hurt. Instead, I focused on the tiny dragon drawing closer to the Cat's tail.

"What are we going to call her?" I asked. "I can't just keep referring to her as Tiny Dragon."

"Why not?" asked the Cat. "She won't be staying long term, just until I can figure out where she belongs."

He went back to eating.

He had a point. I had to give him that. Still, it felt strange not to give the little dragon a proper name. I mean, she was a literal dragon.

She cautiously approached the Cat's tail, her curiosity evident in her wide eyes. The Cat seemed unfazed by her presence, but I couldn't help but wonder what they really thought about each other.

"It wouldn't hurt to give her a temporary name." I took another bite of my fajita, chewed, and swallowed. "Just something to use until you discover why she's here."

The Cat paused to glare at me. "Names have power."

"I know. You've said that before. After I named Betty."

I didn't care what the Cat said. Betty deserved her name. She worked hard each day to keep us caffeinated. And I called the Cat, Cat. I didn't have anything better to call him, though now I wondered what the Cat's name was and why he hadn't told me. Or better yet, why I hadn't asked.

"It can just be temporary," I added, the thought already vanishing as I focused on the tiny dragon.

The Cat huffed, his fajita gone. "She's a baby dragon.

If you give her a name, it won't be temporary. It will be part of her forever."

"That just means we need to give her a good one."

The Cat's mouth opened, but nothing came out. The dragon had grabbed hold of his tail. The Cat's head twisted around to look at the dragon. Both of their eyes widened again, and the dragon let go of his tail. Then, they slowly took a step backward from each other.

"Do you have a name?" asked the Cat.

The dragon nodded.

"Can you tell me?"

The dragon shook her head and opened her mouth, but nothing came out but a chirp.

"I don't speak baby dragon," muttered the Cat.

"Woah, I thought you couldn't speak to anyone." I flicked my gaze between the Cat and the dragon. "That's why I'm here, right?"

The Cat shook his head. "Dragons don't listen to fate's rules any better than I did."

"How about Indigo?" I asked the tiny dragon. "Just for right now."

The dragon sat back on her rear, chirping. I glanced at the Cat, who nodded.

"At least you didn't go with Violet," mumbled the Cat.

He turned and jumped off the end of the island.

"Good luck with the dragon," he said over his shoulder as he left.

Indigo chirped as he vanished down the hallway, her tiny wings flapping with excitement.

"Well, I just need to get the kitchen cleaned up, and

then I'll show you my room. Maybe we can find a book to read before bed."

I turned back to the stove, but the pan, along with everything else I'd used to make dinner, was gone. The dishwasher was slightly ajar, and I found everything inside.

"You know, you could have left them for me." Rolling my eyes, I grabbed my boba tea and held a hand out to Indigo. "Ready to check out my room?"

Indigo climbed into my hand and then motioned with her wings to lift her higher. I did and eventually understood that she wanted my shoulder. She carefully climbed onto my right shoulder and snuggled close to my ear.

I blinked a few times while I adjusted to her proximity then headed up the stairs in the hallway to the second floor. The bookshelves here were full of the types of books I liked to read. Now we just needed to find a book to read while in the tub. I kept away from the spicy fantasy books and started searching for something clean, but fun.

Indigo leaped off my shoulder and glided toward the bookshelf. My heart jumped in my chest, but I didn't try to catch her. I let out a sigh when she landed on the wood. She scrambled down the shelf, stopping to look at different spines before continuing on. Whatever she was looking for, she didn't find it, and she climbed up to the next shelf.

I swallowed hard but let her do it herself. Her tiny little claws dug into the wood without a problem, and they didn't seem to leave a mark behind.

Finally, she paused next to one book, tilting her head one way and then the other. Then she gently nudged the book with her snout before pulling back and shaking her head, moving on. She nudged two more before, on the fourth book, she sat back and chirped at me after nudging its spine.

"Okay, we can read that one," I said.

Hopefully, it was good.

I pulled the book off the shelf and glanced at the cover. It had a dragon on it.

My laughter spilled out over the space. Hopefully, the dragons in it were the good guys.

TWENTY-NINE

I poured the steamed milk into the teacup and smiled at the little book dragon, who kept wanting to sniff it. The Cat glared enough that Indigo stayed away from the cup.

"I don't think caffeine would be good for you, Indigo," I said.

I prayed the Cat agreed. Last night had been long enough. We couldn't go to bed until we'd finished the story about the dragon and the half dragon. Indigo had chirped each time I tried to say it was bedtime.

Indigo leaned back on her back paws, chirping.

"That might work with reading, but it won't work with coffee," I mumbled.

The rest of the steamed milk I poured into my dark-blue coffee mug with speckles of golden stars. This was my second cup of caffeine for the day, and I would enjoy every drop. Hints of vanilla and almond filled the air from the brew.

"So, what's on the docket for today?" I asked the Cat.

The Cat lapped at his coffee but paused long enough to look at me. "Nothing as exciting as the last couple of days. A routine day, then hopefully a guest who can give us more information on the book dragon."

"Indigo, you mean," I said, glaring at the Cat.

The Cat glared back, then he went back to drinking his coffee.

Indigo chirped again and jumped off the counter. She glided across the opening to the large wooden table in the center of the room. On top of it lay various books, stacked nicely. A second table in the center had various books arranged upright. Most had something to do with dragons.

Indigo nudged one of them, then she vanished in between two of the stacks, heading for the stoop under the second level.

I leaned closer to the Cat, keeping my voice low. "Can 'you know who' be out during this routine day?"

I didn't want anything to happen to the cute little dragon while she was in my care.

The Cat glanced up, his teacup empty. "It should be fine."

He looked pointedly at his cup, and I grabbed it.

"I'll make you another."

"Good. We don't have long before our customer comes in."

I got to work pulling another shot of espresso. The extra shot I tossed into my cup. It'd throw the balance off a little, but I wasn't going to waste a perfectly good shot. The current espresso beans the shop provided were top of the line. The logo didn't make sense to me, and I guessed they weren't from Earth, but some other world that also grew coffee beans.

"What if she heads out the door?" I asked.

My nerves tickled from the center of my chest, which annoyed me. I'd finally felt like I had a decent handle on this job and all the weird situations I found myself in. The little book dragon had knocked that feeling sideways.

"If she leaves, she leaves."

My eyes grew wide.

"But she won't. You are feeding her, reading to her, and taking good care of her overall. This place is safe, and she knows that."

I let out a sigh and nodded.

"All right, I trust you. I'll stop worrying." I slid over the teacup so that he could get another dose of espresso and then cleaned up the area around Betty.

The bookshop this morning was in a slightly different arrangement. The big center table was pretty normal, but the bookshelves were in a different order. Instead of going back and forth perpendicular to me, the aisles were aligned so that I could see down each of them. A row of shelves still lined the far wall, but that almost never changed.

"I think I'm ready to open the shop."

The Cat didn't respond, and I turned to look at him, but he'd gone from the counter.

The bells on the door jingled as a middle-aged man walked inside. He had a bright smile but a slightly disheveled appearance. The blue tweed jacket he wore had elbow patches, and the glasses on his face had smudges. Between his hands, he held a crumpled piece of paper, which he hadn't looked up from.

"Good morning!" My call caused him to jerk upright and glance my way.

"Oh, good morning," he replied. He held up the list. "I'm Harold. Don't mind me. I'm just going to start my search."

Then he went back to the list before going up to the first bookshelf near the door. He meticulously scanned the shelves, searching for titles on his list.

I shook my head and sipped my coffee, trying not to stare at him too much. No one liked to be watched in a bookstore. To me, it always felt like the watcher judged me.

I pulled out my most recent online order—an adult coloring book. I'd tossed it and some markers under the counter.

My gaze returned to the table in the center of the room. Bright-green eyes peered at me from the shadows.

Given that the Cat wasn't here at the counter, I assumed Harold must be a guy from a normal world.

I pointed to the guy still reading down the bookshelves and motioned for the dragon to come my way. The bright eyes disappeared, and I leaned forward, trying to spot Indigo.

"Where did you go?" I mumbled to myself.

A flash of purple caught my eye as she glided across the room toward the side of a wooden bookshelf. The one that the guy had just turned away from. Indigo landed on the side of the wood and climbed up the front to the very top.

Oh no.

I must have made a sound since Harold glanced my way, but I quickly started flipping through the pages of the coloring book. Totally inconspicuous. I grabbed a purple marker from the tub and popped the cap off before daring to glance back up.

The dragon was nowhere to be seen.

Harold held two books in his arms but kept going, searching the titles meticulously.

I returned my focus to the bookshelf that Indigo had climbed with her tiny claws, but I couldn't see the top of it. I shouldn't have pointed to the man.

Her snout poked out over the edge, and she glanced at the top of Harold's head.

Please don't land on him.

She gazed at the pile of books he had in his arms, but he turned as he got to the end of the row and looped around to the other side.

Indigo launched herself off the bookshelf and glided to the top of the next one. My heart pounded until she landed safely.

I let out a sigh and wondered where the Cat was.

Harold grabbed another book off a shelf and added it to his stack. He paused, glanced up at the top of the shelf, and then shook his head. He turned in my direction and headed my way.

I flipped the coloring book closed and slid it back under the counter.

"I just want to drop these off while I keep looking," said Harold with a smile as he set the books on the counter. "Usually, I don't find so many on my list."

"No worries. Take your time," I said. "I'll keep these safe and sound until you're ready to check out."

Indigo took that moment to jump off the bookshelf and glide back to the center table. I fought the urge to react and instead gave Harold a nod.

He turned back to the shelves, the crumpled list still in his hands. Thankfully, he continued past the table and back to the shelves.

I pulled the books that he had left with me closer, but I couldn't puzzle out a theme. There was a history book, one on art, and the last was a cookbook.

Something hit the front of the counter, and I swallowed hard, resisting the urge to look up. Almost silent claws walking across the floor sounded. They moved around the front of the counter to the side then behind it.

Indigo walked on the floor, glaring at the counter.

"Did you not make your jump?" I asked quietly.

The book dragon nodded with frustrated eyes. She waved her wings at me, and I bent over to pick her up.

When I rose again, Harold stood at the counter, and I thrust Indigo onto the shelf under the counter.

"Oh, is that everything for you?" I asked, wondering if he'd seen the dragon.

"Ah, yes, I found two more." He nodded enthusiastically. "Your selection is fantastic. I think this is my largest haul yet."

I grabbed the stack of books, which now totaled five, and moved to the register. Something clicked into a teacup, but I didn't react.

Harold's eyebrows went up.

"We have a cat," I said.

"I figured, with a name like Meow," he said.

"How would you like to pay?" I quickly rang up the books, using the prices listed on the title pages written in the upper corner in faint pencil.

Harold slid his hand into his pocket and pulled out a handful of gems. He spilled them on top of the counter, and my jaw dropped. Brightly colored, everything from a deep purple to a bright yellow, each gem was about the size of a marble.

"Ah, I'm not sure..."

Laughter broke out from him as he pulled a credit card out of his other pocket. "I had you for a moment. You can put it on my card."

I shook my head, lightly chuckling as I used his card. "You got me. Do you need a bag for these?"

"Oh no, not at all." He picked up the stones, then he grabbed the books off the counter. "I hope you have a good day."

The Cat leaped onto the counter, making me take a step back.

"You too!" I gave him a little wave as he headed toward the front door.

The bright eyes of the Cat gazed at Indigo as she climbed up onto the top of the counter. "You should have taken the gems. They were worth more."

Harold walked out the front door, the bells jingling as it closed behind him.

"Wait, what do you mean?" I asked the Cat.

"The gems," he said, while watching the book dragon come closer. "They were real and worth more than you charged on the card. You should have accepted them as payment."

I blinked a few times. "How was I supposed to know that? He bought some normal-looking books, had a regular name, and dressed like an old man."

The Cat didn't say anything, but his tail flicked in the air.

"You could've been up here with me, letting me know all of that. Watch, the next thing you'll tell me is he was some sort of wizard." I threw my hands up in the air and then went back to my stool and coffee cup.

More caffeine would solve the problem. I didn't like this feeling; it crawled up inside me, like I had failed at a task I didn't even know I was supposed to do. Being the shopkeeper was a job, sure, but I finally felt like I understood it and could handle the challenges. Then something like this happened, and all of that washed away in an instant.

Had the Cat set me up to fail?

THIRTY

Harsh chirping cut into my thoughts, and I turned to see what Indigo was up to. The little dragon looked every inch a queen as she sat back on her hind paws, flaring her wings at the Cat. She glanced at me, then back at the Cat, chirping even louder.

The Cat sat to face her, but I didn't hear anything from his side of the conversation. Still, his ears lowered, and his body hunched forward. His tail flicked low near the countertop. His green eyes went wide as Indigo kept chirping.

The dragon cut off suddenly, and the Cat's ears flattened even more.

I darted my eyes back and forth between the two. It was clear that while the Cat didn't speak baby dragon, he understood whatever Indigo was telling him. Or enough, at least, to have a reaction.

"I am sorry. I didn't provide you with enough instructions," the Cat said, his green eyes on me. "It was not my intention to..."

Indigo chirped something.

"What I mean to say is that might have come out a little harsh. I should have explained the situation a little more."

I didn't know what to say. The Cat had just apologized to me. I didn't think that could happen. The failure sitting inside my chest felt a little lighter, but it'd take some time before it vanished completely.

Indigo turned toward me and scrambled across the counter to where my fingers were wrapped around my coffee cup. Her head cocked one way, and she chirped once.

"You're forgiven," I said to the Cat. "Since you weren't at the counter, my assumption was that this was a normal bookshop day. Well, a non-magical bookshop day..." I glanced at Indigo. "You know what I mean."

The Cat avoided eye contact with me. "I do not like how Harold smells. You probably can't smell it, but I can."

I reached out to scratch behind his ears, and he stretched his head out for the contact.

"How does he smell?" I asked.

Indigo chirped again.

"Yes, little one, like raw meat that's been sitting out too long," answered the Cat.

I pulled my fingers away and took a sip of my coffee.

"Next time, just give me a heads-up that you're avoiding someone because they smell and to accept the gems." I turned my gaze back to Indigo. "And you, almost giving me a heart attack as you flew around behind him!"

Indigo didn't look bothered at all. Instead, she

glanced between the two of us, her mouth open, her eyes happy.

"So, who's next on the docket?" I asked.

The Cat rolled his eyes. If you've never seen a cat roll his eyes, it's definitely something to see. "Someone you've already met."

The bells on the door jingled before the Cat could say more, and in walked Alas. He was the leatherworker who should have a pair of boots that we'd specially ordered. His dark-brown hair was perfectly in place, and he had on worn jeans with a linen shirt. He looked like a model.

Inside, I swooned.

"Welcome back, Alas," I said. "Coffee?"

"Yes, please," he said, walking up to the counter with a smile. He paused, his gaze landing on Indigo. "Now, that isn't a cat."

The Cat just glared at him.

"That's a Book Dragon."

Indigo chirped twice at him.

I pulled out a teacup from beneath the counter and got started on pulling shots of espresso. Maybe now we'd get some information on who Indigo really was.

"Where did you find her?" he asked, keeping his distance.

"She just showed up one day. We're trying to figure out where her home is." I set the teacup near Alas. "Any ideas?"

"I mean..." He ran his fingers through his deep-brown hair. "Well, I know someone I can ask to stop by, but they're a little intense." Alas leaned closer to Indigo. "She's just so small. Are you reading enough to her?"

"*Reading* to her? I read to her last night. A long book, and we had to finish it before she'd go to sleep."

He shook his head. "No, you need to be reading plenty of books to her. The more, the better, but you might want to stick to books for a younger crowd. Maybe a little shorter than whatever you started with last night. Book Dragons need stories, just like they need food. They crave knowledge, so toss in some non-fiction as well, maybe some how-to books or histories of various worlds."

He stopped to take a sip of his espresso.

I could read to her, but I didn't know how to fit more books into the time we had after the shop closed. Maybe shorter works would help.

"This is the stuff." He drained the cup.

Then he pulled a bag out of nowhere and set it on the counter, opening it. Carefully, he pulled out a set of boots —leather calf-highs. They looked amazing, and immediately I resisted touching the leather. It didn't matter that I wore socks while in the shop; those boots called to me.

"All they need is the Cat to do his thing, and they're good to go."

"Does this mean we get to do magic today?" I asked the Cat.

It'd been a while since he'd done magic in front of me.

"A little." The Cat moved closer to the boots and sniffed. "Tell him the boots look good. Then go grab a box from the storeroom."

"He likes the boots. They're the best pair he's ever seen," I said with a grin.

Alas laughed, and it spilled over the shop like a warm blanket.

I blinked a few times while I soaked in that sound before heading to the door off of the hallway. When I opened the storeroom door, a box sat on the shelf just inside. It was a fancy box that almost felt like satin, with *Meow* scrawled across the top in gold script that glowed in the light.

Now this was a gift box. I brought it back to the counter and set it down, careful not to hit Indigo, who stared at Alas.

"Well, I'm going to get out of your hair." Alas's gaze landed on me and flicked briefly to the Book Dragon. "Be careful, lass. Your life is starting to turn into an adventure, and adventures can be dangerous."

His brown eyes reflected worry, but it vanished as he turned and headed out the door, leaving the boots on the counter.

"He's a strange man," I whispered to myself. I picked up one of the boots and twisted it, getting a good look at the soft brown leather. "These are definitely boots for an adventure. So how do we do this magic?"

"There is no 'we' with this magic," said the Cat, moving closer to the boot still on the counter. "Alas put his charms on it, and now all I need to do is hide the compartments."

At least I could watch.

"Set the boots on the counter side by side."

I did as the Cat directed and stepped back. Indigo moved closer to me, and I held my hand out so she could climb into it. She made her way up to my shoulder and cuddled in close under my ear.

The Cat approached the boots from the top down and touched the first one with his nose. Bright golden light spilled from him like warm honey. It flowed over the boot and covered the brown leather, making it look like it glowed from within. The light cascaded from one boot to the next, then it increased.

I turned away, my eyes watering from the sight.

Then the light vanished, leaving the boots and Cat on the counter.

"That was it?" I asked in disbelief.

"That was it."

All of that buildup for magic, and it appeared as a bright light before vanishing.

"What did you even do?"

"I placed an enchantment on them. A glamour. No one will be able to find the secret compartments except for the one wearing the boots."

"But what if someone steals them?"

"There's always a catch with a glamour." His tail flicked to the box. "You can put them inside now. They shouldn't be hot anymore."

I rolled my eyes and picked up the box, opening it. Tissue paper sat inside, and I tucked each boot in and wrapped the tissue paper around them.

"Do you know when Carter is going to show up for them?" I asked.

The bells on the front door jingled.

THIRTY-ONE

In walked the same blond-haired and blue-eyed guy who'd placed the order to begin with, but something about him was different. His face looked younger, less gruff.

"Hey, Carter, you have good timing," I said, setting the box down on the counter. "We just finished packing the boots up if you want to look."

I motioned to the box and moved closer to the espresso machine. I automatically began to make a mocha, since that's what he'd had last time, using one of the to-go cups.

The Cat watched as Carter entered, sitting next to the box. Indigo chirped right into my ear, and I jumped, which startled her. She went flying, just barely gliding to the countertop.

"Sorry, Indigo. That was a little loud right next to my ear," I said.

The tiny dragon chirped again much softer, but her attention flicked to Carter, who hadn't moved.

"That's a little dragon," he said. "I didn't... Where... Actually, not my business."

He gave me a nod, but his eyes went back to the dragon instead of the box of boots.

"So, you have the boots?" he asked.

The Cat nodded and tilted his head toward the box.

"And you're not going to bankrupt me, right?" asked Carter.

I rolled my eyes and placed the lid on the mocha.

"That's what he said." I set the coffee next to the box. "Check them out..."

He pulled the box closer to the edge and opened the lid, revealing the tissue paper and the boots.

Indigo inched closer to him, and Carter froze, just for a second. Then he pulled out one of the boots.

"These are really nice. And the compartment is hidden?"

"He did the magic this morning. A glamour," I said, trying to sound smart.

Carter's eyes zeroed in on the Cat. "I thought glamours were fey magic..."

I shrugged. "Pretty sure that's what he called it. It glowed all bright before vanishing. It's limited to whomever is wearing the boots. So unless you put them on, you won't find it."

Indigo chirped in agreement, or at least that's what I took it to mean.

"That works," he said, tilting the boot up. "They shouldn't be coming off her feet all that often."

He set it down back in the box and closed the lid

before turning back to look at the Cat next to the cash register.

"So, what's the price?" he asked cautiously.

I turned to the Cat and waited to hear whatever he was going to charge the young man. Hopefully, it wasn't going to be something like the gems Harold had tried to pay with. Carter wasn't from Earth, after all, and I didn't know what they used to pay for goods here.

"Tell him I want a feather from him after the Demon King is dead," said the Cat. "There is an envelope under the counter that he can use to mail it back to us."

My lips parted, but I didn't know what to make of that bargain.

"Are you sure?" I asked the Cat, not caring how it looked to Carter.

The Cat just nodded and kept his eyes on the man.

I let out a sigh. "So this is a weird one. He wants a feather from you, after the Demon King is dead."

This was the second time I'd heard of demons. The first had been from Alas, who'd warned of a war that was coming. Somehow, Carter had something to do with it if this was the payment.

"To be clear, from my wings?" asked Carter, his face blank.

The Cat nodded. "His and no other."

"Yes, from you and no other."

What the heck were we bargaining for here? Also, Carter didn't have wings, or if he did, I couldn't see them. People came in here all the time looking like normal people, but that didn't mean that was what they really were, or looked like all the time.

"Okay, it's a deal." He nodded. "Do we need to shake?"

He held out his hand toward the Cat, but the Cat turned to face me.

I took the outstretched hand, and we shook. A rush of energy flowed through my fingertips as our hands glowed. A faint hum rose then vanished, along with the light.

I yanked my hand back and stared at it. "That was weird."

"Magic is a thing," said Carter.

"Wait, do you really have wings?" I asked before I could catch myself as I pulled the envelope out from under the counter where the Cat had said it was.

Carter smirked. "I do. I didn't always, but now, yeah, I do."

He picked up the box with the envelope on top and gave me a soft smile.

I connected the dots and wondered how someone who traveled between worlds helped someone get their wings. It sounded like a really naughty commercial or something.

"Thanks again," Carter said with a grateful smile.

"No problem," I replied. "I hope she enjoys the new boots, and good luck with the demons?" I shrugged a little on that one before pointing to the mocha. "Don't forget your coffee."

He snorted and grabbed the coffee in one hand, and the boots went under his arm.

The Cat seemed pleased with himself as he watched

Carter leave the store from the counter, his tail flicking back and forth.

As soon as the door closed behind the young man, I spun to face the Cat. "He has wings!"

"Yes, he's descended from angels."

"Angels? For real?"

Indigo chirped, and I nodded.

"True, if Book Dragons exist, angels might as well, too."

THAT WAS NOT what the little Book Dragon had said, but I would not translate for Sable.

If the little one wanted to read, she could figure out a way to make Sable understand that. Though, she had done me a favor and pointed out that I had treated Sable poorly.

Somehow, I'd missed the hurt in her eyes when I'd commented about the gems. It had not been my intention to hurt Sable. I only wanted to point out that they had been worth more than what she charged on the machine. My language had been insensitive, but hopefully she would forgive me.

The Book Dragon moved closer to Sable and nudged her hand, which was placed on the counter.

"That was our last client for today," I said, thinking of the information Alas provided. "We are now closed."

At least the boots were where they needed to be. That universe was on its own for the next bit; it didn't need any of our meddling. As things were, I'd done more than I should, but I couldn't help it. Hopefully, the young Traveler would make things right.

Sable's hand came down on my head and scratched my ears. I couldn't help the purring that came from my center.

"You seem a little lost. Are you okay, Cat?" asked Sable.

I nodded. "Time to rest."

The Book Dragon chirped, asking if I was okay as well. Concern radiated from the little one, and I frowned. I needed to find out where she belonged. This wasn't the place for someone who could ignore the Fates.

"Remember to read to her, like Alas said."

The little one was little, after all, and not used to being around people who couldn't understand her.

The Book Dragon chirped her thanks before twisting back to watch Sable.

I jumped off the counter and headed down the hall.

It was time to do some research about the book dragon, and who she might belong to. With Alas asking his friend, the Book Dragon should be out of my hair before long.

THIRTY-TWO

The Book Dragon stayed on my shoulder as I moved over to the children's section of the shop. It was a small area where the floor had a fluffy carpet and a beanbag chair. The shelves sat low, and mostly picture books filled them.

Yet, on the highest shelf, there was a section of chapter books. Some about real-world events and others about bedtime stories and places to escape to.

The Book Dragon jerked and chirped next to my ear as she launched off my shoulder and glided toward the beanbag. She landed softly on it and dashed excitedly toward a book. It hadn't been there before, when I'd thought about coming over here to read to the dragon before dinner.

Dark-blue cloth covered the book, which had thick pages. Indigo jumped up and down on top of it with her head flicking to me. She chirped twice, which was our signal for *yes*. A single low chirp was for *no*.

"Okay, we'll read from that one. Just let me sit down on the beanbag," I said.

She dashed off the chair to give me room, and I picked up the book as I sat down. It was heavier than it looked. Once I'd firmly planted my butt, Indigo climbed up my leg and to my shoulder to look at it from my point of view.

I flipped open to the first page, and gold letters shimmered the title.

"*Primer for the Beings of the Tree*," I said, reading aloud. "What's the tree?"

Indigo bobbed her head and rubbed a claw along her snout.

I kept going. The table of contents made it look like a guide to the different beings someone might run into in various places. The first entry was for humans, which made me want to giggle.

"*Humans are one of the most numerous species of the Tree. They inhabit various planets and places, springing up in the most random locations. They come in a variety of colors, shapes, and sizes. Some even have access to magic. The most important thing to know about humans is that many other species can breed with them. Sometimes, this is the only model of reproduction a race has. This has led some universes to work hard to protect the humans in their midst.*"

I jerked back, blinking as what I'd just read registered. Humans had kids with other species and had to be protected in certain parts of the universe?

I didn't know how I felt about that, but I stored it away in the back of my mind.

Indigo chirped a few times with a question, but I could only guess what it was.

"Yeah, I'm human, but on my world, we don't have magic. It's a pretty boring place. I didn't know magic was real until I got this job with the Cat."

The next section in the book listed the different humans you might come across.

"*Some humans don't have magic*—that's like my world," I added before continuing. "*Other humans have magical abilities and might be witches, wizards, or have elemental powers. It all depends on the world they are born on and how magical it is. Approach humans with care. The non-magical ones don't have long life spans, but ones with magic often live longer.*"

Indigo nudged me under the chin, rubbing her head.

"Awww, don't worry. I'm not going to die soon. I'm young for a human. Like, even in my non-magical world, I have another sixty or seventy years." My voice stayed soft as I tried to calm her down.

I wondered how long Book Dragons lived. Was she going to be small for the next fifty years?

I flipped back to the table of contents to see what other beings were in the book. "How about we see if we can find more information about Book Dragons?"

THEY FOUND THE BOOK, which was good.

I hadn't been sure they would head in that direction, but I'd hoped they would. It would help Sable, and the little Book Dragon, learn more about the worlds and themselves. The book was special; it only showed species that someone had come across before. Here, it was tied to Sable.

I should have given the book to her before now, but I wasn't sure she'd be ok with it. The last shopkeeper hadn't even been given a chance to look at the book.

But Sable was different. That spark of magic glowed inside her, like an ember. Now and then it brightened, expanding. Especially after she used the magic inherent to the shop.

I'd snorted when she mentioned she didn't have magic. Still, she hadn't figured it out yet. Her brother had a spark as well, and while her world was mostly magic-free, there were places where those who had magic gathered. Plus, the portals to other places were on all the worlds in the great Tree, and she had no idea.

That made me nervous.

I pulled away from the railing on the balcony and headed toward a door my size. I stepped through and into a much larger room. Bookshelves lined the walls, with gaps for arched doors with various symbols etched into them. A giant wooden table stood in the center of the room.

I jumped up and landed carefully on the surface, making sure to not rattle the bowl in the middle of the table. The wooden bowl glowed, with power running through the carvings of vines, leaves, and trees covering the outside of it. The rim wasn't high, just low enough for me to peek over the edge into the still water inside.

"Show me what I have of Book Dragons," I whispered, the quiet words rolling off my tongue.

The spines of different books around the room glowed as their words floated across the surface of the water. I touched my nose to the edge and let the knowledge flow through me.

The Book Dragon had entered with the man searching for the Book that we'd imprisoned within the shop. It had taken all that Sable was to get that Book in a safe room. What did he want that Book for, and what did he want with the dragon?

A thought touched the edge of my mind, something so horrendous I jerked back. My eyes widened, and I hissed at nothing in front of me. What little power I had left darted around the room.

Burning fire inside me roared to be let free. To blaze through the worlds until I found that creature in red. Until I reduced him to nothingness.

Then it flickered out.

My mouth gaped open as my chest burned, trying to get enough air into my tiny lungs. My whole body shuddered, and a glow caught my attention.

The book, the bane of my existence, softly glowed golden, but I ignored it.

"Well, there's an entry in here for Book Dragons..." I mumbled and flicked through the pages.

Most were blank. They didn't even have headers on them. One section had information about Trolls, and I recognized the drawing. It was of the tribe that we'd sold the spears to. I kept going, even passing a page on winged beings, and finally stopped on Book Dragons.

"All right, let's see if the other books we found are right." I skimmed the page before going back to the top. "All right, here we go. *Book Dragons are a subspecies of Dragons, but don't let them fool you. They are still living and breathing Dragons, creatures that can ignore the Fates and control magic in ways that others cannot. The only other beings so independent, capricious, and powerful are the Fey Lords. And like the Fey Lords, Dragons have their own code that is only truly understood by their own kind.*

"*If you ever find yourself in front of a full-grown Dragon of any type, be respectful and honest.*" That was good information to know. "*What makes Book Dragons so special is that they love and crave knowledge. In fact, they need it to grow. Book Dragons require a steady diet of new knowledge to age. They love trading books, true stories, and memories.*"

Indigo nodded as I spoke, her eyes tracing the words on the page. I wasn't sure if she could read them yet.

"*Book Dragons speak many languages, and most often hoard enormous libraries and trade information. Bards tend to be their favorite type of person. Not much is known about the breeding and hatchlings of Book Dragons. They keep their little ones close, raising them with the knowledge in their hordes until they reach adolescence and seek to build a hoard of their own.*"

Indigo chirped sadly.

"Don't worry, Indigo. We'll find your people. You weren't tossed away. Someone is out there looking for you, and we'll keep you safe and sound until we can find them."

Indigo chirped again, but I didn't know what she was saying.

"Tell her we both will," said the Cat.

His voice carried down from above, and I glanced up.

His green eyes stared at me from between two of the banisters. "Keep her safe. No matter what."

THIRTY-THREE

I sat on the stool and took a bite of the breakfast taco bowl.

The eggs were spicy, and they had a vibrant-orange hue from the spices mixed in with the diced jalapeños, which added a pop of green. The potatoes were a light-brown color, crispy and seasoned perfectly. On top, the guacamole was a bright shade of green, dotted with chunks of onion and tomato.

This was a winner. It was too bad I only had to heat this up in the microwave then add the guac. I couldn't take credit for this amazing meal.

Indigo enjoyed eating the scrambled eggs, she snuck the first bite from my plate and it didn't seem to do anything bad to her. Now she took giant bites, leaving little bits of yellow on her snout. I'd piled a little bit of my bowl onto a small plate so that she could eat them. That way, she wasn't trying to steal food from my plastic bowl.

The Cat dove practically headfirst into his own, though he didn't like guac, which left more for me.

"This is tasty," said the Cat. "Make this more often."

I chuckled at the demand. Ordering more groceries was simple, and this made a tasty breakfast. Still, maybe on my next day off, I could figure out how to make something like this from scratch.

"So, what's on the schedule today?" I asked.

"We have a visit this morning from someone who might have information on the little one," said the Cat in between bites.

He suddenly sat up, his bowl empty. His bright-green eyes stared at my bowl, but I'd put a ton of guac on it, and he seemed to decide it wouldn't be worth it.

"Then, this afternoon, we have a few deliveries from a non-magical world. The little one will need to be out of sight."

A sad chirp came from Indigo.

"It's a world that doesn't know of magic, little one. You will learn the rules," said the Cat.

"What type of deliveries?" I asked. "Can I place a grocery order, then?"

"Yes, it should be your world, or something close to it."

I nodded, going over the mental list I'd been keeping. While the stockroom had piles of things, fresh food was harder to keep track of. If I put it into the grocery order, I knew the shop would have that item in stock.

Somehow, I also didn't need to worry about anything going bad. Dates didn't mean much in the fridge. Things were as fresh as the last time I'd closed the door. I'd tested it out with a half-eaten peach on a plate. Three weeks later, that thing still looked like I'd just taken a bite out of it.

Indigo finished the food in front of her and curled up, blinking a few times like she needed a nap.

I smiled. If she wanted to nap, she could nap. We'd stayed up too late last night reading books. After we'd read about Book Dragons in the Primer, I'd pulled a few kids' books off the shelf to read. She'd had me keep one open on the desk in my room. I didn't know if she figured out how to read it, but this morning I found her curled up next to it.

"Well, I'll make some more coffee, and we can get this started," I said. After tossing the plastic bowls in the garbage and putting Indigo's cup in the sink, I picked her up carefully in my hands and carried her to the front.

I set her down on a small cushion I found in the storage room. Then I turned my attention to Betty.

Time to make a fantastic drink. Something chocolaty and caffeinated, plus maybe some mint. Peppermint mocha it was.

I pulled out the Cat's favorite teacup, along with my now-empty mug, and got to work. The smell of chocolate and peppermint filled the air, making me think of snow, the winter solstice, and my family.

That hit hard in my chest, and I made a mental note to send an email to my parents. They'd been really good about sending messages every couple of weeks, but my replies had been shorter and shorter. There was just so much I couldn't talk about. At least they weren't pressing for answers.

Still, I should send a longer reply and maybe have a call with my mom. I'd need to check and see what the date was back home.

Once the mochas were done, I moved the teacup in front of the Cat, then I took a sip of my own. The warmth felt amazing, and I closed my eyes, feeling gooey on the inside.

The bells jangled on the front door, and I snapped my eyes open before glaring at the Cat. He kept his gaze fixed on the newcomer.

A tall woman entered the shop covered in a long bright-red cloak. Her ears tapered to long points on either side of her head, and as she walked, it seemed almost like she glided over the floor. Her dark eyes glowed a deep-orange color as she stared at Indigo, sleeping on the counter. She had a sharp jawline, which gave her a regal appearance.

"She does not belong here!" Her voice rolled through the space with a growl.

I jerked forward, yanking Indigo off of the counter and pulling her to my chest. The sleeping dragon purred contentedly.

"You'll scare her! Keep your voice down. She's napping." My voice came out as a harsh whisper.

Her orange eyes studied me, then flicked to the Cat.

"What is happening here?" asked the woman.

For a moment, the woman flickered, and I saw a dragon standing between the table and the front windows. Bright-red scales reflected the morning light, and those same orange eyes glared at me out of an enormous head. Then the image disappeared, and the red-coated lady stood there again.

"You should explain the situation to the Lady before she gets angry," said the Cat.

"Explain? But she almost woke Indigo up," I replied.

The Cat glared at me, then he looked pointedly at the woman, who stood three feet away from the counter.

"Fine!" I turned back to the woman in red. "She appeared in the shop a few days ago, and we've been trying to figure out where home is for her."

I snuggled Indigo, who stayed curled up. "I've been learning all that I can and reading her books. Plus, feeding her normal food," I added.

The lady glanced at the Cat, who nodded.

"So you did not steal her from her family?" she asked, taking another step forward, her eyes narrowed.

My eyes widened. "Of course not!"

"Tell her someone entered the shop, and you banished him," said the Cat. "I am certain he was the kidnapper."

"Wait, you think that creepy jerk was how Indigo showed up? He was horrible."

"Creepy jerk?" growled the lady.

Her eyebrows rose, and her hands clenched into fists.

It finally dawned on me that this might really be a dangerous situation, and I should probably explain everything in more depth. The passage about treating full grown dragons with respect suddenly flashed through my mind, and I gulped.

"Yes, there was this creepy guy in red. Totally freaked me

out. I had to banish him from the shop. I found Indigo later that evening and made sure she had food." My voice came out as a ramble. "Since then, the Cat's been trying to figure out where she came from so we can get her home. Until then, I'm keeping her safe, happy, and healthy. Though today, she's been really tired. I think she stayed up late reading."

The lady's shoulders lowered. She took a step back, and the tension in the room relaxed somewhat.

"That would do it. Did she eat?"

"Eggs for breakfast. Then she tuckered out." Now that I thought about it, I wondered why she wasn't up and interacting with the lady dragon more.

"Can I see her?"

"Do you promise to not steal her or cause her any harm?" The question slipped out automatically. "I promised I'd keep her safe, and I don't know you. The Cat might, but I don't."

The lady blinked three times, slowly.

"I am Lady Borsal." She bowed her head toward me ever so slightly. "And you?"

"I'm Sable, the Shopkeeper." I held out Indigo. "And this is Indigo. It's only a nickname, not a real name, since I couldn't keep calling her Book Dragon. The Cat didn't want to name her."

She snorted and took the little sleeping dragon in her hands. Her fingers had talons on the ends of them.

"She's young. Too young to be away from her mother... You're doing well feeding her. That's why she needs to sleep." She nodded to herself. "Growth spurt."

The Lady pulled her closer and growled softly at Indigo.

Indigo's eyes fluttered open. Her bright-green eyes turned and met the older orange orbs. Indigo chirped a few times, and then the Lady responded in a strange language.

They could talk to one another. I found myself slightly jealous.

"Does she have a name? A real one I could use?" I asked. "I don't want to call her the wrong name. That's rude."

Indigo's bright-orange eyes flicked toward me, and she chirped, drawing the Lady's attention again.

"We name ourselves when we get old enough. She likes Indigo for now." Lady Borsal cuddled closer to Indigo, then she blew hot air over the dragon.

The little one's eyelids fluttered, and she curled back up into a ball.

"Indigo needs to rest in a warm, cozy place. She might sleep for a few hours, or maybe even a few days." She held Indigo out toward me.

I took the sleeping dragon from her and pulled Indigo close.

THIRTY-FOUR

"I know just the thing." I turned and headed toward the stairs, leaving Lady Borsal behind.

The Cat coughed. "You should stay down here until she leaves."

"She's a dragon, and she told me what Indigo needs. I'm going to make sure Indigo is comfortable first. Otherwise, I'll be worrying about her the whole time we're talking." I moved faster up the stairs and to my room.

On my bed, I tucked Indigo in with my pillows and pulled out an old heated blanket I'd kept from my place. After I turned it on and placed it around her, I headed back.

Yet, I paused at the door.

"Hey, can you make sure she's comfortable?" I asked the room.

Part of me was sure the Cat controlled the shop, but a smaller part of me wondered. Just in case, I figured I'd ask.

Then I headed back down the stairs. Lady Borsal

stood in the same spot, staring at the Cat, who stared back.

"Sorry to make you wait, but I wanted to make sure she was comfortable."

The Lady nodded. "I want to know more about this person in a red cloak."

The Cat let out a sigh and broke the staring contest. "Sable, please go into the storage room and grab a mirror out."

My mind went blank for a moment since I couldn't remember him ever using my name before, but then I turned around and headed to the door in the hallway. Inside were the same old metal shelves, and on the closest shelf next to the door lay a hand-held mirror.

I lifted it, surprised at its weight, and brought it to the counter. The mirror was small and compact, ornate and beautiful, with a smooth silver surface that reflected the sunlight coming in from above. The frame had an intricate design etched along the edges, and the surface was pristine. It looked like a prop from a Victorian-era movie.

"Set it down on the counter," said the Cat.

I did, and he moved closer before touching his nose to it. Light flickered between his nose and the mirror before an image appeared. I leaned in, along with Lady Borsal, as the image of the man in red appeared.

Shivering, I stepped back. "I didn't like him one bit. Creepy."

"Hmmm," mumbled the dragon Lady, leaning in closer. "I'll remember his face. Do you know what he smelled like?"

"Metallic, with an overtone of burned cheese," said the Cat.

I snapped my head toward him. "Really? That's just gross."

I caught Lady Borsal staring and relayed the information.

"I'll spread the word among the clans," she said, nodding. "I'll also mention the little one that has been found."

"Do you think you can find her family?" I asked.

"Yes," she said, her eyes glowing. "We are most protective of our young. The mother must be searching. We rarely have dragonets, and they are cherished. Don't worry. The Clans of Lore are secretive by nature, but they have ears everywhere. They will learn of this."

"Good. Everyone deserves to be loved by a family."

The Cat's ears dipped, but he said nothing.

"You are a strange one, Shopkeeper, especially to be found here."

The Cat's tail flicked in the air.

"The dragons will remember you doing this." With a nod, she marched out.

The image of a large red tail flicking behind her, filling the doorway, washed across my vision, but then vanished.

Then the bells clanged as the door shut.

"How dead do you think that guy is?" I asked the Cat.

"Very."

I paused for a moment, my gaze still on the door. "Good. Indigo is just a baby, and she was taken away from her home and family. That's not right." I shook my head, thinking again of my own family. "I'm glad you found Lady Borsal. At least I know I need to keep Indigo warm and cozy while she sleeps."

The Cat had a look I couldn't describe.

"What about you, Cat? Do you have family somewhere out there?"

Every single hair puffed out on the Cat.

I let out a sigh and moved closer to the coffee machine. Immediately, I went about making another peppermint mocha, and I pulled his teacup back out.

"It's okay if you don't want to talk about it." I poured the espresso into the cup, then I steamed the milk with the chocolate sauce and peppermint.

I filled the cup the rest of the way, making sure to put plenty of foam on it.

The Cat hadn't moved.

I refilled my mug, using what hadn't gone into the Cat's cup.

Sitting back on the stool, I reached over and picked up the Cat. He didn't resist.

"I'm sorry. It wasn't my goal to upset you." I pulled him close and scratched under his chin and then between his ears.

Very slowly, he relaxed.

"I miss my family. Not like all the time, but I miss getting to visit them. I'm going to give my mom a call later this afternoon after the deliveries. It should be fun. I'll get caught up on all the drama with my brothers."

The mirror sat on the counter reflecting the sunlight, and I wondered what else it could be used to look at.

Could I use it to see things outside the shop? How had the Cat used magic to pull up that image?

Then again, the Cat clearly wasn't in a place to answer those questions. Maybe I could ask him later. I hoped so, but I wouldn't press.

After all, he was my friend, too, and I didn't want to upset him.

SABLE COULDN'T KNOW that the conversational area she had stumbled into was off limits.

I could only talk about bits and pieces of my past. Really, only the smallest, least important bits and pieces, and even then, not freely.

Yet, the underlying joy she had while talking about her family filled me with guilt. I knew she couldn't stay after her contract was up, but part of me wanted her to.

Her fingers scratched at my ears like my paws couldn't. My teacup sat on the counter, filled with the chocolate coffee thing. The first had been delicious.

Eventually, my body relaxed, and I stared at the cup.

Sable couldn't stay. I would need to keep reminding myself of that. We had bigger issues to deal with. The baby dragon was going into a growth cycle, and once she woke, she needed to be fed both food and books. This cycle would continue until she was fully grown. It could take decades for that to happen. Sable didn't have decades to spend with the dragon. We needed to find the Book Dragon's mother.

Lady Borsal would do most of the heavy lifting. All

we could do was wait until the little one woke, do our best to keep taking care of her, and keep her safe. Until then, we had to do our jobs and follow orders.

I cuddled under Sable's chin then moved toward the counter. She let me jump to the wooden surface, and I headed to the cup.

"Thank you for the coffee," I whispered, before lapping at it.

I couldn't bring myself to say more.

She scratched at my ears again. "You're welcome, Cat."

THIRTY-FIVE

Indigo was right where I'd left her, and it made me smile.

I grabbed my laptop and added a few things to my cart for delivery. They would make the next couple of days easier for her, especially if this would take a while before she woke up.

I leaned back in my chair, pulling up the last email from my mom.

It mentioned Cyan's birthday, and I already knew I'd send him some book, so I wasn't worried about that. This was the first family birthday I'd miss, though.

I texted my mom and asked if she was available for a video call since I had some time. A notification that I had an incoming video call on my laptop popped up, and I opened it up after making sure my bed wasn't in the frame. I didn't need Mom to see Indigo.

"Hey, honey!" Her voice sounded just like always.

"Hey, Mom," I replied. "I got your email and just

wanted to chat. How are things going with planning for Cyan's party?"

She rolled her eyes and let out a sigh. "He doesn't want one. Instead, all the boys decided they will celebrate on one day this year to make sure you can visit. Somehow, all of them agreed after his visit with you."

My mind froze for a second as I tried to process that. My brothers loved having birthday celebrations separately. It helped that they were mostly spread out over the year, and they were great excuses for the family to gather. Yet Cyan had somehow gotten them all to agree to have one celebration. What the heck was going on?

"So, this wasn't your doing?" asked my mom.

"Not at all," I muttered. "I'm a little in shock."

A soft smile came over her face.

I leaned back in my chair, wondering if I needed to call him next. "Are you still doing monthly dinners?"

"Of course," she said. "There isn't a chance I'd stop doing monthly BBQs, roasts, and such. It's the only time Umber lets me go all out. Otherwise, he's always dropping off some food or a little something for us to try."

Her dark eyes searched over me. "You're looking good. Is the job still going well? You haven't mentioned much in your emails."

I nodded. "It isn't too exciting. A bookshop is a bookshop, but I do like getting to plan out specials. Plus, I'm learning how to bake cookies."

My mom flinched.

"Don't worry, the dough is already made. Though I have learned how to cook some things."

My mom knew I wasn't handy in the kitchen, but I was proud of the progress I'd made so far at teaching myself. Now I could handle things like tacos, steaks, and even some stir-fry, all with reasonably edible results.

She nodded, but her lips tightened into a line.

I braced myself.

"Do you think you'll be home for the holidays? The winter solstice is your favorite." She paused. "Maybe save up your vacation days so you can spend a day here?"

I didn't want to destroy the hope on my mother's face, even though I knew I couldn't do what she asked.

"I can talk to my boss and see what he says, but don't get your hopes up."

We had plenty of time before winter came crashing down, though it was hard for me to keep track. Time passed by differently in the shop, and by default, I didn't think we were on Earth. Or if we were, it was always in a sunny, warm location on my days off so I could enjoy the rooftop deck.

"Oh, shucks," said my mom, scratching the back of her neck. "Your dad's calling. I better answer that. We miss you and love you."

"I love and miss you too, Mom."

The call ended, and I let out a sigh.

I had time to figure this out.

Hopefully.

THIS DAMN PLACE.

Every time Sable tried to have a private conversation

with her family, it made sure I listened nearby. I knew she had a family who loved her, and they wanted her to visit. It wasn't like I was the one who enforced the contract. Yes, she'd signed it, and so did I, but the rules were more than that.

I stayed sitting on the carpet outside her room, hoping the conversation would go quickly.

When she'd asked about my family, everything inside of me had thought of my children and the war they now faced. I shuddered, praying that they would survive and, someday, maybe even forgive me.

The urging I felt from the shop was to find out some way to bend the rules. To be the person I was before, the person who had gotten me into all this, and find a way to allow a visit.

Too many things to do. I had to keep the baby dragon safe, figure out a way around the rules for the holidays, and most importantly, keep Sable safe.

Even now, I felt the icy darkness trying to break from its chains, calling. It had been quiet, but bringing the book dragon in had slowly awakened it.

That worried me. Its energy needed to be drained faster.

Whatever that creature had wanted to do with the book and the book dragon, the book knew about it.

Somehow.

AFTER LUNCH, I waited behind the counter for the

deliveries. It was the last thing on the list for today, and it was on my Earth.

The Cat wasn't anywhere to be seen, and I'd left Indigo upstairs, sleeping. I even checked the chair by the front window, but the Cat wasn't napping. Indigo hadn't stirred during the call with my mom, or when I'd made sure she was still tucked cozy under the heated blanket.

The door jingled open, and in walked John with a large box.

He flashed his too-white smile at me. "I got a ton of boxes for you today."

He set the first one on the counter and then turned to head back to the door. The door had stuck open, and he kept going.

The first box had to be the normal stuff since it wasn't big enough for the things I had gotten.

John brought in a much bigger box, and my eyes widened. Perfect. Absolutely perfect.

"I have one more in the truck. You definitely piled everything up for one day," he said.

I quickly pulled out a to-go cup and ground some beans for an Americano. As John walked in with the last box, I poured the hot water into the cup.

"Would you like cream or sugar in your coffee?" I asked.

He smiled again, setting the last box down on the floor next to the big one. "Some sugar would be perfect. How are things working out with this place? I haven't been stopping by as much as normal."

I shrugged. "Business is good. We had some fun events. You know how it goes."

I added some sugar and gave it a stir before putting a lid on top.

"Here you go." I set the cup on the counter in front of him, but his gaze wandered around the shop before landing back on me.

His eyes were a bright green, but I could have sworn last time they were brown.

"How about we go out sometime?" he asked.

The hair on the back of my neck rose, and everything inside me wanted to take a step away.

He reached out and grabbed my hand, which rested on the counter. My skin turned icy at the contact, and I wanted to scream.

His eyes almost glowed, his lips parted, and sharp teeth flickered in and out of existence.

A roar came from above. A bright-gold light jumped from the railing, aiming directly for John.

"Sable, close your eyes!"

I snapped my eyes shut and jerked back, crashing to the floor. The shop shook, and something roared again. Then everything went silent.

"Sable, are you okay?" asked the Cat.

I blinked, then glanced up from where I lay sprawled on the floor. He sat on the counter, staring down at me.

Quickly, I climbed to my feet. "What was that?"

I ignored his question for the moment. I didn't even know how to think about it, much less answer it. And I had no idea how to think about what had just happened, either.

"Not John," said the Cat. "John's outside on the side-walk. It looks like he slipped and got knocked out."

"Wait, what?" I asked.

I gazed out the window, but it was hard to see outside if you weren't right in front of it. The guy who had been in the shop was gone.

"What happened to the not-John?"

"You don't need to worry about him anymore," said the Cat as he moved closer to me, rubbing his side along my arm on the counter. "Are you okay?"

"I think so. He made me feel cold, like I couldn't do anything," I whispered.

The Cat nodded and leaned up against me. "I am sorry I wasn't down here."

"Not your fault," I said, picking up the Cat. "Not at all. It should have been a normal delivery, just stuff from online shopping."

I shivered and cuddled the Cat closer. "Thankfully, Indigo is sleeping. I wouldn't want her around something like that."

Sable held me close, and the ground became more solid under her feet.

Fire still rolled through me. That creature had dared touch her, touch my Shopkeeper! He would suffer, slowly.

I could feel him under the floorboards, the shop containing him in a cell for the moment. The cell's location was as far away from the book as possible. The cold that rose from him was too similar to take any chances.

I purred in Sable's arms, doing my best to calm down and help her calm down, too.

"Cat, who was that?" she asked quietly. "*What* was that?"

"I will find out."

It was in the rules, after all. It was even the first rule.

Do Not Upset the Cat.

THIRTY-SIX

I peeked out the door of my bedroom, trying to spot if anything was different.

Indigo slept inside a cozy box in the cat tree I'd put together the night before. Well, one of two. The other one sat inside my door, waiting for a good moment to give it to the Cat. Hopefully, I wouldn't insult him, but cats liked cat trees and catnip. I might have sprinkled a little inside the cozy box of his cat tree as well. It was the delivery I'd gotten before things went south with the not-John.

Sunlight streamed in from the skylights overhead as I moved out into the hallway. As soon as I peered over the railing, I saw that the entire downstairs had been rearranged.

Yesterday, bookshelves had lined the walls and formed rows like a normal bookstore. Today, the center of the store had wooden tables. All the tables held various objects. Oak bookshelves still lined the back wall and the wall to the right. To my surprise, a glass case I hadn't seen before stood directly in front of the wall to my right with the shelves behind it. The wooden counter, the cash register, and Betty still sat directly below me.

I let out a sigh of relief. When Betty was missing, things went sideways rather quickly.

I glanced at my phone, which was clenched in my right hand. It still had service.

"MEOW!"

The sound from the Cat echoed upstairs. I rarely heard him meow.

My heart beat quickly as I darted down the stairs in my sneakers. I rushed into the very short hallway that led to the area behind the register. He sat in front of the enormous book, the one he didn't want me to look at and that vanished when he wasn't reading it. It was bigger than him.

I paused in my panicked rush. Light glimmered from the pages, and I took a step forward. He was a shadow of darkness against the light, just the suggestion of the shape of a cat before he solidified.

The Cat glanced over his furry shoulder at me, his green eyes glowing, and then a loud bang sounded from the kitchen.

My heart leapt again, and I spun to face the kitchen. "What the—"

A can had fallen from a shelf and rolled across the floor toward me. I bent over to pick it up.

"Cat? What's going on? Are you okay?" I turned back, holding up the can of corned beef hash.

The glowing book had vanished. The dots connected in my mind, and I glared at him.

"Real smart…"

It took a moment for me to calm down. He only needed to say something, and I'd back off from the book; I thought I had proven that already.

"You should make breakfast." He glanced at the can in my outstretched hand.

"Don't you usually prefer bacon?" I asked.

His black tail flicked in the air, but he didn't respond.

"Whatever! I am going to make coffee first, then breakfast. You know, the normal order of operations."

The Cat moved toward the espresso machine as I did. He stayed out of my way but watched me intently.

"In the teacup, please…"

His request was familiar, closer to a normal morning in the magical bookshop, so I went with it. I reached under the counter to the row of teacups and pulled out a chipped one; it fit his current mood, along with mine.

Then I got to work. I stuck with a vanilla latte—a very large vanilla latte. The scent of freshly ground coffee beans filled the air, and it caused me to smile. I steamed extra milk to top off the espresso in his dainty teacup.

"So, what does today look like? More buying and selling books? Or something more magical?"

My gaze landed on the display case on the right-hand side of the store. The glass sparkled, blocking most of my view, but I could see a couple of books. Other objects sat on top of a strip of purple cloth, but I couldn't make out what they were.

I kept my voice light and careful after what had already happened this week. "Or something more mundane?"

He immediately headed to the teacup. His head hovered over the top as he lapped at the frothy milk.

I hated the silence; it was strange this morning. He had to respond at some point, right?

"How is the latte?"

"Good, thank you."

I rolled my eyes and headed to the kitchen. Now I had to figure out how to make corned beef hash. I was pretty sure I just heated it up in a pan and put fried eggs over the top.

In the kitchen, I grabbed a frying pan and cranked up the heat. The can opener had appeared on the counter. Thankfully, I knew how to work a can opener. I sprayed the pan with olive oil, waited five minutes, and then dumped the contents of the can into the hot pan.

"That looks like cat food," said the Cat.

"You're the one who magically knocked the can from the cupboards. So, you get to eat it... Well, we get to eat it 'cause I am not cooking two breakfasts this morning." I smoothed the corned beef down in the pan until it lay flat and quickly grabbed my phone.

My eyes widened when I realized it was still connected to the cell network. Most mornings, it was a useless piece of tech in my back pocket. When I cooked something new, I usually had a recipe book open on the counter, but I was sure I wouldn't find a recipe book with instructions for canned corned beef. I wanted help from the internet with this one.

"All right, the internet gods say I brown it on both sides and top it with fried eggs. That doesn't sound too hard..."

"Don't tempt the Fates like that," whispered the Cat.

His tail twitched as he paced around on the counter. His eyes darted toward the front of the shop and then back. When nothing seemed to happen, he sat down.

"You seem a little tense. Like, way more than normal, even before breakfast. Is everything okay?" I held out my hand to pet him on the head or give him scratches.

This week, he'd been closer to me than usual. It made it hard to hide working on the cat trees from him. Yet he didn't respond to the question. Whatever was bothering him wasn't my problem, but I couldn't get that loud cry from earlier out of my head. He had sounded like he'd been in pain.

"You might want to flip that," said the Cat.

I spun back to the stove and grabbed a spatula. Time to make an awesome breakfast.

Ten minutes later, I set two plates down on the island. Small charred bits spotted the pile of corned beef on each plate. On top of each pile sat two sunny-side-up eggs for each of us. Somehow, I'd managed to not break the yolks. The scent of the crispy beef hung in the air, along with pepper. I might have accidentally used too much.

I still didn't understand how much food to cook for the Cat. I made him slightly less than I served myself, and he almost always cleaned his plate. Wherever he put it had to be magical, since he wasn't a particularly large cat.

"That looks strange," said the Cat, staring at the food.

He stuck his nose over it and sniffed. His whiskers trembled.

"It should be tasty. I followed what the internet said."

"The internet is wrong occasionally."

I ignored him and sat on the closest stool. Time to try it. I broke my egg yolk and scooped up a bit of corned beef and egg. The texture was slightly crunchy but also not. It wasn't bad, but it did have a little too much salt.

"It's edible."

The more I ate, the better it tasted. Who knew that could happen? I hadn't used too much pepper, which was comforting. This was not something I'd tried eating at home—my brother hated things that came from cans. It reminded me of roast beef, but the texture was different.

"Bacon is better."

"This is all on you." I glanced over at the Cat.

He had egg smeared on his nose and whiskers, which was strange. Normally, he was a very clean eater, almost magical in nature. His plate was empty.

My lips parted, and I blinked rapidly at the plate. "So, you liked it?"

"It wasn't bad."

"Do you want a napkin?"

Instead of answering, he turned his butt toward me and jumped off the counter.

I wouldn't rush my breakfast just because he did. Plus, this was way more filling because of the little potatoes in the corned beef.

My phone still lay on the counter, but now the cell service was gone.

"Really? You couldn't keep the service on until I finished breakfast?" No more videos or social media while I ate.

If there was no cell service, we weren't on Earth anymore. I needed more caffeine to deal with this. Big time.

I finished breakfast with the goal of getting another cup of something with espresso before we opened the shop for the day. The Cat was nowhere to be found when I entered the front of the shop. His teacup was gone, more than likely already in the dishwasher.

He pounced up on the counter and stared at me.

"I would like steamed milk." His face was egg-free—less adorable, but still cute.

"No problem," I said as I pulled what I needed from the mini fridge. "Do you want vanilla in it, or cinnamon?"

The Cat studied me. I felt his green eyes on my back.

"Let's go with cinnamon," he said after a moment.

"Coming right up, boss." Maybe his weird mood had gone?

He snorted.

How does a cat even snort?

I pulled a few shots of espresso into my empty coffee mug as I steamed milk for him. Usually, he didn't ask for a second drink.

The steamer whined louder than normal.

I patted the top of the machine. "Hey, Betty, it's okay. The Cat isn't mad at you..."

Yes, I talked to Betty like a person. I didn't have many people to talk to besides the Cat, who wasn't a person, but might be a person.

"Names have power," said the Cat.

"I know, I know... Leave me and Betty alone." I waved my hand in the air before pulling out a different teacup.

The smell of cinnamon filled the area. I poured in the cinnamon-steamed milk and moved the cup in front of him.

"Here you go." The rest of it, I poured over my espresso. It should be tasty.

I took a sip, swallowed, and then inhaled deeply, my fingers tightening over the warm mug. I could do this. I'd dealt with trolls, aliens, dragons, regular humans, and a whole menagerie of others. Plus whatever the book had been.

"You can change the sign. I'm ready to open."

After my first panic attack from random creatures coming into the shop, I now told the Cat when I was ready. He didn't understand my panic, but then again, he somehow knew what was coming each day.

I held my breath, but nothing happened. He had promised that nothing in the shop would ever harm me, and I still didn't know what'd happened to the guy who had impersonated John. I believed the Cat would keep me safe, though.

He lapped at the milk foam, his back to the door. I gave his head a few scratches, and he momentarily stopped drinking to rub against my hand.

Sunlight streamed in through each window, showing the dust floating through the air and the streaks on the surface, as well as highlighting the writing on the front glass. *MEOW: Magical Emporium of Wares.* Despite the light, I couldn't see any of the outside world from where I stood.

The sparkling glass case to my right drew my gaze again. It definitely meant something. The purple cloth glowed in the sunlight. Whatever today was about, it had to involve that case. Large dusty tomes sat on the bookshelves across from me. None had writing on their spines.

I kept looking over the room, trying to figure out what was coming since the Cat wasn't being helpful. From here, I could see the table in the center of the room. I leaned forward to get a better look at the crystals, bowls, and candles that were every color of the rainbow, all lined up.

"Oh, I didn't know we had candles in stock. Those pillars must be hand-dipped..."

"They are. Each can be used in magic."

"Can you teach me how to use them?"

The Cat spun around to stare at me, but the jingling bells on the front door interrupted his reply.

I held my breath to see who our customer would be.

THIRTY-SEVEN

I smirked as the Cat stumbled over his own paws to face the front door.

A hand held the door open as the figure made its way inside. The woman was human. Or at least, she looked human. Her hair was a silver white, and wrinkles covered her face.

She took her time, slowly shuffling into the main room, and I studied the robes draped around her. The cloth was a deep blue with a white motif on the edges by the floor and around her sleeves. The motif looked like a geometric rising sun. I couldn't see her feet.

I looked back up and caught her smiling at me. Her eyes were bright green, almost like the Cat's. I blushed.

"Welcome to the Magical Emporium of Wares," I said quickly.

The Cat didn't add anything, just watched the woman.

"Let me know if I can help you with any of the items."

She nodded at me and turned toward the table I had been eyeing with the candles and crystals. Unlike me when I entered a store, she didn't touch anything. Instead, she held her hand two to three inches over certain items. She slowly made her way around the room, and then the case seemed to catch her eye. Her body jerked as she quickly moved in front of it.

I didn't know if I should stay behind the counter or go behind the case. Normally, I stayed behind the counter; it was safe here.

The Cat nudged my hand, and I almost jumped out of my skin. He usually didn't touch me, so I stayed put.

"Ask her if she wants something to drink," he whispered.

"Would you like a hot drink? We have coffee and several different teas." I leaned over the counter to see her better.

The woman turned from the case and made her way over to me. I quickly leaned back.

"What teas do you have? Oh, that's a good selection." She eyed the wall behind me, and I turned.

At some point, the wall had changed to three shelves with canisters on them. The first shelf had a small tag with *Tea* written on it. The second shelf was labeled *Herbs*, and the third, *Blends*. The labels for the shelves and the canisters were all handwritten in a feminine script.

"I will have a cup of the spicy cinnamon tea as I shop."

I nodded and took down the canister. On the lid was a set of instructions. I let out a small breath. It was an easy brew, and I programmed the hot kettle for the correct temperature.

"It won't take long. I just need to get the water up to temp." I scooped the specified amount of tea into the metal tea ball.

The woman nodded as she studied the electric kettle with wide eyes. "You have strange magic in this shop."

"We do," I said.

Electricity was magic, depending on where we were in the universe.

"You guard it well," she added with a sharp look.

The Cat meowed at this and drew our attention.

"Tell her we listen to the Fates," he said, "and we hear the call."

I really hated being his voice, but it was part of the job.

"We listen to the Fates," I said.

The kettle beeped at temp, and I poured it into a ceramic mug over the metal tea ball before setting the timer.

"And we hear the call. Your tea will be done in a few moments."

The woman paused and then pulled several items from her robes. The first couple of items were crystals, then came a wooden box, a wand with a crystal tip, and finally a blue bag.

"I have several items that need to be protected. My age is great, and I do not yet have a successor."

The Cat moved and sniffed at each object before nodding.

"What do the Fates say?" he asked.

I quickly repeated the question for him.

She jerked. "They led me here. I know several who would kill for these. I have seen it, but I can't bear to destroy them."

Her voice sounded soft and a little heartbroken.

The Cat nodded again and sent another statement, which I repeated.

"We will safeguard them until the Fates say it is time." The timer went off, and I quickly removed the tea strainer before setting the mug in front of the woman.

She took a sip of the tea, and her face relaxed.

Before she could say anything, the Cat whispered, "Ask her if she has any other burdens we can relieve her of, any other objects we can safeguard."

I stared at the Cat then turned to the woman. "Is there anything else we can safeguard for you? Any other burdens?"

I kept my voice soft, but inside, I was a whirlwind of confusion. That Cat knew much better what was going on. Clearly. I wished he'd clue me in.

The Cat moved closer to me, and in the process, his tail lightly touched the coffee mug I had given the woman. The contact glowed for but a second. Her eyes stayed on me, and she frowned.

"No, there is too much I still need to do. Maybe someday I will be back, but I think this is all for now." The old woman took another sip of her tea.

The smell of cinnamon filled the air and my eyes watered. I blinked back the moisture, then the spicy scent vanished.

The frown disappeared from her face.

"Are you okay?" I asked.

"Fine, dearie, just fine. I always thought I would have a student by now. The Fates still might bless me with one, though time is getting short."

Before she could finish speaking, the Cat gave me another question to ask. "What do the cards say? Have you asked them?"

I repeated the question, but I didn't understand what I was asking.

The woman hesitated before opening the wooden box she had set on the table. Inside, something lay wrapped in a blue cloth. She carefully unfolded the item. It was a stack of what looked like tarot cards, although these were circular. She pulled the three cards off the top and set them down on the counter.

I couldn't read the writing amid the brightly colored pictures. The first was facing the woman and had a glowing ball in the middle with a ring of bright stars surrounding the edges. The second was facing me, and it looked like a trail up a mountain with an altar at the top. The last had an oak tree in the background, a giant leaf in the center, and bright-green writing along the edges.

"Every time it is the same," she whispered.

The Cat peered at each card and nodded. His paw tapped the one with the orb. I didn't need to say anything as the woman nodded. She reached into her robe yet again. This time, she pulled out a ball—or rather, an orb. It was milky white and bigger than her hand. She placed it on the counter, and it stayed where she put it.

"The Orb of Seeing. It was supposed to go to my

successor. My student. I still see her now and then, with bright-green eyes and blonde hair. I swear she is an angel, but that's not possible." She let out a sigh. "Yet I haven't come any closer to finding her."

The Cat moved back to nudge my hand. This time, my mouth opened without my input.

"Maybe she comes after you, and you guide her from the lines." Somehow, my voice sounded male, and the words came out choppier than normal.

He broke contact with me, and my lips snapped shut. That had been incredibly strange, but then again, a lot of what happened in my life these days was incredibly strange. Still, taking control of me like that was out of line, and he knew it.

A sniffling sound broke me out of my feelings toward the Cat. The old woman had tears running down her face.

I reached across the counter to grab her hand, but I brushed the edge of the orb. On contact, it flashed a bright white and hummed. I jerked away, trying to blink the spots away.

The Cat jumped back, too, but the woman didn't move.

"Oh, you're right. How could I have been so blind?" She took several deep breaths.

I grabbed a napkin and held it out.

Instead, she pulled a cloth from her robes. "You must guard it, Lord Felimid. Promise me."

The Cat padded back toward me, and I jerked my hand away.

"Tell her, I promise."

"The Cat promises to guard it," I said. His voice continued in my head, and I repeated the words. "And he promises to make sure it makes it to the one the Fates intend."

He had a name. She knew his name! What had she said again?

The woman nodded.

"Good enough. It will have to be." She wiped at her face one last time, and her gaze switched from the Cat to me. "You have more than a spark of the gift. If you practice, you might be a witch someday."

The Cat froze for a moment, but then relaxed, sitting back down.

"Good to know," I said.

Me, a witch? I mean, I did ask the Cat if he could teach me magic.

The woman took one last look at the items on the counter, and her smile softened. Several years seemed to lift from her shoulders. Then she turned around. This time, her pace was quicker and more purposeful.

"Wait," I called after her.

But her robes had already vanished outside.

"What was that?" I asked the Cat. "We didn't pay her."

"Oh, that was the Prophetess of the Fates," he replied in the same tone as when he described the delivery guy.

I shook my head. That title meant nothing to me.

Sensing my frustration, the Cat continued. "She could see the future. She directed her world in accordance with the Fates. It led to peace and prosperity over the last several hundred years. She has no children or students strong enough with the gift to pick up her mantle and safely use the items here."

"So now you're chatty, since you literally used my mouth to speak?" I raised an eyebrow.

The Cat hung his head. "I used magic on you. I needed to talk more easily with her."

"Why?"

"She didn't want to give up the orb. She knew her death was near, but she didn't want to place her responsibility on another."

A memory of the spark when his tail touched her teacup came back.

"What did you do?"

"What the Fates told me to do."

I darted out from behind the counter before my mind caught up with my actions. My hand landed on the door handle, and I tried to turn it.

It didn't move.

"You magicked her to get her to give up the orb?! That isn't right, Cat!"

"I know." His voice caused me to let go of the door.

It wasn't like it would open if he didn't want it to.

"Then why did you do it?" I asked with my hands on my hips.

"Because I had to."

"That isn't an answer!" My voice echoed loudly, and the shop seemed to rumble in response.

The noise shook the shelves, but nothing else happened. It stopped as quickly as it started.

The Cat shook his head and jumped behind the counter.

"Don't you run from me!" Yet by the time I reached the counter, he had gone. The objects the prophetess had left behind were still there. "You... You're a scaredy cat!" I yelled after him.

I slumped against the counter and breathed. I couldn't hold on to my anger once someone was gone. My brothers had used it against me all the time, and here the Cat was benefiting from it as well.

I picked up the orb and held on to it. It didn't change this time. No flashes or anything. I set it down on the counter and shook my head.

The crystals on the center table again caught my eye, and I stepped forward. I knew nothing about crystals, and while they looked pretty, they didn't seem to do anything. They sat right next to the pillar candles in their rainbow of colors.

Something glittered to my right, so I headed over to the glass case. Inside were a variety of objects. A few daggers, a bowl, and several decks similar to the one sitting on the counter. To the rightmost side were three books. The titles were in a script I couldn't read.

"I bet all of these are magical, like what she brought," I whispered to myself.

The case itself seemed to be magical. There didn't seem to be any way into it. The case folded at the seams, and the back didn't have an opening—magically protected magic?

I turned back to see if the Cat had returned to the counter, but no such luck. Yet something had changed. The items on the counter were now gone, and a book rested in their place.

I moved forward. The book sat next to my blue mug, which was still half full, heat rising from the top. *Candle Magic for Beginners* was written across the front, and a single candle was stamped into the cover in gold foil.

"Ugh, why are your bribes this good?" I didn't expect a response, but I grabbed the book.

At least I would be able to keep busy this afternoon, and this stuff probably wasn't on the internet.

Maybe Indigo would like me to read to her about candle magic.

THIRTY-EIGHT

I had been lying on my stomach on my bed with my feet in the air for over an hour when something shifted in the bookstore.

The longer I lived here, the easier it was for me to tell when things changed. The book on candle magic was interesting, but I needed to grab some candles from below if I wanted to try anything, plus maybe some oils, if I could find them.

Part of me wondered how real this book was. The book felt cheap, and it was published on Earth. Or at least, somewhere that had a London, England.

I hopped off the bed and walked to my open door. Once I peered over the balcony, I immediately spotted what was different. The orb sat in the center of the table below. Nothing else had changed.

"Cat!" My voice sounded loud in the space, but nothing answered.

That orb should've been in storage and protected.

I narrowed my eyes as I walked toward the stairs. We

needed to have a talk, and this time, I was not taking silence for an answer.

The storefront was empty, including the chair in the front window. Usually, it dripped with sunlight, but now the skylight showed clouds. The dark store felt different. Sconces that I hadn't noticed before flickered on and brightened things up a little. Still, the gloom fit my mood.

"Cat! Where are you? We need to talk!" I stopped in the kitchen, but he wasn't anywhere. "This isn't funny…"

The bells on the front door rang, and I froze. This wasn't how things worked. People didn't randomly come into the shop unless we were behind the counter.

I darted down the hallway and to the register. The memory of the fake John grabbing my wrist flashed inside my mind, but I pushed it away.

Two young ladies were peering at the dusty tomes on the bookshelves. Given how similar they looked, except for their clothes, they had to be sisters. One wore a blue dress, while the other had on slacks. They both had their hair braided and pulled back from their faces. Both had brown eyes, though one had eyes that were a bit closer to green.

They giggled as they pointed at various items before turning toward the center table that held the orb.

"Welcome to the Magical Emporium of Wares," I said before they saw me.

Both twisted in my direction.

"Let me know if I can help you with anything or get you a drink."

The one with the hazel eyes headed my way.

Where was the Cat?

"What do you have to drink?" she asked.

"I have coffee and teas." I motioned over my shoulder to the shelf of teas.

She leaned forward on the counter and peered at the wall. She had to be about my age.

"How about a coffee? Andrea, do you want anything?" she called out.

The other girl jerked from touching the stack of candles. "I'm good, sis."

"What type of coffee do you want? An Americano? Latte?" I asked with a forced smile.

Her eyebrows drew together. "I don't know what that is... Just a coffee?"

Okay, so we still weren't back on Earth. I should have gotten the memo since they weren't wearing jeans, but then again, who knew?

I turned back to the coffee machine and grabbed the container of instant coffee next to it. I quickly made a mug with some hot water and mixed the finely ground beans in.

Where was the Cat? I didn't want to do this on my own.

"Here you go." I set the coffee in front of her. "So, where are you from?"

The young woman in front of me was the one wearing the pants and a linen shirt. As she reached out for the cup, I noticed a tattoo on the inside of her wrist. It was a compass rose, with something trailing off of it.

"You could say I'm from everywhere. I travel a lot." She took a sip of the coffee and smiled. "This is really good. I haven't had it like this. Usually, it tastes almost burnt."

"It's better with some cream or some vanilla, but I kept it basic since I wasn't sure what you liked." I couldn't help but smile.

Coffee was something I could talk about all day. Now, instant coffee wasn't my favorite, even though it had improved quite a lot since the original Folgers days. Normally, I made people an Americano when they just asked for coffee, but I had been grumpy, so she got instant. Now I wished I had made her something special.

"I haven't ever seen the shop before. Is it new?" she asked.

"You could say that. It's hard to find. Can I help either of you with anything else?"

I couldn't monitor the other woman with her sister right in front of me.

The woman took another sip of her coffee. "We're just looking, trying to get a feel for this town."

"Good to know," I said.

I spotted a streak of black near the sister and relaxed. The Cat had to be near the second woman. He could take over that encounter.

"When I move somewhere new," I said, "the first thing I do is look for the best places to eat. While I make good coffee, cooking is not a strength of mine."

"Ugh, cooking is the worst. I hate it. Give me some other project or task any time. I am much better at those. Isn't that right, Andrea?"

Her sister murmured in agreement.

The young woman set the mug down. "Well, we

better get moving. We don't want any of our stalkers to catch up with us."

"Stalkers?" I asked, looking up.

I paused in surprise when I realized Andrea stood near the door. What had happened to the Cat?

"Of course! Hopefully, I threw them off our trail." She waved at me, and the bells rang at the door.

Andrea headed out before I could blink, and her sister quickly followed. My gaze landed on the table— the table that was now missing an orb.

I didn't stop the swear word from passing my lips as I raced to the door.

"Cat! They stole the orb!"

The door wouldn't open.

"I know." His voice sounded sad in my head.

I spun, almost tripping on my feet.

He sat on the counter, staring at the ground.

"How could you let them steal it? We were supposed to protect it!"

"I protected it and made sure it got to the person it needed to."

"That girl? The one on the run?" I stomped over to the counter and towered over the Cat. "She didn't have green eyes or blonde hair!"

"No." His tail flicked in agitation, and he still didn't look up. "But it will go from Andrea to the one who needs it."

"But how do you know that?!" I slammed my hand down on the counter, shaking.

He had promised that old woman!

The Cat let out a sigh, his head hanging low.

"I just do," he said as he turned and padded to the edge of the counter. "Today has been a hard day. I'll close up. You should get some rest."

"I... I...don't want to rest! Cat, I need answers! I feel like I broke a promise!"

"You did not break your word." He paused. "I would not put you in a situation to tarnish your honor. This, I swear."

He glanced at me, and his green eyes glowed in the darkened store. "The Fates are fickle, and we do their bidding. Some days are harder than others. It's the curse of this place."

He jumped out of sight, but his voice continued. "Order pizza, take a bath. Try to let it go. That's all we can do."

He sounded tired, more tired than I was angry, and that gave me pause. He padded off toward the kitchen, moving slowly. His fur seemed dull in the flickering sconces as he walked away.

What was wrong with him?

SHE KNEW IT WAS A BRIBE. We both did. Yet I didn't know how else to comfort her.

Today we'd both walked the fine edge of truth and honor. I couldn't stand to see the accusation in her eyes.

I turned before I entered the kitchen and climbed the stairs. These days didn't come often, but each time they did, it hurt.

Sable moved around the counter as I padded down

the balcony and around the corner toward the conservatory. Her voice rose as she made the call to the pizza place. It was the only good pizza that delivered to the store. We had shifted to Earth as soon as I mentioned her ordering pizza.

The shop wanted her to be happy as well. Her anger had darkened the windows and chased away the normal sunshine. The shop didn't like it.

Green leaves and the smell of dirt filled the room. Potted plants were scattered all around under the windows and near the window-filled wall.

I stopped in front of one little pot. The pot itself looked like all the others; it was a deep green. A small oak tree grew out of it, still missing a leaf. I stared at it, taking a breath.

"You are worth it. Someday, I will return home..." I couldn't even touch the pot before I fled back the way I had come.

Someday, my debt would be paid, and I would once again be what I was.

CHAPTER

THIRTY-NINE

I hated to say it, but the pizza helped.

The Cat hadn't appeared as the guy knocked at the locked door. I grabbed the pizza from him and signed the slip with a large tip. More than I should have left, but it wasn't my money I spent. It wasn't anger churning in my gut, not exactly. More like a hollow ache, of deflated expectation.

I had a few guesses about what had happened.

When the Cat had meowed earlier, he had been upset at the book telling him to get the orb and let those young women steal it. Hopefully, the Prophetess of the Fates would forgive him, since he had promised to protect it.

That reminded me—she knew his name and had called him something. It had slipped through my mind, and I couldn't grasp it, like someone had whispered it, and I'd only seen their lips move.

I tore bites of cheese off my slice, and I wished I'd written it down to ask him about it later. He didn't answer questions about himself often, and I felt awkward asking for his name at this point. After all, as he kept reminding me, names had power.

Indigo still hadn't woken up; the smell of pizza or reading aloud about candle magic hadn't been enough to stir her awake. I hoped she would be up soon. While Lady Borsal had warned me she would sleep, I still worried.

It was easier worrying about that than whatever was going on with the Cat. First, I'd found him passed out by the plants, then I'd been attacked in the shop, and now he was depressed about using magic on the Prophetess.

The greasy pizza sat like a lump in the middle of my stomach. It had been good, but I preferred eating with someone, and he hadn't shown up. I picked the pepperoni off the last slice on my paper plate and ate it before pushing the rest away. Maybe I should have remained downstairs to eat in the kitchen.

The cat tree by the door mocked me. I hadn't mentioned it to the Cat, and now I didn't know if I wanted to give it to him.

Yet, maybe it was better to give it to him right now. We both were having a shitty day, him more so than me.

I crawled off my bed and peeked out the door, but I didn't see him anywhere. I slid the cat tree out of my room and down the balcony toward the conservatory. It slid pretty easily on the hardwood floors, and I sped up.

After moving several plants, I situated it in a spot where a few of the platforms would catch the sun from the windows, but he could still look out over the store.

The little oak tree stood next to it, still in the optimal sunlight location. The other plants I moved around until the cat tree appeared like part of the grouping. Hopefully, the Cat wouldn't feel the need to push any of the plants off the edges I set them on.

The overcast clouds had lightened, and sunlight peeked through in various places.

I hoped he would like his present. The carpet-covered tree looked good in its new location, and I couldn't help but smile. Now I just needed to write a note and leave it in a place where he would find it.

A chirping from my room drew my attention, and I dashed inside.

Indigo peeked out of the hole in the box, her green eyes wide as she glanced at the cat tree she stood inside. She saw me and chirped loudly before climbing up the side of it to the top of the box. Then she leaped onto the even higher platform.

"Do you like your perch?" I asked, smiling at the little book dragon.

Indigo chirped twice and stretched her wings out to either side.

I moved closer to see if anything looked different. Lady Borsal had mentioned a growth spurt, but she didn't look any bigger.

"Did you have a good nap?" I asked.

Again, she chirped twice, and she sniffed. Her eyes zoomed in on the slice of pizza I had left on my bed. Before I could say anything, she leaped off the platform and glided to the paper plate. Then, without preamble, she started eating the pepperoni-free slice, taking a bite out of the cheese.

"Please let pizza be okay for you..." I mumbled as I joined her on my bed.

Hopefully, she wouldn't make too much of a mess.

"It's easier if you take bites out of it from the side."

Her head came up as I approached, and her snout had sauce all over it. Dragons probably didn't eat pizza normally, but I wasn't going to take it away from her.

"How about we head downstairs where I have more pizza, and napkins?"

Again, two chirps.

She knew how to say yes in a way I understood.

THE SHOP POKED me as I stared at the book. My to-do list was still so long, yet I couldn't stop staring at the golden book. I hated it so much, especially on days like today.

I had disappointed her. Sable.

Still, another entry done, and so many more to go.

The shop poked me again, and I resisted the urge to growl.

Whatever the shop wanted had to be important since it poked me yet again. I jumped off the table and exited the room. My workshop was protected, and Sable wouldn't be able to casually find it.

The balcony appeared in front of me, and I peeked in between the railings, though I didn't expect to see her in the shop. The shop directed me toward the plants.

I closed my eyes and opened them again, smelling something sweet. Seeing the tree once already today was a lot. I wanted to resist going in that direction, but I followed the scent. Something was different among the plants, and I yowled, not seeing the tree in its normal spot.

But I caught sight of it next to something new.

A piece of paper lay on top of a box with a hole in it, which was mounted on a pole. I jumped up to the top, feeling the carpet under my paws. The paper was folded in half with black writing on it.

Today sucked, for both of us. I hope you like the cat tree. - Sable

The sweet smell came from inside the box I stood on top of. From here, I could see out the window and look at the tree if I wanted.

She had gotten this thing, this cat tree, for me.

I wasn't sure if I should be insulted or pleased.

Warmth flickered through me as I sat here, hoping she would forgive me. This wouldn't be the only time the Fates told me to do something I didn't want to do. But maybe she understood that somehow. Humans were strange, after all.

Why was this called a cat tree, though?

I liked the carpet under my paws, and it gave me a nice place to sit. Also, what had she put into the box that smelled so good?

I crawled down the side of the box into the hole. The cozy dark box smelled fantastic. Almost like the forest had smelled before.

My breathing slowed, and I stuck the tip of my nose out of the box, resting it on the comfortable edge. From here, I could see the top of the tree and the rest of the plants surrounding me.

I let myself drift off to sleep as sunlight streamed down from the window.

At least she must not hate me, and that had to be enough. For now.

FORTY

I was ready, or as ready as I could be.

"So, today is a short day?" I asked the Cat. "And it's fine that Indigo is flying around?"

"It is," he replied.

I sipped my coffee from my blue mug with stars on it while looking out over the store. Indigo had woken up a few days ago, but she'd been taking it easy, resting in my room in her new cave until I finished each day. Today was her first day back in the shop, and I couldn't help but worry.

The little purple dragon sat in one of the coffee mugs, her head sticking out of the top. I'd filled it with hot water to make myself some tea, but she'd plopped inside, chirping.

"All right, then. I think I'm ready."

The shop was in the basic bookstore formation, with shelves along the back wall, but the large table stood in the center of the room. It had stacks of books on it, but I couldn't read the titles. My guess was it wouldn't be Earth we stopped at, given the strange language.

The bells on the door jingled as someone walked inside. I forced myself to relax as I glanced at the Cat and then the person.

It was a cat person. They looked almost like a human, but they had pointed ears on the top of their head, and fur completely covered their exposed skin. It seemed as though it continued under the clothing. The nose was a cat's nose, and short whiskers shot out from it to either side.

Their eyes widened as they entered, and they went to one of the bookshelves immediately. Large yellow eyes darted around as they reached out with paw-like hands.

"Welcome to Meow. Let me know if I can help you with anything," I said.

The Cat added nothing, just stayed sitting on the counter by the register.

The customer's head snapped toward me, and its eyes narrowed before it took a step in my direction.

"Oh, it's a human!" It moved quickly toward me, and I resisted taking a step back.

"Yes, I am human, and I'm the Shopkeeper here," I said.

Its eyes flicked to the Cat, and it stared at him for several moments.

"That's...a cat!" It took a step back, but then straightened itself before bowing to the Cat. "Your Highness!"

It bowed again at the waist, its tail flicking up behind it.

"I apologize for not seeing you." It stayed in that awkward position.

"You should tell him to get up," said the Cat. "Otherwise, he'll stay there all day."

Indigo chirped twice.

I blurted, "You can rise."

This was officially weird.

"Can I help you find anything in the shop? Or maybe some coffee with cream?"

This person had to be here for a reason. Everything in the shop happened for a reason.

It glanced at me as it rose from the bow. "You speak to the Cat?"

He bowed his head toward me with respect, but only his head, not his full body like he had with the Cat.

"I would be honored for your help, Shopkeeper." The cat-creature's gaze skipped over Indigo, who still basked in her mug. "I'm a painter, and I'm looking for books on the topic."

I didn't know what was on the shelves, or where. They changed too often, depending on who would be visiting.

"Tell him to search the table," said the Cat. "He should find what he's looking for there."

I nodded at the Cat then turned to the painter before motioning to the table. "The table behind you is your best bet. The Cat said you should be able to find what you're looking for."

He was moving before I finished my last sentence, but he wouldn't turn his back to the Cat. He walked backward instead, positioning himself to look over the titles.

The Cat quietly sighed and laid his head on his front paws. A shiver went through the painter, but he said nothing.

"This place we're at always ruffles my fur," said the Cat. "At least this stop is a quick one."

The painter reached out, making a sound of joy and snapping up a book larger than a normal hardback. He seemed so excited he almost bounced back to the counter.

"This, please."

"Tell him it's five blue gems."

I repeated the message to the painter.

He nodded and quickly set five blue gems on the counter. "Thank you for your help. I won't forget this!"

He placed another blue gem next to my coffee cup before I could say anything. The painter moved quickly to the door, this time dashing away from us without a concern. The bells on the door rang softly as it closed.

"That was weird. Weirder than usual. What's the deal?" Both Indigo and I glanced at the Cat, who rolled his eyes. "Come on. That was weird, Your Highness."

"Don't call me that," he grumbled. "Fine. They used to be human, and they worship cats, like to the extreme. Eventually, the whole race used magic to become more cat-like. That was probably the first time he'd seen someone not changed."

I didn't know what to say.

Indigo chirped a few times, and the Cat nodded.

"Yes, they consider cats to be their ruling class. I

don't know how the whole place is still standing." He studied the look on my face. "You can read about them. I have better things to do."

"Wait, was that it for today?" I asked, then I pointed at the extra gem. "What about that?"

The Cat flicked his tail. "It's yours. He tipped you."

I picked up the first five and put them inside the register. The other I held up. "What is it even worth? Like, at home?"

"It's a pure sapphire, so around a thousand dollars, if not a little more," said the Cat, jumping off the counter. "I wouldn't lose it."

I clutched it to my chest, my eyes wide. This little stone was worth a thousand dollars? I couldn't believe it, and it was mine because I'd talked for the Cat.

Normally, I wasn't someone who was money driven. Besides the fact that I watched my loan balance get paid down each week, which was amazing enough, I basically didn't pay attention to my bank balance because it made me nervous that this wasn't real. I didn't need anything more than the shop provided, but this on top of that?

I could buy so many holiday presents with this. For the first time, I could be the person who gave the really amazing gifts. My mind started racing, but I pushed that to the side. We had a few months until the holiday season back on Earth.

Indigo chirped in a way that felt like a question.

"Of course you can look at it." I held it up closer to her face.

She bumped it with her nose, still not climbing out of the water.

"Was that what you asked?"

She chirped twice.

I was learning, though it was mostly by whatever my gut thought she was saying.

"Hmmm, so what do you want to do today? Should we read?"

Something that the Cat had said came to me. He said we could read more about the strange cat people. I bet the *Primer for Beings on the Tree* would have more information on them.

Indigo chirped once.

"What about baking? I can make cookies."

Was it really baking if I used pre-made cookie dough?

I said yes, it was still baking.

SABLE KEPT TALKING to Indigo as I padded up the stairs toward my workshop. My to-do list was still longer than I would like, and I'd been monitoring the prisoner to see what he would do.

So far, nothing, but enough time had gone by that I needed to see if any information would come to light. He had something to do with the book, and that other man had brought Indigo here.

Everything inside me said it was connected, and important. I had to figure out what was going on; it was the only way to keep Sable safe. First, I had to see if my instincts were correct and if he really was after the book.

I knew how to do that, and then we'd see what came next.

FORTY-ONE

Baking cookies was an interesting process. Well, it was a straightforward process, at least for me. The ovens preheated themselves to the correct temperature, and all I needed to do was place the cookies on a baking sheet. Then, of course, put them in the oven.

I pulled the peanut butter cookies out, along with some of the chocolate chip, and decided I'd bake two batches. The first came out perfectly, and I set the pan on the island carefully, so as not to burn myself.

Indigo crawled across the pan without a problem. The cookie dough had gotten her out of her hot mug of water. I couldn't wait to show her the bathtub, though I wondered if I could get it hot enough for her. Maybe we could get a hot tub on the roof. One of those that used salt water... I'd need to ask the Cat about that later.

I slid the second pan into the oven, this time peanut butter, and the oven door snapped shut once my hands were free.

"These need to cool a second," I said, looking at the chocolate chip cookies.

Yet Indigo had disappeared from the pan. The cookie she had poked had one side of it pushed in, but she wasn't here.

"Indigo? Where are you?" I didn't see her on the island or any of the countertops, so I headed toward the front of the store.

The hair on the back of my neck rose, and I stepped back into the kitchen. I had the feeling I shouldn't go that way, but I didn't know why. Shaking my head, I moved back toward the oven to peek at the cookies through the glass.

When I turned on the light, green eyes locked with mine from inside the oven.

"Indigo!" I yanked open the door, but she kept sitting there on the center of the pan, watching a peanut butter cookie get baked. "You shouldn't be in the oven..."

I didn't want to pull the pan out and knock her into one of the baking cookies, but she didn't look distressed.

"Are you okay?"

Indigo chirped twice.

I shut the door and watched the timer on the front of the stove. Butterflies gathered in my stomach, but I tried to ignore it. She was a dragon, so an oven at 350 degrees shouldn't do anything to her.

I let out a sigh. There was no way the bathtub could be hot enough for her.

Finally, the timer dinged, and I used an oven mitt to pull the pan out. It was heavier with her on it, but not so bad that I couldn't handle it. She only weighed a little.

She chirped several times, but I didn't have a clue what she was saying.

"I hope you had a good time watching them bake, but you worried me. I couldn't find you."

She chirped once, a long note, and I took that as an apology.

"It's okay. I need to remember you're different from me. I wouldn't be safe in the oven like you were."

Indigo tilted her head, looking at her claws, then at me, before nodding. She glanced at the chocolate chip cookies.

"Those are ready to eat now."

Before I'd completed my sentence, she scrambled across the counter toward the cookie she had pushed out of shape before. First meat, then eggs and now cookies. So far human foods didn't bother her.

I giggled and grabbed one from the pan. Slightly crispy on the edges and soft in the middle. They were perfect. I finished the cookie in two more bites, then I grabbed one of the peanut butter ones. They were better than perfect.

I hummed in pleasure as Indigo made a sound I hadn't heard before. She glared at the peanut butter cookie she had taken a bite out of, then she looked at the one in my hand like it was evil.

"You don't like peanut butter?" I asked.

She gave a single chirp.

"That's okay. More for me, though we shouldn't get stuffed on cookies. It isn't even lunchtime yet."

I flicked my gaze to the front of the store, and that feeling from before returned.

The Cat was up to something, and whatever it was, I didn't want any part of it.

THE NOT-JOHN HAD CHANGED shape over the course of the last twenty-four hours. He no longer looked like the delivery guy.

Instead, he had scales covering his body under the human clothes he wore, along with talons on his hands. No tail, but bright-red eyes that focused on the book in the distance. His claws dug into the wall as he tried to get to the book.

I wasn't stupid enough to have it be the actual book. It only felt like it. Even so, it confirmed my suspicion. The demon wanted the book.

They shouldn't even know it existed.

The Bookseller always kept moving, ever since he'd left my home. He'd never stayed in one place long, and no one could feel it outside his basket.

Yet the demons knew it was here, and for the second time in my memory, I worried about someone else. I needed to reach out to the Bookseller and see if he was okay.

The frigid book drained of energy as time went on, but the process took a long time, and the book had a lot of power. At this rate, it would take hundreds of years, if not longer. I needed to speed up the consumption of the book and the power imprisoned inside.

To do that, I had to speak to Sable.

The image of the book vanished along with its sense of presence.

The demon roared before he tumbled over, encased in stone.

He would be consumed first, and much more quickly.

I DIDN'T KNOW how he did it, but at the sight of it, I squealed with joy.

In the rooftop garden sat a wooden hot tub. It looked like cedar and had several new plants situated around it. I set the book and drink down by the edge and dashed back toward my room to put on a bathing suit.

Indigo clutched to my shoulder as I took off.

"You are going to have so much fun!" I said, setting her on the top of her cat tree. "That was full of nice hot water."

She chirped in reply.

"Not like the oven, or the mug, but warm for me, and you'll have plenty of room to swim around." I paused, looking at the dragon. "What are your thoughts on audiobooks?"

This afternoon would be amazing.

By the time we made it back out to the steaming hot tub, I had downloaded several books onto my phone to play while we soaked. Then I slowly slid into the water, moaning as the heat soaked into my muscles. This was heaven.

Indigo stayed on my shoulder, staring at the amount of water like it would bite.

I sat down in one corner and held up my hand, which she climbed into. Then I slowly lowered her into the water. Hopefully, she could swim, since I wasn't sure how to teach the little one how to do that. Maybe I could show her videos of a dog swimming.

It turned out my worries were misplaced as she bobbled on top and then started paddling with her paws. Her wings stayed close to her body, and her tail steered. It only took a few minutes before she was zooming around the giant tub without fear.

"I told you so..."

She chirped back twice.

I chuckled as I dried my hand before hitting play on the first book. It was a children's tale about a magical cupboard and traveling to a magical land. As soon as the book started, Indigo's head rose, and she glanced around for the source of the sound.

"It's an audiobook. It's reading the book to both of us."

Happy chirps came from the dragon, who flipped over onto her back and floated on top of the water.

The Cat jumped up on the ledge of the hot tub, watching us with amusement.

"You look like you are enjoying your soak."

FORTY-TWO

"Do you want to join us?" I asked the Cat.

The warmth soaked into my bones, and for once, I felt completely relaxed.

Indigo swam around like a fast little fish, even diving and then shooting into the air. It was the most adorable thing ever. She stuck pretty close to my phone, listening to the story playing, but clearly also enjoying the water.

"No, thank you," said the Cat. His green eyes sparkled as he watched the little dragon. "Wet fur is strange..."

He paused, and I waited for whatever bomb he looked like he was going to drop on me.

"Just say it. The anticipation is a little much here."

"Thank you for the cat tree," he started. "I appreciate the gift."

He bowed his head toward me.

I blinked several times before smiling. "Of course. I'm glad you like it. I wasn't sure if you would, but that spot had the best sunlight, even better than the chair by the front window."

The smile stayed on my face, even though I could barely believe he liked the gift. I had been so worried he'd find it dumb. My day couldn't get better.

The Cat added nothing, but Indigo splashed close to him and started chirping at him, faster than I could follow. It was interesting since the Cat had said that by being in the shop, it translated everything spoken to me into English.

For some reason, the dragons had so far been the exception, though. Something was special about them, but they were dragons, so I guessed it made sense. The book about creatures of the tree had mentioned that dragons lived by their own rules.

Bright sunlight poured down from above, and I grabbed my drink and took a few sips.

"Oh, I forgot to mention. There are some cookies in the kitchen for you. I made chocolate chip and peanut butter."

The Cat looked over from his conversation with Indigo and nodded at me.

"Indigo did not like the peanut butter, so there should be more of those left." I loved the peanut butter, but I could share them with the Cat.

Indigo chirped in agreement, and I got the impression she told him to eat all the peanut butter and leave the others for her. It reminded me of how kids sometimes acted.

Lady Borsal had said she would go through a growth spurt, and Indigo had grown from barley the size of my palm to filling my open hand. In addition it seemed she'd gotten smarter. That was both a relief and a worry, since it meant she was a lot more curious and talkative.

"When you have a few moments, I need to speak with you about that book we locked up, but it doesn't need to be now." The Cat laid his head down on his front paws as the sunlight hit his black fur.

It looked almost a deep blue, with a slight green undertone in the direct sunlight.

Remembering the icy touch of the book caused me to sink a little deeper into the water.

"How about after lunch? I'll want to shower after we get out of the hot tub."

"Sounds good."

I couldn't help but wonder what was going on with the book. Moving it into its prison had been the hardest thing I'd ever done in my life, and I didn't want to touch it again. If I needed to move it to a different location, I didn't know how I'd raise my courage.

Last time, I hadn't known what I was doing. This time, I would. I hoped it would help.

Indigo climbed onto my knee, which poked above the water. She chirped at me. I wanted to understand what she was saying so badly, but I just didn't. It had something to do with food. I knew that, at least. I was pretty sure, at least.

"Lunch? I'm not sure what we'll have. Maybe tacos..."

She nodded.

I'd gotten it correct. It had been something about lunch. That was progress. Someday I'd understand the language she spoke.

"Your tacos are tasty," said the Cat.

I looked at him, but his eyes were closed. Something was up. First, he'd thanked me for the gift, and now he warned me we needed to talk about the book. Add in a compliment about my cooking, and my suspicions raised.

I wasn't going to like the conversation this afternoon.

Still, Indigo was enjoying the audiobook and kept swimming around the tub. I, at least, had a few hours to keep relaxing.

THE TACOS TURNED out really tasty.

It helped that I had stocked up on seasoning packets, and I just needed to brown the ground pork with the seasonings in the pan. Everything else just needed to be diced. Plus, someone recommended limes in a cooking app, so I used some juice on top. I cooked the rice in the microwave.

Even Indigo cleaned her bowl, so I knew I'd done okay.

"All right," I said, letting out a sigh. "Let me make some hot cocoa, and we can talk about the book."

I moved toward the front of the store and paused as the main shop came into view. The counter still stood there, along with Betty, but the rest of the store looked drastically different. A couch and two chairs sat centered in the room in front of an enormous fireplace. Inside burned a small grouping of crystals that blasted heat into the space.

I quickly heated some milk and melted the chocolate in the mug.

Indigo watched from my shoulder, but she didn't seem interested in having any. Instead, she took a marshmallow and took tiny nibbles out of it. Each time she took a bite, her eyes grew wide, and she shook her tail in pleasure.

The Cat jumped onto the rightmost chair, which was a deep-velvet green. I sat on the couch, which was directly in front of the fireplace and an intense purple color, careful to make sure I wouldn't knock Indigo off my shoulder.

"So, what's going on with that book? Did you figure out what the not-John was after?"

The Cat turned to look at me. "He will no longer be a problem, but he is a part of this."

"How do you know he's gone for good?" I asked, clutching my mug.

"I made sure of it." The Cat's voice sounded certain, and it took a few moments to realize why.

"Oh."

"The first and last rule is to not upset me, and he upset me by hurting you."

That made me feel warm and fuzzy, even though it shouldn't have. In most cases, in any relationship, that would be a large red flag waving in the breeze.

Yet whatever it had been, the not-John had tried to hurt me. Now it couldn't anymore.

"What did he have to do with the book?"

"He was a demon, and his goal was to take the book," said the Cat.

"What even is the book?" I asked.

For once, he seemed to be actually giving me answers, and I would ask all the questions I could before he stopped.

"Let me tell you a story about how the book came into being." The Cat shifted in his seat and jumped out of the chair and onto the armrest on the couch.

It put him right next to me, and he sat down facing Indigo and me.

"It started with a Fey Lord, many years ago...This Fey Lord was the father of the Elves in the Fey Wilds. He protected his children as best as he could. Upon this time, so long ago, there came a Demon Lord who killed several of his children, and he chose to act."

FORTY-THREE

Sunlight streamed down on three elves eating bread and butter, sitting on a blanket in a clearing. The wind gently blew through the bright-green and blue leaves in the trees.

One female elf laughed at something the male elf whispered in her ear. The other younger woman rolled her eyes and finished her bread.

"I'm going for a walk," she said, shaking her head at the pair.

Harsh laughter spilled across the clearing, and all three of them froze. "Look at the tasty lunch before me. Luck is on my side."

Darkness crept out from underneath a tree, forming into a creature that stood taller than the elves. Bright-red eyes shone from below deep brows, and scales covered the being. He had two large horns jutting out of his forehead. He had a sword strapped to his side and armor over his chest and legs.

It was not a creature of this place.

The male elf stood up in front of the two ladies. "You are not welcome in these lands."

The Demon Lord laughed again. "Who will stop me?"

He drew his sword, and suddenly, the male elf crumpled to the ground.

The woman who had been laughing earlier stood and summoned a sword.

"Awean, go!" she yelled to the younger one.

The younger elven woman vanished into the trees.

The older elf glowed as she pointed her sword at the demon. Bright-white light streamed off of the sword toward the great horned beast.

"Your kind is not welcome here. My Lord comes!" she shouted.

"Then he will also feed me!" The demon swung at the woman, and icy-blue light sliced through the air.

She blocked, but he rushed forward, swinging his sword from the side. Again, she blocked, but the blue light ate at her sword, and the bright-white light of her own magic vanished.

"You will be a tasty meal!" He licked his lips, and she swung at him.

This time, he caught the blade with his hand and swung with his sword. She crumpled to the ground.

Bright light flashed across the clearing, and a figure appeared. Its features were not clear, but it was humanoid, with pointed ears and long hair flowing out behind it. The figure pointed at the Demon Lord, who chuckled.

"Is this the best the Lord can send me?" asked the Demon.

He rushed at the figure, but streams of white light wrapped around the demon as it approached, and he vanished into the light, along with the two elves' bodies.

A book appeared on a table in front of the glowing figure.

"Now you will serve me, and repay my people for the harm you have done," the figure said.

Then the book, table, and Fey Lord all vanished, leaving the clearing to repair itself from the violence it had witnessed.

THE CAT'S voice trailed off.

"So the Fey Lord bound the Demon Lord into a book?" I asked, trying to make sure I understood everything. "Why didn't he kill him?"

"The Fey Lord did kill the Demon Lord, but then bound the demon's power to repay his people. He should have destroyed the power, too," mumbled the Cat. "What he didn't know was that plenty of people wanted control of a book that had the power of a Demon Lord. It gave him nothing but grief until the Bookseller tried to steal it. The Fey Lord let this happen, in a way. But, while the Bookseller had the book, he was cursed by the Fey Lord's magic to keep it safe and keep it secret, and to never use it. The burden was heavy for many years, until you took it from him and placed it here in the shop."

I swallowed, trying not to think about how I had touched a Demon Lord, whether or not he was encased in a magical book.

"What does this have to do with the book now? It's locked up."

The Cat let out a sigh and glanced toward the fireplace. "It is locked up, and over time, the shop will consume the energy from the book until it is no more."

I blinked a few times. "The shop is eating it?"

I tightened my fingers around my mug, a slightly nauseous feeling creeping into my stomach. The shop ate demons. Yet, that magic had been horrible; could I really say that eating it was a bad thing? I didn't know enough to judge the shop.

"Yes," said the Cat. "The shop can eat magic. It gets its magic from a variety of sources."

I really wanted to ask about those sources.

The Cat turned back to look at me, his green eyes glowing in the flickering firelight. "The problem is, it is too slow. The not-John was a demon who somehow traced the magic of the book to the shop."

"You think more demons are going to show up to get the book back. Would that work? Could they free the Demon Lord?" My heart pounded in my chest, and my hands shook just thinking about that cold magic creeping into my fingers.

"No, he can't be freed, no matter what they think. The Demon Lord is dead, only the power remains. The demon situation in that universe is a bit weird right now, though, and the demons are gathering power, so they will keep trying. I need you to help me encourage the shop to consume the book faster." He paused, and then his words came out in a rush. "Right now, the shop's passively eating it, just using it as another source of magic when it needs to. If we work together, we can convince the shop to actively eat it first, destroying the Demon Lord's evil once and for all."

Indigo chirped, saying something to the Cat.

"Yes, the book only contains the power of the Demon Lord, not its soul," answered the Cat.

"Did the fake-John get eaten?" I asked, setting my mug on the coffee table.

"Yes. He hurt the Shopkeeper and has already been dealt with."

What had I gotten myself into? The shop could eat people to use as energy. Not people, but demons who tried to hurt me. Who did hurt me. I knew nothing about demons, but the thing in the book had killed those elves who had been eating lunch in a forest. It had wanted to eat them. That seemed reasonably evil.

The fake-John had wanted that book and would have hurt me to get what he wanted.

But wasn't the book going to die? It clicked.

"You want me to kill someone..."

"No, the Demon Lord has been dead for almost a millennium. All that's left is the power in the book, which could, and would, if given a chance, corrupt someone. The Fey Lord killed the demon. He should have destroyed the power as well, but he was a fool."

"So, it's the Fey Lord's fault that the book is even here," I said. "Dumbass."

The Cat froze, but then nodded. "Yes, he was."

"Can't we have *him* deal with this?" I asked, an idea coming to mind. "Or would he just want the power in the book?"

Maybe I wouldn't need to deal with this situation and could offload it to the Fey Lord. Plus, maybe I could actually meet a Fey Lord.

"He is no more," said the Cat, his voice very soft.

"This act, creating the book, was the beginning of his downfall, the first mistake that led to many others."

I leaned back on the couch, and Indigo nuzzled my neck. I pulled my knees up and wrapped my arms around them.

"What would I need to do to encourage the shop to eat it first?"

"Just ask it to. Tell it you would feel more comfortable if it did so. But you need to mean it." He leaned closer to me. "I wish I did not need to ask this of you."

"Can it break free?"

"Enough of its power can be detected that fake-John discovered it was here, but no, it can't escape its prison." The Cat moved closer and jumped to the back of the couch.

He walked along the back until he climbed over my shoulder and onto my knees. Warmth radiated off of him.

"I will not force you to do this. I will only ask."

FORTY-FOUR

"I'll do it."

I couldn't believe the words that came out of my mouth. Yet, I'd always read stories about heroes, and here was a book literally filled with an evil power that I could defeat. Could I leave it alone and deal with any other demons that tried to take it? I could, but even with the Cat protecting me, that was a terrifying thought. The easier answer was to have the shop eat it faster.

Indigo chirped in agreement, and I gave her a pat on the head for keeping her volume down. She was learning.

She snuggled closer to my ear.

The Cat stared at me from my knees, his face super close to mine, and he nodded.

"It will keep you both safer." He nudged my hand, which rested next to him on my knee.

I scratched behind his ear.

"We don't need to do it now."

"I think I'd rather get it done now. Get it over with, you know?" I whispered.

The Cat purred at the scratches and reluctantly pulled himself away.

He twisted to look at the fireplace. "You might want to close your eyes for this."

I snapped my eyes shut just as the fireplace glowed. Then I peeked since I couldn't help it.

The fireplace had changed. The crystals were gone, and where the fireplace had been stood an archway that led to the room where I'd stored the book. Each step I'd taken to get the book in that room had been ingrained in my memory. My fingers ached from the remembered chill.

Cold air streamed out of the room, and Indigo whimpered. She crawled behind my hair and neck, shaking.

The Cat stared at the book. "You can do it from there. Just ask the shop to focus on the book. Think it. Will it."

I wasn't sure how to think something at the bookstore, but I tried anyway. Inside my head, I pictured a tiny dino eating the book. It wasn't the greatest picture, but I hoped it got the point across.

The room that the book sat inside shrank, and the cold coming off of it increased. I shivered. As the room continued to shrink, second by second, the air grew heavier. The table inside the room got smaller, and then the book shook, like it was resisting.

The Cat didn't look away, and I could feel his paws trembling on my knees at the sight.

"Focus, Sable," he whispered. "Picture the shop devouring the book, consuming its cold magic."

I closed my eyes and let my mind focus on the shop itself.

Betty popped into mind, and the espresso machine transformed into a knight in shining bright-red armor. Its helm opened, revealing large metal spikes that chomped toward the accursed book. With each breath, I willed the image to become reality.

"Come on, Betty. You can do it," I whispered, urging my knight on.

A freezing gust of wind swept through the room, and my eyes snapped open. As soon as my gaze fell on the book again, the scent of freshly brewed coffee drifted over me, pushing the cold back. The hot air of steaming milk and the warmth of a sip of my latte in the morning filled the area around me.

The Cat's back arched, his fur standing on end as he prepared to pounce.

As if answering my call, the low sound of a growl rumbled through the bookstore.

Inside the room, the book flinched again, shrinking further. Mist rose from the cover, but something pushed it back, forcing it to retreat, to be reabsorbed into the book.

A loud boom shook the space, and in a single instant, the book vanished. Everything seemed to freeze in place, and the archway shuddered. Then, slowly, the doorway changed shape, forming back into the fireplace that had been there before. The crystals inside the fireplace slowly re-appeared, pushing warmth back into the room.

The Cat turned toward me, his eyes wide, his fur still stuck out all over. "What did you do?"

I shook my head. "What you asked..."

Indigo climbed out from behind my hair and moved closer to the Cat.

The Cat closed his eyes, and his fur slowly relaxed as he let out a sigh. "It is done, at least."

"You're sure?" I asked.

"Yes, it is gone," he whispered, but it almost sounded like a whimper.

His eyes opened, and all the tension seemed to leave his body.

Indigo moved closer to him, and I petted him slowly.

"Thank you, Sable. You have done something I couldn't accomplish on my own, and that evil power is no more."

Why couldn't he do the same thing?

A sense of peace washed over the room, and warmth, like the shop was happy to no longer have the book either. Yet, that couldn't be the case, right? It was a shop, and I couldn't feel what it felt.

I shook my head slightly.

"I'm glad it's gone." I petted the Cat a little more before I leaned forward carefully and picked my mug back up from the coffee table.

The hot cocoa was still warm.

"Well, we defeated the evil, and now we get to drink cocoa," I said.

Indigo chirped, and the Cat chuckled.

"She wants more cookies," he translated.

"You can go get some more," I whispered to the book dragon.

She climbed up onto the back of the couch and jumped off, gliding through the air.

"I'll go make sure she doesn't eat all of them," the Cat said before jumping off my lap.

I turned to watch them go, and they both vanished out of sight behind the counter. My gaze landed on the espresso machine on the counter.

I smiled. "We did it, Betty. We defeated the evil monster."

I chuckled at myself, turning back to the fireplace. Somehow, it didn't seem strange that I spoke to inanimate objects.

After all, Betty was definitely a hero here, too.

I PADDED after the little book dragon to give Sable a moment. The amount of energy she had pushed at the shop to focus it on the book had shocked me. I didn't even have a chance to do anything before the shop leaped to help her.

Something red with armor had charged at the book, striking it with steaming air. I didn't understand what she had done.

Yet the book was gone, and the shop had consumed its magic. She'd lifted the weight of the book's existence.

"Cookie?" asked Indigo.

I tried not to think of her like that, with a name. She had to be just the little book dragon. Though she had accepted the name, it was dangerous for a dragon so young to take on a name. Magic was strange like that, and names had power.

Sable still didn't understand that, but then most

beings didn't. Not really. Even those who had powerful magic often didn't really understand it.

Like me, I thought bitterly.

"I'll grab a chocolate chip one," I mumbled, jumping to the island. "The peanut butter is Sable's favorite. I want to leave those for her."

Indigo nodded and grabbed a cookie in her jaws. It was half the size of her, but she beat her wings hard to take off from the counter. I shook my head as she rapidly headed toward the floor.

I took a moment to eat one of the chocolate chip cookies. The sweetness filled me with joy, and I froze at the sensation.

For the first time in a long time, I'd felt joy. Almost as soon as I recognized it, it shifted into confusion.

I wondered what it meant.

FORTY-FIVE

My coffee was the perfect temperature, nice and warm while not scalding my mouth. The vanilla flavor made me smile as I stirred the oatmeal on the stove.

The instructions were simple. *Add salt and water, oatmeal, then mix as it comes to a boil.*

After that, you could add all the toppings you wanted. I thought I might add maple syrup and some brown sugar. It sounded amazing; now I just needed the oatmeal to finish cooking.

A flash of purple in the corner of my eye made me giggle. Indigo danced to the soft music I had on. Something classical to fit the mood I was in. The little dragon looked like she was slow dancing to the music. Her eyes were closed, and now and then, she flared her wings. Her purple scales sparkled in the kitchen light.

Way too adorable.

This was the first time I'd had music on like this, and Indigo looked like a fan. I put a note on my mental list to play more music. At first, she'd been curious, then she'd gone directly to dancing on the island.

She swirled around as the song ended, fading into silence.

"Bravo!" I clapped my hands, but then warmth washed over me.

I turned back to the stove. Smoke rose from the pot, and I yanked the pot off the hot burner.

"Shit, shit, shit!"

I used my wooden spoon to stir the sticky mess, but the oats had scorched on the bottom of the pan.

"Well, that sucks."

Chirps from the island sounded like concern.

"It's okay. I'll figure something else out. Maybe some muffins or something... Let's just not tell the Cat about this." I put the pot with the burned oatmeal into the sink and took another sip of my coffee.

Already, the smell of the burnt oatmeal had faded. By the time I turned back to Indigo, she chirped next to a plate of muffins on the counter.

"What the...?" I stepped forward, noticing the cranberries in them, along with some sugar crumble on top.

These were one of my favorite muffins that my mom would make. There was no way the Cat could know that.

I blinked a few times as Indigo kept looking back and forth from me to the food.

She chirped once, like she was asking a question.

"Yes, we'll eat them." I grabbed one, along with a paper towel, took the paper wrapper off the outside of the muffin, and set it in front of her.

She dove in headfirst, taking a nibble out of it.

I broke mine in half and took a bite.

Indigo copied me by sitting on her rear and using one of her front claws to pull off a chunk and then eating it. I had to remind myself not to giggle, that she was learning. Kids did that. They mimicked their parents.

The Cat jumped onto the counter, surprising me. His head tilted at the muffins.

"Oh, muffins. They look good." He eyed Indigo and her neat eating.

I set a muffin out in front of him with a paper towel as well. He started eating, in that weird way, with food vanishing when he took a bite.

I shook my head and glanced back at the sink. The pot with the burnt oatmeal had vanished, along with the wooden spoon and the toppings I had set out on the counter. I swallowed but didn't say anything.

"The muffins are tasty," said the Cat.

I turned back to where he was sitting, and his food was already gone.

"Thanks," I mumbled. "Do you want some coffee?"

He nodded, and I glanced once more around the kitchen. Everything had been cleaned up from the oatmeal, and any crumbs on the counter from the Cat or Indigo were gone. Only three muffins sat on a plate in the center.

Indigo leaped off the island and glided toward the hallway.

The Cat paused mid-turn on the edge of the counter. "Are you okay?"

"Yep, doing good." I quickly nodded. "Let's get you some caffeine."

I headed to the front of the shop, taking a quick glance around the store. The layout looked like the boring Earth layout. Bookshelves along the back, and the kids' section with the beanbag and toys in the corner.

"Are we on Earth today?"

"We are. Indigo will need to hide." The Cat leaped up on the counter, though Indigo had beaten him there.

I tilted my head for more information as I frowned.

"We have some deliveries, but I will stay at the register," the Cat added quickly.

I nodded and pulled out his teacup.

"Okay, sounds like an easy day."

I tried to think if anything I'd ordered would show up today. It was hard to guess, since time moved strangely in the shop. I had several outstanding online orders, but it all depended on how much time had passed on Earth.

"I might have a few things arriving."

The Cat nodded. "Yes, you and I both have things showing up."

I quickly got started on a latte for the Cat. My cup only had a few last sips, and I needed a refill as well. It didn't take long for me to set the teacup in front of the Cat then refill my mug.

Indigo chirped, asking for her own morning drink. I snagged a teacup out and filled it with some steamed milk and vanilla for her.

Indigo immediately stuck her head in it, getting foam all over her snout.

I couldn't help it as I giggled. "It's tasty, isn't it?"

She chirped twice.

"I'm glad you like it." I waited until both the Cat and

Indigo finished their coffees and then put the teacups into the wash bin.

"All right, I think I'm ready," I said to the Cat. "Indigo, be a champ and make sure you stay out of sight."

Indigo nodded and launched herself into the air, then she climbed up one of the bookshelves. She was pretty good at not being seen if she didn't want to be.

The door unlocked, and I took a deep breath. It didn't take long for the door to open, and a small girl darted inside.

"I get a book today!"

I chuckled at Molly's singsong voice. I recognized her from the prior times she had come into the shop. The kid loved books.

Seconds later, Molly's father entered as well.

Molly dashed right to the kids' section with a big smile on her face. She had on a knitted hat that looked like a dinosaur. She plopped to the ground and pulled a few different dinosaur books off the shelves.

She caught me looking and smiled at me. "It's my birthday, and I get a book today!"

"Happy birthday, Molly," I called across the store.

Molly's father had a smile on as he headed to the kids' section, talking to Molly about what book she wanted.

I grabbed a small cup and started making a hot chocolate for Molly. Snatches of their conversation kept reaching me, and Molly went back and forth between two different books on dinosaurs.

I grabbed the whipped cream as they headed in my direction. "Big plans today?"

Molly's father nodded. "Yes, we're headed to an event."

He winked at me, then he noticed the hot chocolate.

"It's on the house for her birthday," I said.

"Hey, Molly..." he said.

Molly held a kids' book in her hands, but she stared wide-eyed and open-mouthed at the bookshelf by the back wall.

I bet she'd seen Indigo, yet she didn't say anything.

"Molly, it's time to pay for your book. And look!" he said.

Molly's head jerked toward me, and I winked. She nodded frantically at the hot chocolate. Molly's father took the book from her hands so I could ring it up. He paid with his credit card, and he put the book in a backpack I hadn't noticed he was carrying.

Molly tugged at his sleeve. "Dad, I saw a dragon!"

FORTY-SIX

The Cat snorted, and I glanced at him then checked out Molly's father's reaction.

I couldn't believe the Cat had made such a human sound, but the Cat ignored us and curled up in a ball next to the register.

Molly's father's forehead wrinkled for a moment as he stared at the Cat, but then he shook his head.

"Well, we all know dragons are dinosaurs that haven't been discovered yet," he said in a singsong voice to Molly.

"Yep, dragons are dinosaurs with wings," I said quickly.

I darted my eyes to the back bookshelves, hoping that Indigo would stay out of sight until Molly and her father left. I did not need to deal with the drama that would undoubtedly follow if Molly's father saw the book dragon. Then again, would he even believe what he saw?

Molly gazed back at the shelves, squinting, her bright

eyes searching for something. Her head snapped back to her father.

"Where did my book go?" she asked.

"It's in my backpack so you can hold your hot chocolate," he said, pointing toward the counter.

Molly's eyes widened, and she glanced at the cup. I had put a tall point of whipped cream on top from a can, along with a little cocoa powder so it looked fancy.

"Oh...that looks so yummy!"

The counter stood too tall for her to grab it, so her father moved to pick it up and hand it to her.

"Can I give you a hug?" she asked me.

I nodded and hurried around the counter before crouching down.

Molly hit me like a truck, almost knocking me to the ground, but I quickly steadied myself. She smelled like pancakes and maple syrup.

"Thank you for the chocolate!" she said loudly in my ear, but I smiled.

Little kids were strange but mostly adorable, especially when they liked chocolate and dinosaurs.

"You're welcome," I said.

Before she pulled back, she whispered in my ear softly, "I know I saw a dragon by the shelves."

I didn't say anything, only winked when she pulled away and kept the smile on my face.

As I stood, I gave her a nod. "I hope you have a happy birthday!"

"I will. Daddy has a surprise for me!" She walked back to her father's side, and he held the hot chocolate out to her.

Molly carefully licked most of the whipped cream off before taking a sip.

"Thank you again," he said, placing a hand behind Molly. "Come on, Molly. We need to get moving if we don't want to be late for your surprise."

"Oh, wait, I have a lid for the cup." I darted back behind the counter, grabbed one of the to-go lids, and held it out to him. "Here you go."

He smiled at me, grabbing the lid, then motioned for Molly to walk to the door. Both of her hands wrapped around the cup, and he had to open the door so she could head out. He waved as the door closed behind him.

"Well, that was close..." I mumbled, leaning forward on the counter.

"Children are special when it comes to magic," said the Cat.

That reminded me of the trick-or-treating and how kids reacted to the bookstore during that time. I wished Indigo had been around to be a part of that.

Indigo flung herself across the room from the top of one of the shelves. She chirped frantically, looking worried.

The Cat nodded. "She saw through your hiding spot. It happens. Molly is sensitive to magic. It's one of the reasons she comes here. It's like she knows when the bookshop is in this place."

Again, Indigo asked something, but it was too fast, and I couldn't follow it. The Cat chuckled, and I glanced between the two of them.

He sighed. "The little book dragon would like to learn

about dinosaurs. The dragons without wings from your world."

I nodded slowly. "That shouldn't be a problem. We have plenty of books about them, and I have some movies."

My mind went to the movies about a little long neck and star leaves. Though, given what happened to its mother, maybe that one wasn't a good idea.

Indigo spoke again, but it was to the Cat.

"She wants to know more about kids, and why she is so small."

Now that was a harder question, but I had an idea on how to answer it.

Indigo sat on the counter, ready for me to speak.

"Well, kids are little. Like you are a little dragon. Do you remember Lady Borsal? Molly is like you, a little one who needs to grow up. Like the Cat said, magic is weird around kids on my world. We don't have much magic where I'm from, but some kids are sensitive."

Now I was making things up based on what the Cat had said, but it made sense. And, I figured, if I got anything really wrong, the Cat would correct me.

"We don't have dragons like you there, but we did have dinosaurs."

I hurried over to the kids' section, and Indigo watched me grab a book. I brought it back behind the counter and cracked it open. It was a picture book, with the different eras of dinosaurs.

"See? They were big creatures who lived on our planet a very long time ago."

Indigo's green eyes went wide at the pictures, and

she put her head right up close to the pages before taking a step back.

"They were much bigger than the whole store." I flipped through several of the pages with her.

"The delivery guy will be here soon," muttered the Cat.

I nodded, thankful he'd given me a heads-up. "How about I leave this open in the kitchen for you?"

Indigo nodded and climbed onto my shoulder.

I placed her and the picture book in the kitchen. "Maybe, if you're lucky, the bookshop can turn the pages for you…"

Hopefully, the Cat wouldn't mind. I didn't want any of the delivery people to see her. Molly was one thing, but people who regularly came to the bookshop as part of their job was another.

It made me think of my family and how they would react to the little book dragon. My mom would completely be in love, though my father, who wouldn't stop reading stories to us when we were kids, would get a kick out of reading to the little dragon. My brothers were a little more complicated, but Cyan loved to read. Umber would teach her how to cook since he knew I wasn't that great at it.

I still couldn't believe I had burned the oatmeal.

That left Onyx and Cerulean, and I didn't know how they'd react. Cerulean lived for the adventure on high peaks. He'd probably be excited if Indigo ever got bigger, especially if she could take him flying. Onyx, I wasn't sure. He was quieter, and such a steady presence. He'd probably nod and not make a fuss.

"Sable, are you all right?" asked the Cat, startling me out of my reverie.

"Yeah, I'm fine," I said. "Just thinking about my family for a sec there."

The Cat stared at me like he had something else to say, but the bells on the front door rang, and someone pushed it open.

My heart froze as John carefully walked in, carrying one large box and two smaller ones. He flashed me a smile as he moved across the shop toward the counter.

I dug my nails into the palm of my hand. A quick glance at the Cat reminded me he was right here and that this was the actual John, not some monster that looked like him.

FORTY-SEVEN

"Hey, Sable, I've got some packages for you." He approached, set them on the counter, then leaned against them with a large smile. "It's good to see you. You won't believe what happened last time I delivered here."

I bet I would.

He shook his head and then shrugged. "I stumbled out on the sidewalk on the way back to my truck, totally hit my head, and I was down for the count." He literally fluttered his eyelashes at me. "Today's my first day back on the job."

"Oh, that sucks." I swallowed. "Are you okay?"

His bright-blue eyes stayed on me. "Yeah, I'm all good now. I just had a minor concussion, but there were some boxes that were stolen from the truck."

I shook my head, trying hard to keep myself from shaking. "Glad to know you're okay."

"It's a dangerous job being a delivery driver," he said.

I couldn't keep standing there like nothing was

wrong, and I turned toward Betty and quickly started grinding beans. "Let me make you a coffee..."

"Oh, I'd love a coffee." He smiled even brighter. "So, how are you liking this job? It doesn't seem like the shop is ever super busy."

"I love working here." I pulled the shot then added some hot water, a simple Americano that I could make with my eyes closed. "I wouldn't decide to do anything else."

"You sure? There's a position that opened up at dispatch. Great benefits and time off." He tilted his head when he said "time off."

I set the to-go cup on the counter next to him.

"No thanks. I get great benefits here." I leaned forward as if to tell him a secret. "They're even repaying my student loans."

"Woah, no wonder you're not interested..." He grabbed the cup with a frown, running his fingers through his hair. "I wonder how the owner can afford it..."

"Not my problem, though I think this is a sentimental shop for them. They must have money."

The Cat bumped into my hand, and I scratched his ears.

"Plus, who can resist a shop cat? He's the best."

"I get that." John nodded, glancing down at the Cat. "Cats are cool."

Especially this Cat, but I resisted saying anything.

"I appreciate the coffee. Good luck with the inventory." He took a sip of his coffee, smiled as he motioned to the boxes, and then turned toward the door.

I let out a sigh as soon as it shut behind him. It locked automatically.

"Are you okay?" asked the Cat.

He nudged my hand when I stopped petting him.

"I am. It's just...seeing him made me anxious, though I know it wasn't his fault." I eyed the boxes. "What did you order?"

The Cat moved away from my hand, dodging around the boxes.

I pulled the two smaller ones toward me. They were both in my name. "These look like they're mine."

The Cat sniffed them. "They must be. Mine is just odds and ends for some projects I need to finish up. What did you order?"

I leaned close to the Cat. "A surprise for Indigo, but let's get the work out of the way first."

The bigger box was sent to the store, so I opened it first. I didn't have a chance to pull anything out before the Cat jumped inside.

"Yes, this is what I ordered," said the Cat from inside the box. "We have the roll of leather, the larger crystals we'll need, and... Why did I order this again?"

I pulled out the larger crystals, and they hummed when I made contact with them. I shook my fingers after I set them on the counter. The leather was a light-brown color, wrapped in a roll about a foot long. I added that to the crystals.

Beside the Cat, all the box contained was a small container of seeds. Warmth radiated from the plastic container, and I picked it up to read the label.

"*Sunflowers—Rising Sun?*" I asked.

The Cat stayed in the box for a moment before jumping out.

"I don't think I ordered them." He moved closer to me, and I set them on the counter before breaking down the cardboard box. "I wonder why they added them to the order."

"Where did you even get this stuff from?"

The box didn't have any labels besides the shipping label, and there wasn't an invoice or anything inside.

The Cat flicked his tail.

"A source of mine." His nose touched the container of seeds, and he jerked back. "That's strange."

I didn't like the sound of that and resisted picking the little packet back up.

His head snapped to me. "They're not for me. They're for you."

"Me?" I quickly picked the container back up to look at the back. "I don't really have a green thumb. My brother does, but not me."

My thoughts went to the garden beds on the roof. Some pretty sunflowers would brighten up the place.

"Maybe I'll plant some in the rooftop garden." I shrugged. "Not sure what else to do with them."

The Cat stared at the container, his tail flicking all over the place.

"I'll put everything else in the storeroom."

I tossed the leather and crystals into the storeroom, then I grabbed my two much smaller boxes. One was a set of earbuds with a short cord. The other was the smallest MP3 player I could find with a touch screen. I snagged out the charger and got it charging while I dashed upstairs to get my laptop. When I came back down, the Cat was studying the device carefully.

"It's a music player, so she can listen to audiobooks and music when she wants."

The Cat slowly nodded. "I've heard of such things."

I began the slow process of getting the player hooked up to the network and the program on my laptop to send stuff to the device. I added a few books on dinosaurs and some classical music.

"It has headphones, or it can be used without them."

His head cocked to the side. "How is she going to use headphones?"

"I'll figure something out," I mumbled.

Indigo came to investigate several minutes later. I showed her the device, but she didn't understand until it started playing some music. Then she wouldn't stop dancing. She poked at it but couldn't get it to do what she wanted.

"You should show the instructions to her," said the Cat.

"No one reads the instructions for tech."

The Cat glared at me, and I pulled out the small booklet and set it on the counter.

Indigo raced to it and carefully peered at each page.

"Wait, can she read English?" I asked as she struggled to flip the page.

I did it for her.

"She's learning."

My lips parted, but I just shook my head instead of saying anything. She was smart if she could understand the instructions for the device already. Maybe the kids' books were becoming too low-level for her? I'd leave it for now, and maybe put a few books for older audiences on the device and see which ones she listened to more.

"Hey, Indigo, I got these headphones for you as well." I held up the earbuds that I had twined together like a small set of headphones with some wire. "I need to see if they fit."

She sat down in front of me as I adjusted the wire so they could sit on top of her head, near her ears but not inside. Then I plugged them into the device and turned it down.

Her eyes grew so wide.

"This way, when you can't sleep, you can listen to things without me. I know I can't always keep up with reading you new things."

Indigo started chirping rapidly, and the Cat nodded.

"What was that?" I asked, not following.

I needed to get better at her language.

"She thinks you are amazing," said the Cat.

Indigo jumped up onto my shoulder, knocking the headphones off. She looked at them with wide eyes for a moment, but then she snuggled the side of my neck.

"You'll have to figure out how to carry it around. I got the smallest I could find," I whispered to the small dragon.

And with that, Indigo had a new mission, one she accomplished in less than a day.

The next morning, she flew through the air with headphones on and the player clutched in her tiny claws.

I wondered what changes those tiny headphones would bring into our lives.

FORTY-EIGHT

Today I opted for cereal. Indigo was thrilled. The Cat, not so much.

"What is this?" the Cat asked.

"It's cereal in milk," I answered. "Cats like milk, so I figured this would be up your alley."

I poured the cinnamon cereal into my own bowl all the way to the top. The Cat and Indigo had smaller bowls in front of each of them. I poured milk into my bowl and then sat down on the stool.

"Are you okay?" asked the Cat, after staring at the bowl then back at me.

"Yeah, I just had some weird dreams." I shrugged and dug my spoon into the cinnamon-crunchy goodness.

Cereal was a treat for me, since it felt like you could never have enough, which meant you'd start with a bowl of reasonable size, and then the next thing you knew, the box was empty.

The little squares soaked up the milk, and I ate with glee.

The Cat finally started eating the pieces, and he nodded. "This isn't bad. Not as sweet as I thought it'd be."

Indigo chirped in reply, standing in the center of her bowl.

I blinked but didn't say anything. She was feeding herself, and I could always rinse her off in the sink later.

"So, what did you dream about?" asked the Cat.

Somehow, his bowl was completely empty in the time it took me to look at Indigo. No milk, nothing left, like he'd licked it clean.

"Uh," I started. "Something about dragons, and my brother, plus the sunflower seeds I got in that box yesterday."

Indigo started frantically chirping and knocked her bowl over. I quickly righted it before milk went everywhere, and she sheepishly gave me a smile.

"Eat first, then words." I looked at the Cat. "She asked what kind of dragons, right?"

The Cat nodded with a grin. "See? You're learning how to speak dragon."

"Maybe Indigo-speak," I mumbled before shoving another spoonful into my mouth.

I let the conversation pause as both Indigo and I finished our cereal. Part of me wondered if I should have made something with a little more protein for her, but I just didn't have the energy. Hopefully, she would be fine with a carb-heavy morning. Lunch would be something better.

The Cat moved across the island toward the doorway.

"All I remember about the dragons is that there was a red one and a blue one. The red one was bigger," I explained to Indigo.

The Cat froze. Then he slowly turned to face me. "Red and blue, you say?"

"Yep, but that's all I remember." I stretched upward and gathered the bowls into the sink. "Is that important?"

I turned back, but the Cat had gone. Indigo stayed on the counter, milk gathering under the spot where she sat as it dripped down her body.

"Let me rinse you off quickly before you grab your MP3 player."

She nodded.

I picked her up and brought her over to the sink, which was already empty. The water was warm as I ran her under it. It didn't take long to clean her, and then I dried her off with a hand towel.

Indigo chirped her thanks then jumped into the air to glide to where I had set the player on the counter, away from breakfast. The milk puddle was already gone from the counter. The Cat was on fire today with the magic.

I smiled, looking around the clean kitchen before heading towards the storefront. Making coffee was the next order of business. I had opted for sugar before coffee this morning because I'd woken up starving, hence the cereal.

I yanked my mug out from beneath the counter and started grinding beans. The Cat sat next to the register, looking thoughtful. His tail moved about randomly, twitching this way and that, which usually meant he was thinking hard about things. I pulled his teacup out as well and decided to go with a basic vanilla latte today, with extra foam.

I frothed the milk with the syrup and smiled as the warm hints of vanilla filled the space. Once I filled both cups, I topped them off with shots of espresso. Only one in the Cat's, and three in mine. No designs this time. I moved the teacup closer to the Cat, then I took a sip of my own.

It was on point.

"This is way too tasty," I whispered to myself.

The Cat stood and tried his coffee from the teacup.

"It is good today." He glanced at me. "You might want to make two more in teacups."

"Oh, what's on the schedule today?" I asked, moving back to Betty.

"Lady Borsal is visiting, with a friend."

My stomach dropped. It had to be an update on Indigo. Maybe she'd even found her family.

I nibbled on my lip as I pulled out two more teacups and started the process of making more milk. What if today was Indigo's last day in the shop?

Indigo glided across the room from the bookshelves on the wall. She had claimed a small area near the door that gave her a fantastic view of everything. She had a small fuzzy pillow and a vase that she could hide behind if whoever visited wasn't from a magical world. Her headphones dangled around her neck, and her little claws clutched the MP3 player as she made her way over to the counter.

"It sounds like you have visitors today," I said, forcing myself to smile.

She held up the MP3 player and chirped something that I took to mean she was going to show it off.

That made me relax a little as I pulled the espresso shots.

"Are you ready?" asked the Cat.

"Yep, let's do this."

The door unlocked, and I finished up the two drinks just as the bells rang.

"Welcome to Meow," I called out, catching sight of Lady Borsal.

Red scales flickered into my vision for a second before her robes came into view. Her orange eyes glowed as she smiled at me.

She noticed the teacups and Indigo sitting on the counter. "Just the ones I was looking for," she said.

Behind her was an older man. His hair was white, and he had bright-blue eyes. He stood slightly shorter than Lady Borsal, and walked with a cane. Despite that, his face wasn't heavily wrinkled or anything, though he still felt old, carrying a weight of centuries through the door with him. He slowly made his way after Lady Borsal, who approached the counter.

She reached out for Indigo, who held up the MP3 player, chirping rapidly.

The Lady's face softened, and she nodded along to whatever Indigo was saying before replying in more chirps.

The Cat shifted uneasily next to the register, and I moved a little closer to him.

The old man approached Indigo with a smile, then a small frown.

"She isn't the one," he said, his voice soft, and he sounded hurt. "But it was worth a try."

I couldn't help but keep my eyes on him, wanting to give him a hug.

He noticed my gaze. "My name is Lord Bennit."

"I'm Sable, the Shopkeeper, and this is The Cat." I motioned to him. "It's nice to meet you. Though, I'm sorry Indigo isn't the one you're looking for."

He nodded softly. "It was a long shot, as it's been many years since we lost my daughter."

I resisted the urge to lean over and pat his shoulder.

"Don't let your coffee get cold," I added in a soft voice. I motioned to one of the cups. "It will help warm you, at least."

I assumed he was a dragon, and probably never got cold, but still, good manners were important.

He chuckled, watching Lady Borsal chat with Indigo. "Did you design the machine she uses to listen to books?"

"I used something that exists in my world and just made it fit her a little better," I said, blushing.

"Something like that would be useful to my kind. I'd like to order several of them for my clan." He studied the device in Indigo's hands. "The older ones could make a project out of it."

"I was just talking about it with Indigo," said Lady Borsal. "It would be useful to record some of our stories in our language, to make sure we don't lose them with time."

I could never have guessed this would turn in this direction; I had just wanted to make sure she had enough reading material when I slept.

"Yeah, we can order more," I said, turning to look at The Cat.

He nodded. "That should be fine, but it will take a few days."

I relayed the information then added, "Any updates on her family?"

Lady Borsal frowned. "I'd hoped that Lord Bennit would have some insight. He tracks all disappearances of our kind, and has for centuries."

"Don't worry. We will find her mother," said Lord Bennit. "I am calling a conclave of the Clan of Lore. It is time we all met and took a roll call of new members. This is just giving me a push to bring everyone together. It will take some time, though."

I swallowed. "Should Indigo go?"

An icy cold crept through me as I thought about her leaving the shop. I couldn't go with her, since I couldn't step outside the door.

Lord Bennit glanced at Lady Borsal before returning to me. "That shouldn't be necessary. You are doing a fantastic job protecting the little one. She is growing at a good rate and learning what she needs to."

A light pressure gathered around me.

"The Clan of Lore offers you friendship. If you need us, we will come."

A weight filled the air with his words.

The Cat didn't move as he stared back, his green eyes glowing.

Lord Bennit turned to the Cat, and the pressure vanished. "No matter what."

FORTY-NINE

ndigo chirped, breaking the suddenly heavy mood.

Both dragons looked at her and smiled.

"Don't worry, little one. We don't mean Sable any harm," said Lord Bennit.

Indigo nodded, but glared at them both, like she'd take them down if they tried anything.

I resisted the urge to chuckle. To my surprise, she set down the MP3 player and dashed over to me. She jumped onto my shoulder then crawled up near my neck, careful to not stab me with her claws since I only had a long sleeve shirt on. She stayed there under my hair, nuzzling me.

"It's all okay, Indigo. Don't worry..."

She chirped, "All right." Or at least that's what I assumed she said.

Lord Bennit chuckled again.

"Well, I need to get a move on since I'm going to be calling the conclave." He turned to look at Lady Borsal. "Thank you again for bringing this to my attention."

He then turned and strode out of the bookshop. This time, he didn't use his cane at all, and for a moment, the outline of a bright-blue dragon tail appeared as the door snapped shut behind him.

"He can be a little intense," said Lady Borsal, picking up her teacup. "He is protective of the little ones."

"What happened to his daughter?" I asked. "If that's okay to ask."

Lady Borsal sipped her coffee, then she let out a sigh. "It was a dark time in our history. We still don't know what happened, really. Lord Bennit and his mate had a litter of three dragonets, which should have been a great cause for joy among all dragons."

I couldn't imagine three like Indigo all at once. The cuteness would be too much to handle.

A soft smile came over her face, the teacup still in her hands. "Lord Bennit was calling for all the clans to gather. To bring us together under one council."

Her face darkened. "His home was attacked, and one of his daughters went missing. He went on a rampage, along with all the other Clan members. All the Clans, not just the Clan of Lore. It pulled us together like nothing else would."

"But she was never found?" I asked.

"No." Lady Borsal shook her head. "All of us have searched far and wide. His other two children are grown, with dragonets of their own."

I petted Indigo, who still stayed under my hair. Too bad hiding from the story didn't change it.

"I should head out," said Lady Borsal. "Make sure you place the order for more of these."

She pointed at the MP3 player.

At least my experiment would help more than just Indigo.

"The Cat can get word to me to stop by to pick them up." She finished her coffee in one swallow, then she headed out.

After the door closed behind her, Indigo climbed off my shoulder. She went back to the MP3 player and picked it up. Indigo leaped into the air and returned to her spot on the top of the bookshelf.

"That was a meeting," I mumbled.

"You are making powerful friends." The Cat turned to look at me, his green eyes glowing. "Lord Bennit isn't someone people will cross. He heads a Clan of over a thousand dragons. Even the Fates would hesitate to cross him directly."

"He didn't seem to like you," I added.

The Cat's tail flicked. "He made it clear that you are a friend. Nothing will change that. What he doesn't understand is that you are under *my* protection."

For a second, I got the image of the Cat and the dragon growling at one another over a toy. Me being that toy.

I pushed that thought away. My place was at the bookstore. I had a contract to fulfill and a little book dragon to protect. I could leave the rest of it to the Cat.

"For lunch, I wish we had some steak tacos," I said. "Quick, easy, and the steak cooked to a medium rare."

I sat down on the stool behind the counter, sipping on my coffee.

"You make good tacos."

"Maybe I can order them from somewhere." I didn't have the energy to cook something that big for lunch, not after meeting with the dragons.

Once I finished my coffee, I planned to soak in the hot tub and try to relax.

I shivered, thinking of Lord Bennit's gaze on me. It had felt like he had done something, but I didn't know what. Before I could ask the Cat, he glanced toward the kitchen then back at me. His head tilted to one side.

"What?"

The Cat quickly shook his head, but I turned to look into the kitchen. Something sat on the counter, and I got up from my stool, heading in that direction.

Tacos. Steak freaking tacos with a little cheese and some cabbage with a small pile of guac on the platter. There were at least fifteen of them.

"Cat, you didn't need to do this…" I turned back to the front of the store.

The Cat stood on the counter. "It wasn't me."

I jerked back and moved closer to the Cat. It was early for lunch, but I bet they would keep. Though I could totally eat one right now. They were tacos; they were an anytime food.

"What do you mean? You're always doing the little things around here, like cleaning up and such."

The Cat sheepishly shook his head. "It's the shop, listening to you. You're the one who causes those things to happen."

"*What?*" The metaphorical ground shifted under my feet, and I reached out to the wall behind me.

"Are you okay?" The Cat jumped down from the

counter and moved closer to me. "You don't look okay, and the shop is freaking out a little."

He moved closer. "You should sit down."

I slid down the wall, noticing the front of the shop had gotten darker. The sun streaming in from the skylights had dimmed.

I swallowed. "The shop is worried?"

"Just a little. It doesn't want you to be afraid of it."

"I just didn't know..." I mumbled, then patted the wooden floor. "I'm okay... I swear. I just need a moment to adjust."

The sunlight streamed in the front room again, just like before.

Holy smokes, the store responded to my words. This was what had happened with Betty when I'd asked the store to speed up processing the horrible book.

"I'm okay. It was just a shock, is all."

The store brightened back to normal, and it almost felt warm under me for a moment.

I carefully stood and glanced back into the kitchen with the steak tacos.

The shop had made steak tacos for me because I'd wished for them.

"These look amazing; by any chance, can you store them for a few hours? It's a little early for us to eat lunch..."

Now I was talking to the store. It'd started with talking to the Cat, then a little book dragon, and now the store. Was I losing it? No clue.

But the only thing I could do, really, was roll with it.

FIFTY

"Yep, I'm going to go soak in the hot tub on the roof."

I waved at Indigo, who chirped but didn't move from the far wall. From there, I headed up the stairs to change, my legs still a little shaky.

I ignored the Cat; I couldn't handle anything else that he might put on my plate.

My brain just needed to soak all of this in first.

THE SUN SPARKLED DOWN on me, and I closed my eyes, trying to let my thoughts wander. Steam rose from the hot water all around me as it soaked into my muscles. I could smell flowers on the breeze that flowed across the rooftop area, even with the high walls on every side.

Deep breath in then out. Sink into the moment.

The bookstore was the magic, and I had been having it do things for me. It wasn't the Cat at all. The Cat was just a talking cat. Maybe. I still wasn't sure about that one.

I cracked open my eyes as I acknowledged my failure of just being able to relax. The Cat hid somewhere, doing his thing, while Indigo listened to a new book that hadn't come from my world.

It'd appeared randomly, but given how excited she was and that it featured dragons, I assumed it was from them, and magic had helped move it to the device. If not, I'd need to figure out what was going on, but the audiobook was in the dragon language, so I decided not to worry about it for now.

My gaze landed on my empty cup that had been filled with iced tea. It still had a few ice cubes in the bottom. I had more in the fridge, but that would mean getting out of the tub and heading down the stairs, making sure to not leave a dripping mess anywhere.

If the shop was magic, and I could control the shop, maybe I could ask it to do me a favor?

"By any chance, can you please grab the pitcher of iced tea from the fridge? I don't want to get water every-where..." I kept my voice low, not wanting the Cat to hear me if he was nearby.

Sometimes, he liked to lie in the sun out here, and I wouldn't notice him if he didn't want me to.

Next to my glass on the wooden table, the surface rippled, but my glass didn't move. Instead, the pitcher rose out of the wood like it was water. My hand covered my mouth while watching it actually happen. Most of the magic of the place meant I never saw it, just the result.

The pitcher stopped moving and sat there. Moisture pebbled on the cool surface since it was warm and toasty on the roof.

It really was the shop doing things to help me out. Not the freaking Cat. What else could the magical shop do? It had eaten an evil book and protected me from not-John, not to mention handling all of the chores.

"Oh my god, thank you so much," I said in a rush.

I reached out and poured myself a full glass of tea before setting it back on the table. It rippled, then sank into the wood, vanishing, and I assumed it appeared back downstairs in the fridge.

"You've been doing everything." I leaned back in the hot water with my glass in my hand, my thoughts racing. "The laundry, the dishes. You even make my bed…"

I took a sip of the cold beverage, trying to calm down a little.

"You are amazing." I chuckled. "And here I thought it was the Cat, when you should have been getting credit all along."

I took another big swallow of the iced tea to give myself a moment to think.

"Thank you for making me feel welcome and at home in the shop. I don't know if this would have worked as well without you." I shook my head with a small smile, feeling like I'd made a friend.

"Wait." I sat up. "Is Betty a part of you?"

Warmth then cold pulsed under my feet. I took that as a yes and a no. I had named the espresso machine, and I loved the name. The machine was a name brand, and I'd wondered if it was real. I assumed so, given the yes-

and-no answer, but since it was inside the shop, it was technically a part of it. I bet the shop couldn't use it, or the Cat would have had much better coffee than when I got here.

Yet Betty was what I had pictured helping me take down that evil book.

"Well, is it okay if I call *you* Betty? I don't want to only call you the shop. That feels weird to me."

There was no response for a moment, then a great rush of warmth rippled across the roof. The sun shone down even brighter before it dimmed back to its normal sunny-day mode.

That brought way more questions to mind, like was I really outside right now, or was this just another part of the shop? The shop—well, Betty—controlled the sunlight. That made my brain hurt, so I shoved it to the side. I had to pretend that this was outside. No matter what. The illusion of some freedom was just too important to me.

I leaned back in the tub and finished off the iced tea. My hand hung over the side with the glass, and I smiled.

"This is amazing, Betty. You, me, Indigo, and the Cat. That's pretty awesome."

We were almost like a family.

A thought crossed my mind then, and I set the glass down. "You know, you do so much for me, so what can I do for you? This shouldn't all be one-sided. I know you have lots of magic, and I have no idea what you might need, but if you need something, I'm here."

A cloud crossed over the sun, and an uncertain whisper brushed at the back of my mind.

"I mean it, Betty. If I can help, you just need to show me how. I'll do whatever I can. That's what friends do."

My towel appeared on the edge of the tub, and I took the hint. I stood and wrapped it around myself before stepping out. I quickly dried off before grabbing the coverup. I'd gotten it to make sure I didn't burn while laying out in the sun.

Though, if it wasn't real sun, would I burn?

That thought vanished as the glass door slid open on its own.

Betty had something to show me, and I couldn't let my new friend down.

FIFTY-ONE

Inside the doorway, I smiled at the various plants and the cat tree I'd gotten for the Cat. I was pretty sure he loved it, and I'd caught him a few times napping inside the box near the top.

I'd refreshed the catnip once, but I didn't want to get the Cat addicted to the stuff. It seemed to help him sleep, and the day after, he seemed more relaxed and friendly.

The plants closest to the cat tree seemed to grow bigger, faster, but that could just be my perception. Their leaves were a brighter green and reached toward the box, as if it were a light source.

The small oak tree had a tiny acorn growing on it. It was still small and green. I hoped the new life was a good sign for the little tree.

A doorway leading to the left on the balcony caught my eye. This was the first time I'd seen it. That whole stretch of wall normally stood empty. Opposite the new door was the balcony over the register area, which was where my bedroom was, then eventually the stairs.

Doors didn't appear on that wall. The runner down the hall was the same one as always.

It had to be where Betty was leading me. I crept to the entrance and glanced inside, but the room was dark, like a haze filled the doorway so people couldn't peek. As soon as I stepped inside, the room brightened, but the haze still stretched across the doorway behind me. While I couldn't look out, no one could see me inside either.

Then again, this doorway didn't normally exist. Hopefully, if the Cat found me, he wouldn't mind.

Giant bookshelves lined the walls, rising several feet above my head. A library ladder rested on a rail that encircled the entire room. On the far wall sat a giant stone fireplace with a small fire burning inside. The fire looked comically small compared to the stone it sat in.

Over the wooden mantle, attached to the wall, rested a large shield. Some kind of symbol emblazoned it, but I couldn't tell what it was from here.

The room wasn't dark, as lanterns sat next to the fireplace, and some light drifted down from above, though I couldn't see any source. There weren't any windows in the room. It almost felt like a cavern, yet the wooden floor gleamed despite the scratches and wear, indicating this room was well used. I couldn't even guess who was using it, though.

In the center of the room stood a large wooden table. A golden book glowed at one end, and I took a step away from it. I knew that book; it was the one the Cat could read, filled with magic.

His concern over it hurting me had been very real, and I moved around the table in the opposite direction. It lay open, and its pages fluttered up and down. Light drifted up from the pages, as if the book begged me to read it.

"No..." I muttered to myself, shaking my head.

Whatever Betty wanted me to see was in here, but I wouldn't ignore the Cat's warning about the book. Today was not the day to ignore the Cat.

Books covered the shelves, mostly put away properly, their spines straight and even, but in a few areas, stacks of books took over.

It made me smile, and I ran a finger along one shelf. Most didn't have titles on the spines, and the ones that did weren't in English.

I caught something glittering out of the corner of my eye and found myself drawn to the shield over the fireplace.

Slowly, I walked around the table, keeping away from the book at the far end, to get a better view of the shield.

"Betty, what am I looking for?"

It almost looked like a golden outline surrounded the shield, and I nodded.

That was the target.

Heat from the small fire flowed from the fireplace, and sweat started forming on my brow as I neared the shield.

Once I stood in front of it, I could see what was carved on the wooden surface. The shield was beautiful. Whoever had carved it knew what they were doing, and I wished I could get closer. Fine vines covered the edges of the shield, and in the center was a giant oak leaf. The edges of the leaf lifted, as if someone had set a real one in the center and turned it into wood.

Other figures stood in the shield's background, but from here, I couldn't see what they were. I stepped forward again, and my foot hit something soft. Glancing down, I spotted a cat bed. Or what I assumed was a cat bed. A pile of blankets lay on the edge of the stone surrounding the fireplace.

"This is his room. The Cat's..."

Other doors branched off, but all of them were shut.

"I should leave."

The room felt warm and loved, but also lonely.

Golden light teased at the edges of my sight, but I turned away from the book. I trusted the Cat, and he said the book was dangerous.

I pulled myself away from my perch in front of the fireplace and glanced at the large table. In the center sat a mirror lying flat, reflecting the wooden ceiling. It reminded me of the mirror the Cat had used to show the one who had brought Indigo to the shop.

"Who are you watching?" I asked.

Behind me, the shield glowed again, and I glanced over my shoulder at it.

"The shield represents someone. Now I just gotta figure out who."

More importantly, why whomever it was mattered to the Cat.

There wasn't anything else on the table that drew my attention, nothing else that I wanted to look at, so I slowly made my way back to the only open door in the room. Two other doors were closed, tucked away within bookcases, but shut. One was a bright green, the other a sky blue. Yet I didn't go snooping.

I paused at the doorway I'd entered through, glancing back over the room. Something nagged at the edge of my attention.

Finally, it dawned on me. This room felt like it didn't belong in the shop, like it had come from somewhere else. Part of it was the floor. It didn't match the rest of the store.

The other was how it smelled. Almost like the wooden shelves were still alive. Even with the fire burning in the fireplace, it didn't smell like smoke. Instead, it smelled like I'd walked around outside in a forest.

Where did this room come from?

Betty had wanted me to see the shield. Now I had research to do and a riddle to solve.

What did Betty want help with?

And more importantly, how did it involve me and the Cat?

FIFTY-TWO

The bacon in my belly felt heavy, even though it had been perfectly crispy. Indigo had eaten a pile bigger than her, and the Cat had asked for seconds. We finished two entire packages of the stuff. The scrambled eggs had been tasty as well, but I felt off.

Part of it was that my mind kept going back to that room and whatever Betty was trying to get me to figure out. I didn't want to let the shop down. She was one of my friends, practically family.

I doodled on a napkin a rough outline of an oak leaf. That had been the center part of the shield.

I tapped my fingers on the counter, and a part of me wanted to ask the Cat about it, yet I resisted. This I wanted to do without his help.

And, to be honest, I wasn't sure he'd help me anyway. Betty had shown me his room, not the Cat.

Shaking my head, I caught sight of him out of the corner of my eye. I set my mug down on the napkin and grabbed a teacup.

"Would you like some coffee?" I asked.

The Cat's tail twitched as soon as he landed on the counter. He didn't answer, but his ears were flattened just so. Something was bugging him today. Hopefully, it was only too much bacon.

Indigo zoomed around the shop from all the bacon. The Cat, not so much.

I quickly made a mocha and refreshed my mug as well. On top, I added some whipped cream, thankful that nothing ever went bad in the magical fridge. At least I knew the reason now. The Cat loved whipped cream, but I didn't pull it out very often.

"Here, this should be tasty."

His green eyes landed on the teacup, and his whiskers flickered. "Thank you."

That worried me even more. He rarely thanked me for things.

He dove into the whipped cream, getting it all over his face. I knew better than to offer to clean him until he was done. Somehow, it would all get cleaned up.

The mocha was a little less chocolatey for me since I'd still had a quarter cup of an Americano in my mug, but I didn't care. The chocolate was still good.

"What's on the schedule today?" I asked after a couple of moments.

"Deliveries, then dragons." The Cat licked his face, getting the last of the cream off.

My mind raced, trying to figure out what might be delivered today.

"Oh, the MP3 players are coming in? That'll be good.

And then the dragons on the same day." I shrugged. "Keeps things straight."

The Cat almost flinched at the word dragons.

I narrowed my eyes.

The dragons were upsetting him. That's where the trouble came from.

Indigo continued to fly around the shop.

"Hey, Indigo! You're gonna need to hide for the deliveries. Do you have a story to listen to?"

Indigo chirped once and headed to her spot on the bookshelf near the door. Her little hidey-hole was there, and slowly, the shop was expanding it into the wall, like her own little cave. She still slept in the cat tree in my bedroom, but anything shiny ended up in the hole.

The Cat nodded to himself as Indigo vanished. His bright eyes landed on me, and I smiled at him. Then the door unlocked.

"I'm assuming it'll be John?"

When the Cat nodded, I took a deep breath and let it out.

"Don't worry. I'm here..." mumbled the Cat.

He moved closer as I eyed the door, and his shoulder touched my hand near my mug.

I petted between his ears; his fur was super soft.

It didn't take long for the door to jingle open, and John darted inside with a large box.

"Hey, Sable, cat..." He moved faster than usual and gave us both a nod as he approached. "Today is a busy day, so no time to chitchat. Working on a promotion!"

He smiled at me, set the box on the counter, then left. In and out before I could even say anything.

I blinked in shock, staring at the box as the door shut behind him.

"That was... Okay." Shaking my head, I grabbed the box cutter under the counter and quickly opened it.

Packed inside were MP3 players, along with things that looked like digital recorders.

"Woah, this is more than I thought we'd get."

"I added more to the order," said the Cat. "They will be needed."

Indigo glided across the room and almost landed directly in the box. At the last second, she slammed into the counter.

"Indigo!"

She chirped once and wobbled, then she shook her wings as she folded them before climbing toward the edge of the box.

"Dragonets," muttered the Cat, rolling his eyes. "She's fine."

I dug around in the box, looking for an invoice, but didn't see one. "Do I just hand over the box?"

"Pretty much," replied the Cat. "The dragon will pay us a fair price."

"That's good to know."

Everything looked in order, and Indigo nudged my hand before crawling up my arm to my shoulder. I scratched under her chin as she nuzzled me. The Cat gave her an approving nod, and I wondered what he had said to her about the dragons coming.

The bells jingled again as Lord Bennit walked inside. The sunlight in the room felt like it shifted, and a breeze entered with him. His blue robes flowed around him, and today he didn't have a cane. Instead, he strode inside like a young man, though it was still him.

It was a little odd, an old man prancing in like he was in his twenties, but I had no doubt that it was the great dragon himself.

"Good morning, Lord Bennit," I called. "Would you like a mocha?"

An eyebrow raised, but then he nodded and smiled at me. "That sounds like a great way to start the day."

Another chocolate lover. Maybe it was a dragon thing.

His gaze landed on the box. "Are those the story players?"

"Yes, along with some recorders," I said.

I quickly grabbed a mug and started pulling a shot of espresso.

Indigo peeked out from underneath my hair and chirped a few times. The dragon started laughing and responded in that language.

I focused on the mocha and set it on the counter.

"I've come with a proposition for you, Cat."

I froze, then turned to look at the two of them. The Cat looked regal, sitting on the counter in a sunbeam that hadn't been there before.

"I want to host the conclave for the Clan of Lore here in your shop."

Indigo dashed off my shoulder and took to the air. She started flying in a circle around Lord Bennit, chirping nonstop.

"Why?" The question slipped between my lips, and both of them turned to look at me.

Bright-green eyes from the Cat, and warm blue eyes from the dragon.

"Why here?"

"Well, it would allow both you and Indigo to attend. All dragons of the Clan of Lore will be attending, no matter how young. Plus, this will allow some of our more reclusive dragons to spend some time out in the wider world. See things that have changed."

His gaze stayed on me, and I felt like he really meant what he was saying.

I looked at the Cat. It was his shop.

Indigo chirped rapidly at the Cat, but he didn't respond immediately.

Lord Bennit frowned. "Of course, I guarantee nothing will happen to either of them. Both are important to the Clan."

I nudged the Cat, who still sat close to me.

Finally, he nodded. "Looks like we will host the conclave."

"Perfect," said Lord Bennit. "Absolutely perfect."

Indigo cheered and zoomed around the room even faster than before.

"I need to distribute these and get working on planning the event." Lord Bennit nodded at us, then he headed toward the door.

As soon as it shut behind him, the Cat slumped to the counter.

"Cat! You could have said no," I whispered, picking him up in my arms.

Indigo didn't even notice.

"No, I couldn't. The book said yes."

I petted him, feeling a quiver before he calmed, hiding his head against my chest.

How bad could a bookstore full of dragons be?

FIFTY-THREE

I pinned the phone between my shoulder and my ear as I listened to the music on hold. It was one thing to say yes to a clan of dragons coming to visit. It was a whole other thing to get all the preparation done.

And everyone in the building knew I was not the person to cook for this. Not at all.

Instead, I had a pleasant lunch of sandwiches catered. I'd ordered cookie dough, brownies, and other sweet things. The last thing on my list were charcuterie boards. Given that they were dragons, having meat as a snacking option seemed prudent. I wanted to make sure that no one got hangry at any point during this meeting.

When I asked the Cat how long we should plan to host the dragons, he'd said only one day. Any longer than that, and they would never leave.

"Hello, this is Boards and Meats. How can I help you?" asked a female voice on the phone. Finally.

"Hi, I need to order five of your largest available

boards, with an emphasis on meat." I crossed a line through the next item on my list.

"Five?"

"Yes, it's a big crowd we're hosting." I knew this was going to be a hassle, especially since I didn't want to explain what was really going on.

"I mean, our largest are grazing tables. Is that what you mean?" she asked.

"Wait, grazing tables?" I frantically clicked around on their website. "Sorry, I'm on your site right now. You can do whole freaking tables? Can I get two?"

"Sure!" Her voice suddenly sounded very excited. "They are eight feet long by three feet wide."

I tried to imagine how big that was and repeated it to myself. Measurements were not my strong suit.

Suddenly, the table in the center of the bookstore stretched. The books on top of it shook as the wooden table kept moving. One side got shorter while the other got longer before it stopped.

I nodded.

"Betty, you are amazing," I whispered.

I needed more than that. It would be at least twenty dragons, plus Indigo and the Cat.

"Let's make that three. I'll have two other tables covered in sweets already," I said into the phone. "How much time do you need to prepare? Like, how does this work?"

I wasn't used to having people in the shop.

"So, I show up the day of the event and set everything up. It will just be me. I'm just getting started at doing large events like this."

"Okay, so I can get you into the bookshop beforehand, and I'll have the three tables set up." I took a deep breath. "Am I crazy if I ask you to do that tomorrow?"

The woman went quiet. "Tomorrow, as in Sunday?"

"Yeah, I'm so sorry for the late booking. I didn't know I was hosting until today. Last-minute events, right?" I crossed my fingers.

"No, no, I can do that. I need to head to the store immediately, though. Can I send you an invoice? Please make sure you pay it online. I usually require a fifty percent fee up front, but since it's tomorrow, I'll send the whole thing."

"That's perfect. It's the Meow Bookstore. I'll send over the address and get that paid ASAP. Thank you again."

"No, thank you!"

The phone beeped, and I set it down.

"Okay, Betty, I hope you can keep the grazing tables in stasis. I don't want someone here the same day the dragons are showing up."

The shop's lights flicked once in agreement.

"You are the best."

"Did I hear stasis?" The Cat jumped onto the counter, eyeing the notebook I had my list on. "That looks long."

"Well, I have sweets showing up later today, meat and cheese plates tomorrow, plus the lunch catering." I motioned to the list. "That means I need our lovely shop to stop time on the food like they do with the fridge."

"Oh, that's smart," said the Cat. "Making sure there is enough food for them. I didn't even think about providing food."

I blinked. Twice. "You wouldn't have provided food?"

The Cat shook his head.

"Well, too late. They're getting snack foods and lunch." I set my pencil down. "I want to be an excellent hostess and show that I'm a good person to look after Indigo."

Speaking of the dragon, she lay passed out on a pillow at the end of the counter. The non-stop excitement of yesterday had worn her out big time.

"Have you checked out the space yet?" asked the Cat.

"Not yet. The cookie stuff should show up at any moment. After that delivery is done, I'll check out the space." I scratched the back of the Cat's head. "Sandra from Cookie Master should be showing up. She recently expanded into brownies."

The Cat purred.

The door jingled and then popped open as Sandra walked in. Her dark hair was pulled back into a ponytail, but this time her apron looked clean. The logo for the Cookie Master decorated the front—a cookie in a chef's hat.

"Ah, Sable! My favorite customer." She carried several plastic tubs in. "You need to give me all the feedback on the brownies. You're the first one to try them."

She set down the tubs on the counter. "I have one more stack. Be right back."

I looked at the pile of plastic tubs. About half were already cooked, which was what I'd ordered. I had called her this morning, and she'd brought over a good amount of what she had.

Sandra popped back into the shop with several more tubs.

"You know, you could have just given me dough," I said with a smile.

"There is no way you would have had enough time for the event to bake that many cookies." She shook her head with a smile. "Plus, I didn't mind. My niece is helping at the shop now, so she is replacing all of what I brought."

Sandra motioned to the cookies. "Not to mention, we didn't have any major orders pending, so you're letting me clean out my freezer."

"Whatever you say, Cookie Master," I joked.

"Oh, look at the beautiful cat!" She reached over to pet the Cat, who suddenly became super friendly with her. "I just love cats. If the shop could have one, we would."

She gave him several more pets.

"But I gotta get going. Thanks for the order. I hope the event goes well. I'll pick up the tubs later this week." Sandra headed toward the door. "Remember, feedback on the brownies!"

"I won't forget."

"Brownies?" The Cat sat on the counter, glancing at the giant containers.

"We have three types of brownies to try: deep chocolate, s'mores, and peanut butter." I grabbed three of the containers off the top of the baked cookies.

The rest sank into the counter like magic.

I smirked and headed toward the kitchen. "I need to

get to baking some cookies and maybe testing some brownies."

"I can give you some input as well," said the Cat.

I paused on my way into the kitchen and glanced towards where Indigo slept on the counter, right next to where Sandra had set the plastic cookie tubs.

Should I wake her? Then I realized. There was no way Sandra hadn't seen the dragon, yet she'd said nothing. Absolutely nothing.

FIFTY-FOUR

I'd been worried about how I would get the food into the room, but in the end, I didn't need to do it. The shop did it for me.

After the lovely lady had pulled together the grazing tables in the main part of the shop, I asked Betty to move it all in here. Not a cracker trembled.

Everything sat perfectly laid out, with swirls of sliced cheeses, fruits, and cut meats rolled up like flowers. The lady at the charcuterie shop had not charged enough for this. I took several photos and planned on writing an epic review for the food.

Indigo flew over the table, careful not to land on it.

The young book dragon's gaze kept going to the other tables, the ones set with mountains of brownies and cookies. They looked a lot less fancy, but that was because I had pulled them together.

I could smell the sugar from here, and my mouth watered. The brownies were chocolaty, rich, and the edges looked slightly crunchy. They were going to be a bestseller in the shop. There was no doubt about it. I could keep them stocked on the counter under a cake dome. They went with coffee just way too well.

Speaking of coffee, I moved closer to Betty. She gleamed in the back of the room, not in her normal spot. The front of the shop felt weird without her there, but a duplicate of the counter sat in the back of the giant room, next to the large archway that led to the front of the shop.

Indigo chirped.

"We have time," I answered. "Until I say I'm ready, the door won't unlock. I just want to make sure everything looks perfect."

I spun around, looking toward the front of the room. For that area, I had to trust the Cat. The very front had a slightly raised stage area, while terraces surrounded the stage in half circles. The terraces had comfortable lounge chairs, almost like love seats, on them, with a large space surrounding each chair. Some spaces had more than one chair, almost like couches instead.

I tested one toward the back to make sure it was comfortable.

A sigh escaped my lips, and Indigo chirped again.

"I'm good, just nervous. This is a big event."

"You have nothing to be nervous about," said the Cat, his green eyes glowing as he gazed at me. His dark form stood in the middle of the archway. "It is almost time. Do you want to be in here or in the front?"

I hurried toward the archway, away from the secondary counter at the back. "In the front, at least until Lord Bennit is here."

"You know, we can have the door to the shop open directly into this room," added the Cat.

I paused and glanced around the space. "That might make the most sense."

Instead of heading farther toward the archway, I turned around and moved back toward the back counter. The wood gleamed under my hands as I rested them near Betty. I took a deep breath and let it out.

Indigo flew directly at me and crashed into my chest since she didn't want to let go of her MP3 player. I wrapped my hands around her and anchored her to my shoulder.

The Cat jumped up on the counter. The archway opened right in front of the counter with Betty on it. Automatically, I started pulling an espresso shot to give my mug a refill.

"I'll take a coffee as well," said the Cat.

Indigo didn't say anything, but I pulled out two teacups from under the bar. I didn't know if these were duplicates from the other counter, or if this was the same counter, just in two places somehow. Still, I made a simple vanilla latte for me and the Cat then a hot chocolate for Indigo. The Cat almost dove into his drink, but instead of watching him, I gazed at the archway. It hadn't changed; it still looked like it opened to the shop.

Indigo stayed hidden under my hair. I carefully took a sip out of my mug, letting the heat from it relax me.

Finally, I nodded.

The Cat sat next to his coffee cup, and the sound of the front door unlocking echoed through the space. Then the bells over the door jingled.

Lord Bennit walked through the archway with a smile on his face, entering directly, without going through the shop. It looked weird, but I was glad it worked.

Somehow, the ancient dragon appeared even younger. His bright-blue eyes traced over the space, including the tables of snacks in the back. His white hair almost sparkled in the light. The blue robes surrounding him swirled.

Then I noticed the person behind him.

He had the same blue eyes, but his hair was dark. His robes were blue but a slightly different shade. He snapped his gaze toward us instead of around the room, but he paused to let Lord Bennit approach first.

"You have outdone yourself," said Lord Bennit. "This looks perfect."

"Thank you," I said with a smile. "Can I get either of you some drinks?"

"Let them know that water is also at each of the seats," said the Cat.

The sudden interjection threw me off my game a little, but I nodded.

"Water is provided at each seating place."

Lord Bennit nodded and moved closer to the counter. He motioned to the man still standing slightly behind him. "This is my son, Adre. He is my right wing, you could say."

I gave Adre a nod and a smile.

His gaze went to the dragon hiding under my hair before looking away when Indigo flinched.

"I will claim an area for our kin," said Adre.

He bowed to his father before heading toward the steps and starting down toward the front.

"I would love a cup of tea, if you have it," said Lord Bennit.

An electric kettle appeared next to Betty, out of view of Lord Bennit. I only noticed it because of the sudden movement out of the corner of my eye.

I pulled out a large bright-blue mug and a tea ball. "Just a black tea or something fancy?"

"Surprise me." He turned toward the front of the room, watching Adre taking a seat next to the stage off to the right in one of the areas with multiple couches.

A canister labeled *Dragons* appeared under the counter, and I glanced sharply at the Cat. He watched Lord Bennit intently. I made the tea according to the directions on the inside lid of the container. The tea leaves vanished when I mixed them into the water, so I put the tea ball away.

"Here you go," I said, setting the mug closer to Lord Bennit.

His nose twitched, and his smile grew even wider.

"Thank you." He picked up the mug and took a sip. "You continue to surprise me."

He turned toward the archway. "More will arrive soon. The opening will be a welcome to everyone attending, plus some general chitchat. The first genuine item on the agenda is the story players, then this afternoon will be about Indigo."

I nodded.

"If anyone gives you trouble, just let me know. You are an honored friend." He gazed at me with his blue eyes until I nodded again. Then he glanced at the hidden space that contained Indigo. "She is getting good at shadow magic. You are doing well, little one."

Indigo chirped. It was the first time she'd made a sound since the dragons had entered the shop.

Lord Bennit chuckled, a warm, happy sound. "Well, Sable might not know about dragon magic. It's why she wouldn't notice. Plus, Sable is special in her own right. It might not work on her."

The Cat chuffed.

Lord Bennit chuckled again and then headed toward the stairs. "This will be fun!"

I remembered Indigo sleeping behind the counter when Sandra had come. Maybe that was why the Cookie Master hadn't reacted? Yet, I still saw her just fine.

Lord Bennit might be right, I didn't think it worked on me. And I couldn't help but wonder why.

FIFTY-FIVE

As soon as Lord Bennit stepped away from the counter, I whispered to the Cat. "Shadow magic?"

"Indigo uses it to hide from regular customers. She is very good at it for someone of her age. Her size also helps."

Indigo chirped twice at the Cat, whose tail flicked in the air. She stayed hidden under my hair, but she nudged my chin.

"She wants the hot chocolate, but doesn't want to move," added the Cat.

I rolled my eyes as I picked up her tiny teacup and held it awkwardly up near my shoulder. Nothing got on my shirt as she stuck her head into the cup. I set it back down when half of it was gone.

It was an extra small teacup for a reason. Last time I'd used one of my mugs, she swam in the hot chocolate as she drank it. That had been just wrong, reminding me of a kids' movie or something.

Shadows appeared in the doorway as three more

people walked in. None of them paid any attention to us. Instead, they headed directly toward the seats, like students who wanted to get the front row on the first day of class. They didn't give off the same feeling as Lord Bennit, and each of them felt young.

Then again, I could be completely wrong. And even if they were young, I had no idea what that meant really. They chatted to each other in that soft language that Indigo knew and that I couldn't translate.

Several minutes after that, a steady stream entered the archway. Their eyes and clothes represented all the colors of the rainbow, plus some blacks, whites, and even metallic colors. Some stopped for coffee or nodded at the Cat. Others headed to the snack tables or toward the brownies. A few skipped all of that and went straight toward the seats.

I recognized one person when she smiled at me. Lady Borsal, with her bright-orange eyes, headed directly to my counter.

"Sable, Indigo, Cat." She nodded at each of us in turn. "How are you doing today?"

She leaned back on the counter, facing the front of the room, but I didn't mind. The number of dragons wanting drinks had subsided, and most who hadn't rushed to get seats at first now slowly settled in and headed for chairs or couches.

"Things are going smoothly," I said. "Would you like a coffee?"

"Not today. I want to be clear-headed for this conclave." She glanced over her shoulder at me. "Not that your coffee isn't amazing. It is. I just don't need a caffeine buzz."

I chuckled. "I don't think I get one anymore. I just drink too much of it."

Indigo chirped, and her head poked out of my hair.

"Ah, little one, you're getting good at that," said Lady Borsal with a sharp grin. "You like the chocolate drinks? Those are too sweet for me."

"She would love a good chocolate drink," rumbled an old voice.

My head snapped toward the archway, where the oldest person who had entered so far stood. Her bright-purple eyes glowed with laughter, and white hair covered her head. She stood about my height and clearly looked older than even Lord Bennit.

Indigo rapidly started chirping.

"Yes, yes, you are the same type of dragon I am." A soft smile covered the woman's mouth as she approached.

Lady Borsal bowed her head. "Honored Elder, it is good that you honor us at this conclave."

Her head stayed lowered until some signal passed between them that I couldn't see.

"Ah, I wouldn't miss it," she said after Lady Borsal raised her head.

She turned her gaze to me, and it felt like my soul was being examined.

"You're the one to thank for these little things." She held up one of the MP3 recorders. "I've been telling stories for days, our oldest histories, both the good and the bad."

Indigo moved out from under my hair and jumped down to the counter. She carried her MP3 player in one claw. She held it up, then glanced at me and the recorder.

The Elder chuckled. "Yes, I will make sure you get a copy. All the young ones will, though I expect more Elders and young ones to show up anytime now."

Her gaze traveled to the Cat, who gave her a nod. "Ah, I wondered when I would see you, Lord."

She nodded several times at the Cat and spoke that language I couldn't understand. It tickled at the back of my mind, like the magic of the shop tried to translate it, but it couldn't.

The Cat's eyes went wide, then he slowly blinked. "Thank her for me, Sable."

"I caught that. Don't you worry," said the Elder. "The Fates will not restrict me. They tried once, and now they respect me instead."

The Cat twitched, but he stayed seated.

Indigo chirped again, drawing the attention of the Elder.

"Of course. We have a few young ones coming. While Bennit asked for the entire Clan to come, many of the youngest and oldest are in hiding. Being protected, they are. This would be too good of a moment for our enemies to attack." She let out a deep sigh. "But plenty will show up, and this will change the Clan for the better."

I couldn't help but wonder what a dragon would hide from. All that came to mind were the demons.

Her eyes sparkled. "It will be progress! Finally!"

A few of the dragons who had already claimed seating areas were chatting and glancing back at us.

"Time for me to take my seat and see what the young folks want." She smiled at Indigo once more, who held up her MP3 player with a soft chirp. "Oh, all right, you can get them first."

The old woman did something on her player, and a light glowed around it. The light then bridged to the MP3 player in Indigo's claw.

My eyes widened. "Woah, you're doing that with magic."

"Of course I am. I wasn't going to figure out how this new tech worked without it. I have many spells that use it now."

As soon as the purple light connecting the two items vanished, Indigo hurried back toward my shoulder.

"Thank you for sharing the stories," I said with a soft grin. "She listens to all the dragon stories she can, since they are her favorite."

The Elder nodded then turned toward the stairs.

Lady Borsal's shoulders relaxed when the Elder finally found a seat.

Lord Bennit jumped up onto the stage, and chatter reduced in the seating area.

"Welcome, everyone, to this conclave of the Lore Clan. Please, help yourself to refreshments and renew connections with others. I am expecting a few more Elders to show up, along with some additional members. My official agenda will start in several clicks."

As soon as he stopped talking, several dragons got up to join others, and the chatter increased.

"So, everyone is getting reacquainted?" I asked.

"Yes, he's waiting for the rest of the Elders to show up. They tend to come at their own pace."

I nodded at Lady Borsal, who turned in my direction.

"You impressed the Elder. She likes you. Good job."

I shrugged. "That's good. I'm just glad she seems to like Indigo."

Lady Borsal leaned in. "I bet she will offer to be one of her teachers, since they will share similar magic."

Indigo wasn't paying attention at all. She had on her modified headset and was already listening to one of her new stories, her eyes wide and her mouth open in awe.

"That's great news, right?" I glanced at the Cat to find him gone.

"It's fantastic news for Indigo. For the rest, well, as you heard, she isn't limited by much, if anything. But she is fair, and she likes you, so everything should be fine."

"Having a teacher like that will help her learn higher-level concepts with her magic faster," continued Lady Borsal. "I worked with..."

Her voice trailed off as four people entered. All of them had white hair and had that same heavy presence as the Elder. All but one of them had deep-purple eyes. They glanced in my direction, but headed toward the platform at the front.

One of them, a stately gentleman who looked quite old but still vigorous, had bright-red eyes, and Lady Borsal bowed her head at him.

He flashed a sharp smile in her direction before heading toward her. "Little Borsal, will you join me in my area? I'd love to chat with you about some new ideas I have."

To call Lady Borsal 'Little', just how old was this dragon?

FIFTY-SIX

"Of course," Lady Borsal responded with a smile and held out her arm to him before leading him to the seats.

The other three Elders were already seated in the same terrace as they approached.

That left me alone with Indigo, since the Cat still wasn't anywhere to be seen.

The chatter from the seats increased again as another group of dragons entered the archway. This time, I almost froze before I tapped Indigo to get her attention. Two little dragons flew around this group, accompanied by two adults. One was a deep blue and the other was orange. The blue one was bigger than Indigo, while the orange one was her size.

Indigo peeked out from my hair and watched with me as the adult dragons guided the young ones toward an area right in front of the stage.

My attention snapped back to the arch again as

another person entered with a young dragon, this time on her shoulder. This one was a bright green.

They headed to the area with the other two young dragons, leaving the youngling there before the adult headed to talk to other adults.

The next couple of people didn't have young dragons. They stopped at the snack table.

Indigo climbed down from my shoulder and glanced over the edge of the counter at the group of young dragons playing on the couch. They were flying about, chirping, and looked like they were playing some sort of game.

"You can join them, you know," I whispered to Indigo. "You can make friends."

Indigo said nothing, but her tail stuck straight out, pointed behind her.

I glanced over the crowd and caught the gaze of one of the Elders with the purple eyes as she glanced in our direction. I pointed at Indigo, then the young dragons. The Elder nodded with a smile.

"See? The Elder says you can. I bet you will have fun."

Still, it wasn't enough to get her moving.

"I bet you are the first one with a story player, and you can tell them all about it."

That got her staring at me, then the MP3 player, which rested on the counter. Instead of picking it up, she nudged it closer to me.

"I'll keep it safe. No one will take it from here."

Indigo nodded, then launched herself in the air, flying toward the group of kids.

A few dragons noticed but quickly looked away as

Lord Bennit glared at them. Still, I could tell people were watching the unknown dragonet.

She made it to the couch that the others were playing on and joined in. As far as I could tell, the other little dragons didn't have a problem with it at all. They mostly seemed happy another had joined them.

A weight I didn't know I was carrying slid off my shoulders, and I let out a breath.

Now I truly was left alone at the back with nothing really to do. I wondered where the Cat was, but he'd seemed very spooked with the Elder. Hopefully, he'd show up again.

No one else arrived, and I grabbed my handy stool to sit behind the counter. My coffee mug was still warm, and I took several sips while watching the crowd below.

Eventually, I pulled the drawing of the shield out of my back pocket and laid it out on the counter. It still wasn't right, but it was closer than the last time I'd worked on it. Betty wanted me to figure out what it meant, and that was what I needed to do. Yet, I didn't know where to even start.

It didn't take long for Lord Bennit to appear back on stage.

"Ah, it seems everyone is here. Welcome to our conclave! It has been many years since we have gathered. It was time. While I wish everyone was here, I understand why some are not." His gaze flicked around the room. "It is good to see someone from every family line, and almost all our Elders."

He nodded at the group of Elders. "I called this

conclave because of a new item that was found that has the ability to spread our stories."

Lady Borsal stood, and she held up the recorder. "I have spent the last several weeks recording our oldest tales. Those passed down to me from my grandmother, and her grandmother. The stories of our beginnings."

Mutterings broke out across the room.

Lord Bennit held something up, and then the dragon language filled the room. The one that I didn't understand. Lady Borsal spoke softly, and it only ran for a few minutes before he shut it off.

"This gives us the opportunity to pass knowledge to our little ones, even when our Elders are far apart. Or when our scholars are lost in a project."

"How does it affect their development?" called out a voice.

I recognized it as someone who'd entered with younglings.

"Like normal, but it lets them listen to the story again and again. Not that I am encouraging our Elders to not tell our stories, but this lets the young ones listen as much as they want. We all know how they want to hear them all the time."

Chuckles came from the parents of the group.

"I'm hoping this will save our stories from being lost. We have lost Elders before it was time, and our histories have gaps because of it. This will let us stop that from happening again."

More chatter started between dragons.

"Let's chat about this in our groups. I will be available for questions."

Immediately, it got louder in the room as people moved about. A crowd went to surround Lord Bennit, while another surrounded the Elders.

Some got up and headed to the snack tables. I stood from my stool as a few headed in my direction for warm drinks. Most ordered some of that tea that Lord Bennit drank, which was a quick beverage to pull together.

The dragons chatted to each other in their language, even in front of the counter. Most thanked me before they headed off to stand in other groups.

Lady Borsal paused at my counter. "I'd love one of those teas."

"Sure," I said, grabbing her a mug for the hot water. "How come everyone broke off into smaller groups? I figured Lord Bennit would talk about the MP3 players for a while."

Lady Borsal chuckled, but to my surprise, a green-eyed dragon answered.

"Some of us don't have a problem with the MP3 players, as you called them. Sure, let's use them, some say, while others will want to chat for a long time about them. This lets the rest of us catch up with old friends and matters we care about much more."

I nodded to the green dragon. His hair was cut close to his head, and his eyes almost looked oversized for his face.

"What I don't understand is, why are you here?" he asked.

"Sable is the host of the conclave," said Lady Borsal. "We are on neutral ground here, protected by powerful magic. I'm sure you felt it when you entered."

He nodded with a frown as he studied me.

"She also introduced the devices to us. Sable is a friend of the Clan."

Again, the dragon's tall, pointed ears twitched, but he said nothing. He only picked up his tea and headed off.

It didn't take long for me to get several more teas in people's hands.

Lady Borsal stayed behind.

"What's that drawing there?" She pointed toward the rough drawing of the shield.

I looked down, realizing I hadn't put it away in the face of customers.

What should I say?

FIFTY-SEVEN

I tapped on the edge of the napkin. "It's a riddle I'm trying to figure out."

I met Lady Borsal's eyes, and she smiled.

"Do you want some help?"

I nodded.

"It looks like a Fey Lord Crest, one of the old ones. That should get you moving in the correct direction..." She glanced toward the archway.

The Cat appeared under the stone archway, moving slowly.

I slid the drawing into my pocket before the Cat moved in our direction. It took him forever to jump onto the counter.

"So many dragons are here," muttered the Cat.

I couldn't tell if he sounded annoyed or not.

Lady Borsal gave us both a nod then turned back toward the crowd.

"You okay?" I asked softly. "I didn't expect you to vanish."

"I had to check on something." He glanced at the dragons walking about, then at the small dragons flying around down near the front. "Is anyone giving you any trouble?"

The Cat turned to look at me, his eyes glowing green.

"No, everyone has been very polite. Indigo is having a good time playing with other younglings." I motioned toward the purple streak darting around the others.

The Cat snorted. "We'll see how long that lasts. I bet she gets annoyed with them quickly."

He moved closer toward me and sat right next to my cup.

I couldn't help myself, and I scratched between his ears. He purred and closed his eyes.

"Why do you say that?"

"Indigo is very independent," said the Cat while leaning into my touch. "She likes to be in charge, or at least feel that way. Right now, they are new and interesting, but I bet she will come back to us shortly."

I frowned, glancing over at the dragons playing.

"He isn't wrong," said the purple-eyed Elder.

I almost jumped. She somehow stood next to the counter, and I hadn't seen how she had gotten there. This Elder was a sneaky dragon.

"I didn't mean to scare you, but the Cat is correct." The older woman smiled in Indigo's direction. "Us purple dragons are fiercely independent and like being in charge. That's going to be hard with a few of the other little ones who think *they* should be in charge."

"At least she's meeting others that look like her and

can fly." I jerked back when Indigo snapped at another dragon, this one blue.

Then she tackled them in midair.

"Is that okay?"

"Yes, they're trying to figure out who is in charge." The Elder sounded like she wanted to chuckle.

A few other dragons watched the exchange between the little ones, including Lord Bennit, his eyes glittering in amusement.

"How serious is this?" I asked softly.

"To them, very. To us, it's interesting, or maybe entertaining is a better word. They have a long time to grow up. The blue has a few years on Indigo as it is." The Elder stepped closer to the counter. "But she is putting up a good fight."

The Cat nudged my hand, breaking my concentration on the fight. "The break looks like it's almost over."

The Elder chuckled, drawing my attention back to the fight. The blue dragon had backed off, away from Indigo.

"Looks like Indigo made her point," she said over her shoulder.

The little dragons began chasing after one another again.

"I'm going to grab some snacks then head back to my seat. The second part of this little conclave will be inter-esting." Her purple eyes met mine, and she smiled.

For an instant, I saw the dragon she truly was. She stood as big as a car, and her scales glittered a magenta color under the stars. Her wings gracefully lay against her back, with her tail wrapped around her. Scars ran along her side, a deep black contrasting with the shining scales.

In a blink, the vision disappeared.

I gripped the edge of the counter, and the Cat bumped into my wrist. I let my fingers relax.

"Dragons," huffed the Cat.

The two big groups chatting at the front broke up, with people heading toward the food table and the desserts. Most of these dragons stuck with water instead of coming to talk to me. Conversations in many languages started, and I even understood some of it. Most wanted to get their hands on more MP3 players and recorders.

The energy and excitement thickened in the room.

Lord Bennit headed in my direction, and no one got in his way. In fact, a few people stepped to the side to let him pass up the stairs. He spoke as soon as he reached the counter.

"I'm going to need a bigger order of these wonderful devices." He chuckled at my grin. "Everyone is excited to try them out. I already gave out what I had, but given the ones who decided not to join us, we need more."

"We can get right on that," I said, turning toward the Cat.

He nodded at me. "I already placed another order."

That was helpful.

"Next up after the break for food is Indigo," said Lord Bennit. His voice softened. "I will introduce her to the Clan, and then there is the test to take."

"Test?"

A purple streak headed in our direction, and my shoulders relaxed.

"To see who she is related to."

My heart froze in my chest, and the entire world seemed to pause.

"Breathe, Sable," said the Cat.

I sucked in a deep breath, and everything moved again when Indigo landed on the counter.

Frantic chirping directed at Lord Bennit made him smile.

"We were just discussing you and a blood test so you can find your family," I said.

The little dragon growled angrily at the older dragon.

"Woah, Indigo. He's trying to help. Just because you find out you're related to someone doesn't mean things need to change. We talked about this." I glanced at Lord Bennit to confirm.

"Sable is correct. I promise no one will try to take you away from your home." His words hung in the air, so forceful in their presence that they almost appeared in the air.

The Elders all glanced in our direction, and the purple-eyed one gave me a nod.

"You love Sable, and she is a suitable guardian for you."

Indigo calmed down a little, but quickly moved closer to me, chirping softly.

"Hey..." I picked her up, and she cuddled toward my chest. "I will always be your aunt. No one can change that. Even Lord Bennit agrees. Blood doesn't mean every-thing. Family is about the bonds you form by choice, and keeping them strong. That's like saying the Cat can't be family because he's a cat. He's still part of my family. Just like you are."

She chirped hesitantly.

I took a deep breath. "This test just means that you can find out if you have brothers or sisters or maybe more aunts or uncles. That's more people who want to teach you and help you grow strong, because that's what families do... Though, let's hope for sisters. I have all the brothers anyone needs."

Indigo chirped, asking about my brothers.

"I don't doubt that someday you will meet them, and they will be happy to meet you." I turned back to Lord Bennit. "So, what does Indigo need to do for the test?"

"One of the Elders will use magic and will need a drop of her blood. It will show her closest blood relatives, and then we will know."

CHAPTER

FIFTY-EIGHT

The purple-eyed dragon Elder made her way over to us.

She gave Indigo a reassuring smile and held up what looked like a crystal. "I just need to prick you, then the crystal will guide us to your closest relatives in the conclave."

Indigo stayed near my arm and nodded before closing her eyes. She placed her scaly head against me and stood as still as she could.

The Elder reached over and lightly pricked her with a needle. A single drop of blood gathered at the end, and she touched it to the crystal. The drop of blood vanished, and warm air pulsed from the crystal. The Elder's hand opened, and the crystal dropped, held only by a chain dangling from her finger.

Chatter around the room continued, with many not even paying attention to what was happening in the back of the room.

The crystal glowed, and I found myself petting

Indigo behind her horns. Her head twisted around to see what I was looking at. Then she realized she had already been pricked and tried to see where, looking at herself in odd ways before seeing the dangling crystal.

The crystal kept glowing, and a dark light cascaded from the Elder's fingertips. Her lips moved, but no sound came out.

The Cat moved closer to me, his eyes also focused on the crystal.

The Elder started walking down the steps. Lord Bennit followed her, keeping his distance.

As soon as they got to the stage area, he faced everyone.

"The second item on our agenda must now be addressed; the ritual has already begun. It is time to find out what Clan lines the little Indigo belongs to." He motioned to the Elder with a soft smile before stepping off the stage and joining his family to the left.

The other blue dragon moved close to him.

More magic gathered around the Elder, and then she transformed into a dragon. Bright-purple scales glowed under the lights, and her green eyes flashed. She was enormous, bigger than the whole room, but she also fit on the stage in a way my mind couldn't really accept. The strangeness was almost too much, but I had to know who Indigo was, just as much as she did.

The chain had tangled within the dragon's right claw, and her tail flicked behind her. Folded against her back sat giant wings, and her focus stayed on the crystal, which hung directly down.

My fingers tingled, and I swore I could feel the magic pulling together. The Cat nudged my arm.

Indigo froze as light sparkled out from the crystal. The crystal pointed to us in the back of the room, and Indigo shook. Energy gathered around her, reaching out to me.

Then the crystal moved.

It pointed to the left, right at Lord Bennit's family. Immediately, each of them spread out, making spaces between them.

The Elder dragon stepped closer to them, still staying on the stage in that strange way.

I couldn't see who the crystal pointed to, and I leaned forward for a better look.

Murmuring picked up as the Elder took another step closer. This time, two people stepped forward: Lord Bennit and his son. The crystal hovered between them before pointing to Lord Bennit.

Light flashed around him for a moment. Then the magic vanished, and the great purple dragon changed back into her human form.

Indigo chirped, not understanding why it pointed to Lord Bennit. Her question hung in the air as dragons chatted among themselves.

The Elder approached him, whispering, and the rest of his family gathered around him.

Indigo climbed up my arm, asking about Lord Bennit.

"I bet he is your grandpa, Indigo."

She hid under my hair again, nuzzling me.

"Just like he said before, you don't need to leave me. He promised." I stroked the top of her head. "Plus, grandpas are the best. They can teach you important things about life, and they always have the best advice."

Indigo chirped again, but I couldn't understand what she asked.

"She asked about *your* grandpa," translated the Cat.

"Ah. My grandpa was amazing. He taught me how to fish and stand up to bullies. Not to mention the best ways to get along with my brothers. He passed away last year, and I miss him."

Lord Bennit took the stage, and everything quieted down in the room. "I want to thank everyone for attending the conclave. It has been decided we won't wait so long before the next one. As you can imagine, this has been a shock to my family, as it brings up painful questions concerning my daughter. As we find more information, we will reach out to those who can help. You can stay as long as you want to chat, but the official agenda is now complete, and this conclave is closed."

As soon as he finished speaking, several dragons moved toward the steps and headed out of the archway. Others moved to continue talking amongst themselves.

Indigo stayed in her current location, perched under my hair on my shoulder. She hummed lightly to me then nudged me.

"I'm okay. I just miss him," I whispered to her. "You should get to know Lord Bennit. I bet he's an amazing grandpa."

The little dragons near the front of the room started flying around again, and Indigo noticed. She chirped once.

"Go play. We can talk more later," I replied.

She launched herself into the air, heading across the room toward the younglings.

Lord Bennit tracked her progress but didn't say anything or stop her. He slowly made his way up the stairs toward me. For a moment, his sharp eyes dimmed, and receded into hollowed shadows. Then he nodded to himself and moved faster. The Elder walked behind him, following closely.

"Sable…" he started.

"This has to suck for you," I said. "You just promised she could stay, and now she's your grand-daughter."

He sucked in a deep breath but nodded. Then he motioned to the Elder who stood with him, her purple eyes glinting in the light. The crystal still dangled in her hands.

"That is true, but what I said still stands. Indigo is safe with you, and I trust you to take care of her. With the crystal, I hope to find her mother."

My eyes widened. "Can you do that?"

"I can try," said the Elder. "The connection between the two of them is strong enough, and relatively fresh."

I nodded, hoping that it worked out. "What does that mean for Indigo?"

"Nothing," said Lord Bennit. "If we find her, she…"

"Will need time to heal," completed the Elder.

She gazed at Lord Bennit, her eyes soft.

I reached out to touch Lord Bennit's hand, which rested on the counter. "I hope you find her."

"Me too." His blue eyes sparkled, then dimmed.

Indigo landed on his shoulder and nudged the side of

his face. She chirped twice right next to his ear then launched herself toward me.

Lord Bennit glowed for a moment, and he responded in the dragon language.

Indigo chirped again then landed on the counter, turning to look up at both of them.

"She called me Grandpa and asked about fishing."

I chuckled. "I told her some stories about my grandfather. Though I don't know if dragons fish."

"Not how you would," explained the Cat.

He had stuck next to me this whole time, a calm, strong presence, just keeping me company.

"Think of a bear fishing with his claws," he continued.

The image popped into my head, but I did not giggle.

It was close, but I resisted.

SABLE MISSED HER FAMILY. That much was clear, yet she was dealing with the dragons well enough.

It took a moment for me to realize I was proud of how she was doing, especially dealing with Lord Bennit. The old ones were often difficult, but she wasn't having any trouble.

I sat there, trying to help any way I could, though I was more than ready for all the dragons to leave. They smelled and left traces of their power everywhere. While the shop would enjoy eating the lingering energy, it gave me a headache.

I felt sorry for Lord Bennit, though. The likelihood of

finding his daughter alive was very small, especially given Indigo was no longer with her. Mother dragons did not let their little ones stray far if they were alive to prevent it. Something must have happened, and I knew how hard it was to lose your children.

Yet I didn't dwell on it. There was nothing I could do. So I stood there, trying to will Sable to make the dragons leave. I couldn't do it, but maybe she could. She wouldn't, though. She was too nice, and while their presence annoyed me, I found I was proud of her for that, too.

CHAPTER

FIFTY-NINE

More and more dragons made their way out of the archway as Indigo chatted with Lord Bennit. She listened as he explained things to her in the dragon language.

I could only catch a few words here and there, but concluded that he was explaining to her about how they were related. And fishing.

The purple dragon had moved to stand near the archway, talking to other Elders as they headed out. She still clutched the crystal in her hands. It glowed every now and then as certain dragons left—those related to Lord Bennit and, in turn, to Indigo.

I stayed behind the counter and petted the Cat. He had nudged me twice after the fishing conversation, and I'd picked him up in my arms. It helped with the worry I tried to hide.

Indigo needed to know who her family was and how to be a dragon. I couldn't teach her that, but still. I didn't want to lose her. I loved her so much.

"She isn't going anywhere," whispered the Cat. "She loves you, too."

He said the words softly, whispering under his purring.

I smiled at him and looked around at what was left in the room. Almost all of the food on the grazing tables was gone, but there were a few cookies and brownies left. It shouldn't take long to clean everything up.

"Hey, Betty, do you think you can put the leftover desserts on a plate in the main shop?" I asked.

The grazing table sank down into the floor slowly. Then the dessert table did the same thing. The farthest parts of the room near the stage went dark, like the lights had dimmed.

The group of dragons near the Elder shrank again as a group exited the archway. Then it was down to three dragons, including Indigo.

Lord Bennit chuckled then turned toward me. "It is time for me to go, but I will stop by with news as I have it."

"Good luck," I said with a smile.

Indigo chirped at him then flew off his shoulder and landed on the counter. Lord Bennit headed toward the archway, taking the Elder's arm as he exited.

As soon as he passed through the archway, it changed. The opening now showed the inside of the shop, as it had before the dragons had begun to arrive.

An immense weight lifted off my shoulders, and the Cat jumped out of my arms.

"All right, I need some food," I said, taking two steps forward. "What are you guys's thoughts on food?"

Somehow, I had skipped lunch during this whole thing. It was early afternoon, and now my stomach definitely demanded food.

"I ordered Chinese," said the Cat.

I almost stumbled as I stepped through the archway. He jumped up on the counter across the room into his usual spot.

"How?"

"An app thing," he said, shaking his head. "I don't know if it will be correct, but they should be here soon."

I nodded in appreciation. I usually called in our order or ordered pizza via the app on the register. Not having to think about what to make was such a relief.

The Cat sat down next to a plate with some cookies and brownies on it. While I had baked a ton, there were only a few left for us to eat over the next couple of days. It seemed all the preparation had been worth it, though, and our guests had enjoyed what we'd been able to offer. That felt good.

Indigo flew across the room and landed on the counter next to the Cat. She almost hit the plate, and I swore her head hit a brownie.

"Actual food before a brownie," I called out.

Someone knocked on the door before I could add anything else, and I twisted toward it. The delivery man held up a bag, and I moved in that direction and quickly unlocked the door.

"Sorry about that," I said.

"No worries. Have a good afternoon." He handed over the big plastic bag then took off. "Thanks for the tip!" he yelled over his shoulder.

I blinked a few times then closed the door and locked it before heading toward the counter.

"All right, let's regroup in the kitchen so we can eat off real plates." I moved around the counter, and both Indigo and the Cat beat me to the island in the kitchen.

From there, it didn't take long to dish out noodles, some hot soup, and lots of various dumplings. It wasn't our normal order, but I didn't care. I found the sesame chicken and couldn't help but giggle. The Cat had ordered way too much food for the three of us, but I appreciated it.

Indigo loved slurping on noodles, while the Cat and I tackled the chicken and dumplings. Once we'd all eaten our fill, and Indigo took off flying toward her little hideaway, I put the leftovers away.

"Thank you for ordering the food," I said to the Cat.

He nodded, then hopped down from the island and vanished out of sight.

With the last of the food in the fridge, I headed upstairs. I was tired, but not in the normal way. Dealing with all of those people—well, dragons—had taken a lot out of me. Usually, social events weren't particularly stressful, but playing host to dozens of powerful magical beings must be something different.

I flung myself onto my bed and grabbed my phone. I opened my chat with my mom and sent her a quick message asking how she was doing.

The reply came quickly. *Good, but busy. How about a call tomorrow night?*

I sent a thumbs-up then stared at the ceiling a bit, letting out a sigh and shifting on my bed. A crunch came from my back pocket, and I pulled out the paper with the crest on it.

Lady Borsal had said it was a Fey Lord's Crest. Maybe it was time to find out what a Fey Lord was. My first stop was the *Primer for the Beings of the Tree* book. It might have something in it, and if not, I would ask Betty for any books we had about them.

My phone buzzed again. This time, a message came from Cyan asking if now was a good time for a call. I quickly hit the call-now button.

"Hey, what're you up to?" I asked with a smile.

I didn't immediately notice the book that appeared on my nightstand.

I SAT on the wooden table in my great room, staring at the Book of Fate. Warmth and light floated out of it, which could have been pleasant.

Right now, though, I would burn the damn thing if I could.

All these centuries, and I hoped that I'd be used to the capricious nature of the Fates. After all, it wasn't like frustration at the Book was a new thing.

Despite that, I couldn't help myself. My tail flickered in the air as my claws dug into the wood.

We had hosted the dragons and found Indigo's family, yet the book didn't have anything else to say about it.

Nothing. Not a clue about what I should expect next. Not even any real acknowledgement that this had been important or necessary, though if it was in the Book, it must be.

Instead of anything useful, it only said that tomorrow would be a normal day in the shop with a customer stopping by.

I jumped down off the table, twitching my tail as I headed for the cat tree Sable had bought for me. Perhaps a nap in the sun would help relax my mind.

After all, I didn't want Sable to notice my mood. I'd just gotten her calmed down, and I was pretty sure she was speaking on the phone with someone.

SIXTY

I marched out of my room toward the balcony with a smile. Today, I remained hopeful that things should be normal, or as normal as they could be.

Indigo flew over the railing, then started chirping.

I paused, then looked down below, my eyes slowly widening.

This... This was different.

All the bookcases were gone. All the woodwork, except for the counter below me, had disappeared. Stone replaced everything else. The floors and the walls looked like they were made of some sort of brick. Even the lights had changed into yellow crystals that glowed. Thankfully, the skylight above still filled the room with bright light, but it dimmed slightly as I took in the differences.

The room itself also appeared smaller. The far wall was somehow closer, with the area in the center of the room limited.

The door would open pretty close to the counter, much closer than I'd ever seen it before.

I hurried down the stairs, wondering who the heck would show up today. Someone who didn't like wood; that was for sure.

The Cat wasn't on the counter, and I quickly made myself an Americano before heading into the kitchen. That was normal, at least.

The Cat and Indigo sat on the island. Both turned to look at me as I entered.

"So, who likes all the stone?" I asked.

"After breakfast, our customer," answered the Cat.

His green eyes glowed as he turned to face the stove. Uncooked bacon and eggs sat on the counter, and I couldn't help but chuckle.

It didn't take long to make breakfast; the bacon was crispy, and I scrambled the eggs. Simple enough, but tasty. We finished everything by the time we all headed toward the front of the shop.

Bacon did not last long, no matter how much of it I made. It was hard to resist making more than one package when I knew the last grocery order had at least ten packages in it. The fact that I didn't have to pay for any of the food made it easy to splurge.

"So, do I get any more info than 'our customer'?" I asked.

"Can I get a coffee before we discuss work?" replied the Cat.

I rolled my eyes and pulled out his teacup.

Indigo chirped, asking for a hot chocolate. She kept glancing toward the area where her little hideaway was, but it had vanished. Instead, she stuck close to my elbow, and I had to be careful not to hit her while making beverages.

I went with the chocolate theme since it seemed like I might need some fortification. Two mochas, one in a teacup and one in my mug, then a hot chocolate for Indigo in a teacup.

She did not get a whole mug of it, no matter how much she looked wistfully at my large coffee mug. If she did, she would swim in it as she drank it, and hot chocolate would get everywhere.

Sitting on my stool, I sipped my beverage as the other two quickly consumed their drinks. I didn't understand how someone could drink something that hot so fast, but neither the Cat nor Indigo seemed to have any problems.

"The customer today is a special case. We are their last hope for items they need, and for once, I actually have them. Last time they visited, I didn't. It will be nice to fulfill the request," said the Cat.

I paused, sipping my beverage. "You mean, you sometimes have people visit, and you can't actually help them? Doesn't the book tell you to get the things?"

The Cat snorted. "The book gives instruction, but that doesn't mean we can get our hands on everything. Even being able to visit almost any world, time isn't always on our side."

My lips parted, but I still didn't get it.

The Cat shook his head. "Time is linear on each world. We can switch between worlds, but we can't go back in time. If we go too far into the future on a world, we lose that time in between."

I froze. It made sense, but another thought came to mind.

"What does that mean for my contract? Is the year based on 365 days in the shop, or a year on my world?"

"It's based on your lived time," said the Cat. "That's also why you can't leave the shop. Time could break."

Indigo chirped.

"If you leave, I don't know if you can come back," answered the Cat.

I thought that the contract was to protect not letting people know about magic, but now that I knew that I could mess things up with time, the restrictions made a little more sense. Same with why room and board were included. Protection and safety for not just me, but the various worlds.

"Are you ready to open the shop?" asked the Cat.

Indigo chirped before I could answer.

"That's my job," I answered, scratching her on her head. "Yeah, let's do this."

The door unlocked, and then several moments later, it swung open.

I'd slightly lifted my coffee mug, but I lowered it, trying to let my brain catch up with what I saw.

"Welcome to the Magical Emporium of Wares." The words spilled out of my mouth like rote as the creature moved closer.

Whatever it was, it had to be related to Swamp Thing from the old movies. It was mostly humanoid, with two legs and arms, plus a nub for a head, but they were made of vines and leaves. The being moved fluidly across the floor, and the vines shifted on their body.

"Do you have it? Have the Fates blessed my people?" asked the creature.

I glanced at the Cat. This was not how this normally went.

"Yes, we have what you need."

The Cat looked at me. "The metal canister behind you on the shelf. Pull it down."

I turned around, and in the place that usually held tea, now only one metal canister rested. I groaned as I hefted it from the shelf to the counter.

The creature quivered, and the vines retracted along the nub of its head. Two purple eyes that looked like petals peeked out.

Its gaze landed on the counter reverently. "The Life Tree blessed you for a reason. I needed to trust that. I am sorry I doubted you."

"Tell them I understood," said the Cat. "You can open the top."

I quickly relayed the information, opening the top of the canister. The smell of earth rose, and for a moment, the scent reminded me of walking through a forest. Then it was gone. Inside, pulsing green moss sparkled, and a green light rose out of the canister.

The creature shook with glee.

"You have found it! You have saved my people." The vines crawled across the counter toward the canister but paused. "May the Life Tree bless you with its power."

The wood of the counter glowed a soft yellow, with the individual grains pulsing with power, and Indigo leaped off and flew toward the kitchen. The Cat stayed put and nodded his head.

Each pulse of power pulled at me, and I couldn't help but touch it. Warmth washed up through my fingertips, and suddenly I saw the Cat's room again, with the book glowing on the table.

A soft whisper from a female voice tickled my right ear in a language I couldn't understand.

The Cat nudged me, staring at me with his green eyes. The glow from the counter had gone, along with the voice.

"Are you okay?" he asked.

"I'm fine," I quickly answered, before looking at the creature and the moss.

The Cat didn't look like he believed me, but he turned back toward the vine creature. "Let them know about the pebbles. They're inside the canister as well."

I peeked inside at the glowing moss and saw pure white round stones sitting on the edges of the canister. Nodding, I smiled at the creature. They took a step back at my look.

I quickly stopped smiling. "The Cat also included white pebbles. They're inside with the moss."

Every single vine on the creature paused, then slowly they turned to face the Cat. "This is a blessing we cannot accept. Our people..."

"We wouldn't offer them if you couldn't take them," I added. "They are meant for you."

"This…" The vines trailing over them moved again. "Gift. I have a gift for you. It will need dirt."

"Dirt?"

"Check the storeroom," muttered the Cat. "It should have what you need."

I turned and hurried toward the door. When I opened it, I found a small table with a green ceramic pot filled with thick black potting soil. I picked it up and headed back to the counter. The creature peeked into the canister, and pink petals floated out of them, fluttering all over the shop.

I crept forward before slowly setting the planter on the counter.

The creature closed the canister lid softly.

"Here." The vines on the counter pulled the pot closer, and more petals drifted out of the mass of vines.

Then the vines on their chest parted, and they pulled out a bright-pink and purple flower. Five petals surrounded a round pure-white object. A single vine trailed off from it. Carefully, they tucked it into the pot, then stroked the petals. The warmth of magic pulsed around the flower, and I couldn't keep my gaze from that perfectly round orb in the center.

"May it bring you as much joy as the offspring the moss and pebbles will give my people," said the creature.

They bowed at me and held the pose for too long before pulling up. The creature nodded at the Cat.

Then they picked up the canister and headed out of the small shop.

"Cat, did that creature just give us its heart?" I asked, as my hands trembled.

The Cat turned to glare at me. "What?"

"It looks like the pebbles from the jar, and they were going to be used to make more plant people. I assumed... Just tell me I'm wrong."

"Only partially," said the Cat.

I sat on my stool and grabbed my mug, still half full of mocha.

"Hit me with it."

"The pebbles help the offspring grow stronger, but they aren't required. Over time, they form their own pebble as they grow up. The moss is needed. Otherwise, they are lucky to have offspring at all. The planet they live on has slowly become inhospitable to them. It is time for them to procreate, then find a new world."

"And the kids will adapt better to the new world, right?"

"Yes."

I stared at the flower, hoping I wouldn't accidentally kill it. I wasn't really very good with plants.

"So we did a good thing today."

"A very good thing," said the Cat, rubbing his head on my hand. "We saved their race."

"What about the flower?" I clutched my mug tighter. "Do I add it to the ones above?"

The Cat chuckled.

"That flower is one of the most valuable magical plants in the universe. It will produce one fruit with a seed. That fruit, when consumed, will dramatically increase one's magical abilities. The seed, when planted, might become a Life Tree." The Cat jumped off the counter and headed toward the kitchen. "We will have some normal deliveries after lunch."

"What's a Life Tree?" I asked. "Wait, what do I do with the plant?"

"It feeds on love," said the Cat, "and they gave it to you. Keep it in your room."

A plant that fed on love and produced magical fruit plus some important seed for some tree that the Cat wouldn't talk about.

It sounded important. Too important to just sit in my room, but I wasn't going to argue with the Cat, who had already left.

I sipped more of my mocha as Indigo flew out of the kitchen with a brownie clutched in her claws.

She carefully landed on the counter then sniffed it before she ate little bites. She glanced toward the door and chirped twice.

"I just need to head out of the room, then it should shift back. Your cave will appear then." I picked up the small pot with one hand and the mug with the other, then I headed toward the staircase.

By the time I made it to the top of the stairs, the bookshop formation had come back. Indigo already sat on top of the bookshelf by the door that had her little hideaway on it. At some point, it had changed from a small area behind a vase to an actual small hole in the wall.

My room looked like it always did, but a sunbeam

landed on the far nightstand where it hadn't before. That would be the perfect place for the flower. Hopefully.

Yet, a book I hadn't seen rested on the top.

"Is that a new book?" I placed my mug and the pot down before picking up the book. "*Tales of the Feywilds...*"

I checked out the index really quickly, with interest.

I glanced around the room, knowing it had to have been the bookstore who gave it to me. Maybe this would give me some more information on Fey Lords and their crests.

The sunlight landed on the plant perfectly, and I swore it perked up.

Loud chirping came from below, and I set the book on my bed before grabbing my mug. I'd have to read it later, once I got a break.

From the balcony, the chirping sounded louder. It came from the kitchen, and I hurried down the steps.

The Cat and Indigo sat on either side of the plate of leftover cookies and brownies from the conclave. Indigo kept glancing at another brownie.

The Cat turned to look at me. "She wants another brownie..."

"Indigo, you already had one this morning. I can make you a better snack. The book said you shouldn't have too much sugar..." My mind raced, trying to think of something easy I could make. "How about BLTs for lunch today? I'll make extra bacon."

The Cat's head tilted, and Indigo chirped, asking what a BLT was.

"Oh, BLTs are magical. You have nice and crispy

bacon, with fresh tomato, lettuce, and a good white bread. Plus, a little mayo. It's one of the best sandwiches known to man."

"Magical?" asked the Cat.

"The closest we can get on my world, I promise."

SIXTY-TWO

The Cat looked intrigued.

The smell of frying bacon filled the air again, even though I cooked it in the oven.

I sliced a tomato on a cutting board, while the Cat and Indigo watched me with awe. Neither of them could slice things, and Indigo had asked more than once when she would get a Sable form. I made a mental note to ask the next dragon that stopped by about that.

I laid out enough slices of white bread to make four sandwiches. The Cat stared, and his tail flicked, but he resisted asking any questions. Indigo didn't notice.

The timer went off, and I pulled the bacon out of the oven. I let it sit while putting mayo on one slice per sandwich and adding tomato to that side as well. Then I added the lettuce before turning back to the bacon and using tongs to move it over to a lined plate.

I used paper towels to get the bulk of the excess grease off before laying the slices on top of the lettuce. The final touch was topping it with the untouched slice of white bread. The first sandwich I cut into four triangles and set in front of Indigo.

Despite her obvious enthusiasm, she waited to eat. While waiting, she danced in place, her tail swinging back and forth then lifting her front claws up. It was adorable, and warmth glowed inside my chest at the sight of her waiting for us.

The next sandwich went to the Cat, and the third to me. The fourth I cut into quarters as well, but I left it off to one side.

Indigo took that as the signal to dive in. Not literally, but she did her best to pick up the quarter and take a bite. She hummed in glee. The Cat didn't pick it up but ate in that weird, magical way, where bites appeared, but he didn't have food in his mouth.

I ate the first quarter in two bites. Crunchy, salty bacon, with ripe tomato and crispy lettuce—absolutely perfect.

We were quiet until we'd cleared our plates. Indigo plopped down on the counter, a few bites of her sandwich left and her eyelids fluttering as she fought off a nap. The Cat and I both eyed the last sandwich, and I set half of it on his plate.

"I figured we'd both want a little extra."

The Cat nodded regally before diving into his extra half. I finished mine off quickly as well before grabbing a glass of cold water.

"Thank you for lunch. While not magical, strictly speaking, I understand the sentiment," said the Cat.

I nodded and picked up Indigo. "Gonna take her up to her sleeping area."

The Cat jumped off the island and vanished.

I turned around, and all the dishes had disappeared already. "Thank you, Betty. You are the best!"

Warmth flowed up from my toes, making me smile. The shop was amazing, and I wished I could make them as happy as they made me. It reminded me of my quest to figure out the Fey Lord Crest.

I carried the snoozing Indigo up the stairs in my arms and into my room. I placed her in her cat tree and turned the heated blanket on before tucking it around her. Her little snores increased.

I smiled to myself as I sat down on my bed, wondering how to fill this weird lunch break. The book on the Fey Wilds caught my eye. I hadn't had the chance to really look over it, besides skimming the index, since Indigo had created such a racket while begging for another brownie.

Pulling it open, I glanced down at the contents. From what I could see, it had chapters on what the Fey Wilds were with some stories about them. It didn't speak of specific Fey Lords, just how things worked.

I read aloud the first bit. "*The Fey Wilds are a magical world, usually one of the most magical in any given branch of the Tree. Each land has a Fey Lord, a representation of the land itself and those it creates to live with it. These Fey Lords are some of the most powerful in any world. They are on the same level as dragons. Do not cross a Fey Lord, for even the Fates have difficulty restraining them.*"

I blinked a few times. "Well, I hope I don't run into one of those. The dragons are intense enough..." I muttered to myself. "But who are the Fates?"

The book continued to talk about how Fey Lords had specific rules they followed, but the rules themselves depended on the Lord. Lots and lots of information that contradicted itself. Then a sentence popped out at me.

"The Fey Wilds and Fey Lords are connected to the ley lines, which can lead to conflicts with the Fates."

This was the second time I had seen a mention of the Fates. The Cat and others in the shop had mentioned the Fates. They had everything to do with the glowing magical book that the Cat had. That had to be the clue. I needed more information and stories about Fey Lords and the Fates.

My phone buzzed, making me jump. I quickly grabbed it.

"Great timing, Mom..." I set the book down then answered the call. "Hey, Mom."

"Honey, I'm sorry I forgot to call the other night. It's been crazy here. You know how it goes with your brothers."

I chuckled. Something was always going on in my family; that was just how it worked.

"I wanted to know if you wanted me to ship your birthday present to the shop."

I swallowed hard. "That would probably be best. Though maybe Cyan can stop by for a visit? Or Umber?"

"Umber's the one in a bit of a pickle. He's trying to figure out a few things on the farm. You know him and how he's always changing his mind. Goals are only momentary directions for him, bless his wandering soul."

"What's wrong with the farm?" I leaned forward, my eyes wide.

My mother snorted. "Nothing. That's the problem. He's a little bored. I told him to think about babies, not changing what he's growing."

"Babies? I thought he was going to build a house on the farm... Is he even dating anyone?" It took a moment for me to realize my mom was laughing. "You're messing with me."

"Just a little. He's working on the plans for the house. There's talk of them starting the foundation next week. It should be quick to go up."

"I'm sorry I'll miss it."

"You'll see it during the holidays, I'm sure."

The Cat jumped up on my bed, making me jump. His green eyes stared at me.

"We have the deliveries this afternoon. Just a reminder." He nudged me, and I scratched his ears while mouthing, "Thank you."

Then he jumped down and vanished.

"My lunch break is almost over, but it was good to talk to you."

THE SHOP WAS GETTING TOO nosy. Making me stand outside Sable's room yet again while she had a conversation with her family.

Then the bomb dropped, and I had to figure out what to do about it. Sable's birthday was coming up. Clearly, the shop intended me to do something about it because it had put me here to eavesdrop on the conversation.

Was that a big thing for families? Her brother had mentioned a big party for his twenty-fifth, but I didn't know if this was a big one, or even what "a big one" meant.

I needed to find out.

Somehow.

SIXTY-THREE

By the time I made my way back to the counter, the shop looked normal again. The long row of bookshelves along the back had reappeared, with the large center table filled with stacks of books.

"I love this layout," I mumbled under my breath.

"That's because it's your world's layout." The Cat jumped up on the counter. "How about something cool for the afternoon?"

The Cat rarely requested a change, so I paused while thinking about it. We had plenty of ice in the cooler.

I turned around to look at the wall of teas and pulled down three different options. "Do you want fruity, citrus, or minty?"

The Cat tilted his head. "Fruity."

I put two teas back and pulled out a pitcher I hadn't used before. I measured out the loose tea into a bag then added hot water. Just around four cups would do it, and I set a timer. I had to think about how I would present this to the Cat. He couldn't use a straw after all.

Once the timer went off, I filled the pitcher with ice and some cold water before taking out the tea bags. I sniffed it and inhaled the scent of peach, plus some sort of berry.

With a smile, I headed to the kitchen. Inside the freezer, I found the real treat. I pulled out two packages of tapioca boba. Both went into the microwave, and once that finished, I stood back at the counter. The pitcher of tea was suspiciously ice cold, but I said nothing.

Instead, I pulled out a tall glass for me and a teacup for the Cat.

My boba went into my glass, followed by ice. For the Cat, I added the ice first then a bunch of the boba so it sat on top of the ice. Then I added the iced tea to both cups. The boba was already lightly sweetened, and the fruit infusion wasn't bitter, so I didn't need to add sugar.

For me, I pulled out a thicker than normal straw.

Then I moved the teacup in front of the Cat, careful not to wiggle it too much. "Here you go. Boba tea."

"I've seen you drink this before." He sniffed it then lapped at the tea.

"You can eat the black boba balls," I added.

His tail twitched, and then one of the balls vanished from the teacup. It was probably about the size of his mouth. Hopefully he didn't choke. That'd be bad.

"It's chewy," he said.

My panic vanished. How did he eat the boba?

"But tasty," he added.

I took a long sip of my tea, getting a few of the boba balls with my straw. At least Indigo still slept upstairs, so I didn't need to worry about her choking on the boba.

Once the Cat finished with his tea, he turned to look at me. "Ready?"

I nodded.

It didn't take long for a new person to enter the store.

"I think this is the right place," said the guy.

The blond-haired, blue-eyed, gorgeous man entered the shop with a box in his arms, plus a few envelopes on top.

It took me a moment to figure out who this was.

"This is MEOW, right?" he asked, pausing near the door.

"You found us! Welcome! You must be new," I replied.

He nodded, walking the rest of the way inside. "Yep, John got promoted, and I was assigned this route."

"He mentioned something like that might happen. I'm Sable."

He set down his package.

"I'm Adam. It's nice to meet you." He glanced around the shop, catching sight of the sign warning people not to upset the Cat. "He said there was an awesome cat here."

The Cat stepped closer to him, sniffing. Adam reached out, and the Cat nudged his hand before purring. I immediately relaxed. Adam was what he said he was.

"I better get going," he said with a smile.

Then he headed out.

"He's good folk," said the Cat as he approached the envelopes. "These are for you..."

My gaze still stuck on the door that had closed behind Adam. "What?"

"You got mail."

I shifted the box and picked up the cards. "Birthday cards from my family, though they're a little early…"

There were three cards, or what I assumed were cards. One from Cyan, another from Umber, and the last from Cerulean, which surprised me. He often forgot birthdays if he was traveling. I hadn't asked if he was home, but I bet he was helping with the construction for Umber's house.

"Early?"

"Oh, yeah, a week early." I chuckled. "Normally, my brothers are pretty late, but I think everyone's at home right now. I bet one from Onyx will come soon. Plus, Mom said she'll mail my present."

I put the cards together so I wouldn't forget to bring them upstairs, then I turned toward the box.

"So, what's in the box?" I asked the Cat.

The Cat said nothing, so I grabbed a box cutter and opened it up. The Cat jumped inside before I could peek.

"Ah, just some supplies." The Cat jumped out, his whiskers drooping.

I looked inside to see some stacks of paper, and more of the MP3 players and recorders for the dragons filled the whole bottom.

"Oh, we'll need to let them know they're in."

The Cat nodded.

I picked up the box and added it to the storeroom. "So, that wasn't hard at all. Though we have a new delivery guy…"

The Cat didn't look concerned. "They change every so often, but John lasted the longest. Hopefully, Adam will stick around."

"Can they always find the shop?" I asked.

"The shop shows up at the same place for the deliveries, and we know when they are going to happen," explained the Cat.

The Cat had been willing to answer my questions much more lately. I hoped nothing was up with him, but I was glad to be getting answers instead of only more questions. The conclave seemed to have done something to him, but I didn't know what.

"So, can we appear in other places on my world?"

"If needed."

I squashed the thought of my hometown, and appearing there.

THE DRAGONS WERE THE ANSWER. All I needed was for Indigo to ask one of them about human birthdays.

The timing of the arrival of the MP3 players was perfect. I just needed to be patient, and then I would have my answer.

After that, I could make my plan.

SIXTY-FOUR

I rubbed my eyes and stared up at the ceiling. My dreams had been strange, filled with dragons, golden light, and the Cat staring at me. None of it made sense, and I didn't feel like I'd slept much, yet I wasn't tired.

Even so, my bed was comfortable, and a small dragon at some point had curled up next to my right side during the night. Her little snores were adorable, and I peeked under the covers at her with a smile.

It was time to get up, though, based on the sunlight coming in from my skylight. The beam of warm light hit the beautiful flower on my nightstand, making each of the petals almost glow. The round white object in the center glittered.

Finally, I pulled myself out of bed and headed to the bathroom.

By the time I'd dressed, Indigo had vanished from my room. The door stood open a crack. I chuckled as I headed out onto the balcony, excited to see what type of day I would have.

The shop looked different. The tall bookshelves were the same, but everything else wasn't. More tables filled the space, along with other objects like dressers. Each flat surface had things on it like bottles, books, or signs. The front display had changed, and beside the wingback chair stood a lamp along with a large planter.

I shook my head, trying to figure out what it reminded me of as I headed downstairs. My first stop was the coffee machine, Betty. She, along with the counter, stayed the same, and I quickly made a latte before heading into the kitchen.

Then it dawned on me. An antique store—that was what the shop reminded me of. My fingers twitched, wanting to dive into the stuff and see what treasures I could find.

Antiquing was one of those things I did with my mom. We would spend hours checking out new shops near and far during high school. I loved the thrill of the hunt, finding an old quilt or the perfect coffee mug. Maybe I'd have time after breakfast to do a little browsing.

The Cat sat at the counter, staring into the open fridge. "We forgot to do the shopping."

"What?" I paused, thinking of the last time I'd placed a grocery order.

It had been well before the conclave. While we had a ton of bacon in the freezer, we'd run out of eggs.

"Well, we can do cereal with milk, and I can place an order this afternoon."

The Cat nodded.

I pulled a box of cereal out of the cupboard, along with three bowls, one smaller than the others.

"Do you know where Indigo is?"

"Listening to a lesson in her hut," answered the Cat. "She received a new one this morning from that Elder."

I nodded, wondering how the dragon magic sent the stories.

"I'll get her in a moment, then." I poured cereal for each of us, followed by milk. Then I headed to the hallway. "Indigo, breakfast! It'll be quick."

By the time I ate my first bite, the dragon flew into the kitchen, her MP3 player clutched in her front claws. She landed better than last time, using her back feet more. She still had the headphones on her ears, and someone speaking filtered from them.

She moved toward her bowl.

I held up a hand. "You might want to pause that. If you ruin the headphones or the player, you will need to wait until I can get you a new one."

Indigo paused, glared at the bowl, then she took off the headphones and set the player down carefully.

Then she jumped into her bowl, too fast for me to stop her. Milk went everywhere, but nothing got near the player.

The Cat growled at her as he ate his own breakfast. She sent a sheepish look his way before gulping down bits of cereal.

I quickly downed my bowl, but Indigo beat both of us, draining the milk in her bowl.

The question of *where did all the milk go?* echoed through my head as she flew over to the sink to rinse off.

The tap turned on automatically, and she literally washed herself off in the stream before shaking off. Then she grabbed the MP3 player before carefully putting the headphones back on and flying out of the room.

"You're staring," said the Cat.

"That was impressive," I replied as I finished my own cereal.

"Dragons learn fast."

I nodded slowly. She used to not even think about the fact that if she swam in her food, she'd get dirty. Now she could clean herself off all by herself.

"What does today look like?"

"We will be buying...then selling."

"Okay, might as well get started..." I paused after standing up from the stool. "Do you think the shop has any quilts out there? I used to love hunting for nice quilts with my mom."

The Cat blinked. "No idea. I can check..."

"That would take the fun out of it." I set my bowl in the sink then went to grab the others, but they were already gone.

The plate with a few extra brownies and cookies on it still sat in the middle of the island. I grabbed the plate, along with my latte, and I headed back to the front of the shop.

The shop even smelled slightly dusty, like an antique shop. Those were some good days shopping with Mom before I felt overcrowded by my family, and everyone decided I needed to be meddled with.

"Sable, you ready?"

The Cat's question knocked me back into the present, and I nodded, setting the plate of goodies on the counter. I pulled out the glass dome from underneath to set on top. Less dust that way.

The door unlocked, and whatever open sign we had outside went into effect. The door opened almost immediately. In walked a woman who, from her puffy eyes and pink, slightly damp cheeks, had clearly been crying. Her brown hair was pulled back in a ponytail, and she looked like she was my age. She carried a cardboard box.

"Welcome to the shop!"

She nodded as she made her way to the counter. "Thanks. I saw in the paper that you buy stuff. I have some antiques and just some weird stuff I inherited. Basically, the things I thought I'd try to sell before the garage sale."

"Yeah, we can take a look and see what you have…"

"We?" she asked.

The Cat meowed, drawing her attention.

"Oh, you are so adorable." She reached out to give the Cat pets.

I opened the box to look inside.

"Just buy the entire box. Offer, like, $500," said the Cat while purring for the lady.

"How about I make you a coffee, and you can have a brownie as I look through things," I said to the woman.

"Oh." Her face brightened. "That would be wonderful!"

I quickly got to work on the coffee.

"Things have kinda sucked since my grandma died.

She left her house to me. It was all so sudden, though. I didn't even know she was sick."

I set the to-go cup in front of her.

"I'm trying to deal with her stuff as quickly as possible. I got offered a great internship across the country. At least if I can rent the house out, it will help with bills. But I have to empty it out first, and she had so much stuff!"

"Oh, I totally understand. You chase after that internship—they are invaluable." I grabbed a brownie and set it on a small plate before putting it next to her. "You dig in. Chocolate always helps. I'll look through the box."

"You could just offer her the money," muttered the Cat.

After she left, I'd have to explain social niceties to him yet again.

"She had these weird collections," she added, before taking a bite of the brownie.

Then she went quiet as she munched it.

I took my time looking through the box at the crystals, feathers, candles, and other things her grandmother had collected. All of it looked like the stuff people would sell in an occult bookstore. None of it looked special.

Yet I touched one of the crystals, and it shimmered. For a split second, it looked different. Magical.

I began to suspect that Grandma was more than a collector.

I touched one of the feathers next. As soon as my finger grazed it, it changed into a leather-bound book with strange letters on it.

Now the Cat's comment made more sense. All of this

was magical, but she didn't know it. The items in the box were all glamored to protect their secrets.

I turned to look at her. "I think we can take the whole box off your hands for, say, $500, if that works?"

SIXTY-FIVE

"Oh, that'd be great." The woman had finished the brownie, and the Cat purred under her fingertips again.

I moved over to the register, hoping the Cat wasn't using magic to make her want to accept the price. Though, given what I could see without touching the items, the box wasn't worth even that much. I counted out the twenties twice to make sure it was all there, then I pulled a bill of sale. I signed it, and she signed it as well.

"Thanks for this," she said, putting the money away in her pocket.

Then she picked up her coffee and headed to the door. It closed quietly behind her, the bells silent for once.

I slowly pulled things out of the box. As I set them on the counter, they changed. Feathers turned into books and scales. Candles turned into tools, and the crystals just became more energized.

"She really didn't see what all of this was... Also, just

offering her the money without looking would seem strange, just so you know."

The Cat's tail flicked as he looked over the items. "True. I hadn't thought about that. She was clearly a regular human who didn't know her grandma was a witch."

"How often does that happen?" I asked, frowning.

"More often than not. Magic doesn't always pass from parent to child, and it's safer to not tell the child about magic until they show promise. This is for worlds where magic isn't the norm, like yours."

"Wait, are we on my world now?" I patted my pocket for my phone, but I'd left it upstairs.

I'd stopped carrying it in the shop, since it really didn't work most of the time.

"Yes, though not in our normal location," answered the Cat. "You should leave the items out. The buyer will be here shortly."

After I took everything out of the box, I placed the box behind the counter. "That seems rather quick."

The bells on the door rang as it opened. In hurried another human, this time with a wide eyed look. She searched around the store before her gaze landed on the counter.

"Oh, thank the Fates. She came here."

That comment broke my normal train of thought. "Welcome to the shop..."

"Yes, yes." She hurried to the counter. "I can't believe that Hazel left the house to Alice without saying anything to us. We didn't even have time to remove any of the coven's gear! We all figured we had time to clear it out, but she's rushing for some reason."

I glanced at the Cat, and he nodded.

"Well, Alice has an internship offer that she needs to take. Renting the house is going to help her pay her bills in the new place. She sounded really worried and sad."

The woman let out a sigh. "I feel like we got off on the wrong foot. My name's Beth, and I am part of the coven that Hazel ran. Alice should know that we would take care of her... I'll send some of the others to stop by. She knows us as her aunties."

I nodded. "It sounds like she could use some family."

"We're all she has. Her mother passed when she was young. We've tiptoed around, making sure we didn't break the protection, since she doesn't have magic." She shook her head sadly. "I'm hoping I can buy all of this back from you. It belongs to our coven. We're lucky enough we figured out where it went. Some of this has been passed down for generations, even centuries in a few cases."

The Cat nodded. "Sell it at cost."

"It's all yours for $500," I said. "That's what we gave her."

Her eyes softened.

"Thank you for being sweet to her." She quickly pulled the money out of her purse. "I promise we will do better by Alice."

"I hope so. Make sure to give her a good hug."

Beth held out her hand for me to shake, and I did.

"Oh, you have some magic as well... I guess that

makes sense, given this shop." She hesitated before she pulled her hand away.

"I'm just a Shopkeeper," I said with a smile.

I grabbed the box, but she held up a hand.

"I'll just put the things in my storage. I have plenty of room." Beth put things one by one into her purse.

Somehow, it all fit, like magic.

She paused again and stared at me.

I almost asked what was up, but then she spoke again.

"I think this belongs with you." Beth pulled a bright-orange stone out of her purse. It hadn't been one of the items in the box. She nodded twice. "For the help you gave to dear Alice."

"It was just some advice."

Beth shook her head and patted her bag before heading toward the door. "Thanks again, sweetie."

"So, what did we accomplish there?" I asked, ignoring the fact that she'd said I had magic. "They were going to lose their tools?"

"Some of those crystals and books had been passed down for centuries. It would have been devastating for any coven," said the Cat.

"How did they let something like that happen?"

"No idea, but they weren't careful. They are lucky the Fates helped them out."

"Or helped Alice out..."

The Cat turned to look at me.

"Maybe it was her who needed the help. She got $500, and her remaining family got a kick in the pants to not forget about her, even though she doesn't have magic." I shrugged. "But who knows what the Fates are thinking?"

I picked up the stone, which heated in my hands. "And I got a stone that's warm."

Chirping from across the room caught my attention as Indigo dive-bombed me without her headphones on. She went directly to the stone and picked it up, even though it was almost the same size as her. Then she headed back to her hideaway before I could say anything.

"Well, that was rude."

The Cat chuckled. "Guess the stone was for her. It was a Dragon Stone, after all."

"Dragon stone?" I asked, but the Cat had already vanished from the counter.

SIXTY-SIX

Today, the shop looked normal enough as I sat on the stool behind the counter. The grocery order had come through yesterday, so I'd made scrambled eggs and more bacon. Indigo was sad all the brownies were gone, but I resisted placing another order for more.

My focus stayed on making another boba tea. It was supposed to be a hot day on Earth, but that meant little since more than likely, we wouldn't be there until the day was over with.

Still, I hoped after the workday, I could get some sun on the rooftop and maybe get some reading in. Several more entries had shown up in *Primer for the Beings of the Tree*, and I wanted to get caught up on some of the different species we had met.

I planned to read it with Indigo, since she had finished the most recent story that the Dragon Elders had sent over to her.

The Cat jumped onto the counter as I added ice to the pitcher of tea. "Can I have something with coffee?"

"Yeah." I nodded. "This is for me for later."

I stuck it into the mini fridge and tried not to think about how it actually fit before pulling up his teacup along with my mug.

I wanted something sweet this morning. A vanilla latte with brown-sugar syrup sounded perfect, and I quickly started on the latte part, steaming the milk with the flavors already added.

Indigo made her way over to the counter and chirped at the Cat.

"Yes, today is dragons," replied the Cat in a cheery mood.

Which was strange. He wasn't usually cheery about dragons.

"Oh, are they here for the players?" I asked.

Indigo started making chirps faster than I could follow, but I focused on the coffee. Caffeine first, then I'd get the players from the storage room.

Next came the espresso, and I pulled my shots first then more for the Cat. He only got one, and I added his second to my mug. Then I took a sip, enjoying the flavor.

"So, what did she say?" I whispered to the Cat.

He lapped at his drink before responding. "She's excited."

I tapped a finger on the counter and resisted glaring at him. Instead, I sipped my delicious latte while sitting on the stool. The sunlight blazed from overhead, and it gave the entire shop a warm feeling. It was magic that I wasn't sweating, and I appreciated every moment of it.

Indigo sat next to the Cat, her tail moving back and

forth across the counter. Her eyes stayed on the door. As soon as the Cat finished with his drink, the lock clicked.

I moved his teacup off the counter but kept my mug out. I had plenty of coffee yet to go, and it wasn't uncommon for me to have a drink in hand when customers came to the shop. It helped with the overall ambiance, if I did say so myself. The Cat could slam his all he wanted, but I would enjoy mine slowly.

The bells on the door jingled as Lady Borsal stepped inside. Indigo started chatting immediately. The dragon chuckled as she made her way toward the counter.

"Good morning to all of you." Her gaze landed on Indigo, who almost vibrated as she spoke. "And you are a very excited little dragon."

Indigo leaped off of the counter just before Lady Borsal got to it and flew around her head twice.

"How about we discuss the conclave first, then we can chat?" she asked the little dragon.

Indigo landed back on the counter with a smile.

Lady Borsal's orange eyes drilled into me as she gave a toothy grin. "You did a fantastic job winning over several important dragons in the clan. Lord Bennit said it was a success. He is busy, along with a few of the other Elders, tracking down some leads."

Her head tilted toward Indigo, and I got her point. They were searching for her mother.

"So everyone was happy with our hosting! Good! I'm glad to have met everyone's expectations." I knew I had done a good job, but hearing it from her helped.

"You did more than that."

"Are you here for the extra players?" I pointed toward

the door that led to the storeroom. "I got a bunch of them in, ready to go."

Lady Borsal shook her head. "No, that's the other reason I'm here—to tell you one of the Honored Elders has offered to teach Indigo about her magic. She will arrive at some point and will be the one to pick up the players."

"The purple-eyed one?" I asked.

"Yes, she has taken an interest in Indigo." Lady Borsal smiled at the little one. "You are very lucky. She is the strongest dragon in the Clan."

Indigo chirped twice in agreement. Then she asked a question.

"Lord Bennit will be by as well, but not as soon as the Elder. He wants to spend time with you. Don't you worry."

I really wished I could hear both sides of the conversation, but I could follow along well enough.

"Will I need to set anything up for when the Elder visits?"

Lady Borsal gave me a soft smile. "I don't have any suggestions. You did well at the conclave; follow those instincts."

Indigo jumped up on Lady Borsal's arm and climbed up her shoulder.

"All right, this one has a ton of questions."

I nodded and stood. "There is a chair in the reading area over by the kids' books." I motioned toward the correct area of the bookstore. "You can get comfortable there. Do you want anything to drink?"

Lady Borsal shook her head. Indigo was already chatting faster than I could follow. She headed toward the reading area, so I sat back down.

"Well, that was easy…" I muttered.

"Dragons are never easy to deal with."

I scratched the Cat's head as he moved closer to me and my mug. "Don't think I'm going to share just because you finished your coffee already."

The Cat chuckled. "I had my fill."

My eyes stayed glued on Lady Borsal and Indigo on her shoulder. From here, I couldn't hear what they talked about.

"I hope Indigo learns what she needs to. I don't want her to be behind others her age because she's here," I whispered.

The Cat head-butted me.

"Don't be stupid. It is beneath you." He paused, staring at me. "Dragons live a long time. There is no such thing as a dragon being behind, not in any terms mortals could really understand."

I could hear the conversation between Lady Borsal and Indigo from the counter when Sable wasn't saying idiotic things. She nodded at me, and I let her keep petting me.

Indigo played her part well, and Lady Borsal promised to find out more about how humans on Earth celebrated birthdays. So far, we knew they involved cards, along with gifts, but I needed more.

It needed to be perfect.

I purred, knowing it wouldn't be much longer.

CHAPTER

SIXTY-SEVEN

It felt cozy when the shop was in my favorite arrangement. We were on Earth and would be doing something rather normal today. Deliveries, maybe, or at least something involving humans.

Not that getting to meet other species wasn't fun, but I had a bit of a headache that I prayed would go away, and it would be nice to not have to worry about the weird.

The Cat lapped at his coffee, slower than normal.

I clutched my mug to my chest and watched as Indigo napped. She'd asked for a basket to sleep in, so she slept on the floor hidden behind the counter. Ever since the BLTs, she had been sleeping more. My assumption was that she was growing again.

This time, I wasn't sure how much she would grow. All of those stories she listened to helped feed her soul, which was good, but I worried about how she would feel about not fitting in her hideaway anymore.

The Cat finished his coffee, and I moved the teacup

under the counter. He crept closer to me like he didn't want to spook me. Then he licked my hand that held the teacup.

For a moment, I couldn't believe he had done it, then I realized my headache had gone. I couldn't even put two words together to thank him as I quickly inhaled at the sensation.

The Cat had magicked my headache away. Magic was amazing.

"Are you ready for today?" he asked.

I nodded, and the door unlocked.

The bells jangled as the door shot open, and Molly dashed inside.

I petted the Cat in thanks for getting rid of the headache as Molly's giggles filled the store. She headed to the children's section with glee.

I grabbed a small to-go cup, along with a larger one, and started on a hot chocolate and a coffee for her father. I glanced up in time to see her flop to the floor and pull a book on dinosaurs off the shelf before flipping through it.

Yet as the bells rang again, it wasn't her father who entered. Instead, a woman with short brown hair and eyes that held a panicked expression walked in. She caught sight of Molly, and her shoulders relaxed.

"Molly, you need to be careful about racing ahead," she called out to the girl.

Molly completely ignored her.

That wasn't good.

I kept going on the hot chocolate and the coffee, though I wasn't sure if the woman would want it.

She slowly walked over to where Molly was and

squatted down next to her. "We need to get to school before the bell rings."

Molly ignored her again, and the woman gritted her teeth before standing up with a snap.

I had to do something.

"Hey, Molly," I called, keeping my voice nice and sweet. "I have your hot chocolate ready to go, but you gotta get moving so you aren't late for school!"

The little girl glanced my way with a big smile, then she carefully put the book back on the shelf. It was the same one she always looked at first, and I swore it was also the one she had bought for her birthday. Molly got off the floor, dodging around the big table in the center of the room, and darted up near my counter.

"Really?" she asked, her eyes almost glowing as she peeked over the counter.

"Of course," I said with a smile, pointing to the small to-go cup. "It has whipped cream on top, but it will be warm. Just be careful with it and make sure you listen to..."

I glanced at the woman, who quickly mouthed, "Aunt."

"Your aunt."

The girl's hands crept to the edge of the counter, but I didn't hand it over yet. Her aunt had to get involved, or this would not work. I wondered where her father was, but it wasn't the time to ask. Hopefully, he was okay.

I motioned to the larger to-go cup.

"I have a coffee for her, too. Do you think she wants it?" I asked Molly in a serious tone.

Molly glanced at her aunt then at the coffee cup, her

eyes squinting. "I think she likes coffee. Most tall people do."

"Well, that's good." I resisted the urge to chuckle at the "tall people" comment.

"I'd love a coffee," said her aunt with a look of relief after glancing at her watch. "We should have just enough time to walk the rest of the way to school."

She held out her credit card, and I pointed to the reader. She tapped it and then picked up the coffee along with the hot chocolate. Molly carefully took the hot chocolate from her with both hands.

"What do you say?"

"Thank you, Miss Sable."

"Of course, Molly. Have a great day at school."

Molly walked beside her aunt and out the door, which closed quietly behind them.

I glanced down at the Cat. "So, what's the deal with Molly?"

The Cat didn't answer, but his tail flicked in the air. I shook my head at the non-answer but scratched behind his ears, which he liked.

"How about another cup of coffee?"

This time, he nodded, and I pulled his teacup back out.

As I started working on it, I noticed the children's section had disappeared. "Oh, so we have another visitor this morning?"

The Cat nodded, but flicked his tail.

I put extra effort into his coffee, topping it with more frothed milk than normal. Indigo hadn't stirred in her basket, so she was good.

I sat on the stool and sipped more of my coffee. With the headache gone, I felt more normal and hopefully ready for whatever had made the Cat annoyed.

"It's them again," muttered the Cat between lapping at the teacup.

"Them?" I asked curiously.

"The cat people."

I didn't need to ask more. Last time, an artist had shown up asking for art books. The experience had driven the Cat crazy. The people worshiped cats, and so the person's entire focus had been on the Cat. More than that, he had looked like a cat himself, which had clearly increased the annoyance.

I drank more coffee to prepare myself, yet as I looked around, nothing else had changed. The shop didn't have as many stacks of books as last time, and I had to admit I was a little confused as to what we'd be doing.

I shook myself and remembered that the Cat and the shop had been doing this a long time. They'd tell me what to do when I needed to do it.

I only had to hope no disasters struck that I couldn't handle.

SIXTY-EIGHT

The door was still unlocked, so I expected the next visitor any moment, but that wasn't what happened.

The Cat finished his coffee, and I finished mine. I ended up making a second cup for myself, with lots of cream and vanilla to prepare myself for this meeting.

Indigo kept on sleeping. Now and then, a little snore would grow louder, and I had to resist chuckling about it.

I caught myself just watching her sleep, then I noticed the Cat watching me.

"She'll be okay, right?" I asked.

"Yes, she is a growing little dragon."

"But will she get too big for the shop...?" Concern filled my voice, and the sunlight coming in from the skylights dimmed a little.

The shop reacted to my emotions, and I could feel like the shop could, and would, get bigger if needed.

The Cat chuckled. "She has decades before she grows bigger than me."

I glanced at the Cat, then at Indigo. Somehow, she was about half the size of him now, if I didn't count her wings spread out behind her. Hopefully, he was right, and she wouldn't grow too big too fast. As she was now, she wouldn't fit into a mug again because of this growth spurt.

The bells on the door jingled, and I snapped my head up. Yet all I could see was someone struggling with a large rectangle that had to be at least three feet by two feet and wrapped in brown paper. It clearly looked like a painting. He made it past the door before I jumped out from behind the counter to help. At some point, an empty easel appeared near the window.

Ideas sparked at the edge of my mind as the cat-person set the still-wrapped painting on the easel. He carefully used his paws so he wouldn't damage the paper while still managing to hold the painting.

He stepped back and glanced our way.

It was the same cat-person as the first time, with yellow eyes and brown fur. His tail had stripes, and this time, he wore an apron with what had to be paintbrushes stuck in one pocket.

The cat-person caught sight of the Cat on the counter and bowed.

This time, I knew what to do.

"You can rise," I said with a confident voice. "What brings you to the shop today?"

If only I could tell stories to my brothers. They would get a kick out of this.

"A present for Your Highness." The cat-person bowed again toward the Cat, but didn't stay in the position for long. "You have changed my life, lifting me up from my lowest to now being a renowned artist!"

I wondered how much time had passed from when he'd last seen us.

He nodded his head frantically. "I am Meser, the artist, at your service."

"It's nice to meet you, Meser," I said, after a quick glance at the Cat.

He sat there, staring at Meser.

The Cat's voice whispered in my head. "You kid…"

I ignored him.

"So, you brought a present?" I motioned to the painting.

"Yes, yes, I am now known as the Cat artist. I paint only the most holy." His paws clapped a few times. "I am not worthy of the honor, but the Holiness wished for my presence, so I humbly accept. That is why I am here. To give a present to the most holy for changing my life."

He moved toward the painting and tore the brown paper off the frame. Then he stepped back to give us the full view.

My mouth dropped open, and I resisted the urge to chuckle.

The Cat sighed in my head.

The painting was of the Cat. He sat on the counter in a beam of sunlight, his fur sparkling and his eyes glowing with magic. His form filled most of the painting, making him larger than life.

I had no idea how Meser had done it, but it was perfect. I moved around the counter to get a better look. The closer I got, the more detail I could make out. He'd carefully done each individual hair of the Cat's fur in different shades of black. His eyes were the perfect shade of green, and they seemed to glow, even though it was only paint on a canvas. It must have taken forever to get right.

Even the look on the Cat's face looked right. So much pride.

I wanted the painting badly. I'd hang it up in my room and keep it forever, even after I no longer worked at the shop.

Even the frame was ornate. Created out of some golden wood, with leaves carved into it along each of the edges.

"This is amazing," I whispered, unable to help myself.

Meser just about melted into a puddle.

"It's all right," said the Cat.

"The Cat agrees," I added.

Meser shivered in delight, and tears formed at the corners of his eyes. "I can only hope that you enjoy the painting."

I nodded before moving back behind the counter, wondering how the Cat would react. The Cat didn't add anything else, but I glanced his way like he had.

"The Cat accepts the painting and the honor of the workmanship that went into it," I said confidently.

Meser actually jumped for joy and clapped his paws together. He bowed again to the Cat, then to me.

The Cat grumbled in my head.

"Thank you again for your assistance in helping me

grow as an artist." Meser then headed out the door, careful to keep facing us as he moved.

The shop door jingled quietly closed.

"That painting is epic," I said. "I can't believe he painted it. How do you think he holds a paintbrush?"

I glanced at the Cat's paws.

"It is done well," grumbled the Cat, his eyes still locked on the painting.

I wondered if he knew that was what he looked like. The only place that had a mirror was my bathroom.

"It looks just like you. I have no idea how he painted it from memory. Meser was only here the first time for, what, twenty minutes buying that book?" I shook my head. "If you don't want the painting, I'll totally hang it up in my room. It's just so well done."

The Cat turned to look at me.

"You would hang it up in your room?" He blinked twice.

"Of course! It's the finest piece of artwork I'll ever own! It's hand-painted, has a custom-carved frame, and it's a great cat!" The Cat was crazy if he thought I would pass up hanging the painting on my wall.

"You can keep it, then," he said dismissively.

Mine!

CHAPTER

SIXTY-NINE

This morning, Indigo was awake. She buzzed around the kitchen as I made scrambled eggs and took the bacon out of the oven.

"The Elder dragon is stopping by today," said the Cat, leaping up onto the island in the kitchen.

Indigo's excitement suddenly made sense.

I stirred the eggs, doing my best to make sure they didn't get burned. I finally felt like I had perfected the art of scrambled eggs and bacon, even if it had taken me months. Though I wished I could cook it for my brothers; it might shock them.

Still, I missed Umber's cooking. Giant cinnamon rolls and pancakes, sausage, potatoes in all shapes. Umber was an amazing cook.

I bet I could make a decent pancake at this point. I'd learned a lot, after all. I made a mental note to try that later this week. They would be even better if I could get some berries to toss in them, and some real maple syrup.

The timer beeped to take the bacon out, and I quickly

set it on the stove to cool. I hummed to myself as I dished out the scrambled eggs onto the three plates, then I served up the bacon onto one large plate.

My coffee was still thankfully warm as I sat down to eat. Indigo landed next to her plate and attacked her eggs. The Cat grabbed a few slices of bacon first. I swore it was his favorite food. I also grabbed some bacon. It was bacon, after all. It didn't take long for us all to clear our plates.

I headed out front to the counter, but Indigo beat me, landing on the wooden surface with a trill. That sound was new.

The Cat jumped up after her, and with him providing scale, I noticed Indigo's growth. She had definitely grown bigger. She was a little longer, and now she was firmly half the size of the Cat.

Indigo turned to look at me again and then at the door.

"One moment," I said, moving around the counter to check out the space that had formed.

Ever since Lady Borsal had mentioned taking inspiration from the conclave conference room, I had been thinking about what shape the bookshop should be in for training with the Elder. The center of the room stood empty today, and the area across from the door was larger than before. The wall had moved back, leaving plenty of cleared space on the stone floor. In one corner sat one of the large couches from the conclave, and there were plenty of pillows.

The seating arrangement was the best idea I had.

"Hey, Cat, is this large enough for a full-grown dragon? I can't remember the size she was on the stage."

The Cat jumped off the counter and joined me in the center of the room. "Yes, she will have plenty of space if she takes her true form. She won't be able to fly, or even stretch her wings, but I doubt that will be a thing right now. She wouldn't be able to take her Elder form, but that's also not likely to be a thing today."

Indigo chirped, her eyes wide, and I swore she asked about the Elder flying.

That's when I realized Indigo might not have seen a fully grown dragon before. Mentally I sighed as I pushed the thought away. All the dragons I'd interacted with had kept a humanoid form. I assumed it was to keep me at ease. Even seeing the image of the Elder in her true dragon form had made my brain turn sideways.

Indigo, with her cute smaller form, just made me want to protect her.

"All right, then we should be good." I moved back behind the counter as the door unlocked.

The Elder walked in, the bells ringing in her wake. Her eyes glowed, and she smiled at all of us. "Good morning, everyone."

Indigo leaped into the air and flew closer to the Elder.

"Ah, you are excited this morning. That's good." She gazed over the area the shop had created and nodded. "This will work perfectly. I need to talk to Sable for a moment, little one, and then we can get started. How about you get your stone, and I can check it out?"

Indigo shot into the air, heading toward her hideaway.

The Elder marched across the store and stopped near the counter. "I heard you have more players ready for the dragons?"

I pulled the box out from under the counter where I had it ready to go. "It's a large order, along with some recorders for the rest of the Elders."

The box vanished as one claw touched the edge. Then the claw turned into a finger a moment later.

"You have done much for the Clan of Lore." She nodded at me. "You can call me Twilight Moment or Lady Twilight."

My eyes grew wide at the honor. Everyone had referred to her as Elder or Honored Elder, but no one so much as whispered a name. Names had power, as the Cat always warned me.

"Thank you."

"Of course. We are related, after all. Indigo is my great granddaughter. Well, maybe add a few greats." She chuckled at her own joke.

My mouth fell open. "She is going to be so thrilled to find out she has more family. I hope Lord Bennit understands, because she is now calling him Grandpa Bennit."

Lady Twilight's laughter echoed across the space.

Indigo almost dropped her stone as she shot out of her hideaway with it clutched in her claws. It glowed a bright-orange color, spilling light across the shop. Lady Twilight turned to face Indigo and held her hand out for the dragon stone.

"This will do nicely for what you want to accomplish," she said to the little dragon. "Let's head over to the training area and get to work."

She flashed me a smile, then the two of them moved over to the right to the big open area. They were close enough that I could see what was going on, but I couldn't really understand what was being said.

"It's a high honor learning her name," said the Cat. "I don't know if any other mortal knows it."

"Really?"

"The amount of greats she would need to add would be many." The Cat moved closer to me, within reach to give him pets. "That Elder is one of the oldest dragons left in the many worlds."

"Is she older than you?" The question slipped out.

The Cat's head tilted toward me to give me better access behind his ears. "Maybe. It's hard to know for sure."

I kept scratching him, trying not to let my surprise show that he had answered the question. Usually, he dodged questions about himself. Then again, he was much more talkative now than when I'd first started at the shop. It felt comforting.

After a couple of minutes, the Cat moved out of reach and curled up in a ball on the counter. He closed his eyes, and I assumed he'd gone to sleep.

I pulled the book out from beneath the counter that I read when it got slow. Given that this particular book was a little spicy, I had to be careful not to read it around Indigo. There were definitely some things I wasn't ready to explain to her just yet.

Time passed quickly, and before I knew it, my stomach grumbled about lunch.

Lady Twilight and Indigo headed our way, and the Cat perked up. His tail twitched frantically.

"This was a good session. We will need plenty more, but today's progress was good," said the Lady.

Indigo's eyelids drooped.

"We're going to have lunch here, and you are welcome to stay," I added.

Lady Twilight shook her head. "I need to head back to my home. Thank you for the offer."

The Cat steeled himself next to me, drawing attention.

"You should stay," he whispered softly.

Power blossomed out of nowhere, heading directly at the Cat. He froze, like he had been struck by something.

"Cat?"

Pain. So much pain I couldn't move.

I had to trust the dragon and Sable. It had to be worth it.

I had to protect Sable.

CHAPTER
SEVENTY

"Cat?" I asked again, yet he didn't move.

I reached out to touch him, but something blocked my way. It made my fingertips tingle.

I turned back to Lady Twilight, wondering if she had any idea what had happened.

Her head tilted to one side, staring at the Cat. Her eyes had gone completely dragon. Magic pulsed around her, distorting her outline.

My hands shook, and the skylights dimmed. Indigo chirped twice, asking what was happening.

Lady Twilight frowned, then nodded. She took a step back, clearly agitated, but tried to smile at Indigo. "Little one, how about you take the dragon stone back to your hideaway? Stay there and guard it until we say you can come out."

Indigo chirped but glanced at me first.

I quickly nodded. The Elder knew something I didn't, and she didn't want Indigo here right now.

Finally, the little dragon flew toward the far wall and the door before vanishing into her private area.

Lady Twilight took another step back, her form shimmering, then she vanished, except for her eyes. They hovered in the center of the open area, along with that strange power swimming around her, different from whatever surrounded the Cat.

The bells on the back of the door screamed as it slammed open. In stumbled someone in a red cloak, with dark eyes burning like coals. A pale face stared at me, and I realized who it was. The same man who had dropped Indigo. He had been the one asking about the cold book we'd destroyed.

"You!" He pointed a finger at me. "You must call them off. I can't go anywhere! I'm in hiding, stuck slinking from one hole to the next. Dragons are circling closer and closer, nearly on me!"

He actually stood here in front of me. Part of me couldn't believe it.

He stomped toward the counter and pointed at me with a clawed finger. "You will fix this!"

Molten heat flowed from my center to each of my limbs. Power pulsed inside my chest.

"You kidnapped a baby dragon from its mother." The words shot out from between my lips like a physical force. "You are working with the demons."

The man threw back his head and laughed. His form twisted. Pitch-black horns grew from his head, and scales trickled down his face as large sharp teeth formed.

"You know nothing of demons."

The demon, now in its true form, didn't notice the

dragon eyes moving closer, or the sheer, angry power flowing off the hidden presence of the Elder dragon at my words. He took another step toward me.

Suddenly, the form of a purple dragon came into view. Her wings were folded tight against her back, and she held her claws outstretched in front of her. The rest of her body clenched tight, making herself smaller than when she'd been on stage, yet she still filled the whole center of the shop.

"You will pay for what you have done!" My voice rang out again, stopping his forward movement.

The energy inside me waned, and the shop shifted around me, readying itself. Lady Twilight moved faster than I could have imagined. Her claws surrounded the demon, and a low growl filled the room that vibrated in my bones.

The hair on the back of my neck rose, and icy cold trickled down my spine at the sight.

Nothing remained of the strange but kindly older woman. This was a full dragon Elder, in all her power and anger.

Everything in me screamed to run, to flee this creature in front of me, but I stood firm. I had to believe the dragon would not harm me, and I had to be here for Indigo, for the Cat, and for the shop.

"This is the one my Clan searches for," growled the dragon.

I nodded, my words stuck in my throat as I managed to somehow still stay standing behind the counter.

The demon flailed, fire coating his body as his cloak shimmered. A tail flickered out, and magic appeared from his fingertips, spreading down his body. He vanished, but the dragon didn't react at all, only tightened her claws, making the demon reappear right where he'd been.

"Well, such a present you give to me, Lord. I will remember this." Lady Twilight's eyes turned toward the Cat.

He remained in his spot, unmoving.

She bowed her head, and then the two of them vanished.

Nothing remained. Not a trace of her magic, the terror, or the demon.

I let out a slow breath to steady myself as I almost wobbled.

"What just happened?" I asked.

The Cat didn't reply.

I turned to face him and took a step forward.

Then, suddenly, he collapsed onto the counter. It was like all the bones in his body disappeared and he turned into a puddle of black fur.

"Cat!" I touched his side and found him still breathing.

His body trembled, and I didn't know if I should pick him up or not.

I did anyway. I picked him up and held him to my chest.

"I got you. You'll be okay…" I whispered as I held him close.

What should I do?

"I'll be okay," he mumbled.

"What happened?"

He let out a sigh, his small head resting on my shoulder. "I disobeyed."

The words hovered in the air as I tried to figure out what he meant. Who did the Cat answer to? Based on all I knew, the only thing I could figure was it had something to do with the book. He answered to the book?

"And let me guess, you cannot say what you did?"

He twitched at the question but didn't answer.

I nodded and didn't let go of him as I sat back on my stool.

"Hey, Betty, can you lock the door? I think we're done for the day."

The front door's bolt snapped shut, and I relaxed. I realized we had one more member of our family missing, and I wanted all of us here.

"Indigo, it's okay to come out again..." I called out toward her hideaway.

Indigo's head peeked out to check before she launched herself into the air. She circled around us twice, chirping, but I couldn't follow what she was trying to say. She clenched her MP3 player in her claws as she flew upward toward my bedroom.

Once she was out of sight, I got up from the chair. My mind was still racing, trying to figure out exactly what had happened.

"Let me guess, you weren't supposed to ask Lady Twilight to stay, and that was the trigger..." I didn't even phrase it as a question, since it had been the last thing that happened before that weird power had gathered around him.

The book hadn't wanted the dragon to stay. That

would have meant I would have been the one to face the demon. Maybe even alone.

With the Cat still in my arms, I slowly climbed the steps toward the second floor, then I made my way down the hallway to peek into my room. Indigo lay in her cat tree, her tail sticking out of the hole. She didn't seem to be upset about what had happened at all. I continued around the balcony and headed toward the plants and the rooftop deck.

Bright sunlight spilled from the windows and warmed the space, and I sat in a chair next to the Cat's cat tree that I swore hadn't been here before. I scratched behind his ears as he eventually stopped trembling in my arms.

"No matter what, I am here for you, Cat."

SEVENTY-ONE

A teacup appeared on a wooden table that rose from the floor. Warm milk filled the porcelain, and next to it sat my dark-blue mug with the stars. Steam rose from each. I sent thoughts of thanks toward Betty, hoping the shop could feel them.

The Cat stirred in my arms, and his head pointed toward the milk.

I carefully set him on the table and grabbed my mug, wrapping both hands around it.

The Cat moved next to the teacup and lapped slowly at the milk, acting more like a cat than I had ever seen him. He'd protected Indigo and me, and in turn, the book had punished him.

Somehow.

Heat twisted and churned inside me and sat at the back of my mind. I smashed that sensation down, but I didn't let it dissipate. Right now, it wasn't useful. Normally, I could let things go, since I didn't like to hang on to negative feelings. This time, though, I kept it there. I'd use it later.

"You protected Indigo and me, which is part of what you do," I whispered.

The Cat froze, his mouth open, not daring to move. "Hush, Sable... Please..."

It was the please that got me. I nodded slowly. I'd let the conversation drop, but I couldn't let this go completely. He had protected us, and had clearly accepted a lot of pain because of it.

His gaze darted around the space, like he was expecting something else to happen. After a few moments, he went back to lapping his milk.

I took a sip of my drink, not even tasting it. The warm light coming in from the windows increased as I relaxed into the comfortable chair. The Cat hopped over to my lap, almost hitting my mug but somehow missing it. From there, he leaped over to his cat tree.

"I'm going to rest," he said as he crept into the little box with a hole in it and curled up in a ball.

I kept sipping on my drink, waiting. Eventually, his breathing evened out, and I slowly climbed to my feet.

Silently, I crept down the hallway toward the area where the door had been before, the one that led to the Cat's hidden library. I found it, almost like it was waiting for me. I didn't stop until I stood inside the cozy library with the giant table. The book glowed brightly in the center, golden light streaming toward the ceiling.

I glared at it. "How dare you punish him for protecting Indigo and me. Part of what he does is protect me, the Shopkeeper."

My hands shook, one still clutching my mug. I stood there glaring for another moment before turning away. The light flickered behind me as I fled.

I didn't turn back.

Indigo met me in the hallway, flying in the air. She landed on my shoulder, and this time, her chirping came slower. I could partially understand what she said. It had something to do with Lady Twilight and how strong her dragon was.

"She *was* pretty intense in her dragon form," I said.

Indigo chirped.

I ignored the fact that Lady Twilight had scared me senseless when she had appeared in her true form. Hopefully, if I ever saw Indigo that big, I wouldn't fear her. Right now, when she could fit on my shoulder and nuzzle me, she was just adorable.

Still, it was a good reminder that someday Indigo would be that big and potentially that scary. At least she had Lady Twilight to teach her how to be scary. I would stick to the bedtime stories and how to be a good person.

Those things I could do.

Unlike protecting the Cat, which it seemed I couldn't do.

That weighed on my mind as I moved down the steps toward the kitchen. I felt like I could eat a horse, and I wanted *all* the calories. That meant takeout, maybe something with noodles. Life was always better with noodles.

"How does Chinese food sound?"

Indigo chirped excitedly. She loved the wonton soup,

though I couldn't get her not to swim in it. I'd get some for her so at least she'd have her own container, and I already knew what the Cat liked. I pulled up the menu on the tablet on the register. Our last order popped up, and I added some extra egg rolls and spicy noodles before hitting submit.

It didn't take long for my phone to buzz that the delivery was nearby. I headed toward the door, forgetting about Indigo on my shoulder. The guy didn't even blink as he handed over the two large plastic bags.

I froze after the door closed, realizing it had been not even fifteen minutes before the food had shown up.

"What the..." I shook my head and kept going toward the kitchen.

The passage of time in the shop was weird, so I ignored it. Food mattered more.

"Hey, Cat, I got Chinese food if you want some."

Indigo leaped off my shoulder, beating me to the island and dancing around as I approached. Her favorite bowl for her soup already sat in its proper location, along with plates for the Cat and me. I poured the wonton soup into the bowl, and she literally climbed into the bowl, careful not to spill anything. She swam around, drinking the broth. I chuckled as I pulled out my container of soup.

Then the Cat jumped up on the counter.

"Did you get my chicken?" he asked, almost sounding normal.

I smiled, relieved. The Cat was okay, at least for the moment.

"Of course. You want the spicy stuff?"

He glared at me as if to say there couldn't possibly be any other type.

I quickly opened his container and poured a good amount of the spicy chicken onto his plate. I added an egg roll before taking one for myself as well. I couldn't help but giggle as Indigo attacked a wonton in her soup, almost like she was dueling with it.

The Cat flicked his tail. "I thought dragons were refined."

Indigo chirped, but her mouth was full, so it came out muffled.

"Maybe when they're older," I said. "After someone teaches them how to hunt... Wait, do dragons hunt?"

"Yes, they hunt. It's a big deal the first time they hunt in their dragon form."

"Not it," I whispered. "Maybe you can teach her with, like, a mouse or something."

The Cat's head tilted to one side, looking at me like I was crazy.

"It was just a thought," I said before chomping down on an egg roll.

Inside my head, I pictured the Cat trying to teach Indigo to stalk a mouse. I couldn't help the giggle that escaped.

The Cat glared at me, not commenting, like he knew what I was thinking.

That was okay. At least he was acting more like himself, and that had to be good enough.

SEVENTY-TWO

I woke up with a smile on my face while singing a love song under my breath. My dreams had been filled with romantic candlelight, a faceless person, and some superb dessert.

It could all be from the extra-long bubble bath I'd taken before bed. The bubbles had fascinated Indigo to no end. I added bubble-making to the list of activities to do with her one of these afternoons.

Downstairs, I headed directly to Betty. A nice warm silky latte would be the perfect start, then maybe something spicy for breakfast.

I skidded to a halt behind the counter, my eyes wide, looking around the bookshop. "What is this?"

"Trouble." The Cat appeared up on the counter, jumping from somewhere in the store's front. "My punishment continues."

I stared, and I stared some more, before what he said finally registered in my brain.

"How is a coffee shop trouble?" I asked.

A beautiful long wooden table with two benches sat next to the window, the honey wood worn and smooth. A few square wooden tables, with four chairs each, took up the center of the room, but they had plenty of space between them.

The shop had to be bigger, since bookshelves still lined the back walls and the wall to my right. Yet the children's section had vanished, and the shop felt older.

In the front window, plants hung from hooks in the ceiling. The Cat's wingback chair sat there in a beam of sunlight.

My counter looked the same, along with Betty, but next to the cash register, four cake platters with domes covering them were filled with various cookies and brownies. Behind me on the wall stood the shelves filled with different tea canisters. The place was stocked like a full-blown coffee shop for the day.

"It means people," grumbled the Cat. "How about a coffee in my teacup?" After a moment, he added, "Please."

I quickly moved in front of Betty and started frothing milk. We'd both need some energy to get through today, it seemed.

Indigo appeared, flying across the coffee shop seating from her hideaway. She twirled in the air, showing off her flying skills, which had improved. The little dragon landed on the counter and moved closer to the Cat.

Time stopped as she nuzzled him. Her purple snout rubbed back and forth under his chin. He didn't even move before she galloped her way over near Betty.

Once I had a moment, I gave her head a pat, then I

pulled out cups for all of us. The teacup for the Cat with the pretty flowers on it, my thick dark-blue mug with hints of stars, and then a small white coffee cup for Indigo.

I added extra frothy milk into the teacup and then my mug. Indigo looked at her cup forlornly.

"I'm making you hot chocolate. Don't worry. I just want to cheer the Cat up first."

She chirped in response. Something that sounded like "Oh, I agree."

I added more milk to the metal pitcher along with some good dark chocolate. I also got the beans grinding and the espresso shots going. Multitasking for the win with Betty. I needed to remember what that was like if today would be like my coffee shop barista days in college.

The milk warmed and darkened as the chocolate melted. I poured it into Indigo's cup as she eagerly watched. Surprisingly, she waited until I put the espresso into the Cat's teacup and then my mug before touching hers.

She sniffed her cup once then chirped. I knew what she wanted and pulled out the whipped cream sprayer. I put a small bit on top of her cup and then even added a little cocoa powder so it looked pretty.

Her eyes practically glowed as she leaned forward and stuck her snout into it.

I picked up my mug with a smile, happy to see she wasn't trying to climb inside the cup. Maybe she wanted to stay clean for today, especially since at this point, her form was too large to really fit.

The Cat already sat at his cup, lapping at his drink.

"So, is this a magical coffee shop? Or a normal one?" I asked after taking a sip of my latte.

The warmth washed through me, and I sat on my stool. I still needed to make breakfast, but I could take a few moments to enjoy my drink and maybe get some answers out of the Cat about what today would bring.

"Indigo can stick around. No one will mind," said the Cat, pulling away from his teacup.

His whiskers were completely clean, and the cup was empty. Of course he'd answered a different question and not quite the one I'd asked. Still, it was more information.

Today would be a coffee shop on a world with people other than normal humans. It sounded fun.

But first, breakfast. Grabbing my mug, I got up and headed into the kitchen. Hopefully, we had enough time for some bacon and eggs which were quick enough.

The oven was already preheated, and the bacon package lay on the counter. I chuckled to myself.

"Thanks, Betty," I whispered to the empty kitchen.

At least I could feel like I was doing something productive.

I didn't comment on the cookies and brownies already set out on the counter. I bet I would find missing cookie dough from the freezer, along with the extra brownies.

I didn't mind. It would make it an easier day.

It didn't take long for me to get the bacon in the oven and some scrambled eggs going on the stove. By the time the bacon timer went off, both Indigo and the Cat sat on the island near one another.

Indigo cooed at him, but I didn't know what that meant. It felt like they were having a conversation I wasn't a part of, but that was okay. The Cat's grumpy mood had vanished, and I wanted it to stay that way.

I put the bacon onto a plate in the center of the table then dished up eggs for all of us. I added four slices of bacon to the Cat's plate since he preferred to be served. Then we all ate in silence, except for the sound of crunchy bacon.

"How busy do you think we will be?" I asked.

The Cat stared at me, and his tail flicked in the air. "That's the trouble part."

SEVENTY-THREE

The Cat wasn't wrong.

Back in the front of the shop, I sat on my stool next to Betty and took a deep breath.

"All right, let's do this."

The door unlocked and immediately flew open. A troll with dark-green skin, tall horns, and a dashing haircut stepped inside. A linen button-up and jeans created a perfect outfit for the guy, though he looked a bit young for me. He carried a laptop under one arm and a backpack over his shoulder. His brown eyes darted around the space before landing on me.

"Welcome to Meow," I said with a smile.

He smiled back as he made his way toward the counter. He dropped the backpack and laptop off on one end of the large wooden table, then he stood at the counter. His eyes flicked to Indigo, who lay curled up in a ball on the counter, napping. The amount of bacon she'd consumed had done her in. The Cat sat near the register but paid no attention to the troll.

"Can I get an Americano?"

"Of course. Are you going to be here for a while?" I asked as I started on the espresso.

He nodded.

I pulled out a dark slate-gray mug and set it on the counter. It wasn't the one I had been going for, but it felt right, so I filled it with hot water. Then I added the double shot of espresso. I moved the mug closer to him then headed for the register.

He pulled out a credit card I recognized, and I quickly rang him up. I wondered how the credit card companies operated across worlds? Were they in on magic? Was that how some were accepted everywhere?

Before the transaction could finish, the door opened again, and two more people wandered in, breaking my thought process. The two women looked human, except their eyes were a brilliant green, almost like the Cat's, and they had pointed ears. Both wore sundresses and had leather backpacks on their shoulders, and both were stunningly gorgeous.

They dropped their stuff at one of the square tables before heading my way. They nodded at the troll, who headed toward the long table.

Then the door opened again, and two humans entered. Except somehow I knew they weren't human. They headed directly to the line that formed, flashing slightly glowing yellow eyes.

The elven women both ordered hot chocolates and stared at Indigo. Yet the tiny dragon didn't stir.

I quickly got to work making the drinks.

"Will you be here a while?" I asked them both.

"Yeah, we have some studying to do, and the coffee shop on campus is under construction."

I nodded, smiling, then pulled out two dainty green coffee cups. In the time it took for me to make the drinks and for them to pay, a line had formed with some additional folks behind the two not-humans. The yellow-eyed whatevers wanted drinks to go. A vanilla latte and a brown sugar latte, and both kept their distance from the Cat.

The Cat stared at them.

"Freaking wolves," muttered the Cat, even though only I could hear him.

It was the first thing he'd said since we'd opened and I couldn't help but glance over at them. Cats versus dogs was actually a thing, who knew?

From there, it was nonstop action until midmorning, when I finally got through the seemingly unending line. It had been a good mix of people staying and studying and to-go orders, so the shop didn't feel crowded even though it had definitely been busy.

A wolf and an elf had joined the troll at the long table. The two elven girls sat at their table, deep in the study of economics, of all things. They had already gotten refills once, while the troll basically went through an Americano every hour. The last time he had gotten up and brought his mug, I'd been ready, just needing the cup.

Except, of course, I couldn't see the future.

"Can I also get a brownie and two cookies, as well?" he asked super politely, and I nodded.

From under the counter, I took a round wooden plate and grabbed a pair of tongs.

"For cookies, I have chocolate chip and peanut butter..." I added a brownie to his place since there was only one kind.

"One of each, thanks."

I added them to the plate and to the charge on the register.

"You should offer him a discount card," said the Cat.

He lay curled up in a ball, not even looking at people as they came in.

I paused, not knowing what the Cat was talking about. Then I noticed next to the register in a small card holder sat a stack of what looked like business cards. Each one had ten coffee cups on it and the words *Free Coffee*. A hole punch sat next to it.

I quickly grabbed a card and punched out three coffees, plus three more for the goodies.

"Here, you can get a free drink after a few more purchases."

The troll jerked his head back and then smiled. His entire face lit up, and he blushed. "Thank you so much!"

He grabbed the card, the plate, and the mug, carrying it all back to the table with a bounce in his step.

"I didn't know we had a coffee program..."

The Cat's tail flicked across the counter, and it woke Indigo up. She stretched like a cat herself, then she glanced around in shock at all the people.

"I know, boo. The place is busy today," I said.

She nodded, wide-eyed, then launched herself upward toward the bookcases at the far side. It was probably time for her morning lessons using the MP3 player.

The two elven girls had stopped talking, watching Indigo fly across the room.

"So, what's today's goal?" I asked the Cat quietly.

The coffee shop was busy, with lots of chatter coming from the large wooden table, but I didn't want this conversation to be overheard.

The Cat didn't respond immediately. Instead, he climbed to his feet and moved closer to me. I took that as liberty to pick him up and give him some cuddles.

He immediately started purring in my arms. "Something about helping a relationship along. We don't get tasks like this often. They are not my strong suit."

"Do we even know who we're supposed to help?"

The Cat nuzzled my chin, and I took that as a no. He really didn't like tasks that didn't have any detail about them. I suspected he worried we wouldn't be able to do it, since it sounded like he didn't understand what it was we even had to do.

"Don't worry. We got this," I whispered.

He nuzzled me again then then pawed at my hand until I let him go. He jumped back to the counter.

"How about another beverage?" he asked.

I smiled to myself as I noticed my empty mug. It didn't take long for me to make a vanilla latte for me and the Cat. The beverage soothed me as I glanced around the shop, trying to figure out exactly what we were supposed to do. It could be any relationship between any of these people, or even someone who wasn't here yet.

How could we narrow it down?

SEVENTY-FOUR

The door opened again, and another couple of people walked inside. They were in mid conversation, and it gave me a moment to get a good look at them.

One was a surfer boy, with golden blond hair and bright-blue eyes. He reminded me of the guys who the Cat had mentioned were wolves, yet he gave off a playful energy that I could feel from behind the counter.

The woman he entered with was the opposite. She screamed danger, with dark hair and eyes and a body to kill for. Each step she took reminded me of a predator in a forest. Bright golden eyes reflected power around the room.

One of the other wolves sitting at the wooden table nodded at them, then glanced away. He muttered something to the rest of the table before waving at them.

The guy waved back with a white smile. Then they headed in my direction, still chatting.

"I can't believe it worked. They agreed to the

schedule of runs through the neighborhood and to the howling at night." His chatter kept up as they moved closer. "It's amazing how the kids in the school have improved. Like, attendance problems have dropped to zero, and all the kids are coming in well rested."

"It's an amazing program you put together. I'm proud of you," said the woman. She smiled at me, but her look grew a little puzzled as she glanced around. "No menu?"

"Welcome to Meow, and just let me know what you want. I can usually make it. We also have some cookies and brownies." I motioned toward the register.

That's when I saw the Cat staring at the guy.

"I'll take a hot chocolate. Joey, what about you?" she asked.

I moved to get started on the milk for her drink. Then I found Joey looking at the Cat.

"Woah, that Cat is like the Dog..." Joey's head tilted to one side as he studied the Cat.

The Cat moved a little closer, and Joey held out his hand.

"Ummm, I'll take a coffee. I mean, a latte," he said.

I shook my head, watching the scene as I made the drinks.

"For here or to go?" I asked.

The woman glanced back and forth between the Cat and Joey. "To go, please."

"Hey there, buddy," the young man said to the Cat.

The Cat sniffed Joey's hand, and Joey smiled.

"I know I must smell weird. Sometimes cats hate me.

It's all that dog smell, but I don't chase cats." He kept his voice low and smooth.

The woman melted next to him, her eyes softening as she looked at him. They had to be a couple.

I finished up the drinks and set them on the counter. The Cat nudged his hand once and let the blond dude pet him slightly. Then he turned away toward the register.

"The drinks are on the house. The Cat approves."

The Cat's tail flicked in the air.

"Oh, thanks!" said the woman. "Come on, Joey, we don't want to be late."

That snapped him out of his daze with the Cat.

"Of course, love. Let's get moving." He turned to look at me with a smile. "Thank you for the drinks."

They headed out of the coffee shop.

The Cat padded across the counter back to his drink. "He smelled like an old acquaintance."

"I didn't know you were friends with a dog..."

"I wouldn't say friends, just... It's complicated." He cut his sentence off like he would say more, but couldn't.

I didn't press and instead sipped my drink. We were quickly approaching lunchtime, and the place was still busy.

"I'm thinking sandwiches for lunch, since they're easy to eat while working."

The Cat nodded. "You make a good sandwich."

I resisted asking if he had eaten other sandwiches before mine. Then again, who knew? The Cat was strange, and I didn't understand him most of the time.

"I'm gonna pop back into the kitchen to put them

together so we can eat whenever we're hungry. Holler if someone needs help."

Taking my drink with me, I headed into the kitchen and pulled what I needed out of the fridge. We had ham for lunchmeat, and cheddar cheese, plus some tomato, mustard, and a little mayo would make a great easy sandwich. I had almost forgotten the lettuce, but I remembered we had it at the last moment. Then I sliced the three sandwiches diagonally and set them in the center of the island.

I brought one triangle with me to the front.

The Cat sat next to the coffee machine with someone standing across from him, talking. He had almost perfect skin, and I swore he glowed.

"I'd like a large coffee. Black, please."

The Cat nodded then turned to look at me. "You heard?"

"Yep, I can get that. Do you want it for here, or to go?"

His blue eyes practically twinkled as he smiled at me. "To go, please."

He leaned against the counter, and I could have sworn he batted his lashes at me.

I almost leaned closer to him but forced myself to focus on the coffee. It was an Americano, but I figured that was close enough to what he'd asked for. I set it on the counter, careful to keep my hands away from him, jerking back as he moved toward the cup.

He stared at my sudden movement, clearly confused.

The Cat moved closer to him, and a fresh breeze blew across my hair. His green eyes narrowed, glaring at the guy.

The guy chuckled, quickly paid, then left. As soon as the door closed behind him, that feeling from the Cat disappeared.

"Fucking angels," muttered the Cat.

I looked at him in shock. The Cat had sworn. The Cat never swore.

Then his words reached my brain.

"You mean, like that Carter guy?" I asked, remembering the only angel person I had met so far.

"No, Carter's a decent guy. That one was slime."

"He used some sort of persuasion on me, didn't he?" My mind raced, thinking of how I'd wanted to lean closer to him. "That *Primer for the Beings of the Tree* book mentioned they naturally have it."

The Cat nodded and finished his latte.

I picked my sandwich triangle back up and took a bite out of it. Tasty, but simple. I didn't know if it was the food or what, but the little purple dragon dashed across the room, drawing attention. She had her little MP3 player in her claws and headphones on.

The two elven girls gasped at her cuteness, but Indigo didn't even notice. Her eyes stayed glued to the sandwich in my hand.

"Yours is in the kitchen. It has extra ham and no cheese," I said, pointing.

She chirped and flew faster toward the hallway behind me.

I glanced down at the Cat. "You might want to go eat yours as well. You know how she can get."

The Cat jumped off the counter and vanished.

"Make sure you leave the rest of mine alone!"

Things calmed down after that, with the afternoon slowly passing as people finished drinks and headed out. Within a few hours, the shop was empty, and I could only guess what we'd accomplished. I hoped we'd done whatever we were supposed to.

I had to admit that I was starting to agree with the Cat on this one. Days where we didn't know what we were supposed to accomplish were definitely a pain.

SEVENTY-FIVE

The shop looked normal this morning, though at this point, I really didn't know what that meant.

Either way, the bookshop feel had come back when I peeked over the railing. The center table had books piled high, along with something that looked like crafting materials arranged around one side.

I had a random song stuck in my head, and I was starving. Although, even before breakfast, coffee sounded wonderful. I detoured toward Betty to make a strong latte with some brown sugar. Usually, I preferred my brown-sugar drinks iced, but this morning I needed something hot.

That first sip warmed me up, and I closed my eyes, smiling before getting a better look at the shop.

The center table had a basket full of yarn, which I assumed was part of a crafting display. This close, I now saw that the books on the center table were all yarn related. There was even a beginner's crochet kit.

Chirping from the kitchen caused me to head in that

direction faster than I'd wanted to. The Cat and Indigo sat on the island having a conversation. Neither of them noticed when I entered the room.

"So, does anyone have thoughts on breakfast?" I asked.

Indigo's head snapped around, then she flew directly at me. She landed on my shoulder and nuzzled me, all the while chirping so fast that I couldn't follow or even guess.

The Cat turned toward the oven. "It will be a chilly day for our customers."

I nodded, wondering if that was why I craved a hot beverage this morning. The warm weather was slowly winding down back on the planet I was from, but that didn't mean time passed the same way at the shop.

Normally, outside on the rooftop deck, the weather was perfect whenever I got the chance to lay out. Then again, I wasn't working while on the rooftop deck, and my assumption was the shop had found a perfect place with glorious weather whenever I'd wanted it.

"Oatmeal with dried fruit it is."

No one complained about my statement, though Indigo jumped back off my shoulder and headed to the counter.

I pulled out the instant oatmeal and various mix-ins. "What does everyone want in theirs?"

This time, I understood the chirps from Indigo. She wanted chocolate chips, coconut, and milk. A decent order, though I'd put in more coconut than chocolate chips.

"Apples with cinnamon and pecans," said the Cat.

Now, that one I'd make a double batch of and share with the Cat.

After boiling the oats, Indigo's chocolate melted into hers. Again, she ate rather neatly, instead of diving head-first. I filled two big bowls with the perfect combination for the Cat and I. All of us went quiet as we ate, and our meal took a little longer as we lingered over the warm food.

The breakfast warmed me up even more than the coffee had, and I hoped that today would be a great day.

"So, what's on the agenda today?"

"It's a simple day. We have someone picking up goods." The Cat stretched out on the island before hopping off. His voice continued as he traveled to the front. "Hopefully, short, too. A nap would be good."

I quickly followed, as did Indigo. Despite starting behind me, she beat me to the counter. Her flying had gotten a lot better lately.

I'd finished my latte, so I started on another, plus one for the Cat.

Indigo shook her head when I offered her a drink. She had eaten a big bowl of oatmeal with lots of milk, so I wasn't surprised. Instead, she stuck close to the Cat, like she was waiting for something.

I couldn't help but wonder what was up with that.

When I finished making our drinks, I sat on my stool. "Ready whenever you are."

The Cat nodded, but the door didn't unlock yet. Instead, he focused on his drink, quickly lapping it up. Once he drained his drink, the door unlocked. I moved the teacup under the counter.

Nothing happened.

Over an hour later, the Cat napped, as did Indigo, and I was on my third latte of the day. Outside the windows, now and then a leaf would blow by. Thankfully, back home, it wasn't this late in the year, but it wouldn't be much longer until the seasons changed. Soon, the harvest festival would happen in town, and there would be fresh apple cider.

And I was going to miss it.

Most of the time, I was okay with signing the contract. I wouldn't change anything. I especially would not give up meeting the Cat or Indigo.

Both of them napped on the counter, and I snapped a few photos on my phone.

The bells on the door finally jingled, and I glanced up.

In walked a very tall man in a bright-red coat, along with a much younger girl wearing the same colors. Both looked totally human, except for the fact that they each had four arms. The girl looked around thirteen with blonde hair and dark eyes.

The man turned toward the younger girl. "Find yourself something. I need to pick up my order."

The girl smiled and walked to the nearest bookshelf, skimming titles as she walked around.

The man headed toward the counter, smiling at me.

"Welcome to the Magical Emporium of Wares. How can I help you today?"

"Just picking up an order. It should be under Benjamin. Then whatever my daughter picks out. I promised her something for helping with the harvest this year."

"It's in the storage room. The box is labeled," said the Cat, who now sat next to the register, his eyes on the man.

Indigo still napped, not even realizing people had entered the shop.

I headed to the storage room, and on the first shelf sat a cardboard box the size of a shoebox, tied with a string. A handwritten note read *Benjamin*. I carefully brought the box back to the counter.

Benjamin petted the Cat with a big smile.

The girl studied the items on the main table, especially the crafting kits and books on how to crochet. "Father, do you think I could learn?"

He turned toward her. "You can do anything you put your mind to. I bet your mother would love a scarf."

Her smile brightened even more. She quickly picked up the kit that had some yarn in it, along with a skein of bright-purple yarn. She headed to the counter.

"I think this is what I want." She carefully set it on the counter then saw Indigo. "Oh, that's a dragon..."

Her voice went soft.

"It is, though she's napping right now."

"Isn't that lucky, Father?"

"It is, sweetie. It is..."

I moved over to the register and added the crochet kit and yarn. The order was already listed, though the currency was coins.

"That will be twenty-five gold coins," I said, praying that was correct. It felt like a lot.

Benjamin nodded and pulled out a bag, then he began counting the coins. He set each one on the counter. Once he finished, I swept them all into my hand and put them into the register. They were each about the size of a dime and looked like pure gold.

Indigo's head snapped up at the jangle of coins.

The girl gasped as the little dragon twisted about, looking at the two of them. "She is so pretty."

Indigo immediately flared her wings and stretched, giving the girl a good look. Then she chirped at me, but I couldn't follow the comment.

"Come on. We need to get home before dark," said Benjamin, though his gaze also didn't leave the dragon.

The girl grabbed the kit and extra yarn before waving at Indigo. "Bye, little dragon!"

Indigo fluttered her wings in reply.

As the door shut behind them, I shook my head.

"Did you have a good nap?" I asked.

Indigo chirped and then said something that I swore sounded like she was asking about Lady Borsal.

The Cat stared at the door.

SEVENTY-SIX

"She's coming. We just had to get work out of the way first," muttered the Cat.

"What was that about, anyway? What did we sell him?"

"Benjamin? Seeds for next year. He protects a small farming town that stays away from current technology. They are living the same way they have for a millennia. Anyone who wants to leave can, but their immortality is stripped from them."

"Wait, you're saying they don't age?"

"Not once they reach the age of maturity for their kind."

"So, they just stop aging, like magic."

The Cat nodded, his eyes still on the door. "Yes, like many creatures of the Tree. But once they leave their homelands, the magic fades. They can return home, but that doesn't mean that they stop aging. Usually, once something is lost, you can't get it back."

I sat on my stool, thinking about that. Stay home and

never age or leave everything you know but eventually die. That had to be an intense choice. I mean, eventually you would want something more and leave, right?

My thoughts paused as the door opened again. In walked Lady Borsal. Today, she wore a deep-red dress with leather boots and a black cloak. It stood out from her normal robes.

Indigo immediately launched herself into the air, flying right at her before landing on her shoulder, chatting the entire way. I couldn't follow a single chirp of it.

I giggled to myself and turned toward Betty. While I shouldn't have any more caffeine for the day, another warm drink sounded amazing.

"Would you like anything to drink?"

"Whatever you're making..." answered the dragon before she said something to Indigo in the dragon tongue.

I made yet another hot latte.

"Do you want anything?" I asked the Cat.

"No, thank you," replied the Cat. "This is going to be a learning visit for Indigo."

"Good to know." That meant I wouldn't need to hang out down here, though I had a million questions for the dragon, especially about what had happened to the demon and Lady Twilight.

I pulled out a black mug for Lady Borsal and poured in the milk. Then I topped it off with some espresso, putting a flower pattern in the center as I poured. Normally, I didn't bother with such things, but she had dressed fancy today. I hoped it would make her day even brighter.

I set the mug out on the counter, then I worked on my drink.

"Thank you," said Lady Borsal. "The Elder sends her regards and apologizes for her rushed exit last time. The gift is being taken care of appropriately."

She flashed sharp-pointed teeth as she spoke the last word.

"Good to know." I didn't need any more details than that.

A shiver went up my spine, but I reminded myself that the demon had kidnapped Indigo from her mother, and who knew what he would have done with the youngling. It was good that the dragons now had him. Hopefully, they could get more information about Indigo's mother.

"I have some lessons from the Elder to go over with Indigo, including helping with the project they were working on last time."

Indigo chirped twice.

"She will be back to work with you. I am only here so you keep making progress on your lessons. Listening to the old stories is good, but you also need to work on speaking and flying." Lady Borsal stared, her bright-orange eyes almost glowing.

Indigo sheepishly nodded. It seemed like someone was slacking on dragon lessons.

"Well, feel free to work down here or in the conference space." I'd noticed the doorway had opened up in the far wall. "I don't need to watch y'all. So, I'm going to head upstairs and warm up in some sun."

I paused before I headed out.

"Are you going to stay for lunch?" I asked.

"No, thank you," said Lady Borsal with a smile. "I appreciate the offer."

I nodded and picked up my mug before heading to the stairs. I had a fantastic book to finish, and maybe I could find out more about the Fey Lords. Based on my calendar, I had two full days off starting tomorrow. I should be able to make progress on figuring out whatever Betty was trying to tell me.

Whatever it was, it had to be important.

LADY BORSAL CHATTED with Indigo as Sable headed up the stairs.

"Can you grab the dragon stone?" Lady Borsal asked Indigo. "We need to work on the magic to get it to work in time..."

Indigo flew off toward her cavern.

I listened as Sable headed to her bedroom. Then I turned to face the dragon. I gave her a nod. Indigo didn't take long to get back with the giant glowing stone.

"Birthdays! What do we do for her birthday?" asked the little dragon.

Lady Borsal grinned, her eyes sparkling. "Humans, on her world, eat cake and have presents, like we found out before. Also, everyone wears these little hats for the party. It's supposed to be a fun day for the birthday person."

I paused, thinking about what we could do. Placing

an order with the baker wouldn't be a problem, and presents were easy enough.

"Lord Bennit and I would like to join the celebration."

Indigo nodded quickly then asked about Lady Twilight.

"She is tangled up with a project right now, so I doubt she will make it, but knowing her, she will bring the best present when she does manage to get free."

Indigo poked the stone with a frown.

"Your present will be amazing, little one," reassured Lady Borsal. "We just need to make sure it works right. This magic is hard magic, and if you didn't have the bond with Sable, no one would even recommend it."

I knew we could pull this off and give Sable a very good birthday. It wouldn't have her human family at it, but it would have all of us. That had to be enough.

"Let's get to work," said Lady Borsal.

I turned and jumped from the counter. It was time for me to work on my own list and present for Sable. I still wasn't sure what to get her, but it had to be something grand. Something worthy of the person she was.

After all, look what she had done for me.

SEVENTY-SEVEN

This morning, I was on a mission. It was my first of two days off, and I needed to figure out more about this Fey Lord business. I didn't know how it worked, but on my days off, I always seemed to get up early, even when I intended to sleep in.

It didn't matter as I headed to the kitchen to make pancakes. The mix came in a box, and then butter and maple syrup went on top. It wasn't quite bacon and eggs, but it was just as good, in its own way. After all, there weren't many things better than bacon and eggs. Maybe waffles, but I somehow always burned waffles in the waffle maker, so pancakes it would be.

The mix was simple, and it didn't take long for me to flip pancakes onto a plate on the island. The Cat and Indigo were nowhere to be seen, but I made some little ones for Indigo. I even put on a little music to sing with. It couldn't get better than this.

A chirp behind me spooked me, and I sent a small pancake flying.

Thankfully, Indigo took it as a challenge. She dove after the pancake and caught it before it hit the floor. She chomped on it merrily as she headed back to the island. The pancake stack stood bigger than the little dragon. That was mostly because I'd also made a tower of small ones. Still, I'd already made quite a substantial quantity of both sizes.

I decided that was enough and sat down to make myself a plate.

Indigo watched as I put butter on, then I dipped each bite into syrup. Then she tried to do the same thing with the smaller pancake. As soon as she tasted the maple syrup, she started chittering loudly.

"Maple syrup *is* pretty amazing," I said.

The Cat jumped up on the counter. "Pancakes. That's new."

"I figured something different for my day off." I finished my first pancake and grabbed two more off the stack. "Plus, they freeze well, and they make super quick meals."

I tossed one onto the empty plate I had set out for the Cat. "Do you want butter or syrup?"

"Yes, please."

I quickly buttered it and poured a little syrup over the pancake.

The Cat didn't have as flexible digits as Indigo did. Indigo cut her little pancake up into four sections and dipped each one into the syrup. It was adorable. The Cat couldn't do that with his paws.

"So, what's on your to-do list today?" I asked the Cat.

"Not much. Indigo will need to stay out of sight."

The dragon quickly chirped, asking why.

"Sable is having a guest."

"I am?"

The Cat's head tilted to one side, staring at me.

"Yes?" he answered, sounding slightly confused. "One of your brothers..."

I pulled out my phone to check for any messages or emails from my family to say as much, but I found nothing. "I don't think anyone is visiting."

The Cat's tail flicked. "All I know is one will show up."

I ate another couple bites of pancake. "Well, good to know."

"I apologize if I ruined a surprise."

"Not your fault," I said. "I told my mom I had these two days off, but I didn't think anyone would show up."

I shrugged and took another bite. It would change my plans a little, but not by much. I still needed to find more information about Fey Lords. At the same time, it would be great to see one of my brothers.

Breakfast went quickly after that, and I stored the extra pancakes in the freezer in meal-sized portions. It would give me some options for quick breakfasts later this week, in case something tough showed up. The rest of the kitchen cleaned itself, and I headed to the front to make some coffee.

"Thanks, Betty." I lightly patted the top of the espresso machine, thankful that the dishes loaded themselves into the dishwasher.

Sitting on the stool, I wondered if I should message my mother asking about any visits, but I decided against it. Instead, I'd go about my day and be surprised when someone actually showed up. If someone did, at least.

Indigo had taken off for her hideaway, still working on whatever homework she had gotten yesterday. We'd stayed up a little late reading together, but that was for fun. I didn't have a clue where the Cat had gone, though I guessed it was to the room with the big glowing book.

Taking my cup, I moved toward the shelves.

"Well, Betty, if you have any other info on Fey Lords, now's the time to share it," I mumbled under my breath.

A doorway near the far wall appeared, and I moved toward it.

I peeked inside, and even more bookshelves filled it, bookshelves upon bookshelves. They stretched as far as I could see.

"Woah, are these all the books you have? You are so freaking amazing..." I wandered down one of the aisles, looking at the various spines.

All of these were leather and had strange symbols on them. The next section were newer-looking books made with cloth bindings.

The shelves continued. Most of the time, I couldn't read what was on the spines. Some had nothing on the spines at all. Still, I wandered, wondering what I could find here.

Farther down the way, one book stuck partially out of the bookshelf. It immediately caught my eye, and I hurried in that direction.

The book was slim and bound in dark-green leather. Carved on the front was an oak leaf.

"This must be it." I flipped it open, finding thick parchment for each of the pages.

It was handwritten, each line in thick pen strokes that were hard for me to make out. The words weren't in English. That much was clear.

Now all I needed to find was something to translate the book with. Still, it was progress.

A loud knocking rattled through the room, and I hurried back toward the opening. A dark form at the front door caused me to pause, but then I realized who it was.

Cerulean.

SEVENTY-EIGHT

My brother's presence felt fake as I set my coffee cup and book down on the main table and hurried toward the door. Honestly, I'd expected Cyan again. I flung the door open, and he hurried inside, carrying a large cardboard box.

"Sable! Finally, I thought I'd be standing out there forever!"

I motioned for him to set the box on the counter, and I closed the door behind him and locked it. "I didn't expect to see you this morning."

"Did you really think the family would forget your birthday?" he asked with a chuckle. "There wasn't a chance someone wouldn't show up. You're lucky it's me and not Mom."

"Mom never leaves town," I said with a smirk.

Then I found myself wrapped up in my brother's arms. He lifted me off the ground slightly before setting me back down. All I could smell was forest and mountains.

"She just might have, to come see you," he muttered, still smiling. "So, this is your place?"

He glanced around the shop, his gaze darting every which way.

"It is. Do you want a coffee?" I asked, moving behind the counter after grabbing my mug.

I really wished I had a living room I could invite him to. Instead, I had the kitchen or the rooftop deck.

"Sure, I'll take something warm. I'm not picky about my caffeine." Cerulean kept glancing around the shop, like he couldn't believe I lived and worked here. "You know how it is when I'm on my jobs; if it's hot and caffeinated, I'm happy."

I quickly make him a latte with an extra shot of espresso and set it on the counter next to the box. "Come on back into the kitchen. I have stools so we both can sit down."

Cerulean grabbed the big box, so I picked up both our cups and headed to the island.

In the kitchen, he set the box down and then took out a large pastry box from inside. "Mom made you a small chocolate cake with vanilla frosting."

"That is, like, an extra-large cupcake..." The thing looked amazing and much more like a cupcake than an actual cake, which I was thankful for.

He also pulled out two smaller boxes.

"I got you a little something on my last trip, and then Dad, well... He had to get you something as well." He sat on the stool and pulled his cup a little closer.

"I'm surprised to see you. I thought you had a big

tour thing coming up to some deep mountain range or something."

He scratched the back of his head, messing up his brown hair. "Eh, I canceled it. The client gave me a bad feeling."

"Ah, the legendary gut-check of Cerulean," I said with a smirk.

"Hey, my gut-check has saved my bacon many times."

"I know, I know." I took a sip of my now-lukewarm drink. "So, why are you really here? Visiting isn't really your thing."

He shrugged, frowning. "Can't I check on my little sister?"

I kept staring.

"Fine. I needed a break from doing my job. I might be getting a little burnt out." He stared down at his coffee cup. "Plus, Mom wanted someone to come out here, and Cyan has a big project he's rushing to finish for some important company. Like, a six-figure project."

"Woah, that's pretty amazing."

"It is. Plus, you know Onyx wouldn't come. He doesn't like to fly, and this by car would be pretty far for him."

That much was very true.

"Umber is working on the farm and won't be free until the snow flies." He smiled brightly, his blue eyes almost glowing. "So, you get *me*! Aren't you lucky?"

"Of course I'm lucky. I have a great family, a fantastic job, and I get to live here." I motioned to our surroundings. "My life is pretty lucky."

Something clicked in the back of my mind, and I quickly stood. "Actually, I have something for Umber for you to bring back."

I headed to the storage room, and the sunflower seeds in the paper envelope sat inside on a shelf.

Back in the kitchen again, I set them on the counter. "I randomly got these and thought of him."

Cerulean picked up the envelope, staring at it with his forehead wrinkled and his eyes a little scrunched.

"Where did you get these?" The question came out strangely, almost choked.

I shrugged. "It was part of an order, but the client didn't pick it up."

Which wasn't quite the truth, but I didn't know how to explain they'd just shown up one day for me to give to him.

He nodded slowly, still looking way more confused than an envelope of seeds really warranted.

"So, do you want to split this massive cupcake with me?" I asked with a grin.

He nodded, his gaze switching to the giant cupcake.

I got up and pulled out plates, plus a knife and forks. I cut it into quarters and put a quarter on each of our plates.

"This feels like a ton of cake," I said, sliding the plate over to him.

I wanted to make sure the Cat and Indigo got a bit as well, but I couldn't outright say that. The first bite was like a warm hug from my mother. It reminded me of birthdays past, along with big family gatherings. It was so chocolatey it almost melted in my mouth, but it wasn't too sweet, like the perfect balance that my mother always seemed able to strike for me.

"Mom sure knows how to bake a cake," I added, taking another bite.

Cerulean's cake vanished almost instantly. "I swear she puts extra effort into yours."

"Nah, it's just that I ask for less sugar." That was the secret; otherwise, Mom's icing was way too sweet, like make-your-teeth-hurt sweet. "So, if you canceled your next trip, what's on your schedule?"

Cerulean kept glancing around like he was waiting for something to happen.

"No idea. Just kind of seeing where the world takes me. Another trip will come up. They always do." He chuckled to himself. "That's the thing about my job. Someone always wants to go somewhere, and there's always somewhere to go."

"Don't you plan on settling down? I know Umber wants to find a partner. What about you?"

He started laughing. "I doubt I'll go that route with my life. All of you guys are all I need."

His laughter rolled around the space and made me smile.

"You never know," I added, finishing my cake.

My contract here was only for a year, but already I was hoping I could take a quick break then come back with a new contract. Maybe take a two-week trip to see my family then sign up again. I couldn't imagine leaving the Cat or Indigo behind.

"You should open your presents."

I quickly pulled Dad's present in front of me and

pulled off the wrapping paper. It was always a book—that was Dad's thing. Everyone got a book for their birthday. This one was covered in leather and had a clasp.

I flipped the pages open and found them blank. "A journal?"

"Really?" asked my brother. "That's new."

I hadn't ever gotten a journal from him before, but I supposed there was a first time for everything. "It's super nice, though."

Cerulean nodded, looking confused again.

Dad's books usually had a theme or a lesson he thought you should learn. Maybe I needed to figure out my own theme with the blank journal.

"Here, open mine." He eagerly pushed his box across the table.

I pulled the bright-blue box closer and slowly started pulling off the paper. He glared at me, so I moved quicker, laughing as I did so. He had already gotten me a card, so it surprised me to get something else from him. I pulled the lid off the box and paused.

Inside lay a bracelet on a red cushion.

"I know you're not a jewelry person, but I felt like I had to get it for you..." He shrugged.

I pulled it out carefully. The chain looked delicate and had three stones on it. One was purple, one was bright green, and the last was black.

"Woah, this is beautiful." I glanced up at him with a smile. "You didn't need to get this for me."

"Let me put it on you." He leaned across the island and opened the clasp, and I held out my wrist.

It felt almost warm as it rested against my wrist. Loose, but not loose enough to get caught on anything.

"Thank you," I said, meaning it.

It was a magnificent gift.

It wasn't possible.

I watched, hidden in the shadows. His gaze kept drifting my way, even if he couldn't see me. Sable had no clue, of course, but the pulse of power inside this brother differed from the last one. This was much stronger.

The bracelet echoed with power—a protection spell made specifically for her. He hadn't been the one to create it, but he had gotten it made somewhere. Somewhere not on this world.

More questions echoed inside my head, but I didn't have anyone to ask, and I had no way to find out. I didn't trust the dragons with this. They'd been helpful, and counted Sable a friend, but centuries of distrust died hard, and I wasn't particularly interested in letting it die at all. Dragons were unpredictable, followed their own rules, and didn't respect any other being.

It wasn't like her brother's power changed anything, though. I knew Sable was special, and that was why, as soon as her contract ended, I would vanish from her life just like I had for every other Shopkeeper. I couldn't let her be trapped here, like I was.

CHAPTER
SEVENTY-NINE

I didn't want to get out of bed.

Last night, I'd stayed up late reading a fun book while soaking in the hot tub on the roof. My choice of book had bored Indigo, so she'd listened to a dragon story.

My brother had left soon after I'd opened his present. He wasn't one to hang around for long, so I hadn't been too surprised. The only time he'd seemed to relax was when we were in the middle of nowhere camping, and I only knew that because, after begging for ages, he'd taken me on one of his camping trips in the mountains.

It had been an experience that'd shown me camping was not my thing. It was his, but not mine. I loved hot water, fresh food, and fancy coffee, as he put it.

I snuggled under the blankets and cuddled with my pillow. Indigo landed on the bed near my foot and slowly made her way toward my head. At least, I assumed it was Indigo. If not, today would be a strange day. As soon as I thought that, a purple head came into view, and she nuzzled me while almost purring.

"Morning, Indigo."

She chirped softly once and curled up next to me on my pillow. I didn't mind. The sun barely came in through the skylight, making her purple scales almost glow in the dark room. I smiled as I closed my eyes again, letting my thoughts wander.

Sleeping in was amazing when my brain actually let me do it.

A couple of hours later, I finally sat up and stretched. I needed coffee and something tasty for breakfast.

Indigo still slept on my pillow and didn't wake even once I got up. It wasn't until I dressed and opened my door that her head snapped up.

She blinked a few times then flew after me before landing on my shoulder. I'd forgotten to ask Lady Borsal if she should sleep so much or if it was another growth spurt.

The shop was quiet as I made my way downstairs and detoured by the front for a quick latte. Then into the kitchen I went.

On the island sat the Cat. He had an empty bowl next to him and a box of cereal.

"Good morning, Sable."

"Morning, Cat. Did you eat already?" I asked.

Cereal sounded good. I hadn't had any in a while, and the crunchy honey version on the counter was one of my favorites.

"Yes, some of the crunchy stuff."

I nodded and pulled out a bowl.

"Do you want some?" I asked Indigo.

She shook her head and jumped off my shoulder to the island. It took a few moments for her to curl up in a ball, and then she was out again.

I glanced at the Cat as I pulled out the milk. "I think she's going through another growth spurt."

The Cat stared at her and slowly nodded. "Probably. She is learning new ideas from the dragons, and that helps her kind grow."

"I wonder if I'll notice the changes," I mumbled as I took a bite.

"Last time, she only grew an inch or so." The Cat stared at her some more. "Plus, she grew smarter, her language changed, and the edges of her scales deepened in color."

I paused, my spoon halfway to my mouth. "I noticed the physical growth, but she talks more? I hadn't really realized."

"It will be more like that this time," said the Cat. "Physical growth depends on age and surroundings."

I chewed and motioned for the Cat to continue. This had not been in any of the books I'd been able to find and read on dragons. Maybe it was in some of the ones in languages I didn't understand, but that didn't help me much.

The Cat's tail flicked back and forth. "If she wants to stay small, she will stay small. She likes her dragon tree and her hideaway, but those are tiny spaces. Even I wouldn't be comfortable in them, but she is. Plus, even dragons that want to grow big do so over centuries."

I nodded. I hoped Indigo stayed small, but not if it would mess with her development.

I finished off my bowl of cereal while sitting quietly with the Cat, just thinking about Indigo growing bigger.

Eventually, the Cat turned to look at me. "What are your plans for today?"

I smiled and cupped my hands around my coffee mug. "Not much. I'm going to relax and chill in the hot tub and maybe finish that book I started last night. I need to call my mom and thank her for the cupcake. Did you like the cake?"

The Cat nodded. "It was tasty."

"Indigo dived into her slice," I chuckled. "Literally. She needed a bath after eating it."

Indigo had gotten cake and icing under her claws and even some in one of her ears, somehow. It had been absolutely adorable. Though, I wasn't sure how much she'd actually eaten.

I sipped on my coffee.

"Have fun reading," said the Cat as he jumped off the island.

I put my bowl in the sink and picked up Indigo. She remained out, but I didn't want to leave her behind since she had stuck close to me so far this morning.

The dragon slept through me making an iced coffee, changing into my bathing suit, and then heading to the rooftop deck with a book. I placed her on a fuzzy towel in the shade and climbed into the hot tub. Steam rose from the warm water, and the sun glowed softly but not too hot with the cool breeze. Basically, the perfect weather for what I wanted as I flipped open the book.

By the time I'd emptied my iced coffee, I'd finished the book, and Indigo was up and swimming in the warm water.

"You sure you don't want anything to eat?" I asked for the third time.

She shook her head and dived under the water.

I climbed out of the tub, ready to shower off and get back into some real clothes. My stomach growled, and I kept going back and forth in my head about what to order for lunch. Chinese food was always a good choice, but maybe some BBQ would be good to change things up.

Once I showered and changed back into normal clothes, I stepped out onto the balcony, ready to track down the Cat.

"Hey, Sable, do you have a moment?" The Cat appeared in the center of the shop down below. "I have something I want to show you."

EIGHTY

Indigo tossed herself over the balcony and flew down below, her wings glittering in a sunbeam.

"Sure. What are your thoughts on lunch?" I asked loudly as I headed toward the stairs. "I'm leaning toward Chinese or BBQ."

I turned toward the front of the space. An archway glowed on the far side, and the Cat sat in the middle of it. Indigo flew through just as I noticed it.

"Oh, what's that?" I asked, walking forward. As far as I knew, today was a day off, and the shop normally was pretty static during those times.

The Cat almost smiled, then turned and padded through the doorway, his tail flicking.

I hurried and entered the warm, glowing space.

"Surprise!"

I yelped and couldn't keep the giant smile off my face.

People filled a brightly lit room, all wearing small birthday hats. The Cat and Indigo even had them on their heads, though they hadn't been there moments before. A banner hung lopsided across the far wall with *Happy Birthday* written in purple. Crystals flickered around the edges of the space, giving off a soft glow.

Lady Borsal and Lord Bennit were both here, along with Alas, the leatherworker. Plus the Cat and Indigo. A giant cake sat in the center of a round table, along with plates of food. Piles of Chinese takeout covered the table, with tall stacks of egg rolls and wontons, plus spicy chicken and noodles.

"Happy birthday," said Lady Borsal, holding up a glitter-covered birthday hat for me to take.

"Thank you!"

I couldn't help myself and put it on. It was a small hat, meant for a little kids' party, but I said nothing about the size. Everyone looked so proud of the surprise they'd pulled off. The little hat Indigo wore looked way too big, but she clutched it as she chirped from the table.

"I guess lunch is taken care of," I said with a smile.

"There is plenty of food," agreed Lord Bennit. "So many Clan members wanted to join, but I limited it just to us two."

He held out an empty plate, which I quickly took.

Indigo chirped until I took a seat at the table, then everyone else sat down. We passed around plates of food, and I loaded my plate up. The Cat sat next to me on the table itself, with Alas on the other side. Lady Borsal helped Indigo plate up some food, while I put food on the Cat's plate.

Alas spoke to Lord Bennit about something involving

leather, while Indigo chirped at both Lady Borsal and me, who loaded Indigo's plate up with more protein.

The Cat stayed quiet.

Everyone dug into food, but the conversation kept up. Alas was working on a project for a warrior that he was describing to Lord Bennit in detail, Lady Borsal explained something about dragon magic to Indigo, and I just listened. Warmth washed through me while looking around the table at everyone.

"Did you guess?" asked the Cat quietly.

"Not at all," I whispered to him.

He nodded and took a bite of an egg roll on his plate. "Good. I can still be sneaky after all."

The spicy noodles made my eyes water, but they were perfect. "Of course you can be sneaky. You're a cat."

The Cat focused on his plate, and Lord Bennit asked him a question. Alas seemed fascinated that the dragon could speak directly to the Cat without needing to go through me.

"How is that possible?"

Lord Bennit laughed.

"The Fates hold no control over dragons," he explained, before eating an egg roll whole. "The Eldest of us swim through the ley lines and return to the Tree when it is time."

His head bowed for a moment then straightened.

I listened in awe, not having read that in any of the books I had been able to find about dragons. Maybe I'd have to figure out how to read more languages so I could read some of the older books. The truly old-looking ones were definitely not in English.

Everyone focused on food after that, and I quickly cleared my plate.

"So, do we eat cake, or do you open presents first?" asked Lady Borsal.

Everyone turned to look at me.

"Well, how about we do presents first? Let lunch settle a bit before the sugar rush."

She nodded, and then a pile of presents came into view. One moment, there was nothing there, and then three gifts appeared.

Indigo launched herself at a badly wrapped one covered in tape and orange-colored paper. She carefully lifted it off the table and flew it in my direction. Yet as she flew closer, one of her claws twitched. The present slipped, dropping toward the table.

Indigo chirped in panic.

Lady Borsal's hand shot out faster than I would have expected—if I hadn't known she was a dragon—and caught it.

"It's all right, little one," whispered Lady Borsal.

She held the gift out to me, which I carefully picked up.

It weighed a ton, and through the paper, my fingers touched something rough. Slowly, I peeled off the bright-orange paper. The dragon stone pulsed as I touched it.

"The dragon stone?"

Indigo started talking faster than I could follow. Lord Bennit laughed along with Lady Borsal.

"What Indigo is trying to say," said Lady Borsal, "is

that she helped create the magic in this gift. We helped a little, too, but the idea completely came from her."

"What does it do?" I asked.

Lady Borsal's gaze flicked over to Lord Bennit.

He took over. "It will teach you how to understand dragon tongue."

Both the Cat and Alas gasped. Lord Bennit glared at them both, and their mouths shut, though the Cat's eyes had widened.

"You are kin of the Clan of Lore. It is only fitting you can speak with us all," declared Lord Bennit.

I nodded slowly, my eyes focused on the pulsing stone. "How does it work?"

Lord Bennit smiled a very dragon-like smile with too many sharp teeth, but not in anger.

Lady Borsal motioned for me to pull the stone toward my chest. "You need to accept the magic inside it."

I'd accept that magic in an instant.

"It will take time to work. We don't know how long..." She glanced at Indigo, who nodded. "The magic needs time to settle inside you."

Indigo moved closer, not touching me, and she chirped twice.

I smiled at her. "This is an amazing present."

She nuzzled my arm then leaped back.

I pulled the stone closer to myself and tried to do what Lady Borsal had said. The pulsing light felt warm through my T-shirt. Then it flared. Bright red, blue, then purple flashed in the stone before going dim. My chest filled with warmth, becoming almost hot, but it wasn't painful. I had to blink several times to get rid of the spots left behind from the flashing.

The magic from the stone vanished, and it felt cold in my hand.

Lord Bennit held out his hand for it. I gave it to him.

"Like Lady Borsal said, it will take time to settle in your body."

The stone vanished.

"It might be weeks before you understand a word of what you hear."

"Soon, right?" chirped Indigo.

I blinked at Indigo. Her soft voice had sounded inside my head.

EIGHTY-ONE

Indigo leaped toward my arms, and I pulled her close.

"It is an amazing gift," I whispered. "Thank you."

"Smells like me!" she chirped.

My eyes widened at Indigo's words. First, I understood her, and now I smelled like a dragon? Yet I kept it to myself for the moment.

Lady Borsal chuckled at Indigo's words, which I shouldn't be able to understand yet but could.

"She has lots of dragon magic around her right now." She caught my eye. "Don't worry. It will wear off over time as it sinks in."

The Cat nodded. "You do smell a little like a dragon, but like she said, as it sinks in, it will fade."

There were still two presents to go, and I didn't know how someone could top this, or even come close.

Indigo jumped into the air, flying around the table a few times and chirping. Lord Bennit tracked her movements.

Her voice sounded soft in my mind. "Best gift!"

I chuckled at her antics.

Alas picked up a large box wrapped in a blue cloth. "Well, I hope you like my gift."

He held it out to me with one hand.

I went to take it, but it weighed more than I expected, and I almost dropped it. After putting it on the table, I carefully untied the cloth and peeked inside. I gasped as I quickly pulled the boots out of the box. I had asked if it was possible to get a pair of boots from him when he'd made the pair for the Traveler. These boots were a deep forest green, with light-brown laces that laced up to the knee.

"These are amazing..." I said.

"They should fit perfectly, and your feet shouldn't get tired in them."

I gave him a bright smile. "I appreciate the gift! I spend a lot of time on my feet here."

The Cat nodded at Alas. I'd bet the two of them had spoken about the gift. Still, these would go with basically any outfit I had, and I did spend most days on my feet. Well, every working day.

Lord Bennit picked up the last box and held it out to me. For a split second, he frowned, then the expression cleared. "I hope you never have to use this, but just in case."

The Cat looked at the dragon as I took the box.

The present was wrapped in plain brown paper with a string tie. Inside lay a small leaf, coated in something that looked like wax and attached to a thin chain. It looked like a necklace made from a long, narrow leaf.

Lady Borsal's eyes went wide before she schooled her expression.

"You are a friend of the Clan, yet you do not have a dragon roar. Should you ever need our help, crumple the leaf. We will be here instantly." His eyes glowed a deep blue, and I felt the words roll through my bones.

"Thank you. I will wear it every day."

This was unexpected. Even Indigo looked intrigued.

"No need. I here," she chirped.

Lord Bennit shook his head lightly. "Stranger things have happened, little one. Remember, we protect our friends, and our friends protect us."

Indigo landed on the table and nudged the side of my arm.

"No harm!" Her voice wobbled, and I quickly set the leaf down and picked her up.

"Don't worry. Nothing is going to happen to me. Between the Cat, the shop, and the dragons, I'm probably the most protected person in the Tree."

Indigo trembled as I hugged her to my chest.

"I will be fine."

Warmth rose all around me from the table and the walls. Betty was chiming in about my safety as well.

The dragons looked on with interest.

I set Indigo back on the table and motioned to the large cake. "Guess what?"

Indigo chirped once.

"It's cake time!" I said.

Her green eyes grew wide, and she twisted about to look at the cake in the center of the table.

The cake had chocolate frosting with purple writing

on it saying *Happy Birthday*. A tiny purple dragon was on the side, flying.

"We have candles," mentioned the Cat. A small box of birthday candles sat near his paw. "Just blow them out quickly."

I knew the shop didn't like open flames, so I nodded and quickly stuck three of them into the cake's top. I wasn't going to put my actual age on there. Three was good enough. Though I didn't have a lighter.

Lady Borsal caught my eye and reached out. All three candles blazed to life.

Then Alas started singing "Happy Birthday" in a soothing voice, and the others quickly joined in, even the Cat.

I couldn't believe they had done this for me. As soon as they finished the song, I blew out the candles, and Indigo danced in place on the table, excited for cake.

Plates appeared, along with forks and a knife.

"I'll cut everyone a slice."

The cake was chocolate with a white frosting on the inside. It had three thick layers, and the center layer also had chocolate chips. The first slice I set in front of the little dragon.

It was almost as big as her. Her eyes grew so big and her mouth was open with her tongue hanging out.

"This is a special day, so you get an extra big slice. This isn't a normal slice," I warned her.

Indigo nodded, inching closer to the plate.

For everyone else, I asked how much they wanted. Lord Bennit shrugged, so I cut him what I considered a good-sized piece of cake and did the same for Lady Borsal.

"What kind of cake is this?" asked Alas.

"Looks like chocolate, with both chocolate and vanilla frosting, plus some chocolate chips."

He nodded, but it was clear he probably hadn't had a cake like it before. He got the same sized slice as the two dragons.

For the Cat, I didn't ask and just cut him the same amount as me—a good slice, but not too big. The Cat and Indigo didn't get forks, but I passed out utensils to the rest of us.

The first bite tasted like heaven. Sweet, but not too sweet, mostly a good rich chocolate.

Indigo growled in joy, her whole snout shoved into the cake. Icing covered her scales, but she went in for another bite.

I chuckled. The rest of us ate much neater and slower, but with no less delight.

"So, this is birthday cake," muttered Lord Bennit. "I learn something new every day."

"Do you not celebrate birthdays?" I asked.

"When dragons reach the age of majority, we hold a gathering, but not yearly." He nodded at the cake. "I like the idea of cake."

"Everyone loves treats," added Lady Borsal.

Lord Bennit nodded to himself. "I like this idea of celebration, too. Sometimes we forget to celebrate."

I chuckled to myself, wondering about the unforeseen changes my taking care of Indigo would create.

CHAPTER

EIGHTY-TWO

Indigo pulled back from her slice of cake, not even half of it gone, and she slumped to one side, her stomach round. She blinked a few times before she lost the battle with her eyelids.

"Usually, she eats more than that."

Lady Borsal chuckled. "She should be sleeping, but she didn't want to miss your birthday party. Growth spurts will be more frequent as she learns to use her magic."

Indigo drifted off to sleep next to her cake, with vanilla icing still on her nose.

"Well, I'll make sure to let her sleep this evening," I said.

She shouldn't have forced herself to stay up for my birthday party, but I appreciated it. Looking around the table at my adoptive family, I reflected that this had been unexpected, but treasured.

Lady Borsal chuckled. "She might be out longer than that." She glanced over at Lord Bennit, who watched

Indigo with a soft smile. "Her lessons with the Elder will resume, hopefully, in a few weeks."

He nodded.

I wanted to ask for an update on Indigo's mother, but I didn't. This wasn't the time for bad news, or even a no-news update. When the dragons wanted me to know something, I would.

The Cat inched closer to the sleeping dragon, also keeping an eye on the smallest of us. Lord Bennit's gaze snapped to the Cat in surprise, yet he didn't comment.

Alas chuckled awkwardly. "Well, I need to get back to work, but this was a pleasant break, lass. Happy birthday."

He pushed his chair away from the table, and that signaled everyone else. The two adult dragons got up as well, and I followed.

"I appreciate all of you coming to celebrate my birthday." I gave Alas a hug.

"Enjoy the boots, and have an adventure or two," he whispered with a wink before hurrying out the door.

That left Lady Borsal and Lord Bennit, both of whom gave me nods.

Lord Bennit held out his hand for me to shake, which I did.

"Have a good afternoon," he added, before they also left the shop, leaving the three of us.

The Cat sat on the table, staring down at the sleeping Indigo.

I sat back in my chair. "Thank you for doing this."

Part of me still couldn't believe that the Cat had pulled this together. It had to have come from him;

Indigo wouldn't have thought about it. She hadn't been around when the birthday cards had shown up.

"Of course," said the Cat.

His mouth opened like he wanted to say more, but he stopped.

I reached out to give him a pet, but he moved before I could.

"I hope you have a good afternoon. Indigo might need a bath," he said, moving across the table away from me.

I didn't understand why he pulled away, but I scooped Indigo up and grabbed a napkin. It only took a few swipes to remove the frosting from her nose. When I finished, the Cat had gone. I kept the book dragon close, and she stayed sleeping, curling up closer to my chest.

"Hey, Betty, can you put away the leftovers?" I asked quietly.

A burst of warmth rushed through the shop, and the food, along with the leftover cake, sank down into the table.

"Thank you, my friend," I whispered as I headed out of the room.

The Cat wasn't wrong. I could still smell the sugar on Indigo. I needed to get a warm washcloth to make sure she wasn't sticky anymore before I tucked her into her cat tower with a heated blanket. I didn't know how long she would be out this time, but at least Lady Borsal had warned me.

By the time I tucked Indigo away in her tower, all nice and clean, the afternoon was in full effect. Bright sunlight streamed in from the rooftop deck, and I headed in that direction. The tiny oak tree next to the Cat tower caught my eye. One of the several leaves on it shimmered. It went from dark green to bright red, yet none of the others changed at all.

I quickly counted the remaining leaves, and, even including the smallest, there were only ten. The little tree looked so bare. The red leaf stayed attached and didn't fall, but the hair on the back of my neck rose. Something didn't feel right about it at all.

Back on my home world, it was fall, and soon, the harvest festival would be in full swing. Still, it wasn't like the shop had seasons. As long as I'd worked here, it had been consistent. Bright warm skies on the rooftop deck. Sometimes out the front door, the weather looked different, but that was the weather on the worlds we touched, not here in the shop.

The leaf on the tree shouldn't have changed.

Shaking my head, I slid the door open and stepped into the midafternoon sun. Heat washed down on me, and I smiled.

Ignoring the ominous leaf on my birthday had been the right choice. I could deal with it tomorrow. That and the Cat.

It was too bad he was in some sort of funk.

IT DIDN'T TAKE LONG for me to realize I should go talk to Sable. It wasn't her fault I was in a bad mood.

She'd broken all expectations doing this weird job she had magicked into. As the Shopkeeper, she was the best I'd ever had, and considering how long it'd been, that was saying something.

I slunk out of the shadows of the archway of my workshop and headed toward the roof. My guess was that she was in the sunshine, which fit her.

This conversation should be easy. All I needed to say was it wasn't her; it was me. I felt off, but I was glad her birthday had gone so well.

Every scrap of rehearsed conversation left my mind as I padded along the floor, turning the corner. A bright-red object caught my eye, making me freeze. Ice cold shot through my body at the sight, and I couldn't move. Names spilled through my head of each child it could relate to. It didn't help lessen my fears.

The last time a leaf had fallen, it had been sudden. One second it was green, the next dead on the floor. There hadn't been time to even think about the circumstances. This time, a bright-red one appeared.

What did it mean? Were they okay?

What had the Fates chosen to punish me with now?

EIGHTY-THREE

I couldn't find the Cat anywhere once dinner time rolled around. The doorway that led to the hidden room didn't appear, no matter how sweetly I asked Betty for access.

I worried about him, and that worry crept into my dreams, which were filled with conflict, destruction, and, oddly, images of my family.

None of it made any sense.

Despite my troubled night, I woke up just as the sun peeked into the skylight above my bed and forced myself to get up. Today was not a day off, and I had a job to do.

I checked on Indigo, but she still slept deeply, curled up in a tight ball with the heated blanket tucked around her. She hadn't moved since I'd put her there the day before.

"Grow strong and smart, little one," I whispered as I headed to the bathroom to take a long shower.

It felt like a long-shower day, which meant I stood under the spray for way too long since the never-ending hot water didn't give me a clue to get moving. By the time I'd gotten dressed and headed out my bedroom door, more sunlight streamed into the shop from above. But I felt way more human, so I counted my tardiness as worthwhile.

I wore my new boots for the first time, lacing them up over my skinny jeans. Each step felt like stepping on a cloud. The only other additions from my birthday party were the necklace from the dragons and the bracelet from my brother. I'd tucked the leaf necklace under my black T-shirt and had a dark-purple flannel on top.

The red leaf on the little oak from yesterday made me feel like fall really was here. Hence the flannel, though the shop's temperature stayed the same as it always had.

My first stop was Betty, and I quickly pulled a large cinnamon vanilla latte for myself. Something warm and relaxing seemed just right. I frothed the milk perfectly and topped it with a ton of rich foam.

The main shop looked the same. Books filled the big table in the center, bookshelves ran along the back wall, and the children's area was set up. Maybe we'd be getting more deliveries from Adam, since it felt like a "normal" day without magic.

I headed to the kitchen. The room brightened as I entered, making it clear I'd beaten the Cat here, despite my indulgent shower. Bacon and eggs would be easy enough, and it'd let me sip my latte slowly as I readied myself for work. Bacon went into the oven, and I scrambled eggs on the stove with a little shredded cheese mixed in.

None of it took long. Even so, I expected to see the

Cat waiting when I finished, but he was nowhere to be found.

"Cat, breakfast is ready! I made bacon and eggs..." I called out into the hallway, unsure of where he was hiding.

I picked up a piece of crunchy bacon and took a bite. It really had turned out perfectly. I sat down and started on my plate slowly, keeping an eye out for the Cat.

My plate was half empty when he showed up with his whiskers drooping.

Immediately, I knew something was off. "Hey, you okay?"

"I didn't sleep well," the Cat muttered.

His tail hung low, and his ears drooped.

I nodded and motioned to the plate with bacon on it. "I had rough dreams as well, but bacon always helps."

The Cat moved toward his plate, but even the bacon didn't cheer him up.

That red leaf on the tiny oak tree came to mind.

"You know that tree, the one that's special?"

The Cat froze, even before I could get my question out. He said nothing, but the tension emanating from him crackled the air with intensity.

"It has a red leaf. I watched it change yesterday, like magic. One second, it was dark green like the others, then it shimmered to red."

A loud knocking came from the front of the shop, causing me to jerk, almost spilling my coffee.

"That's strange..."

Again, nothing from the Cat, though his eyes went wide.

I jumped up, leaving my plate on the island with food still on it, and hurried toward the front of the shop with my latte in one hand, trying hard not to spill it. Two dark figures stood outside the door. Though I only recognized one of them, I quickly unlocked the door and let them in.

Lady Twilight entered.

"I apologize for the unexpected arrival, but we are on a timer here..." She stepped into the shop without asking, and I moved toward the center, near the large table.

Her bright eyes flicked over the room, searching.

The Cat appeared, jumping onto the counter, his head cocked to one side. "This is unexpected."

"I bring a gift, one of equal value to what you have given me and my Clan." Her voice came out formally, and she directed it to the Cat.

Behind her entered someone with a thick green cloak with the hood up.

I couldn't see who or what was beneath it, but I trusted the Elder Dragon. Of course, with her here in the shop already, I really didn't think I had a choice.

"You have saved countless eggs. Others taken like Indigo from distant clans that normally don't meet with the Clan of Knowledge, and some of our own. All of this by giving me that demon." Her gaze turned toward me. "Dragon-kin, Guardian of Indigo, Shopkeeper, do you accept this gift on behalf of..." She paused. "Lord Felimid Ó Cearnacháin Felix?"

The Cat froze, and Lady Twilight waited for my answer. Magic swirled through the air, so heavy I could almost see it. Like motes of dust. I glanced at the Cat, but it was like he was stuck in time. Nothing moved near him. Nothing moved near the guest either. Only Lady Twilight and I even breathed in the sudden pause.

I'd heard that name once before, but I couldn't remember where, like it'd been removed from my memory. That was the Cat's name. His true name. It rolled around inside my mind, pictures forming, making connections. The red leaf appeared, along with the hidden room, and the shield Betty had shown me.

Everything inside me said it was time to discover what was going on.

There was only one possible answer. "Yes."

Time unfroze, and the Cat growled so deeply that the floor vibrated.

"What did you do, dragon? How dare you?!" Magic swirled along the Cat's fur, and his tail flicked. The edges of his form blurred then snapped back into place. "By bringing them here, you have sentenced them to death! You've killed one of my children!"

The voice floated in the back of my mind, but it was clear I wasn't the only one who it had been intended for.

Lady Twilight simply nodded.

"It is time for change," said the dragon, her eyes glowing a deep green.

I glanced between the two, wondering what the heck was going on, when the cloaked person stepped forward.

"Is he here?" a soft voice asked. "My father?"

EIGHTY-FOUR

An old woman's wrinkled hand pulled down the hood, revealing bright-blue eyes, a hopeful look, and sharp-pointed ears. Wrinkles covered her face, and her hair glowed a bright silver. The weight of time surrounded her as she glanced around the room. Her gaze passed right over the Cat, like she couldn't see him, then her gaze landed on me.

Lady Twilight nodded.

"He cannot interfere." She motioned to me. "She is the one who must be told."

The old Elven woman stepped forward with a smile directed at me.

"I've heard much about you, Sable, keeper of the Fated Shop." She bowed her head. "You seek to right the wrong from ages past. We have much to speak about."

Anger still pulsed from the Cat's direction, but this woman didn't seem to notice it at all.

"We should sit," she said with a smile, glancing around.

"Betty, some chairs would be great," I whispered under my breath.

Lady Twilight nodded and headed toward the counter. The large table in the center of the room sank into the floor, and two dark-green velvet chairs rose in its place.

"This really is it... It's been hidden here this whole time," muttered the elven woman as she glanced at my wide eyes. "Forgive me. I am Liluth Faechid, one of the First."

Faechid?

She bowed her head again at me and motioned to the chairs. "I need to start the story at the beginning." Her gaze went to the dragon. "Do I have enough time?"

Lady Twilight nodded. "Time passes strangely here, and more so under my influence. You will have time enough. It is the least I can do."

She leaned up against the counter right next to the Cat.

I sat in a chair and waited for Liluth to take the seat across from me. "The beginning would be great. I feel like I'm missing so much information."

Liluth sat in the chair, running her fingers slowly over an armrest as she did. She blinked a few times before relaxing into the comfortable seat. "It's so strange, being here. At the edge of my senses, I can feel it."

This did not feel like the beginning, but whatever she was experiencing, it was big for her, so I gave her the space.

Her gaze snapped to mine. "I am one of the last of the First. The First of my people, the Elves, created by our father, Fey Lord Felimid Ó Cearnacháin Felix of the Towering Forest."

A sad smile came across her face. "He created my race in his lands within the Fey Wilds, one of the more magical worlds of the Tree. In the beginning, there were only a hundred of us who lived in the Towering Forest. We learned from our father, and we aged slowly, nearly not at all, as part of his magic. Our people prospered over time, and children were born. Much like us, but without as strong of a connection to the magic of our father. Still Elves, just not of the First."

Her eyes shone as she continued, "The Fey Wilds are wild, each kingdom ruled by a Lord. Sometimes, fighting took place between Lords, or there might be a small war with some other world, but nothing that shook our foundations. Not until the demons appeared."

She paused. "A crazy people, they are, who like to conquer lands. They killed some of our people, the young ones among us who weren't ageless. The loss was felt by all, including our Father. None of us knew his pain, though I wished we had tried."

She glanced down at her hands. "It led him down a dark road, searching for a way to stop them. To stop any of his children from dying, even those generations removed from us, the First."

She swallowed hard.

The Cat had family, children even. My fingers tightened into fists.

"Dragon, you have gone too far." I wanted to attack the creature that stood next to the counter.

Fire burned inside me, yet I could barely move. The iron-strong magical bonds that held me weren't of the dragon's making, but of the Fates'. I knew their power. I had tested it, and I knew that I could not deny their will.

"Liluth will fade now that she's left my lands. Another of my children, gone..."

The rage flickered to ice cold coals. Another child I couldn't protect, even with how old she now looked. In my lands, she would still be young, but outside of those, my limited magic faded.

"There will be no such thing, Lord Felix." The dragon's quiet statement knocked me out of the dark path my mind had started down. "She will join me in my home. That will pause her aging, possibly even return some of her youth. She volunteered to come when I explained to those still on the edges of your lands. Don't you dare take this choice away from her."

I flicked my gaze over the dragon's face, searching for deception. It was their way, as abiding by my law was my own, though I had to admit this particular dragon had always treated me fairly.

"Is that even possible?" I asked.

"Didn't you once say, never make a deal with a dragon?"

"Yes. You always get what you want, no matter the deal."

The saying also worked with Fey Lords, though I couldn't even remember what that felt like. So many ages had passed, I couldn't picture my children's faces.

Some nights, I could repeat the names, letting them linger in the air, living in a ghost of a shadow of memory.

"Well, I wanted to give you a gift. Sable accepted it on your behalf."

"This isn't a gift." I could feel the lie twist out between my teeth even as I said it.

Somehow, it was a gift, though I was also sure the dragon knew my struggle. Whatever they had found because of that demon had led to this. Sable saving a baby dragon had led to others being saved, and this Elder had done everything she could to find something worthy of that.

The story that Liluth told wasn't the full truth, though.

No one knew the full truth but me and the bastard Fates.

CHAPTER

EIGHTY-FIVE

"He turned to dark magic that he knew better than to touch," Liluth said. "Magic forbidden by those who protect the Tree. The pure magic of the ley lines themselves.

"My Lord shouldn't have been able to touch it, but he found a way. The will of a Fae Lord is difficult to thwart, even for the Tree itself. But doing a thing does not always result in what you expect, and there were consequences. The ripples were felt across hundreds of worlds. So many lives were touched, so many threads of fate twisted out of their patterns...and so my Lord was punished."

She let out a sigh, closing her eyes.

"One moment, everything was normal in the Towering Forest. The next, the land trembled as the great tree shuddered. All of us fled as the land under our feet turned cold then faded into nothing. Three voices called out, *This Fey Land is no more. It's Fey Lord is no more. May Felix someday earn redemption, should he seek it and deserve it, as only we may say.*"

Tears rolled down the elven woman's face. "The Forest was gone, a dark mist left in its place. Any time we tried to enter, it led us right back to the edges. The First could no longer feel our Father. Worse yet, the magic had changed. Our children no longer had echoes of agelessness. Over time, the long lives faded. Only the First remained the same, as long as we did not leave. But plenty left, searching for a path to redemption for our Lord, a way to appease the Fates."

My heart clenched in my chest. Leaving my family behind for the year-long contract was nothing compared to this pain, this tragedy.

How many people suffered because of what the Cat had done? I didn't have a clue, but it really didn't matter.

"Did they find one? A way to make it right?" I asked.

Liluth shook her head. "Nothing. No one who left found any trace of what had happened to our Lord. It was like he no longer existed for us." Her fingers tightened on the armrests. "But he is here."

A sad smile covered her face. "I can feel his magic in this Shop, in you. Though it is different, not the Forest, it is still my Lord's power."

It made sense that the Cat had screwed up and gotten himself banished here. Or at least, that's what it sounded like, based on the story Liluth told.

"This is the closest any of us have gotten to him since the Towering Forest vanished. I can feel the curse in the magic. I bet he's cut off from it until he finishes whatever the Fates set him to do." Her face fell. "I'd hoped that I could do more to help him, but if it's a task the Fates have given him, there is nothing anyone can do."

"What about Betty?" I asked. "The Shop. You said it's his power, so how is it also different? Betty is its own entity..."

Liluth's eyes narrowed. "The Shop has a name? Its own personality?"

"Yeah, it can do things. I ask it to do things, and it happens."

"But you call it Betty?" She shook her head. "Did you name it? Or did the old Keeper name it?"

The Cat had warned me about naming things. About how a name could give something power. Maybe I shouldn't have named the espresso maker and the shop? Still, it seemed wrong to not give the shop a name. I couldn't just call it "the shop," that felt completely wrong.

"I named them, but they agreed to it. I think." Warmth rushed up from the chair like a hug, making me feel better. The cloth on the chair almost embraced me.

Liluth noticed and her smile wavered. "The Fey Realm didn't act like its own person when it was whole. It might have something to do with the curse, or the loss of connection with my Lord. While people view them as separate, we First have always known the Fey Lord and his Realm are more like the same thing than distinct beings."

"So, Betty is the part of the Fey Lord that likes me and wants to be my friend?" I asked.

Liluth studied the ceiling for several moments. "I do not know. Though, the magic trusts you. That much is clear. I hope you can figure out how to help my Lord and send him home. So many have lost hope. Generations don't even believe he is real. Most have fled to a different world and settled there. The last of the First... We wait, and we hope, though our number trickles down, as one by one my people lose that hope."

I needed to talk to the Cat.

"THAT'S the conclusion she comes to?" I mumbled. "I like her just fine. I threw her a birthday party yesterday."

Lady Twilight chuckled. "She's young, and what happened here with your Realm is pretty strange. I wonder how to put it to rights." She side-eyed me. "Though you're the only one with the whole true story, as you would put it. Sable might want to know. She might need to."

I rolled my eyes, letting out a deep exhale. If Lady Twilight spoke the truth, my daughter would be safe, though she'd be stuck with dragons for who knew how long. It wasn't any worse than my punishment of being in the store and putting things to rights. The years dragged on all the same, as they would in the future.

"There is nothing to tell. I need to put things right."

"Do you have any indicator of what those things are?"

I shook my head. "All I have is the book. It tells me what the next task is. Though, you were not supposed to show up today. This is detouring us from what should be."

I slowly lay on the counter, not moving any closer to the elven woman I couldn't take my eyes off of. Liluth was one of the First in more ways than one. She had been my First Daughter, the First of my children in truth. She was my dearest Daughter, who trusted me, and I had failed all of them.

When I had been banished, all one hundred of my First children still lived, and now there were only ten. Liluth's time was quickly fading, all because I had reached too high to try to thwart the Fates.

"We need to leave soon," whispered Lady Twilight. "I can feel the welcome ebbing. The magic I used to find this place has limits, even for me."

"They aren't going to be happy with you."

"Dragons have always had our own relationship with the Fates. We mostly act how we wish, and they tolerate it because they have no choice. And because, in the end, we both protect the Tree."

Fey Lords had often acted outside of the Fates as well. Look how that had turned out for me. Then again, I knew my failure. I knew that I had not been protecting the Tree, but protecting my own.

BEFORE I COULD ASK anything else, Lady Twilight made some motion, and Liluth stood.

"Thank you, Sable, for watching over my Lord. I hoped he wouldn't be stuck alone all these years." She bowed her head at me, then the two of them hustled out the door.

The door thudded shut and locked. Silence reigned.

"So, you're cursed?" I asked quietly, without turning to look at the counter.

"I am."

"Until things are put to right?"

"Yes."

"How long have you been stuck here?"

"A very long time…" he said, sounding old, with a depth of age and grief and exhaustion that I could barely comprehend.

"How do we break the curse?" I asked.

This time, I turned to look at the counter, but the Cat wasn't looking in my direction. Instead, he gazed toward the balcony and the potted tiny oak tree.

"You don't." He turned and jumped off the counter, vanishing out of sight.

Continue the series with Keeper & Kindred, Book 2 of MEOW: Magical Emporium of Wares.

TONI'S NOTES

Thank you for reading the first book in the Meow Series.

I started writing this story several years ago as my personal escape - a quiet corner of the world where I could find a warm hug on the page. It's been a dream to share the beginning of this cozy tale with you, and it's your kind encouragement that has kept me writing.

Our little book dragon, Indigo, holds a very special place in my heart. If you'd like a sweet, secret peek into her very first moments arriving at the shop, I invite you to join my newsletter! It's a simple, cozy way to stay in the loop with what I'm currently creating and all the ongoing adventures in the garden. Check out bookhip.com/MMHZKBC to get the story!

For those who want to join me even earlier on the writing path, you can find me on Patreon or Ream. It's there that I share chapters of my new books as they come to life, including an upcoming series about a very special customer from Meow whose life is forever changed by their visit.

May your days be filled with warm tea and even warmer stories.

Cozy wishes, Toni

MORE BOOKS BY TONI BINNS

<u>Nexus Universe - Traveler Series</u>

If you enjoy Urban Fantasy with found family, slow burn romance, and unknown magic, check out the complete story!

- Traveler Forgotten (*Short Story*) - Available at tonibinns.com
- Choice of the Traveler
- Call of the Traveler
- Courage of the Traveler

www.ingramcontent.com/pod-product-compliance
Lightning Source LLC
Chambersburg PA
CBHW030329010826
48973CB00004B/926